AF599235

GOOD
FOR HER

TYLOR PAIGE

Page & Vine
An Imprint of Meredith Wild LLC

This is a work of fiction. Names, characters, places, and incidents either are the product of the author's imagination or are used fictitiously, and any resemblance to actual persons, living or dead, business establishments, events, or locales is entirely coincidental. The publisher does not assume any responsibility for third-party websites or their content.

The author acknowledges the trademarked status and trademark owners of various products referenced in this work, which have been used without permission. The publication/use of these trademarks is not authorized, associated with, or sponsored by the trademark owners.

Copyright © 2026 Tylor Paige

All Rights Reserved.
No part of this book may be reproduced, scanned, or distributed in any printed or electronic format without permission. Please do not participate in or encourage piracy of copyrighted materials in violation of the author's rights. Purchase only authorized editions.

Paperback ISBN: 978-1-964264-34-9

Good For Her *is dedicated to my Great Grandmother, Bonnie Mcleod. Look Nanny, I made it.*

Author's Note

This book is a horror romance. That means that while we do have people falling in love and getting their happily ever after, the plot is very much a horror story. *Good For Her*, like my other slasher romances, is meant to be fast paced, bonkers, and very much an homage to the genres I love. The quotes, the kills, the spills, all of it is completely intentional. Why? Because that's how slashers are. Do they always make sense? No, but that's why we love them and watch them over and over again.

Please keep this in mind when diving into *Good For Her*, and I'll think you'll enjoy this book. And, if you don't....

Beep, beep, Ritchie.

This book is rated R:

Good For Her is a horror romance novel with topics that may be upsetting for some readers. I encourage you to consider this list to know exactly what you are going to encounter while reading this book. This is not an exhaustive list, but I did try to cover the basics. *Good For Her* features murder—on page and off, discussion of gang rape, kidnapping, dubious consent, free use, guns, knives, recreational drug use, thinly veiled homophobic comments (not by a good guy,) callous comments on sex work, blood, gore, single incident of racism, religious trauma, death of a parent, and abuse of power.

CHAPTER 1

EVIE

The Cold Open

"Beep beep, Ritchie." I turned toward the craft services table and picked up a bag of chips, pretending to intensely read the label. Sebastian, my best friend, stood beside me and turned his head and swore as his agent stormed across set to berate him for some imagined infraction.

"I heard that." The brunette woman—wearing hot-pink heels and a matching pantsuit—stepped between us, her back to me. She crossed her arms over her enhanced chest. With the heels, she loomed over us both. All around, members of the cast and crew passed by either snickering in amusement or shaking their heads at Sebastian. He was always getting into trouble with Heather. "I know your guys' little code. What are you eating?"

"Nothing, I was just walking with Evie," he lied.

I rolled my eyes from behind her and stepped farther down to the popcorn machine. I grabbed a paper bag and filled it, tossing a scoop of M&M's in between layers of popcorn. I closed the bag and shook it noisily while Sebastian continued to get yelled at for eating.

"I want you to do another workout tonight before you go to bed."

"I was up at three this morning working out. Come on," he protested. "One bagel isn't going to kill me." He reached for the table, but she slapped his hand away.

"Say that in ten years. If we want a lifelong career, which we do, you need to learn smart eating now. You eat that bagel, and I'll haul a treadmill into your trailer to run it off between scenes."

"You wouldn't."

"Oh, I would."

Popcorn in hand, I stepped back and shifted to the side to watch the shitshow unfold. I'd warned him if he tried to sneak craft services, he'd get caught. Sebastian was Heather's meal ticket. There was no way she'd risk her paycheck being short because he gained an ounce of weight.

His green eyes flicked to me, and he scowled. I popped a piece of popcorn into my mouth, and Sebastian stared at my hand as I mouthed, *It puts the lotion in the basket.*

We had lots of codes to talk to each other, all of them movie lines. What started off as a silly game on set of the first *Simon Says* movie turned into a secret language that helped us communicate around the adults. We were now on *Simon Says Three*, and the code was ever-expanding.

"Are you listening to me?" Heather snapped.

Sebastian turned his attention back to his agent.

"I got you a private screen test with the producers of that apocalypse movie. If you're bloated, you won't even make the shortlist."

"It does this whenever it's told," I quipped.

Heather turned her head and shot me a dirty look. She knew better than to say anything to me. My mom would have her ass dragged off the studio lot and out of Hollywood by sundown.

Sebastian huffed loudly. "Yes, I get it. I'll go drink some water and continue to starve. Go find someone else to bitch at."

Heather stormed off, leaving us alone.

"Come on. I want to relax," Sebastian muttered.

I refilled my popcorn bag, and together we headed to the trailer lot. Instead of heading to the one labeled *Sebastian Shaw*, we walked over to the one that said *Lita Reyes*—my mother's. I climbed up the stairs and hurried inside, plopping down on the red velvet couch.

I didn't have the same restrictions as Sebastian or Lita. I wasn't an actress, just the child of one. However, I'd grown up on set and seen how badly Sebastian was treated. I often wondered, was it really worth the fame? But then he'd light up every time someone recognized him, or he saw his face on a billboard, so maybe it was. I wouldn't know. No one ever paid attention to me.

"Did you hear that bullshit? A treadmill in my trailer!" He collapsed beside me, and I offered him the popcorn. He scarfed it down. "Ooh, M&M's." He smiled, leaned across the couch, and gave me a quick peck on the lips. "I was watching *The Exorcist...*"

Butterflies fluttered around my belly. "It got me thinking about you." It was our way of saying *I love you*. We'd yet to say the actual words, but the movie lines felt just as powerful. They were special and only ours.

Sebastian set the empty bag down and turned back to me, kissing me again. His smile, salty and butter-flavored, curled against my lips as our mouths met again. This time, our tongues touched, and in a flash, the mood shifted from playful to something else. He pushed me down onto the couch, his hands roaming under my shirt. A groan rose from his throat.

"I can't wait for—"

The door flew open, and light poured in, causing us to bolt upright.

"Sebastian Shaw, I know you aren't making a mess in my trailer." My mother came in, hand on hip. She was in costume, a matronly fuchsia dress. Her black hair, normally soft and smooth, was curled and teased to resemble a woman from the eighties. Fake blood had been splattered all over her dress, face, and arms. She kicked off her thick pumps and huffed. "Don't you have something better to do than make out with my daughter and get popcorn all over my expensive furniture?"

I blushed and glanced over—Sebastian was grinning ear to ear.

"Actually, I don't, ma'am. My scenes aren't for another hour."

"Lita," she corrected. She wagged a finger at us. "Just because you two are dating doesn't mean I'm an old lady. And I got done early, so they'll be calling for you soon, I bet."

Her costume suggested otherwise, but I wasn't going to be the one to tell her. She was turning forty-nine this year, but in Hollywood, that was basically thirty.

I patted Sebastian's knee and looked up at him, taking in just how cute he was. I was so lucky. I was living every teenage girl's dream. I was dating Sebastian Shaw, the Hollywood bad boy. He was on the cover of magazines, movie posters, and had already won awards, at just sixteen. With his long, jet-black hair, green eyes, and chiseled jawline, he was easily the most handsome boy I'd ever seen. Even before he'd started getting tall and working out, I'd had a crush on him.

And he was in love with me.

"We have such sights to show you," I said—our secret way of telling him to go with it because it would be worth it after. Which, in this situation meant prepare to shoot a scene. I squeezed his hand. "I'll come see you after your scenes," I promised. Now that my mom was done with hers, Sebastian would be called to set shortly, which meant, if we were lucky, he'd get out early. Reluctantly, he left, giving me one last lingering kiss before running out.

"You two are too cute," my mom sighed as she peeled off her costume and headed to the shower. "Remember, I'm going to dinner tonight. I won't be home."

Oh, I knew.

"These are very important men, and I suspect I may be out all night, so you'll need to catch a ride with Sebastian in the morning. I presume he'll have snuck in to keep you company." She shot me a look that was equal parts motherly warning and sisterly amusement. I cringed. She'd given me the sex talk the day before, and it was just as awkward as one could expect. Made worse by how pro-sex she was. I would have rather had the "stern-purity-bullshit" speech over the "lubrication-is-your-friend" one.

"Maybe."

Despite being far too interested in my pending sex life, I loved the relationship between us. Lita Reyes had spent almost twenty years in the spotlight before deciding to have me. She claimed she wanted a best friend who, in her words, "was more beautiful than she could ever be, but just as smart." While I wasn't so sure about the whole "more beautiful" part, I appreciated the sentiment. My mother was a Latina bombshell. I could only be so lucky to look like her.

Maybe then I could star in movies.

From day one, I tagged along with her to movie sets. The cast and crews always treated me warmly, and many of them, as we continued on with the *Simon Says* franchise, came to feel like family. They played games with me in between their scenes, and I'd help them run lines. I came to the premieres, and they came to my birthday parties.

It was how Sebastian and I met. My mother introduced us on the first day, despite Heather arguing that the talent shouldn't be distracted. We were the only kids on set for *Simon Says*, so the production company set up a trailer for us to attend school in. In between classes and filming, we kept each other company in our trailers, watching movies, pretending we were part of those worlds, and for a little bit—pausing the world we actually lived in. We bonded over existing in a world meant for adults. I'd never hung out with a kid my age before him, so he was special to me. And later, as we grew up on set... I became special to him as well.

Later that night, as my mother was heading out the door in a gorgeous red, skintight cocktail dress, she paused to kiss me goodbye and to remind me to lean on Sebastian.

"Hollywood is an awful yet magical place. If, for some reason, I'm not there, you two need to stick together."

Her eyes bore into me for a beat longer than comfortable. I cocked my head, curious.

"Who are you doing dinner with again?"

She inhaled deeply and looked away.

"Six men who don't deserve the privilege."

I didn't understand. Lita Reyes was like that sometimes. Blunt when she needed to be, cryptic when she wanted to be. I suppose it didn't matter who these men were. Her tone and grim expression told me I should be so lucky to never meet them.

She hugged me one more time and left without another word.

I watched from the window as she walked down the long drive and stepped into a limousine. Then, I called Sebastian.

"Whoa."

Sebastian rolled off me and collapsed onto the mattress. Our bare chests rose and fell in matching rhythm. My skin was slick with sweat, and my heart was beating so fast, like I was the Final Girl in one of the movies we loved so much. My body was reacting as if I'd just sprinted through the woods, only to be caught by the handsome serial killer, and I wasn't mad about it. I'd be Sebastian's final girl any day.

"Was it good for you?" He turned and propped his head up in his hand.

I rolled to face him. "I mean, yeah. It hurt, kind of. It hurt a lot when you first started, but after a while, I forgot about the pain."

"They say that's normal," he offered, running a finger down the middle of my chest, between my breasts. "I love you so much, Evie. I've never loved someone as much as I love you."

"I—uh..." Panic fluttered in my belly. We'd never said those words before. "I was watching *The Exorcist*," I said lamely, too scared to use the real words. It almost felt like a jinx. If I confessed that I loved him, he'd for sure meet some beautiful actress, fall madly in love, and forget about me.

"Groovy," he sighed, quoting Ash from *Evil Dead*, clearly disappointed. After a beat, he finished the phrase from *The Exorcist*. "It got me thinking about you."

We fell asleep, his workout alarm rousing us. I joined him, as my mom had directed, noting that she had, in fact, not come home last night. We went to the gym, did our workouts, and then headed to the lot. He dragged me through the large bare sound stage, over to set. The only lights were the security lights above various exits, creating shadows across the already creepy set. I glanced around. We were in Sebastian's character's bedroom. He paused near his bed, tilting his head toward it and smiling wickedly at me.

"Movie fact—this is a real bed."

I bit back a snarky comment but couldn't contain the eye roll and excited butterflies in my belly.

"We're early, but that just means we can sneak in round two. They say it hurts less and less each—" Suddenly, he stopped midsentence, and his eyes widened.

"Beep beep, Ritchie," he whispered.

The use of our code, alone in the dark, made me freeze. Goose bumps rose on my arms as he reached for my hand, squeezing it tight. Something was wrong—very wrong. I turned slowly, fear sliding up my spine as I tried to keep my steps quiet. When I was fully facing the rest of the room, my blood ran cold. I snapped my mouth shut as I saw a shadow running away, pushing open the emergency door and fleeing.

"Evie, don't look!" Sebastian shouted and tried to turn me away, but it was too late. I saw the body swaying from the scaffolding right where the man had just been. My entire mind went blank as I stared at the familiar dress and high heels.

And then, I screamed.

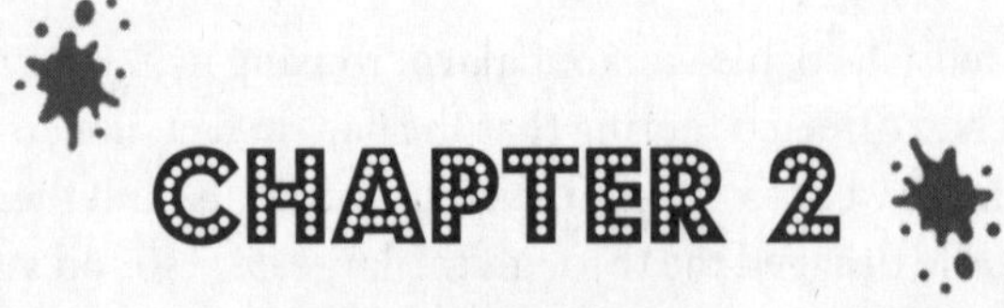

CHAPTER 2
EVIE

The Time Jump

"Hello, and welcome to *Featured Creatures*, the only show where we keep the female gaze at the forefront as we explore all things horror. I'm your host, JoJo Perkins. Today, we have Evie Reyes in the studio, the daughter of legendary Final Girl, Lita Reyes—rest in peace."

JoJo put her hands together in a praying motion and looked to the ceiling. "Evie here has granted us an exclusive interview as she prepares to reenter Hollywood, this time in front of the camera."

She turned her chair, adjusting her bright yellow cocktail dress to better cover her lap. I forced myself to keep up the fake smile as I waved to the cameras. I caught myself starting to slump forward and straightened my posture.

JoJo's hair and makeup looked gorgeous, and the yellow dress complemented her flawless dark skin perfectly. Her stylists were great at their jobs. I, on the other hand, had dressed myself today. Thankfully, I'd recently gotten my hair cut to resemble the Betty Page look, so the maintenance was minimal. I'd curled my black bangs and fluffed my shoulder-length hair and called it good so I could focus on painting my lips red and giving myself a simple smoky eye. The colors complemented my naturally tan skin tone, but they didn't make me stand out like JoJo in her yellow dress. Paired with my ripped black jeans and a black shawl over a lacy black crop top, I looked...boring.

I needed a stylist.

I reached for the glass on the table and took a sip. My hand shook slightly as I placed it back down.

"You left California after Lita's passing," she prompted.

I nodded. "I did. I moved to Michigan. My aunt Yvonne took me in. It was really healing to be around people who knew my mother like I did."

"What did you do during your time there?" JoJo crossed her legs and leaned back in her chair. She was ignoring the cameras altogether, focusing her eyes and smile on me.

"Well, I finished high school. After I got my diploma, I wasn't quite sure what I wanted to do with my life, so I—" Heat flooded my face. I laughed. "I'm going to sound like a man having his midlife crisis right now, but I started a podcast."

The crew on the other side of the room chuckled, but JoJo, ever the expert host, rolled with it.

"Yes! I'm actually an avid listener of *The Body Count Bimbo.* Or was. I switched to the videos when you started your YouTube channel. I love seeing your gorgeous face light up and get all excited about our favorite topic, horror." She turned to the cameras and flashed a megawatt smile.

"It's so fun, going in every week and gushing about horror movies. It's the best job ever." I beamed.

"Mood, girl. You have over three million followers—we've got how many?" She scrunched up her nose.

A cameraman called over to us. "Seven hundred thousand."

"Oof. If you're watching a clip of this on YouTube and haven't already subscribed to our channel, make sure to hit the like and follow buttons so we can attempt to compete with Miss Three Million over here, and you'll never miss a *Featured Creature* interview. Anyway, you've got your channel, what do you plan on doing with it now that you're back in Hollywood?"

"Unfortunately, my channel has to go on hiatus while I'm here, but luckily, there are tons of videos from the last three years to binge while you wait for me to come back."

"And for those unfamiliar with your content, what exactly would they be binging?" She leaned in.

"Over at *The Body Count Bimbo*, I go through the history of the horror genre in detail. I cover every subgenre, trope, famous actor and actress, and historical moment. I talk about what I love, what I hate, all of it. I leave no stone unturned."

"Well, just the one." JoJo gave me a pointed look. "As a fan, I've seen all of your videos, and there is one person and franchise you haven't touched. Can we talk about it?" She shifted to a softer, more empathetic tone. As if I were a scared animal she was trying to lure out from its hiding space.

I rolled my shoulders, uncomfortable. "That is why I'm here, isn't it?" I smiled halfheartedly and looked down at my worn high-tops. The canvas was ripped on the sides, and I'd taken a marker to the rubber. I'd gotten them as a birthday present when I was sixteen. I'd been so happy then, with grandiose dreams and plans for a future nothing like the one that actually happened.

My mom wasn't supposed to be murdered.

I raised my head, trying to exude strength. It was time to stop living in the past.

"Yes." JoJo leaned in again, her eyes full of concern. "Do you want to take a break? Get some air or something before we continue?"

I pushed myself up from the chair. "Actually, yeah. I think that's a good idea." I removed my mic pack.

The assistant director called cut, and the cameras stopped rolling.

"Ten minutes!"

"Thank you, ten!" the crew and I responded as we walked off.

Antoinette, my agent, stepped up the moment I was off the set. She reached for my shoulders and stopped me.

"Are you okay? Talk to me, Evie." She tilted my chin up, forcing me to look at her.

I studied her face, focusing on her short brown hair and

sparkling smile. Her dark skin, matching her eyes, glowed. I needed her confidence to rub off on me. I inhaled deeply, focusing on my breath. I made eye contact and nodded.

"I'll be fine. It's just a little nerve-wracking."

She let me go, and together we walked outside. A handful of the crew were smoking near the doors. They nodded politely, but Antoinette pulled me away from them.

"You can do this. This is what you wanted, remember? Dante said you didn't have to if you didn't want to," she reminded me. "You've already signed on to the movie."

I closed my eyes and sucked in the fresh air while she continued to hype me up.

Ten minutes went fast, and we returned to set. I gulped down a full glass of water, and when I set the glass down, the director called, "Action!"

"So, your mother, Lita Reyes, was a Final Girl. She played the iconic Lana Westcott in the *Simon Says* franchise." She paused then continued. "The world was rocked when, five years ago, Lita Reyes was found dead on the set of *Simon Says Three*—an apparent suicide. You were the one who found her. Are you comfortable talking about it?"

My eye twitched.

Suicide? It wasn't fucking suicide.

It was them.

Thornton. Dourif. Castle. Hodder. Englund. Bradley.

Antoinette stepped onto the stage.

"That wasn't on the list of approved questions. Cut it, or we leave," she snapped.

JoJo's kind expression hardened in an instant. She turned to glare at Antoinette. The two women stared each other down, daring the other to argue. With a deep sigh, JoJo turned back to me, flashing her smile again.

"Despite your mother's sudden death, the franchise continued on, shifting Sebastian Shaw into the lead role instead of replacing Lita with another actress. How do you feel about that?"

I forced a smile.

"I honestly have a lot of respect for the director and the writers for making that choice. I think it honors my mother's legacy without erasing it, and that's exactly why I took the call when Dante reached out."

"Dante Delambre," she clarified, looking at the camera.

"Yes, Dante is directing the next *Simon Says* film."

"This is his directorial debut. He's taking over for his father, who directed the first five movies. And it will be your debut, as well, on the silver screen. Tell us about that call, Evie."

"Well, it came about six months ago. He'd seen my YouTube channel and had just signed on to direct the film. He'd been with the franchise as long as his dad, and he had a vision for how he wanted the sixth movie to go. He wanted me to be involved."

"I'm sure that as an expert in the genre, your insight will be welcomed on set."

I tried to stay focused, but my mind kept drifting elsewhere. I didn't want to be doing this interview at all, but Antoinette thought helping promote the film would help me get a bigger role, and Dante hadn't disagreed. Nothing had been locked in yet, so this was important.

I needed to make sure I was on that set.

"Did you say yes right off the bat to being cast, or were you hesitant to return to a place so... traumatic?"

My mind returned to the room. JoJo was pushing the limit. I glanced at Antoinette, who was already poised to shut down the interview. She'd wanted me to do this, but not at the cost of my emotions. A painful memory from that night washed over me.

Sebastian begging me to look away. Me, staring as my mother's dead body swayed from the rafters. Shoving myself out of his arms to sprint to her, tripping over set pieces as I ran, but it was too late. There was so much blood.

I looked down to find my hands shaking. No, not today. I shoved the awful memory down.

"Sorry." JoJo cleared her throat and started over. "How long did it take him to get you to say yes to the film?" Her eyes flicked to Antoinette, who nodded her approval.

"I did sit with the offer for a while before agreeing," I admitted. "At first, it was a hard no. I didn't think I could handle seeing everyone again. I wasn't sure how they'd treat me or if they even cared about my mom. Had everyone moved on but me?"

When I glanced back at JoJo, I realized I'd gotten too personal. I cleared my throat and sat up, my face flushing.

"But Dante insisted I see his vision for the movie, so I flew in from Michigan, and he was right. Reading the script and seeing his storyboards in person sold me." I finished with a smile.

"And now you're officially signed on as..."

I smiled. "I'm actually not allowed to say who I'll be playing."

JoJo smirked for the cameras.

"All right, girl, keep your secrets. What are you most excited about?"

Revenge.

Thornton. Dourif. Castle. Hodder. Englund. Bradley.

"I think seeing some of the old cast and crew will be fun, now that some of the nervousness is gone. The dynamic will be a little different now that I'm an adult and can finally go to cast parties." I laughed. These questions had been on the list I'd been given last night. They were safe. I was prepared.

"Yes, you were on set with your mother from a young age, weren't you?"

"I was. She started the *Simon Says* movies when I was eight, and up until—" I steeled myself, pushing the heartache back. "Up until her passing, the *Simon Says* crew was like my family."

"Speaking of the cast, how do you feel about working with Hollywood hunk Sebastian Shaw?" JoJo's eyes lit up, and she bit down on her lip, as if having just savored the most delicious treat.

I inhaled deeply. My stomach twisted, and my heart sped up just a fraction at the sound of his name. Even after all these years, his name elicited reactions from my heart and mind that my soul fought against. I didn't want to think about Sebastian.

In my mind, he was just like the rest of them. *Hollywood.* No one had cared about me after she died. They had moved on with their lives as if Lita Reyes had never existed. And I couldn't let myself be dragged off course on my quest for payback. My mother was going to be avenged. Somehow, I'd make it happen.

Sebastian Shaw wasn't on the list of approved questions, but damn if it wasn't a good one.

CHAPTER 3
SEBASTIAN

The Establishing Shot

"Sebastian Shaw? Oh, my God."

My lips twitched. As I spun around, I lowered my sunglasses and flashed a smile at the two women with their mouths open and arms stiff at their sides. The lanyards around their necks told me they were here for a tour.

"Hello, ladies. Would you like a picture?" I strode over to them.

"Would you? Sadie, oh my God. Amy is going to be so mad!" the blonde with the sheer crop top underneath squealed.

I stepped between the two as the brunette on my left stretched her arm out to take a selfie.

"Who's Amy?" I asked, smiling wide.

"Amy is our best friend. She was supposed to come with us, but her sister went into labor, and she had to head to the hospital. She's obsessed with you. She has a tattoo that says *Sebastian Says* on her lower back," the blonde who took the photo explained.

"Bummer. Want to really make her mad?"

The girls' eyes widened, and they nodded.

"You got a pen?"

Two signed shirts later, I reached into my pocket and pulled out my phone. "Sorry, ladies, I have to take this." I left them giggling as I turned and ducked into a sound stage before I could be stopped by any more fans. There'd been no phone call, but it was an easy excuse to get out of talking to people. Just as I was putting it back in my pocket, a text came through from my agent, Anderson.

Anderson

WYA?

I scrunched up my nose at the question. I pushed the call button and brought the phone to my face.

"Hey, sorry. I'll be there in a few. I got distracted."

A loud sigh came from the other side of the call. "I'll order a Red Bull."

"Blueberry." I hung up and left the building, grabbing a golf cart to take me to the lot restaurant I was supposed to be at twenty minutes ago. Once there, I ditched the cart and hurried inside, finding Anderson at a table, sipping on a glass of amber liquid. He was a silver-haired man in his fifties. He didn't tan, bleach his teeth, or participate in any new trend that was running around L.A. His blue eyes were hard but his smile charming. Before he was an agent, he did a lot of security work. Today, like most days out of office, he wore jeans and a tight T-shirt over his muscles. He was a definite upgrade from Heather.

"Sorry about that. I was out late last night. I'm a little hungover," I admitted, sitting down across from him. The restaurant was brightly lit, with lots of windows that let in natural light, and decorated in green and white. A waiter came over and set a blue energy drink in front of me, along with water. I downed the water and then popped the tab on the ice-cold can.

"I assumed as much," Anderson said after the waiter left. "What time did you get home last night?"

"I love that you think I went home." I sipped my Red Bull and tipped it toward him. "It's hard being the hottest man in horror." I grinned. A magazine gave me the title earlier this year, and I'd used that line every chance I got.

"Yeah, yeah. Drink up. I have some news for you, and I need you to pay attention."

The waiter returned with a plate of cheese and crackers. I grabbed a wedge and popped it into my mouth.

"News?"

"I got the script for *Simon Says Six*."

I paused, picking up the menu in front of me. "Oh yeah? Dante is directing, ain't he?"

"He is. The subtitle leaves something to be desired. *Simon Says Six: Six Six*." He rolled his eyes. "But, on the better end, the writers came up with some interesting stuff for Ronny McCoy."

"Anything good?" I asked, feigning disinterest as I scanned the list of lunch items. My stomach rumbled. I tried to remember the last time I'd eaten, but last night was a bit foggy. All I remembered was a pair of soft, tanned—

"Well, your character is an adult now. So, they're adding adult problems."

"Adult problems?" I looked over the menu and lifted my sunglasses. "Like what? Bills, doctor appointments?" I laughed. "Is Ronny gonna have to get a desk job?" I reached for my drink and took a sip. I'd already seen the script. I just hadn't mentioned it to anyone.

"No, he's going to have sex."

I choked on the carbonated liquid so hard it came through my nose. I set the can down and reached for a napkin.

That was a rewrite.

"What?" I coughed, cringing at the burning in my nasal cavities.

Anderson laughed.

"The producers saw you in *Step-Devil*. They know how much that movie made. They noticed that once you became a legal adult, you were up for the challenge. No pun intended. *Step-Devil* wasn't just some cheap horror movie. You showed them what you could do when given the proper spotlight. They want that." He smirked.

I rolled my eyes, but a grin slowly spread over my face.

"Yeah? Well, *Step-Devil* paid for the privilege of seeing my ass plastered in every theater in the world." I sat up. This meeting had just gotten interesting. "How much are they offering?"

"I told them how much we want, and they offered to double it." Anderson leaned back, a smug smile on his face.

My eyes bulged.

Come again?

"Double *Step-Devil*? Do they even have the budget for that? It's the sixth installment of the franchise, for fuck's sake."

"Apparently, they do. The studio thinks that you dropping trou, paired with a killer marketing campaign, will drive sales through the roof. *Simon Says Six—*"

"*Six Six*," I interrupted. I'd been the one to suggest the subtitle and was quite amused by it.

He rolled his eyes. "*Simon Says Six: Six Six* has the biggest budget of any film they're making this year. You need to take the offer before they change their minds."

I slammed the rest of my energy drink just as the waiter came by. He took my empty can, and I ordered street tacos and a beer then returned to the conversation.

"Doubling *Step-Devil* is steep. Why are they offering such a high price for my ass?"

Anderson's blue eyes flicked away from mine.

I narrowed my gaze. "What?"

"Well, for that price, they want a little more than just your backside."

It took me a beat to understand, and then my jaw dropped. "They want me to show my cock on screen?"

"Well..." Anderson shrugged. "Yeah."

I stared down at the table, slightly sick to my stomach. Suddenly, I wasn't hungry anymore. I shouldn't have downed that Red Bull so fast. Full-frontal nudity was bold. Was I prepared to show the world my cock? Would I disappoint, or would I shoot straight up to A-list status?

"We can always tell them no, Sebastian. It's not like you need the money."

No, I didn't. Ever since I fired Heather and the rest of my team, I'd been putting a lot more money in the bank. Between them no longer stealing from me and finally taking on better-paying roles, I wouldn't struggle for a long time if I invested wisely.

"Everything will be by the book?" I looked up, raising an eyebrow.

He nodded eagerly. "Yes. There'll be an intimacy coordinator any time it's needed and a closed set for those shooting days. NDAs will be signed where appropriate, and there'll be a discussion between everyone involved about what you and your costar are comfortable with."

I pursed my lips in thought. I'd been in such shock at the idea of going full-frontal that I'd completely forgotten I'd have someone with me in the scenes.

"Have they cast her yet? Who is the character exactly? I need to see the script." I sat back and ran a hand through my hair. It was still damp from my shower this morning. This was not the meeting I'd been expecting today.

"I can email it to you." Anderson took out his phone and started tapping the screen.

I shook my head in disbelief. He was a good guy overall. A vast upgrade from Heather, who'd managed me my entire childhood. He let me say no to projects without making me feel horrible, but he also knew a good deal when it came across his desk. And this was a good deal.

My phone vibrated in my pocket, signaling a new email.

"Take a look later, and we'll set up a meeting to go over anything you want. Questions, concerns, requests." He leaned in. "Sebastian, you can ask for anything you want at this point and get it."

Really? I smirked.

"Just because I'm hot shit in my genre doesn't mean I'm hot shit everywhere," I argued. I could go to any horror convention and drown in a sea of pussy and cock from fans, but on the streets of L.A., no one noticed me.

"Stop lying to yourself." He waved a hand dismissively. "*Step-Devil* put you on the map, and the producers know it. They are fully aware they could lose you if they don't offer you something good. This could explode your career, Sebastian."

I pressed my lips together and considered it. It wasn't like my cock was unimpressive. I was happy with my size, as were the people I'd bedded. And I worked hard to maintain my toned body. Who didn't like more money?

"Fine. I'll do it."

Anderson clapped his hands together and grinned. "I fucking knew you'd be in. Sebastian, you have no idea how big this is gonna be for you."

I winked at him and laughed. "Right back at you." I pointed to my lap.

We both laughed, and then once we settled down, I realized something.

"One thing, though." I leaned in, a twisted grin curling my lips. "An actor is only as good as his scene partner. Who is the bimbo I'm supposed to fuck?"

CHAPTER 4 SEBASTIAN

The Final Girl

"When is the chemistry read? Bring in everyone you're considering. I want a say in my scene partner," I said to Dante.

We walked across the studio from the parking lot together, at which time he mentioned my costar was basically chosen. They'd gotten it down to two women, of which I'd yet to meet. I was beginning to feel pushed out of the very franchise I was saving.

"It's scheduled for next week, but I doubt we'll need it. We've already narrowed down the roles, Sebastian. I think you'll be fine with our picks." He sighed.

I stared down at the guy directing the next installment in the franchise I'd been a part of most of my life. Dante was in his early thirties, average build, with a creepy mustache and thick-framed glasses. There wasn't anything particularly threatening about him.

"You asked me to flash my dick but couldn't be bothered to ask if I wanted a say in who I'd be doing it in front of?" I shook my head. "You're out of your fucking mind, Dante." I was gearing up to rip his ass a new one when my gaze flicked away from him for a fraction of a second and—

Was that—no. *Was it?*

"Sebastian?" Dante asked, but his voice seemed far away.

"We'll revisit this," I mumbled as I started away, toward the woman who looked startlingly familiar. "Hey!" I called, raising my arm to wave. She was heading into a building. "Hey!" I yelled, my tone more urgent, my pace quickening.

She stopped, and so did my lungs.

"Evie?"

I stared, dumbstruck, at the girl I'd given my heart to when I was young. From a distance, I'd been unsure, but there was no denying it now. Her dark-brown hair was cut to the tops of her breasts, curling at the ends. Her face had matured, but her russet-brown eyes remained just as I'd remembered. Even the clothes she wore had the same casual, grunge style.

I'd been thrown back in time.

"Sebastian."

Her maroon-painted lips curled into a small smile.

I rushed to close the gap between us, tossing my arms around her. "Holy shit. How—why—when?" My brain was short-circuiting. I didn't know where to start. Evie was back.

She stood stiff as I hugged her. I pulled back, running my hand through my hair. "How have you been?" I sputtered finally.

She laughed, and it was music to my ears, like a wind chime in a light breeze.

"I've been good. What about you, Mr. Movie Star?"

I ran my tongue over my lips and rolled my eyes. Suddenly, I wasn't so proud of the *hottest man in horror* title.

"I've been doing good too." I looked around the lot. People were moving all around us, going from sound stages to offices, not paying any attention. I returned my focus to her. "Actually, things have been kind of great. I don't know if you've seen everything."

She leaned against a railing in front of a building and crossed her arms over her chest, tightening her leather jacket around herself. I ran my gaze down her body. Under the jacket, she had on a tight minidress that was a faded reddish-purple. Underneath were fishnets and black boots. Tattoos littered her skin, making me curious about the ones I couldn't see. It was as if someone had taken my wet dreams and crafted my ideal woman from them.

My ideal woman had always been Evie Reyes.

"I've seen a bit. Congrats, Sebastian. You've worked so hard for all of this."

"I have." I nodded. "I fired Heather ages ago. It was the best decision I ever made. I was able to take control of my career. *Step-Devil* was a hit. Did you get a chance to see it?"

"I heard about it." She blushed and looked away. "I didn't go see it."

I brushed my bruised ego off with a wave and a chuckle. "Aw, well, you should. It's a good movie. It got nominated."

"That's the one with the..."

"Sex scene?" I wiggled my eyebrows. "Oh yeah. I had to go twice as hard at the gym to make sure I looked good for it."

"I bet. Well...that's kind of why I avoided watching it. It's a little awkward to see." She rolled her shoulders and tugged on her jacket uncomfortably. Her gaze shifted around, as if looking for an escape. I knew that look, but panic set in. I couldn't let her go so fast.

I just got her back.

"What? My ass? It's nothing you haven't seen before." I laughed loudly, overcompensating for the awkwardness I was creating. "And that's nothing compared to what they have me doing in the next *Simon Says*. They are going to pay me big fucking money—we're talking blockbuster money—to go full-frontal in a sex scene with some chick I haven't even met. I'm sure she's a crazy fangirl or something." I smirked and moved closer, trying to force the old familiarity. She visibly cringed and gave me wild eyes. Heat flooded my face, and I stepped back. My heart began to race. This wasn't right. Since when was I this cocky asshole? I took a breath. I needed to back the fuck up and try again.

"You look great."

My mind, body, and soul were responding to her presence as if I'd been thrown back in time. I was a sixteen-year-old in love. Those three small words seemed to break the tension between us. Her lips slowly curved upward into a smile.

She laughed again, and my cock hardened. Oh God, I really

was acting like a teenage boy.

She brushed her hair behind her ear, revealing stretched lobes with white, heart tunnels. I shook my head, still in disbelief that she was really here, a foot away from me. Her eyes drifted behind me, and her expression perked up. She waved.

"Dante!"

I turned and saw Dante heading toward us. Jealousy rolled through me in dark waves as I stared him down. I'd seen the type of women Dante dated before. They were Evie look-alikes. I wasn't going to give him the chance to steal what was mine. My hand twitched with the desire to pull Evie into my side like I would have years ago, but I forced myself to stand still and feign nonchalance.

"Evie! I see you've found Sebastian. Seb, Evie has agreed to come on as Ronny's love interest."

My eyes widened, and I looked back at Evie. My stomach tightened with mortification as I realized what I'd just said moments before. I'd called her a fangirl.

The woman who'd been cast wasn't someone who wanted to fuck me—she was one who already had.

"One of them, anyway," Dante said, interrupting my thoughts. "We've cast two women in a love triangle situation. Have you read the updated script yet?" he asked me.

I shook my head.

"No, I haven't. Sorry." I turned to Evie, my face still warm. "I didn't realize."

"It's okay," she said, offering me a small smile.

"Here's Johnny." I looked to Evie, hoping she'd remember our code. A flicker of recognition hit her eyes as she took in that I didn't want Dante here. He was an intruder in our conversation.

"Ugh. I forgot you two used to do that. What does that mean? It's from *The Shining*, I know that," Dante muttered. I stared blankly at him. Why would I tell him our code? Sensing the awkward tension, he chuckled nervously. When I continued to glare, his focus went behind us, and his eyes lit up.

"And there's the other girl now. This is perfect. Skye! Over here!" He waved.

I opened my mouth to protest another uninvited guest into this conversation, but a quick glance at Evie stopped me short. Her eyes were lit up, as if relieved. Was talking to me that bad?

I swore inwardly, realizing how hard I'd come on just now. I'd been so excited to see her, and she looked ready to run for the hills.

Reluctantly, I tore my eyes from Evie to catch a blonde with no bra bouncing toward us. My eyes rolled into the back of my head as she skipped over.

"Oh my gosh, what a surprise!" she squealed, thrusting her hand out. "I'm Skye."

"Yes, we haven't finalized the script yet, but one of you"—Dante pointed between Evie and Skye—"will be Sebastian's scene partner for the set piece. I tried explaining this earlier, but you kept interrupting," he said to me.

"Why didn't you tell me who was cast?" I demanded. How could he not have mentioned my ex was one of the leads? He had to have known Evie and I dated before...she left.

He had said I wouldn't need a chemistry test...

"Because we haven't officially—"

Skye inserted herself between Dante and me, cutting him off. "I'm so excited to work with you, Sebastian. I'm a huge fan of the *Simon Says* franchise, and I loved you in *Step-Devil*. I can only hope our scenes are half as hot as that movie."

"It's bold of you to assume it'll be you in bed with me," I said to Skye but was staring directly behind her at Evie. She looked down, which satisfied me greatly. "Considering—"

"Beep beep, Ritchie," Evie said the words so fast they blended together, but I understood.

I cocked an eyebrow. Was I not allowed to say that we once dated? Why didn't she want them to know about our history?

"I was actually thinking that maybe it was better for me not to be the main love interest," Evie said to Dante.

The cocky grin slid off my face.

"You think?" Dante turned to her. "I'm assuming you've read both versions of the script, then?"

She nodded. "I did. I just think, with my ties to the series, the rewrite might be smarter."

"That's the version where you and I hook up and then murder her character," Skye said excitedly.

I ignored her and spoke over her head. "I want a say in this. No decisions get made on the script until I give it a pass," I demanded. "I will not accept a life I do not deserve."

Evie and Dante turned to me. Evie's brown eyes widened, and the familiar spark of passion and rage lit up her face. I was adding to our code, using a line from *MaXXXine*, but it fit, and Evie understood what I was trying to tell her. She was pissed. Good.

"Sebastian, come on. This is a stretch. What's next, a producer credit?" Dante threw his hands up.

I stared him down. "My agent said I could have whatever I wanted, so long as my hard cock was front and center when needed. Evie is my final girl," I said, keeping my eyes on the woman who broke me five years ago.

"Well, I think both scripts are great, and if I got the chance—" Skye started but was quickly interrupted by Dante.

"Fine. But I want your opinion at the table read tomorrow. We'll be going through both scripts. Don't fuck around. If you want a say in who your final girl is, actually come prepared to defend your choice." He stormed off.

Just as I was turning back to Evie to explain that I wasn't always this big of a dick, my phone rang.

Anderson was calling.

I scrunched up my nose. "I've got to take this. Maybe we can go through the scripts together at dinner?" I said, bringing the phone to my ear. I glanced back at the girls and gave Evie a wink. "I'll catch you later, Final Girl," I said before turning away to take my agent's call.

CHAPTER 5

EVIE

The Martini Meeting

"He called me Final Girl." Skye swooned and fell back against the railing I'd been leaning on.

I stepped back, slightly confused. Had we been part of the same conversation?

"He's so fucking hot," she continued. "Did you see him in *Step-Devil*? I need to touch that bare ass." She made a squeezing motion, and I cringed. She didn't seem to notice my reaction. "I have a friend who slept with him a year or so ago. She said his dick is huge."

As if seeing me for the first time, she stuck out her hand for me to shake. "I'm Skye."

"Evie."

"I think I recognize you." She squinted and ran her gaze up and down me. "I feel like I've seen videos of you?"

I rolled my eyes. I got this often in public.

"Probably. I have a web channel, The—"

"*Body Count Bimbo*! Yes!" she squealed as her eyes widened with recognition. "I listen to you when I work out sometimes. Wow, no wonder he wants you as the main lead."

I blushed and offered a tight smile. "I think he was just trying to throw his weight around. I think you'd be better in that role."

Like a spring, her mood popped right back up from

disappointment to excitement.

"Really? This is gonna be such a game-changer for me. Especially if we go with the good script." Her words were casual, but the look in her honey-colored eyes was a mix of threatening and hopeful. Almost as if she were making sure I agreed with her.

"It sounds like they haven't made a decision yet." A sudden flare of jealousy and protectiveness came over me. Maybe I did want the lead role alongside Sebastian. It was my mother's legacy after all. "It could be either of us."

"True, but if you don't even want it, that should factor in." She spun around, flipping her long, silky blonde hair over her shoulder. "If you don't want to fuck him on camera, I will."

I pressed my lips together. She was clearly confident in her status on this project. Who was I to argue? I nodded and stuffed my hands into my pockets.

"Well, it was nice to meet you. I'm going to head to my hotel."

"Ooh, where are you staying? They put me up at the Carradine."

I faltered. Hopefully my mother's home was ready sooner rather than later, and my hotel stay was short. I couldn't quite read Skye, and that made me uneasy. Was she only interested in the role, or something more with Sebastian? And why did I even care? I shook my head, forcing him from my mind.

Suddenly, her competitiveness slid off, and she looped her arm through mine. "If we're gonna be spending the next few months together, we need to become friends fast." She started moving, and I stumbled forward, not entirely sure what was going on but too nervous to protest. She was far more confident in this world than I was, even though I'd grown up on this very lot. I thought about that as we rode to the hotel we were both staying at. How unfamiliar this all felt, despite knowing it shouldn't be. Skye didn't seem to notice me going in and out. She talked the entire ride. She gave me a rundown of her life and asked about mine. I was guarded and kept things vague when she asked about my family. It didn't seem to faze her, though, because she just kept talking. And by the time we got to the hotel, I realized I was the bitch—not her. She was just a girl with goals.

"It's gonna be so much fun, Evie." She hugged me in the elevator. "I hope they pick me," she said, stepping back, her wide eyes searching mine. What did she want from me? Was she waiting for me to say I wished it too?

I wasn't sure what I wanted.

Before I could speak, the elevator dinged, and we turned to see a man holding a giant bouquet of flowers. Skye's face lit up, and she ran to him. I followed behind at a slower pace.

"Dahlias are my favorite! Those have to be for me." She grabbed the mixture of burgundy and pink flowers from the man. He looked slightly startled but waited as she read the card. Her jaw dropped, and she looked at me. "He wants to take me to dinner."

"Who?" I asked.

"Sebastian, silly!" She waved the card.

The delivery man nodded and left.

Skye came back to me, holding the large arrangement. "I knew we made a connection today. He's probably going to go with the good script. I'll have my chance to win him over. Oh, Evie, this is amazing!" She tried to hug me again, but the flowers got in the way.

"That's great, Skye. I'm not feeling too hot. I need to go lie down."

"Oh? Headache? Tummy troubles?"

"Chronic nausea," I told her, which wasn't a lie. I dipped into my room before she could try to help me—or before I had to hear more about her and Sebastian's possible sex scenes. I leaned against the door and let out a breath. Sebastian was taking Skye out to dinner, and I was...disappointed? Why, exactly? I didn't come here for him, and yet...

Had I read everything wrong?

Sebastian had seemed happy to see me.

He'd remembered our codes.

And...so had I.

I fell onto the bed and rolled onto my back, staring at the ceiling. The more I thought about it, asking Skye out made sense. He was so obnoxiously Hollywood now. With his muscular physique and chiseled features, he didn't need plastic surgery. He was one of the rare people who were born gorgeous. Time had only enhanced his allure.

He'd bragged to me about how good his life had gotten after I left, and all I could think about was how bright his green eyes were now. A far cry from the dull, depressed look he wore when we were kids. He'd wanted me to know that my sudden departure from L.A. hadn't hurt him. And I couldn't say the same. This was just another kick in the shin to tell me he was over me.

It was hard not to take that personally. Exhaling, I sat up. Staying here, alone in my room, I'd go crazy thinking about him and Skye. I needed to do something.

I took a nausea pill then showered, changed, and redid my makeup. I waited until I heard Skye's voice in the hall, heading downstairs. Once I was confident she'd left for her date, I exited my room. I went down and wandered into the bar.

"Blueberry lemon drop," I ordered.

"Is this who I think it is?" A handsome man with a sun-kissed tan and slightly long, tousled, sandy blond hair slid over, flashing a bright smile. "Evie Reyes?"

I eyed him cautiously. He wore a dusty blue suit, but he appeared young. "And you are?"

"Glenn Thornton. I'm one of the producers for *Simon Says Six*. It's nice to finally meet you. I was a huge fan of your mom."

Thornton.

I stiffened.

"*Six Six*."

"What's that?"

"The movie is *Simon Says Six: Six Six*."

He eyed me curiously. "Right."

The bartender returned with my drink. Glenn ordered a rum and Coke and sat beside me.

"I'd heard they'd put some of the actors up here, but I hadn't realized you'd be here too."

"It's temporary. I have people cleaning my mom's estate so I can move in."

"They never sold it?" He raised his eyebrows, his tone shifting with interest.

I shook my head. "My aunt wanted me to be the one to decide what to do with it. I was only two years away from being an adult when my mother died."

"Right. My apologies. Lita was highly respected in the field."

A moment of awkwardness crept over us when I didn't reply, but Glenn pushed it away quickly.

"We'll be seeing a lot of each other. I'm one of the youngest producers on the project. I took over for my dad when he passed earlier this year."

"Michael Thornton?" I asked, my stomach tightening.

Thornton. Dourif. Castle. Hodder. Englund. Bradley.

He was on my list.

"Yes. Did you know him?"

"My mom did." I brought my drink to my lips but paused. "I'm sorry for your loss." The words rang hollow, but what does one say when they tell you their parent is dead?

Good.

"Same. Let's not talk about our dead parents, though. The Hollywood gossip circles have done enough to both of them."

"Fair enough." I smiled tightly and made a mental note to look into the cause of death—and why I hadn't heard about it. "So, *Simon Says*, we're second gen. Welcome to the club." We raised our glasses, letting them clink, and then we drank. I was a bit stiff in my movements, and I didn't reply when he said welcome. Instead, I toasted to something else silently.

Thanks to whatever or whoever did Michael Thornton in.

"It's an honor to be here." I lied. I wouldn't be here at all if it weren't for his father and his friends.

"So, tell me about yourself, Evie Reyes."

I eyed him suspiciously for a careful moment and then started in. Over the next hour, I told him about my career as a social media influencer, and soon, after a third cocktail, I'd completely forgotten why I'd come down from my room. I was having a good time with Glenn.

Even if his dad had been one of my mortal enemies.

He was flirty but polite. He teased me, leaning in intimately, but never once did his hand move to my thigh. It was a pleasant surprise. Had I met the only gentleman in Hollywood?

A few hours later, our good evening was interrupted by a squealing voice.

"Evie!"

Glenn and I turned to see Skye and Sebastian returning from their date. Skye ran toward us, but Sebastian stayed back, hands deep in his black suit jacket, scowling. He'd styled his hair back with gel. My breathing hitched slightly at the sight of him.

"Seb—come here!" Skye called, throwing her arms around me. "You look like you're feeling better." She giggled and called to Sebastian again.

Reluctantly, he sauntered over, maintaining the scowl on his face.

"Hey, Sebastian," Glenn greeted warmly. "Glenn. I'm a producer for *Simon Says Six*."

"*Six Six*," Sebastian and I shot back at the same time. We made eye contact, and the corner of his mouth twitched. I laughed, but stopped when I realized I was the only one who thought it funny. Glenn held out his hand, but Sebastian didn't shake it, leaving Glenn to falter and stuff his hand back into his pocket.

"Let's go sit at a booth." Skye grabbed Sebastian by the arm and pulled him to a table.

Glenn picked up our drinks off the bar.

"You want to?" he asked.

No. Not with how Sebastian was scowling at us. However, Glenn was already halfway across the room, and Skye had already sat down and was waving her arm in the air.

"Sure, I guess," I muttered to myself as I hopped off my stool and joined the party.

Skye and Sebastian took one side of the booth, while Glenn and I sat across from them.

"What were you guys meeting about?" Sebastian asked as soon as we sat down. His tone was sharp and carried an air of authority. "Discussing the movie?"

Glenn and I exchanged a look at the cold, almost accusatory question. Why did he care?

"Not at all, actually. Glenn saw me drinking by myself and decided to be friendly," I shot back.

"You look more than just friendly," Sebastian said. "Like we caught you on a date."

"We only just met today, actually." What was he doing? I stared at Sebastian, trying to communicate silently. I scanned my memory for a movie line that could convey what I needed, but I was a tad too tipsy to focus.

"So did we." Skye leaned her head against Sebastian's shoulder. "We had an amazing dinner. Sebastian took me to Tantalus. Have you been?"

"I love that place," Glenn said.

"I've never been," I said.

A waiter came by and took our drink orders.

"Maybe I can take you sometime." Glenn gave me a smile that, ten minutes ago, would have given me delicious butterflies. Now, I was hyper-aware of our audience.

"You can do better than that, Mr. Producer," Sebastian sneered. "That's if Evie's not pretending to have a stomachache. I can't help but notice I didn't even get a thank-you call."

I stiffened. How did he know about me not feeling well? I glanced at Skye, who coincidently was focusing hard on the drink menu.

Thank you? For what exactly?

I was about to ask when Glenn spoke up beside me.

"Well, I mean, it'd probably be more than just dinner." Glenn fumbled with his words. “Maybe a show or something. We can talk about this later,” he said.

I pressed my hand to my forehead. This was mortifying. Poor Glenn. Poor Skye. She had no idea why Sebastian was acting like this. I didn’t either, for that matter. This was exactly why I hadn’t called Sebastian when I returned. Glenn was a producer. He had connections I didn’t, and while his dad was already dead, the others weren’t. I needed to play nice.

Sebastian wouldn’t understand my need for revenge. This was a solo mission.

“Speaking of thank you—Sebastian is such a gentleman. Not only did we go to dinner, but Sebastian also sent me flowers. Evie saw them. They’re gorgeous, aren’t they, Evie?” Skye, seemingly afraid of silence, piped up.

Sebastian’s head snapped toward her. “What?”

“The Dahlias. They were stunning. And expensive. My momma had a saying—if the date costs more than what you made in a full day’s work, then your date deserves to get a little lucky. Thank you for sending them to my room.” She turned from him to beam at us across the table. “He called me his Final Girl.”

Everyone at the table watched as her hand dipped under the table to touch Sebastian.

He didn’t flinch. He didn’t seem to register she’d said anything at all. He was glaring those green eyes at me.

“Those flowers were for Evie.”

CHAPTER 6

EVIE

The Chemistry Test

"I— I need to get some air." I slid out of the booth before anyone could protest.

"Oh, my God. I—" Skye sputtered. "This is so embarrassing. Evie, let me come with you." She stood, but I put my hand up.

"No, I need to—not you. I'll be fine. I just have to go. It was nice to meet you," I said to Glenn.

"Are you sure? It's still early," Glenn protested.

I muttered an apology and rushed out of the bar, freezing in the lobby. Out or up? Pausing to close my eyes for a moment, I opened them and went to the elevator, quickly pushing the button.

"Evie!" Sebastian called to me, but I refused to look back.

I stepped inside and reached for my purse, digging for my room key.

Sebastian caught the elevator, sliding in just as the doors started to shut.

"Sebastian—"

"He's no good for you," he blurted.

I leaned forward and pressed the button for my floor.

"Don't be alone with him again," he ordered.

I raised my eyebrows. "Excuse me? You're not my fucking handler. Where is this coming from?"

"A concerned friend. That man is no good, Evie. Trust me."

"Trust you?" I scoffed. The elevator started upward, and I stared ahead. "I don't trust anyone in this fucking town."

"Then why did you come back?"

The elevator stopped, and the doors opened. I stepped forward, but he grabbed my wrist and pulled me back, allowing the doors to close.

"Sebastian—" I protested, but in a flash, he leaned over me and smashed the emergency stop. I flinched, waiting for the alarm, but there was none. I glanced around. What had just happened?

"Answer me, Evie. Why did you come back?"

I looked up at him. His green eyes, the color of forest leaves, pierced into mine.

"Sebastian, someone's going to come open this door."

"We've got three minutes." He didn't take his eyes off me. "Answer me."

"I was invited. Dante—"

"I don't believe that. You wouldn't come back just to be in a stupid movie."

"It's not stupid. It's my mother's legacy," I snapped.

His eyes softened. "I'm sorry. You know that's not—"

"Look, thank you, I guess, for the flowers." I shrugged. "I'm not going to take them from Skye, but they were a nice gift. I don't have anything else to say. I look forward to our working relationship." I gave him a tight, straight-lined smile.

His eyes widened, and he leaned back against the wall, a short laugh coming from his chest. "You look forward to our working relationship. What kind of line is that?"

"It's a necessary one." I sighed deeply. "Sebastian, I know—"

"Know what? That you ghosted me? Broke my heart and fucked up my brain permanently? Because I don't think you do. If you did, you wouldn't be acting so damn cold."

I opened and shut my mouth.

Ghosted?

He told me to go.

I stood there speechless, taken aback by his accusation.

"Thought so." He smirked and crossed his arms over his suit. "Now, why are you here?"

"You wouldn't believe me if I told you." How could I confess that I was here to murder as many big-shot men in this industry as I could before I was inevitably gunned down? He stared at me as if trying to bore into my soul. They were so intense, I broke contact, my gaze sliding down his body and resting at my own feet. The longer we stood in silence, the heavier the tension grew.

"I never thought I'd see you again."

Same.

"I know. I'm sorry. I should have found a way to warn you I'd accepted a role," I mumbled, stepping back and leaning against the elevator doors.

"Like a phone call? Or a text? You have my number," he said.

I rolled my eyes. "Really? You wanted me to call after five years with no contact?"

"Yes, really. You're acting like we're strangers. Why? What did I do to make you shut me out of your life?"

You stayed.

A heavy weight began to grow in my belly. It had been selfish of me to ask that of him. And looking into his eyes now, I wasn't even sure he remembered.

"You're acting like everything is black and white, and it's not. I—"

"I was in love with you." His eyes grew shiny. "I told you so many times how much you meant to me. How I couldn't do this without you. You never once said it back. You were my first everything, Evie. Do you know what that did to me?"

"I—" Tears welled in my eyes, obscuring my vision.

"Did I mean anything to you?" His voice cracked as he asked, and suddenly, he wasn't the man I'd met this afternoon. The charming, cocky movie star. He'd reverted back to the boy I knew and loved all those years ago.

"Yes, you did," I whispered. I pressed my lips together tightly. Him close to tears had me close to crying as well. "Sebastian, that night changed me."

"I'm not talking about your mom. I'm talking about me. About us. What we did before we went to the studio. Forgive me if I don't believe you when you say I meant something. You left a few days later and never looked back. Tell me, Evie. How long did it take for you to forget me?" He pushed off the wall and stepped toward me, raising one arm to pin me against the doors. As he leaned into me, I could smell the whiskey on his breath. It mixed with his cologne in a delicious, dangerous concoction. My breathing quickened as I tilted my head to look up at him. "A month? Maybe two? We saved ourselves for each other, but we never made promises past that night. Tell me, who was the next guy you fucked? Did he look like me?"

"You're drunk," I said but didn't push him away.

"So? Answer me."

"No," I said firmly. I lifted my hands to his chest to push him away, but when my palms fell against his muscles and I could feel the hard lines of his chest, my resolve fluttered. He must have caught my reaction, because he chuckled.

"That's all because of you." He moved back just slightly, and I breathed in relief as my hands dropped from his body. He reached for the top of his shirt and began unbuttoning it, pulling it open to reveal a spectacular set of abs decorated with tattoos. They were all movie themed, but the one that caught my eye was a large chainsaw on the side of his ribcage, with a bloody ribbon that said, *Groovy*. It was from *Evil Dead*. One of my all-time favorite movies. My vision glossed over the rest of his ink and focused on the muscles. I stared, counting each pack.

Eight.

"With you gone, I stopped fighting this town. I threw myself into work, made sure I could cry on cue. When I wasn't on camera, I was in the gym, molding my body into what they wanted. And man, did they want me. Your rejection did wonders for my career, Evie Reyes."

I tore my gaze from the V leading beneath his pants. "I was in a bad place mentally, and I needed to cut ties with everything in this town." I was this close to telling him the complete truth about why I was here, but he interrupted my thoughts.

"But now you're back." He reached out, his knuckles grazing my jaw.

Delicious shivers slid down my chest, through my stomach, and settled between my legs. I tightened my core and inhaled deeply, trying to steel myself.

This was bad. I turned my head toward the doors. When was someone coming to help us?

He leaned back in, and reflexively, I tilted my face up as he nuzzled his nose against my cheek. "Evie, this feels like a dream. It's been five years, and the moment I saw you across the lot, time went away. It could have been five days or five decades, I won't stop feeling how I feel about you." His hand brushed my hair back behind my ear, and I gasped as he whispered in my ear.

"And I can tell by the way you stare at me that you feel it too. Well, Clarice, have the lambs stopped screaming?"

My heart had slowed, but each beat screamed in my ears. His head moved, inky black hair falling over his eyes. His lips hovered an inch from mine. If I moved even a fraction...

A pounding on the doors rattled the metal, bringing me back to what was about to happen. I shoved Sebastian back and moved away from the door.

"That's from the book, not the movie," I said lamely as Sebastian glared daggers at me.

"Are you okay?" a man shouted from the other side.

A low growl came from Sebastian as he leaned forward and pulled the emergency button back out. The doors opened a moment later, revealing two security guards and a maintenance man.

"It's fine. Button got pushed by accident," Sebastian muttered. The men looked from Sebastian, with his unbuttoned shirt, to me with my flushed cheeks, and embarrassment flooded me. I put my hands over my face.

"Everything good?" the maintenance man asked again.

"Yes, thank you," Sebastian said.

The men left quickly.

Sebastian exited the elevator then turned to me, reaching his hand out. "Come on. Let's go to your room so we can keep talking."

I stared at him blankly, the heat from my face gone. Slowly, my gaze raked up his gorgeous frame. If I took his hand—if we went to my hotel room—there would be no talking.

I shook my head. "I'm sorry, Sebastian. No. I'll see you at the table read tomorrow." I reached out and pushed the button to close the elevator. Only once the doors closed and I couldn't stare into those beautiful, haunting eyes could I breathe again.

Fuck me.

He wasn't going to make revenge easy.

CHAPTER 7 SEBASTIAN

The Table Read

I woke to my phone going crazy. Groaning, I rolled over and put my hands over my eyes. My phone continued to ring, so I swung my arm over and felt around for it. Finding it on my bed, I dragged it to my face and squinted at the screen. Anderson.

Fuck. The table read.

"Hello," I groaned.

"Get the fuck over to the lot, you dick," Anderson hissed.

I sat up and stretched, then dragged myself to the mirror on the wall. Staring, I couldn't help but feel a little embarrassed at my appearance; I looked like a fucking goof, dressed in a suit for a girl who wasn't even interested. So uninterested she sent someone else on a date with me. Nothing about last night went how I'd hoped.

"Where the fuck are you? You were supposed to be here half an hour ago," Anderson yelled.

"I stayed at a hotel last night. Let me shower, and I'll be there." I hung up before he could ask more questions. Then I texted him to send over some clothes, along with my room number, and stripped to shower. I took my time under the hot water. I needed to sober up fast if I was going to see Evie again today.

My Final Girl.

By the time I was clean and headache-free, my clothes had arrived. Jeans, a black tee, and my leather jacket. Anderson had sent someone to my house. I laced up my boots and left the hotel room. Anderson was in the lobby, scowling. He handed me a blueberry Red Bull.

"What are you doing here?" he demanded. "Are you already fucking your co-star?"

"Quite the opposite," I muttered. "Let's go."

I downed the energy drink as we got into the car and let Anderson rant about how I made everyone wait at the table read.

After Evie's embarrassing rejection, I'd returned to the bar solo, where I'd had a drink too many. Still hopeful that maybe she'd come down and pity me with conversation, I stayed far into the night and ended up giving the bartender my credit card to get me a room at the hotel. It was just a tad pathetic.

"People are going to think you're difficult to work with, Sebastian."

"Who are *people*?" I rolled my eyes. "I'm the fucking star of this franchise."

"No one is untouchable. Look at what happened to Lita Reyes. If they're done with you, you'll know it."

My head snapped from the window.

"What the fuck did you just say?"

Anderson shrank into his seat. "I—you know, people talk. It's just rumors. Sorry."

"Put some respect on that name." I thrust my empty can at him, shaking my head. "After that comment, you should be more worried about your job than mine."

"Yes, Sebastian. I apologize. I know you were close to her."

"She was like a second mom to me."

I looked back out the window as we passed through the studio gates. Rumors, hardly. Lita Reyes didn't kill herself. Anyone who was anyone in this fucking town knew her death was murder. Minutes later, we were in the building and heading to the table read, where everyone was waiting for me. I took a large breath and pushed the door open. Everyone looked up and gave sarcastic cheers and claps.

I smirked and flipped them off. "Sorry, guys. I had a rough night with Jack Daniels."

Dante came over and smacked my back. "Happens to the best of us. Take your seat, and we'll get started."

I scanned the room, waving apologetically at Anderson and the others. There were two tables set up. The main table was filled with the cast, writers, and director. The second was the producer's table. The main table was long and arranged for us all to face each other. Off to the side was a smaller one. Chairs were all on one side, allowing everyone sitting to face us. They would be studying us, making decisions we wouldn't even know about until later. Everyone was where they were supposed to be, except for one person. I took my seat and pointed.

"What are you doing over here, *producer*?" I asked Glenn, spitting the title like a curse.

He turned from where he was flirting with Evie. All the chatter in the room stopped.

"Me? Waiting for the *star* to show." He snickered and stood, putting his hand on Evie's shoulder and staring me down. "I'll text you later."

"Everyone have both versions of the script?" Dante asked.

I looked down at my spot on the table and picked up both scripts. I hadn't read the updated one yet.

Dante continued, "Let's start with the first version, in which Riley, played by Skye, is the Final Girl."

Skye squealed beside Evie, bouncing up and down.

"Are we sure we need to bother reading that version?" I said, cutting through the chatter. Again, everyone stopped to look at me.

"What?" Dante asked from the head of the table.

"I want Evie to be the Final Girl. There's no need to read both," I said firmly but cool.

Everyone was watching Dante and me, gazes volleying between us. Who would win, director or lead actor?

Dante seemed to be thinking the same thing. "Be that as it

may, I still want to read through each of them to see how they feel. So do the producers and the studio executives."

I bit my tongue. I wanted to tell him this was all a waste of time. Evie was going to be the lead, no matter what it took. Anderson cleared his throat and came from behind to offer me another energy drink. He elbowed me as he did so, reminding me that I had a job to do, and that job was to shut up and listen to my director.

I clenched my fists under the table. Taking a deep breath, I grabbed the top script and opened it to begin the read.

It was a pretty basic slasher. My character had been through hell and back in the first five movies. In this version, Riley, Skye's character, was my girlfriend, and Lucy, Evie's character, was a siren of sorts, luring me to cheat on her. In between all the body count padding, Riley sets up a dinner and confronts me. We have sex, and right in the middle of it, Lucy comes in and tries to hack Riley to pieces, revealing herself as Simon Says's daughter. Riley escapes, which leads to the epic final battle between Lucy and me. I chop off her head and walk away from an explosion, smoking a cigarette and calling Riley to ask her to move in with me.

Overall, the first updated script wasn't bad. The girlfriend wasn't even a named character in the original version I'd read a few months ago. She'd only had a brief moment in the beginning. This script gave my character depth and would give Skye potential to come back for another movie, but overall, I was bored and found it uninteresting. There was a break between scripts, and before I stepped out to have a cigarette with the others, I paused on the other side of the table to speak to Evie.

"I think my mask of sanity is about to slip," I quoted *American Psycho*, asking her to speak to me privately.

She stared up at me, her jaw ticking, as if she were going to speak. Before she could, Glenn came over and stole her attention, sliding smoothly between us. She completely turned her attention to him, and getting the hint, I stormed off to smoke.

Returning to the table, we opened the second script. The

beginning was overall the same. I began to zone out until I noticed Evie on her phone, causing me to perk up. I glanced to see if anyone was paying attention. A moment later, my phone vibrated.

So, she did still have my number.

Unknown

Sometimes dead is better.

I quickly saved the contact as Final Girl, noting that it was a new number from the one I'd had before. I looked down at the script to make sure I was in the right place, then considered the text. She was telling me she didn't want to revisit our old relationship. I stared at the phone, forgetting my script. If she didn't have feelings for me, then why was she still using our code?

I shot back a text, quoting *Scream*.

Not in my movie.

She snickered as she read, then focused on the table read, driving me bonkers. I tapped my foot under the table, trying to pay attention to my lines. Out of the corner of my eye, I saw her raise her phone, and my gaze shot to her.

Final Girl

The power of Christ compels you.

She wanted me to leave her alone. She texted me first! My mouth fell open, but I snapped it shut quickly as Dante cleared his throat and glared at me for having my phone out.

I shoved it back into my jacket and got back into the script. In this version, I meet Lucy and fall for her. Riley comes in and tries to get me to leave Lucy for her. Lucy gets attacked by Simon Says, and when I find her safe, we have sex. Riley comes in afterward, revealing she's Simon Says's sidekick, and detains me—naked. Then the girls have the epic last fight. Lucy wins, saves me, and we run off together, escaping the villain once again.

During the slow parts, I tried to think of a comeback. I wracked my brain. Dozens of quotes came to mind, but everything felt too creepy. I typed a line from *The Bride of Frankenstein* and hesitated.

I'll make sure we're together forever.

What was I doing? Was this flirting, or could that be interpreted as a threat?

All these things ran through my mind while I tried to stay focused. This was part of my job, and I was being incredibly unprofessional. On any other project, where I wasn't tied to the entire franchise, playing on my phone in the middle of a table read could get me sacked. It was then I realized she'd done this on purpose. She wanted me to not give this version of the script a good read so that the producers would see me as unenthused and choose the version with Skye as the main lead.

I stared at her, unblinking. She sat across from me, smiling like a cat having just ate its mouse.

"Sebastian?" Dante called.

I tore my eyes away from Evie. "Huh? Oh, sorry." I read my lines and fumed silently as we ran through a few more pages until I didn't have any lines. I deleted my creepy message and typed a new one, ditching the movie lines.

He's no good. Drop him.

Final Girl

Why? Because he's not you?

Yes, but also because he's a bad guy.

Final Girl

I like bad boys.

"Sebastian!" Dante snapped.

"Sorry, one second," I said.

"If you don't put that phone away, I don't care what you want. We're going with the script I pick."

I bit down hard on my lip. Inhaling deeply, steadying my rage caused by the woman across from me, I handed my phone to Anderson, who'd stepped forward to take it. Evie cackled and sat back, crossing her arms. Did no one notice her phone being out?

We took a short break, and I bee-lined for my agent, snatching my phone back. Heading outside, I checked my notifications and found a text from her.

Final Girl

Flexing your muscles isn't going to win me over. I'm not interested.

That look you gave me last night when I unbuttoned my shirt says otherwise.

I looked around but didn't see her anywhere.

Final Girl

You really think you're hot shit now, don't you? When did you become so damn cocky?

Five years ago, the same night I made you come.

I shoved my phone into my pocket and stormed back inside. Irritation seeped into me as I walked back into the room. Evie stood by her chair, staring at her phone. The shocked look on her face told me she was reading my last message. She looked up and typed something quickly. Then, just as everyone was sitting down, my phone vibrated.

Final Girl

You didn't.

My mind went blank as I stared at her. She grinned, knowing she'd finally pissed me off. My breathing grew heavy as I tried to rein in my anger, but her relaxing deeper into her chair like a satisfied cat tipped me over the edge. Caught up in the moment, I leaped back up and pointed at her.

"You liar!" I shouted.

The room froze, and I realized what I'd just done. Slowly, I lowered myself back into my seat.

"I—apologize. That won't happen again."

Silence filled the room, and heat flooded my face as I lowered my gaze to my script and kept it there until Dante stopped seething and called for us to resume. For the rest of the table read, I was on my best behavior. When it was over and people stood to go, I rushed to Dante and profusely apologized for my unprofessionalism.

He sighed deeply and rubbed his jaw.

"Don't fuck this up for me, Seb. That's all I have to say." With tired eyes, he gave me a tight smile and patted me hard on the back as he went to the producer's table to defend casting me. I'd seen this before. I was on thin ice.

Anderson caught my attention and motioned for me to leave so he could do damage control. With my head hung, I exited the room.

Going outside, I was surprised to find Evie the only one lingering by the doors. Rolling my eyes, I pulled a cigarette from the case in my pocket and lit up. Taking a long drag of nicotine, I turned to her.

"You're a liar. I know you came."

She had her back toward me, arms clutched to her chest. "Did I? Maybe I was a good actor, even then."

"Well then, you're gonna be one hell of a star in this movie."

She turned and shook her head. "No, I don't think I will. They're going with the first script. I'm not your Final Girl."

We stared each other down until the doors behind me opened and Glenn came out.

"Ready? I'm starving." He went to her, beaming as her face lit up. With a quick smirk my way, he put his hand on the small of her back, and together, they started away.

Rage and jealousy began to creep back into my veins as I watched them laughing as they walked. I wanted to storm over, spin the asshole around, and knock his teeth in, but Anderson joined me outside, and I was forced to listen to him talk about professionalism and how they still want me on the movie. My entire body shook with fury as I tried to stay focused, but all I could think about was Glenn and Evie. I needed to get the fuck out before I punched something.

"Where's Dante?" I asked as the rest of the producers exited, nodding to us as they left.

"Must still be in there—Hey!" Anderson called to me as I stormed back inside.

Fists clenched, vision red, I went back to the room and slammed my hands down on the table where only Dante sat. He jumped as I glared at him, seething.

"Evie's the Final Girl, or I walk."

CHAPTER 8

SEBASTIAN

The Soft Pass

"The producers want to fire you, you know that, right? They didn't like you making threats. They think you have a big head," Anderson said.

"They, or Glenn Thornton?" I asked, trying on the costume I'd just been handed. One thing I liked about the *Simon Says* movies was the costumes. They were nothing fancy, usually just casual clothes. For *Simon Says Six: Six Six*, it was no different.

"How are the pants?" the costumer asked.

I gave him a thumbs-up and raised my arms, moving in a circle.

"Good, good. I'll order a dozen of these. You can head over to makeup."

"Has Dante made the call yet?" I asked as we headed to the next part of my day. Today was hair, makeup, and wardrobe. Tomorrow, I'd start stunts. I couldn't help but notice that neither Evie nor Skye were here for any costumes. That had to be intentional.

"Not that I know of," Anderson said, following close behind while glued to his phone. "You know, they were planning on going with the second script anyway, until you opened your mouth. Now we'll be lucky if they don't kill you off and make them have the sex scene instead."

"I'd like to see them try." I snickered, but inside, I was slightly worried. Had I overdone it? Would I get pulled from the franchise that had given me everything? As we went into stunts the next day, I made sure to check my attitude at the door and do as told. Not just for safety reasons, but because people were watching and reporting back. I was riding a thin line, but I wasn't about to lose my job because I'd gotten too cocky. This franchise meant everything to me.

I apologized to Bryce and the rest of the old guard. Bryce—who'd been playing the character Simon Says since the first movie—laughed it off.

"Hey, no problem. We've all been there once or twice. I've threatened to walk away unless I got my way before. How do you think I got the bigger trailer?"

Everyone else seemed to feel the same, and by the end of the week, I felt like I'd redeemed myself by working hard and shutting up long enough to ask Dante if he'd made a decision about the script.

"I appreciate you giving it your all this week. The producers have noticed."

I gritted my teeth. Every time someone mentioned the producers, I knew they were referring to Glenn—who wanted me off the movie just so he could fuck Evie. The very idea sent my blood boiling. I didn't want him alone with her at all if I could help it. From what I'd heard, he was just like his father; and his father had been a bastard.

"And what about the scripts?" I asked point blank.

"Well..." Dante's eyes shifted away from mine. "I want you to do intimacy tests. With both girls. Next week."

"I don't need them," I said, keeping my tone even. "Look, I'm going to be real with you—"

"It's obvious you've got a thing for Evie. I get it. She's fucking hot, and you were friends back in the day. But with the money these execs are shoveling out for this movie, I have to make sure everything is perfect. I can't pick a script until I know who has more chemistry with you."

I bit my tongue. We had been more than friends.

I left his trailer pissed and with a list of things to go through before next week. There would be three days—one for Skye, one for Evie, and the last for callbacks if they weren't entirely sold on one particular woman. That third day wouldn't be necessary. They were going to see that it had to be Evie and me on day one.

Skye was plenty nice, and in a different scenario, I would have no problem playing opposite her. She'd made her desire for the role clear on our *date*. Getting the role of my love interest was all she talked about.

"We'll look so cute together on screen!"

When I'd escorted her to her room that night after Evie basically pushed me from the elevator, I'd politely explained that the flowers had been for Evie and that I'd be campaigning for her to get the part because we had history. She'd seemed a bit hurt, but otherwise okay. I couldn't blame her, though. Who wouldn't want the lead in the biggest horror movie of the year?

The weekend came and went, and my anxiety over the intimacy tests had taken over my brain. Instead of my usual party schedule, I worked out and sat at home.

Waiting for Evie to call.

She had my number. It was killing me not reaching out to her, but I'd already overdone it at the table read. If I pushed my luck, she'd run even harder into Glenn's arms, and I might never see her again.

Alive, anyway.

I silently begged for a call, a text, or for her to just show up at my house. Something, anything, to acknowledge my existence. But there was nothing.

Monday came, and I was the first one on set. It was Ronny's bedroom from *Simon Says Five*, with some minor changes for the new movie.

Dante arrived shortly after, with the intimacy coordinator.

"Kate is going to be helping with everything. But if you and

Skye want to talk privately first, that's fine too. She should be here any minute." He looked around.

My heart sank. I'd hoped to be with Evie today.

"Did you read my notes and directions?" he asked.

"I did."

The scene was pretty hot, even I could admit. From an artist's standpoint, I admired Dante's vision. I thought it would be good if done right—with the right people. He walked over to the fake door.

"You'll start here, bringing her inside, kissing her, frantic to be with her. You'll fall to the bed, clothes will come off, and that's where your *big* reveal happens." He smirked at the pun.

I rolled my eyes.

"Then it'll just be whatever you and your scene partner want to do. Today we'll play around with different positions and angles. We want to make sure you're comfortable with each other before we go into filming."

Dante stepped away to speak to someone else as a costume designer came in with two satin robes. One maroon, one powder blue. "Here's yours."

Dante, who'd been talking on the other side of the room with Kate, paused to look at me.

"Go get undressed and come back to set," he called from across the room.

I did as told, and when I returned, Skye was there in her blue robe.

"Hey, Seb!" she greeted me warmly.

"Hey."

"What are your hard limits?" Kate asked.

"I'm down for anything." Skye winked. She was entirely too chipper for this. "Sex sells. So, let's sell this baby."

"And you?" Kate asked.

I shook my head. "I'm not sure. I guess we'll see as we go?"

"We can do that. If we do something that makes you uncomfortable, say stop. We'll adjust. That goes for both of you,"

Kate said.

I knew this, as I'd worked with an intimacy coordinator before.

"Let's start with some kissing," Dante said.

I turned to Skye. Her eyes were hungry as they raked over me. Her fingers curled as she prepared to pounce. I shoved the pit in my stomach even further down and forced myself into professional mode. I'd kissed plenty of women on screen. Shooting this was nothing new.

Ruining the take was though.

Even though none of what we filmed today would see the light of day, I needed to make sure Skye and I had zero chemistry.

I closed my eyes and pressed my lips to Skye's. She tried to encourage me by putting her hands on my chest and moving closer, but I gave her nothing. There was nothing to give. My lips moved, my hands ran along her thighs and up her body, but it all felt wrong. Evie was at the forefront of my thoughts.

It was almost painful, knowing that I wasn't trying to be bad at kissing Skye. I just was.

"Okay..." Dante sounded confused, but after a few minutes of being stiff and cold, he moved us deeper into the room, leading us to the bed.

"Let's remove the robes."

We spent the whole day going through every movement, every touch, and every line. I gave them nothing. I couldn't with Evie on my brain! I was fumbling. Dante had to keep saying stop and readjusting us. We were only doing things when directed, and none of it felt natural. My dick didn't get hard once, which Skye took offense to. According to an assistant, she'd gone to her trailer and cried. Guilt riddled my stomach. This wasn't just my career I was affecting. This could be a big break for her. But I wasn't going to allow her to get it. It was a selfish move, but I couldn't risk Evie getting away again. Her getting this part gave us more time together, and every moment I had was another chance at convincing her to stay here... with me.

I tried to do better that afternoon. Give Skye a little more to work with, but it was still lame. I knew I could do better, and yet, I just—didn't. By the time Dante called it, everyone looked pretty defeated.

"Where is the guy from *Step-Devil*?" he asked me after I'd gotten back into my regular clothes. "You know how many times you said stop? Or claimed something was a hard limit? If this were real, you'd be a monk."

"Sorry. I just struggled to get into the scene," I muttered then fled the lot before I could be questioned.

The next day, I arrived first again, the excitement over what I knew was coming too much to contain. I'd slammed a blue Red Bull on the way in and was bouncing on my feet as I waited. Slowly, everyone rolled in, dragging in their moods from the day before. I could see it in the way they gave me tight, exhausted smiles that they expected a repeat of yesterday. I ignored them, keeping eyes locked on the door as I waited for my Final Girl. I went to change, and when I returned, Evie had arrived. She was talking with Kate.

Seeing Evie in just a robe, this one white, knowing she was bare underneath and what we'd be doing all day, my cock sprang to life.

"There we go!" Dante cheered.

I turned, my attention pulled from Evie. Dante was grinning ear to ear. He gave me a thumbs-up, and I realized you could see my erection through the robe. Everyone on the closed set zeroed in on me, and I quickly covered myself with my hands, embarrassed at the sudden attention. My face flushed with heat, and I forced myself not to glance in Evie's direction.

"If that's any indication of how today's going to go, it's gonna be good." His mood from before shifted to one of excitement. "Thank fuck. Let's roll."

CHAPTER 9

EVIE

The Method Act

"How are you feeling, Evie?" Dante crossed the closed set.

My stomach was tight with nerves. I pushed them down.

Keep playing along.

"I'm ready."

"Good, well, Kate has given you the rundown. We'll try to stop only when you say. You and Sebastian run the show. Let's start with some simple kissing."

Sebastian came over, and my brain and nerves went into overdrive. What was he wearing under it? Was he naked, like me? Butterflies fluttered in my belly. I ran my eyes down his frame, and as I brought them back up, they caught his piercing, hungry gaze.

With little direction from Dante, Sebastian grabbed my waist and pulled me in, his lips crashing down on mine with the most lustful, needy force I'd ever experienced in a kiss. His tongue was searching for mine in seconds, and I found myself too stunned to reciprocate. I pulled back and pushed his hands away.

"What?" Sebastian frowned.

"That was a lot at once." I grimaced.

"Okay, Sebastian, take it slow," Dante ordered.

Sebastian's chest rose in a huff, but he came back, this time kissing me slower, softer. I closed my eyes and forced myself to focus on the act—here, today. Not on the memories this kiss was trying to force up and out.

Don't let yourself get distracted. Stay focused on why you came back. You need your revenge.

I repeated the words over and over, and it helped me stay grounded in the handsome man's embrace. However, remaining grounded turned into downright distracted. His hands began to roam up and down. He reached for my ass, and I flinched. He stopped, and we started again. And again. Every time he tried to do something other than chaste kissing, I froze, and we had to stop. After an hour, Dante finally called for a break.

"Let's take thirty to consider what we've tried thus far and how to proceed, hmm?" he said.

I hurried off set and rushed into my trailer, where I paced, trying to settle my heart. Why was I struggling so much?

I'd known when I was offered the role that we'd be doing this. And I'd told myself once every one of those men who had taken part in my mom's murder were dead, it'd be worth it. But thinking of Sebastian and being here with him in real life were two different things.

I couldn't let myself fall. But, I had to sell that I was to Dante and the other bigwigs in order to land the part that would give me daily access to the studio in which all these men worked.

Having spent the morning trying to do it, I wasn't quite sure I could.

I was no Lita Reyes.

A moment later, there was a knock on my door, and I called for them to come in. Dante entered, an awkward smile on his face.

"Hey. Do you have time to talk?"

"Sure. What's up? I know that wasn't great. Skye warned me that her test was bad, so I think I got in my head." I sat on the couch, and he came to sit on the other side, a distance away.

"Definitely. So...I just got an email from one of our producers. He wants us to consider a rewrite, where you're not a lead character at all. You just make a cameo."

"What? No!" I shot to my feet. I needed to be on set for longer.

A cameo didn't give me enough time, enough excuses, to be near everyone. This role was my in to places I might not have access to otherwise.

"I know. I replied back that the change wasn't ideal. I love the scripts we have. If it weren't for Sebastian's little ego trip the other day, we would have already picked you as the lead. They know taking him out of the movie is impossible without fan backlash, but they couldn't let him have his way just to prove a point. That's why the execs are making us do this bullshit. This new email tells me they are not happy with us."

"What can we do?" I stopped pacing and turned to him.

Dante lifted his shoulders. "Show them they're wrong about dropping you from the cast." He leaned forward, putting his elbows on his knees. "Evie, you and Sebastian looked like siblings kissing out there. We need chemistry."

I stared at him blankly, and he continued.

"Give him a chance. Stop pushing him away. Get to know adult Sebastian." He stood. "I think you'll be pleasantly surprised. He's not always the jackass celebrity he pretends to be."

"I don't know if I can believe that." I rolled my eyes.

"Why don't we leave you two on set alone for a while? You can get used to each other in private, and we'll come back and see if we can run some of the scenes."

He left, and when I returned to set thirty minutes later, I found only Sebastian. He was standing awkwardly, his hands in the pockets of his robe.

"Hey, I didn't mean to come in so hot."

I soaked him in, admiring the earnest look in his eyes. "It's okay. It was kind of cute. I'm sorry I've been giving you frostbite."

"Frostbite?" He smiled.

"Cold. Nothing. I'm not a professional actress, and it shows." I sighed. I'd jumped so fast at this opportunity that I didn't realize just how hard it was all going to be. Sebastian came over and put his arms around my waist. I stiffened and started to pull back, but Dante's warning of the recast forced me to push through my nerves and stay in Sebastian's embrace.

"Don't think of it as acting. No one's here to watch and review. Let's just..."

"Talk?" I suggested, stepping out of his arms. I went to the bed and patted the spot beside me. He joined me. We stared at each other, soaking in the moment.

"What do you want to talk about?" he asked.

I stared deep into his jade eyes. Suddenly, the years washed away, and we were back in time, just the two of us.

Everything.

My heart yearned to tell him everything. Every little detail of my life he missed after I left. To pick up right where we left off. To laugh and joke like we were kids. But we weren't. Dante's words ran through my mind.

Get to know adult Sebastian.

If I wanted to stay in this movie, I had to make them see chemistry. And chemistry with Sebastian should be easy. It was, at one time. I raised my hand slowly, touching his shaved cheek. Oh, how I wished I hadn't missed this transition from teenage Sebastian to the man in front of me.

His breathing hitched at my touch, his eyes dipping to where my robe parted, revealing the tops of my breasts.

I leaned in, and this time, our kiss was...good.

Would it be so bad to enjoy my time with him while I had it? Sebastian let me lead, and eventually, I opened up and let our tongues touch. His hands slid up my arms, pulling me closer, not in a forceful way, but a needful way.

"Evie, this feels like a dream. You're here, about to be my scene partner for the hottest sex scene of my career."

This was the Sebastian I remembered. The one I'd left behind. We were each other's firsts, and we'd never gotten the chance to explore that further...

I melted into his arms, shifting so his mouth could find my neck and collarbone.

"You know there's a thing in the industry called unsimulated sex? Most of the stuff you see is simulated, but it doesn't have to be if we don't want it to..."

I moaned and closed my eyes, letting myself enjoy his touch as he continued seducing me with his words.

"Everyone has their favorite Final Girl, Laurie in *Halloween*, Nancy in *Nightmare on Elm Street*, Ripley in *Alien*. My personal favorite was Kirsty from *Hellraiser*, but you top them all, Evie Reyes. You're the ultimate Final Girl."

The doors suddenly opened, and we jolted apart as the limited crew came in. Dante's face lit up when he saw our flushed expressions.

"That looked amazing! Let's keep that up. Can you do that with a room full of people?" he teased, causing us both to chuckle.

The private time had helped. Or made things worse. While I was confident now that I could kiss him on screen, I wasn't entirely sure I was acting. I shoved away the nerves, watching with hungry eyes as Sebastian disrobed.

Anthony C. Hopkins.

He was even more...impressive than I'd remembered. Or imagined. I averted my gaze and allowed him his time. He did the same when it was my turn.

Kate taught us how to use body positions and camera angles to make it look like we were having sex. Unless it was a close-up, hardly anything was intimate or arousing. In fact, oftentimes they'd have us trying out positions that didn't even seem possible. We were essentially playing Twister at times on the bed, but the lack of sensuality in it all often created laughter between Sebastian and me, which helped relax us both. It made the times when we stopped laughing...good.

There were times when the crew was in the room where the lines of acting and reality blurred. Dante had directed me to sit on Sebastian's lap nude and make out with him. It was clear that Sebastian was struggling as well. His erection had pressed against my body almost all day.

Skye had said she hadn't felt it once.

"I'd like to play with blocking for a simulated oral sex scene," Dante said. "Are you comfortable doing that?"

"I'm down for whatever," Sebastian said cheerfully. He'd been in a pleasant mood all day. It was a stark difference from what I'd been expecting, based on Skye's experience. I was beginning to believe it may have been an intentional move on Sebastian's part.

The idea sent nervous butterflies through me, but I quickly forced them away. I wasn't here for love. And this movie was more than just revisiting my mom's legacy. It was for avenging her.

We took lunch, which Sebastian and I ate together in his trailer.

"How are you feeling?" he asked.

"Good. You?"

"Great, Final Girl." He winked.

I stared for a moment as he walked away, my gaze drifting to his backside. Suddenly, I liked being called Final Girl.

We returned to set, and Kate offered us a tray of flesh-colored tapes, bandages, and pouches.

"Let's get new modesty barriers."

I scrunched up my nose.

"What?" Sebastian asked, grabbing his. He had no qualms about opening his robe and putting his pouch in place in front of me. I picked mine out more gingerly.

"They aren't exactly comfortable," I murmured. They were glorified bandages. Pulling them off my skin was painful.

"We have other options!" Kate perked up. She loved her job entirely too much. "We can put you in nude underwear."

I shook my head. Those were hot and itchy. That would be worse. I went to the bathroom and set my patch. I ogled myself in the mirror, slapping on the nipple pasties and turning to get a good look at just how much the patch for my lower regions covered. It was just a simple piece of tape that matched my skin tone. Only if you looked hard, would you see the lines of where it sat. I returned to set, and we started the scene.

The crew in the room was quiet as we got into place. I sat on the edge of the bed, fully nude. Sebastian, also naked, kneeled in front of me.

Dante came over and told us he wanted to see the scene from behind, to check if it would look real from that angle. Once we gave a thumbs-up, he returned to his monitor and yelled for action.

Sebastian began by placing kisses along my thighs. Arching my back, I allowed my breasts to be on full display. When we started filming for real, I wouldn't have pasties over my nipples. I closed my eyes, and as Sebastian's fingers roamed the inside of my thighs, I forgot what we were doing and why we were here. My breathing became labored as I lost myself in his touch. His fingers knew just how to...

"You're so beautiful, Final Girl," Sebastian murmured, his tongue trailing up my thigh.

That wasn't in the script.

Dante didn't correct it.

"Stay with me, Final Girl," he whispered as he continued to do all the things Kate had taught us. He pinched my nipples, and a real moan escaped my lips. He shifted closer to my sex, and when he dipped his head, my modesty barrier shifted.

We both froze. I looked down, he looked up, and for a moment, we stared at each other. He cleared his throat and tried to fix the patch, but it fell to the floor between us. My arousal had caused the adhesive to wear off. Heat flooded my face as I looked into Sebastian's eyes. He knew exactly what had happened too.

"Everything okay?" Dante asked.

I glanced back. It was clear from how they stretched their necks over their cameras that they didn't know the patch had fallen off or how close Sebastian was to me.

"We're fine," Sebastian called, his gaze returning to mine. He was asking me silently what to do. His words from earlier returned to me.

Most of the stuff you see is simulated, but it doesn't have to be if we don't want it to...

I closed my eyes. The heat of his breath on my sex had me

needy for his mouth. This was a dangerous path we were taking, but in the heat of the moment, I didn't care. His confident words and expert fingers convinced me that for just a bit, I could abandon my quest and perform for the cameras. Leaning back, I angled my hips toward him. Slowly, he moved his fingers closer, parting my lips. My body shuddered as he spread my pussy and leaned in, running his tongue along my wetness. A groan escaped my lips, and my hands went to his hair, pulling him tighter. He licked me and sucked my clit. A finger slid inside, moving in and out slowly. I gasped.

We'd abandoned acting altogether, then. I kept wanting to shoot a glance back at the people watching us, but I was too scared. My heart raced madly as I tugged on his hair, pulling him deeper into me.

Although I'd never admit it, I'd watched his career from afar. I'd seen his movies and yearned to be the actress in *Step-Devil.* I'd recalled that one night we'd had many times before...everything. And now, this was that times ten.

I bucked my hips and pleaded for release. Knowing that I had an audience should have made me ashamed, but it didn't. I was reveling in the knowledge that they could all see what Sebastian was doing.

"Sebastian—" I begged.

He chuckled but didn't stop, and suddenly I was shoved over the edge of pleasure, coming in front of everyone in the room. Heat flooded my veins, and my thighs shook as Sebastian continued his beautiful, secret assault on my body. He continued until I came down, and then he pulled back, feigned shock, and picked up the modesty patch, waving it at the crew behind us.

"Oh shit." Dante hurried forward, calling for Kate to come back so I could get a new one applied.

Sebastian leaned over, grabbing our robes and tossing me mine. Standing, I stared at him, stunned at what had just happened. I wanted to be furious, but...I wasn't. I didn't know how I felt. I'd never had public sex before, and I'd certainly never come while surrounded by strangers.

While we waited for Kate to return, Sebastian joked with Dante.

"I'm glad we caught it when we did," he said, referring to the modesty patch. He glanced over at me and winked. "That could have been bad."

CHAPTER 10

EVIE

The Improvisor

"I think we've cast our Final Girl," Dante told me over the phone that night.

"Really?" I could barely contain my squeal.

"Oh yeah. That last scene? It looked so real, we'd be stupid not to cast you two opposite each other. I just got back from my meeting with the producers. Some of them weren't happy, but I told them our decision was made."

"What's next, then?"

"Well, we scheduled one more day for chemistry tests, but we don't need them anymore. Take the day off, come back, and then we can discuss the final script for you and Sebastian. I'm going to sit down with the writers and confirm everything." He went on about the schedule, but I found my mind wandering, disappearing elsewhere.

Returning to that set from this afternoon.

We had two more weeks of preparing before filming. We'd be doing more stunt training, intimacy training, script runs, rehearsals, more hair, makeup, and wardrobe days, along with whatever marketing they came up with.

After I hung up, I found a text from Glenn asking about my day. I told him I got the lead and noticed he didn't admit to being the one who was pushing for me not to. He didn't like Sebastian—

which was fair. Sebastian didn't like him either.

Especially after today, but I wasn't going to be telling anyone about that. After we'd cut for the day, I'd showered and reflected on what had happened. Something about it was exhilarating, yet... coming down, post orgasm, I knew that I shouldn't have done that with him.

He was distracting me.

Eventually, I told Glenn that I'd be spending my day off moving back into my mom's house. I'd gotten word that it was finally ready. He invited himself to help, and in turn, I agreed to order dinner for us. He made a casual remark about being more man than any actor could be, but I ignored the dig at Sebastian. I decided I'd pick a side after the heavy boxes were brought in.

I still had reservations about Glenn. He was the son of one of my enemies, but that particular one had just died. Heart attack in his hotel room, Glenn had said. Could I get publicly involved with someone so close to the people I planned on making suffer? I kept waffling between it being a stellar alibi and it being the thing that gets me caught.

As I lay in bed that night, I stared at the ceiling, trying to decide how I felt about being with Glenn. He was nice, handsome, and charming. But he wasn't...Sebastian.

Not that any of it mattered in the end. Being with either of them long term meant either giving up my quest for revenge or having finished off the six men on my list and survived. Both scenarios seemed unlikely.

But it was nice to pretend...

I clenched my thighs together, thinking about this afternoon. It was the hottest thing I'd ever experienced—people in the room, them not knowing it was real...

I should have stopped him, and I think if it had been anyone else, I would have. I fell asleep with the question still on my mind. Who was I leading on—Glenn or Sebastian?

Myself.

♠ ☠ ♠

SKYE CAUGHT ME the next morning leaning against the moving van in the studio lot.

"Hey! Isn't today moving day? Why are you here?" She gave me a half-smile, half-pout. We'd grown close after she admitted to wanting the lead so badly that she ignored the signs that those flowers and the date she went on with Sebastian had been meant for me.

"Society wants to pit women against women, and I started to fall for the trap. I'm sorry."

Her apology had made me see her in a different light, and I'd started to find her quite fun to be around.

"Yeah, Glenn is on his way. He's gonna help. We're just meeting here."

"Glenn?" She raised an eyebrow and poured herself some juice. "A little birdie told me your chemistry test with *Sebastian* went phenomenally."

"A little birdie?"

Her shoulders fell. "Dante called me last night and told me they're going with you as the lead." She perked up an instant later. "But I'm so happy for you. He said that your scenes were crazy hot. I can't wait to see it. And I can't wait for our epic fight scene at the end."

"Same. I might even let you get in a real hit or two."

We hugged.

"Oh, and Sebastian texted me this morning to tell me too. I think he felt bad that he couldn't...*perform* with me, you know. Ugh, I hate you. You've got both of the hottest men on set vying for you!" she gushed.

I rolled my eyes. "I wouldn't say that."

"Oh, really? That same little birdie told me Sebastian was hard as a rock the entire day of your chemistry test. He was a limp marshmallow with me." She gave a pout. "Not that I'm entirely interested, but it would have been a nice compliment. Oh well." She winked just as Glenn pulled into the parking lot, sliding into the spot right beside us. He got out and flashed a mega-watt smile, causing Skye to giggle. I got into the van and Glenn joined me in the passenger's seat. I rolled the window down as I backed out of the spot and waved to Skye.

"See you on set," I said before taking off to move back into my childhood home.

"It looks just like I remember," I sighed as I stepped inside a few hours later.

"It's...a lot of pink," he said.

I nodded. "It was her favorite color. She used to joke that her heart was stuck in the seventies." I took my shoes off and curled my toes into the shag carpet. It indeed was a lot of pink. The walls had a rosy-pink shade of wallpaper, and she'd gotten the carpet to match. On the walls, scattered in between photos of the two of us, were kitschy items, like vintage clocks, art prints, and plastic peacocks. The furniture was old too—velvet couches and TVs that still had antennas. Old, but not worn down. It was all in pristine condition. Everywhere that guests were welcome, she'd maintained the aesthetic. She'd allowed me to decorate my bedroom, and our home theater had been semi-modernized.

"Are you going to update it?"

"Nope. Well, just a few things. I had them add security cameras, and the TV in my room is new." Shrugging, I directed him to take my box of clothes upstairs.

The home was modest in comparison to many celebrity homes. There were no giant wings or elevators. She and I had rooms on the same floor—down the same hall, even. But now, I couldn't bear the idea of leaving her room empty, so I was taking it as mine and making my childhood bedroom a guest room.

Moving in went fast, so I opted to unpack as well. Glenn

stayed with me, as I had to take him back to his car, and helped where he could. We began in my bedroom, starting with my books. We plopped down on the carpet and opened the boxes to fill the lower shelves first.

"I didn't know your mom, but my dad always spoke highly of her. I think he may have had a thing for her, if I'm being honest," he admitted.

I froze, turning to look at him. Did he know something? Or was this his way of checking to see if I knew anything? This was such a bad idea. I decided right then that I'd take tonight, grill him on details about his dad and my mom, and then politely break it off tomorrow.

As the plan was forming, a text came through from Sebastian.

Psycho Killer

Dinner plans, Final Girl?

He'd mentioned that I was saved as Final Girl in his phone, so I'd changed his name in mine.

Can't. Move-in day. Sorry.

I stuffed my phone into my pocket and returned to unpacking books with Glenn.

"You really like horror," he said, glancing at the titles as he shelved them. He held up *Christine*, by Stephen King.

"It's in my blood."

"Was your dad an actor too?" he asked.

"I don't know. She never told me who he was." I shrugged. I'd never thought to look into it either. A memory of her popped into my mind, and I smiled, hearing her voice.

"What is he like?"

"Who?"

"My dad. Do I look like him? Or act like him?"

"You act and look like yourself, Evie Reyes. The man who helped create you is irrelevant. There's a reason he isn't in our lives. Men aren't important. Let me take a page out of you and Sebastian's playbook and speak to you in movie quotes. From the wise words of Jennifer Check, 'Boys are just placeholders—they come and they go.'"

"But what if he comes looking for me?"

She laughed. "Then I'll toss him into Falls Lake with all the others."

I smiled at the memory. She'd been equal parts wise and snarky. I'd always admired her for being so boldly independent. She was who I strived to emulate every single day.

And she wasn't wrong about men.

It was always my preference that men *came* and went, and most of them were fine with that. Every one of them, in fact, had been more than happy to bounce and forget my name after we'd slept together.

"Interesting. I bet it's someone big in the industry, then. I wonder if you're the love child of some high exec," Glenn laughed, pulling me from my thoughts.

I doubted I was the product of a love affair. My mother was too smart and practical to have gotten pregnant solely because of her emotions.

"Tell me more about your dad," I said, switching the conversation. "You know, other than the heart attack."

Glenn flashed a brief grimace and nodded. "That was just what we told the public. What actually happened was kind of embarrassing."

"Oh?" I paused my unpacking.

"They found him completely naked, with his cock stiff as a metal rod. The autopsy report said he'd taken too many little blue pills, and that's what caused the heart attack. My mom was mortified, so we said he'd died in his sleep. We couldn't let their image be tarnished. They always pretended to have a storybook marriage. It was far from it."

"Oh?" I asked, pressing for more.

He sighed. "I know he wasn't the best husband, but he was a good man."

I held back a snicker. If he was such a good man, then why was he going to dinner with my mother that night? And why did he kill her? None of the men on my list were "good."

Glenn sensed my coldness and shrugged. There was silence for a beat before he spoke again. "Thankfully, we'd already been discussing me taking over his roles in various projects, *Simon Says Six* being one of them. It was an easy transition, and it allowed me to make the calls I wanted without any real fight amongst my family."

"*Six Six*," I whispered under my breath.

"What?"

"Were you guys close?" I pressed, moving on from my joke.

I needed to know if he knew anything about my mom. Was he aware his dad had been one of her killers? Did he know she'd been murdered at all, or did he believe the suicide story they'd given?

He paused, setting the books in his hand down by his ankles.

"Somewhat. He brought me to meetings sometimes. If you're asking about his affairs—yes, I knew about them. All of them."

"All of them?" I raised an eyebrow. I licked my lips as my breathing hitched in excitement. I was so close...

He snickered and returned to the stack of books, filling the rest of the bottom row.

"Yes, even the one with your mother. It nearly destroyed our family." He stood and brushed off his pants.

"He and my mother never had an affair," I sneered, my mood dropping in an instant. Standing to join him, I huffed and glanced down at the hardcover still in my hand.

IT by Stephen King. It was one of the many first editions of his I'd collected sometime during my career. This book was thick.

"Evie." He gave me a pointed look. "You don't have to lie now. They're both gone. I don't hold it against her. She didn't know my mom. She was just a career-driven woman doing what she needed to get to the top. That's pretty common in this town. Ask your co-star."

"Excuse me?" My mouth fell open. "My mother did not sleep her way to the top. And why are you bringing up Sebastian right now?"

He gave me a weird look and pursed his lips, as if trying to consider if he should tell me something or not.

"Let's not get into it. That's his business. I shouldn't have said anything." He bent down to open another box, but I wasn't interested in unpacking anymore.

"My mother was not having an affair with your father," I repeated.

"Well, you tell me, then, why my dad confessed to fucking her the night she killed herself? My mom told me everything, Evie. Sorry yours didn't."

"Your father raped her." The words spilled from my mouth. I had no evidence of this, but in my heart, I knew there was no way my mother would have willingly slept with Thornton. She was smart, career-driven, and kind. She was not a home-wrecker.

My anger had gotten the best of me and was spilling out. He froze for a beat, then stood up straight.

"Rape is a strong word to throw around. You say it too loudly, and you won't last very long here."

"Is that a threat?" I tightened my grip on the book.

He put his hands up and started toward the door, his back now facing me. "I think we're done here. My mom warned me dating you was a bad idea, but I ignored her because you're really hot. We can have different opinions on things, Evie, but fact is fact. Your mother wasn't raped. She was a slu—"

Before he could finish his sentence, I hurled the book at him. It spun in the air twice before the corner hit the back of his head with a loud thump. The eleven-hundred-page hardcover fell to the ground, and a moment later, so did he.

I stared at the limp body in disbelief before creeping toward him.

What had I done?

I went around to examine his head. His eyes were closed, but he seemed to be breathing.

Fuck.

This wasn't part of the plan. I lifted his hand, but it fell limp. Shit, shit, shit. I looked around my bedroom. How did I get him downstairs? He was heavy. Rolling him onto his back, I grabbed him by the ankles and began to drag him. Where to, I wasn't sure. Then, the doorbell rang.

I swore and grabbed my phone to pull up the doorbell camera. My stomach sank. I stared at the screen, then back at the unconscious body I was dragging through my house, then back at the screen.

Sebastian was here with pizza.

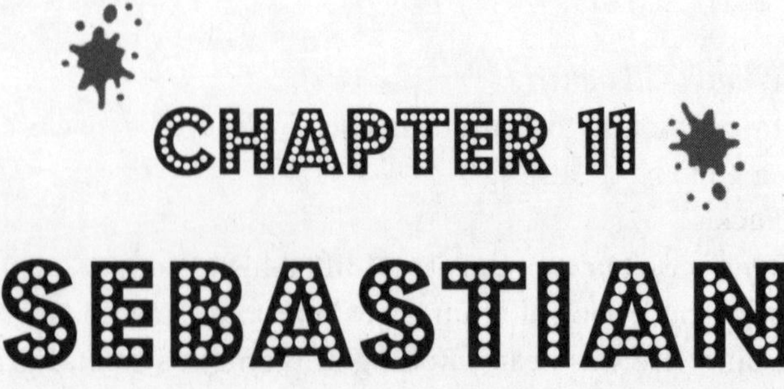

CHAPTER 11 SEBASTIAN

The Producer

I waited at the door, my leg bouncing with nerves. It was bold of me to show up like this, but I hoped bringing food and drinks would soften Evie up enough to let me spend the evening with her. I glanced back at the short moving van in her driveway, telling me she was here.

I shifted my weight from side to side, the hot pizza no longer stinging my hands as it cooled. I huffed, feeling awkward. Maybe she was in the backyard or something. I pushed the doorbell again, and suddenly the door flew open and Evie stood before me, breathing heavily.

"Hey! Sorry, I didn't hear the doorbell. I've been unpacking. What's up?"

I eyed her suspiciously as she wiped a bead of sweat from her brow.

I held up the pizza and six-pack. "I just wanted to say congrats on getting the role. I thought we could have dinner, talk about it."

And, you know, the other stuff. Like me eating your pussy in front of a room full of people.

Something about her demeanor wasn't right. Her smile didn't meet her eyes.

"Oh, sure. Um...okay, yeah." She seemed unsure about letting me in, but eventually moved to the side to welcome me in.

I went in and reflexively took my shoes off, as I'd always done when we were kids.

"It's like stepping through time," I admired. "It even smells the same."

"Yeah, I found a stash of the candles she loved. Vanilla cupcake. I lit a few and stuck them all over," she said, closing the door.

I headed straight to the kitchen and dropped the pizza and bag of drinks on the table.

"I thought, with it being your first time here since your mom's passing, you might like some company," I said, turning to face her.

The panicked look on her face subsided, and she smiled.

"Thanks. That was kind of you to think about me. How did you know I was moving in today?" she asked, opening the box and taking a slice of cheese pizza.

"You told me..." My brow furrowed. "Earlier today, when I texted?"

Her eyes widened. "Oh, right! I forgot."

"I hope it wasn't too forward to stop by. I just knew the address." I cringed inwardly.

Was this a mistake?

"No, it's fine." She waved off my concerns with her hand, blowing air through her lips. "Dante said we should probably spend more time together... It's just been a crazy day."

"Right." I grinned and started unpacking my bag, pulling out beer, a couple of Red Bulls, and water. I grabbed two beers from the six-pack, handing one to her. "Congrats, Final Girl. I knew you'd land it."

She rolled her eyes, and I fell in love.

"Yeah, like you didn't bomb your test with Skye to make sure she wasn't even an option." She set her beer down and turned toward the cabinets, opening them one by one, finding them empty.

"I don't know what you're talking about." I grinned, opening both bottles and a Red Bull for myself. I wasn't ready to admit that the reason I'd bombed so badly was because I couldn't stop thinking about her.

"They must have packed away all the dishes. All I have down here are bottles and bottles of cleaner."

I glanced past her, seeing a few random soaps but no dishes.

She shut the doors and reached for the beer in my hand. "I'll have to ask about them tomorrow."

"You want to watch a movie or something? Is your internet set up?"

"It sure is. Grab the food." She started toward the den. "But just one movie. I still have unpacking to do."

"I can help. I don't have any plans tonight," I offered.

She didn't say anything. Instead, she led me through the house.

"Did you intentionally keep it as it was, or have you just not decorated yet?" I asked.

"I didn't bring a whole lot with me. This is just temporary. Once the movie is over—the press tour and stuff, all of it—I think I'll finally sell it. For now, it feels nice to see my mom everywhere." She picked up the remote and turned on the mini movie-theater-sized TV on the wall. This room, other than Evie's bedroom—for obvious reasons—had always been my favorite in the house. Lita had decorated this room like a real movie theater. Movie posters were framed on the walls. There were candy shelves, a mini fridge for drinks and ice cream, a hot dog cooker, and a popcorn machine. They were all empty now, but she used to keep them stocked for Evie and me. Along the walls sat real theater seats, purely for aesthetic. The center of the room held a ridiculously long red couch and two coffee tables in front of them and two smaller end tables on each side. You could easily fit ten people on the furniture to watch a show.

"I know, it's weird with nothing stocked." She saw me looking at the snack area. "I'll grab some stuff and maybe host a movie night or something soon—with the whole cast."

"Right. The whole cast..." I furrowed my brow. She was really making me work for her attention. I was practically throwing myself at a brick wall.

I set the food on an end table and plopped down on the couch. "Is this your way of telling me I'm not special?" I teased.

She sat on the other side, far away from me, and huffed at the screen as she tried to log into her streaming service accounts.

"This is always the annoying part. What?" She glanced my way, clearly having not heard me.

"Nothing." I sipped my beer then set it down, trading it for my Red Bull. She paused and looked at me with a raised eyebrow.

"Do you ever go without those?"

"Not if I have the choice." I popped the tab and took a swig. "Try one. I brought a few flavors."

She picked one up, reading the label.

"I'm partial to blueberry. The yellow ones are good too."

She set the red can down and opted for the yellow one, popping it open and taking a sip.

"Ooh, I do like this one. Let me try the watermelon." She opened that one as well, took a sip, and grimaced.

I nodded. "Yeah, those are gross. We can just dump it." I took it from her and set it aside to trash later. "Energy drinks are a must have, working long hours like we do."

"We?"

"Well, you're one of us now, Final Girl." I winked. "You might want to ask for some of these in your trailer once we start filming."

I grabbed a slice of pizza and mowed down while she logged into her accounts and began to scroll.

"What do you want to watch?" she asked, automatically going to the horror category.

"*Candyman*? I could go for some Tony Todd action," I said when the picture popped up.

She pushed play with no argument.

As if there were any argument not to watch Tony Todd.

"I need to go check on something," she said as soon as the movie started. She bolted out of the room and was gone for almost ten minutes, leaving me to watch the movie solo. She returned looking just as frazzled as when she'd answered the door.

"Is everything all right?" I asked.

She smoothed her hair and tugged her shirt down. "Yeah, of course. Why?" The last word came up an octave higher, making me think that something was definitely not all right. She must have seen the suspicion in my eyes, because this time when she came to the couch, she sat right next to me, tucking her legs underneath her. She sighed and offered me a small smile as she changed the subject. "This is..."

"Nice?" I offered when she couldn't come up with a word.

I put my arm around her shoulders and pulled her into me.

"Nostalgic," she said. "It's weird, seeing you all grown up."

I gulped as memories flashed before my eyes—specifically yesterday, when I had my head between her thighs.

"You're even more beautiful now than you were before." I reached up, brushing her hair behind her ear to admire her jewelry. She was wearing bright red metal tunnels the shape of hearts in her stretched lobes.

"Getting out of Hollywood did wonders for my self-confidence," she said. "In Michigan, I could be whoever I wanted. I didn't have to worry about not landing jobs because I got a tattoo." She snickered.

"You still got a job here," I argued. "And I have tattoos. You've seen them. What did you think of the chainsaw?" I teased.

She sat up some, and I took note that her cheeks had a flush to them.

"Groovy," she said, quoting Ash's infamous line from *Evil Dead*. "And yes, I have seen your tattoos, but you can't honestly say being a major Hollywood actor hasn't held you back from getting more than just what you can hide under clothes."

"All right, maybe." I rolled my eyes but then leaned in, our lips only an inch apart. "That just makes seeing my tattoos a fun surprise. Did you like what you saw yesterday, Evie Reyes?"

Her breath hitched, her eyes widening.

I started to lean in when something fell upstairs.

The loud thump caused Evie to jerk away and stand. "I need to go check on that," she said and flew from the room.

I stood and followed her. "Is everything okay?" I asked as I went up the stairs. I went to her mom's room, directly above the den. "Evie?" I called.

"Don't come in here!" she yelped. "I'm naked."

I paused at the door. That was the worst excuse she could give me. Her being naked would only make me want to barge in faster. I pushed it open slowly, letting the creak signal my presence. "What's going on?"

A muffled protest came in response, but it wasn't from her. It was a deeper voice. A man's.

Jealousy got the best of me, and I strode in.

"What the—oh, fuck." I paused midstep, the words falling out of my mouth. I took in the scene, not entirely sure what I was seeing. Evie stood there holding a pair of pantyhose, with Glenn Thornton tied to a chair, his mouth gagged with...more pantyhose? He glared at me and continued fighting his restraints.

"Evie...what is going on?"

"I told you not to come in." She crossed her arms. "Why didn't you respect me when I said I was naked?"

I stared, unable to take my eyes off the man she had tied up with what looked like just more nylon stockings. How many pairs did she have? Were they really that strong? "But you weren't. You were... What *were* you doing?" The words came slowly, my brain struggling to process the scene.

Glenn rolled his head until the gag loosened, then spit it out. "She was trying to kill me."

CHAPTER 12 SEBASTIAN

The Twist

Six months prior

"Show me how badly you want the movie."

I tapped my fingers on my knees, beginning my pitch. "Well, *Simon Says* has always made money. I'd like to bring it back but give it an upgrade. Better writers, larger budget. Bigger kills, bigger thrills. All of it. We toss out the last few movies' lore and go back to basics, but with a modern look."

"I see. And how are you getting the funding?" A slow grin spread across the producer's lips, stretching his loose skin. He watched me from across the hotel room, his lips curled in a smug smile, happy that I'd been reduced to begging. I pressed my lips together tightly, looking down at my hands and clenching them. Looking back up, I exhaled then stood and removed my shirt.

"I don't know, how am I, Thornton?"

He ran his tongue across his lips, and I shuddered.

"Good boy." Thornton turned and poured himself another drink, then reached for a second glass, filling one for me. Pulling a small prescription bottle out of his robe pocket, he shook it like a rattle then opened it, pulling out one small pill. "I just need something to help me get started." He laughed as he took the medication with his drink. Setting the bottle down beside the whiskey, he grabbed my glass and walked over to me, staring me down. Pushing the glass against my lips, it was clear I didn't have a choice but to drink. I took it from him and swallowed hard. This man had a lot of pull in the industry. This wasn't our first meeting in a hotel like this. I could take him if I wanted to. And, Thornton did like being man-handled a little—but if I fought back, he'd tell everyone. Every person who I spent time with to get what I wanted would stop calling me. No, they'd start calling each other, canceling auditions, publicity tours, contracts. I could stand up right now and leave this room with no violence at all, and I'd never work again. With that knowledge, I brought the drink to my lips and sipped the whiskey slowly.

He ran his eyes up and down my body. "Relax, take off your shoes, stay awhile."

This part never got easier.

Once we got going, I could turn my mind off and just—thrust. But the lead-up was always torture.

How badly did I want this movie made?

Very.

I didn't care what they wrote. I just wanted to step back into the franchise that had started my career. With a big budget, we could do *Simon Says* justice and make so much money, and I could become a household name.

I leaned down and unlaced my boots, kicking them off. The moment my feet were free, Thornton dropped to his knees, reaching for me. I froze as he took my foot, lifted it to his face, and inhaled deeply. I bit back a grimace. I put the thoughts of what I was about to do out of my mind. Once I slid the condom on, I could close my eyes and pretend I was elsewhere.

This is just work, Sebastian. Clock in and clock out.

Heather's words echoed in my brain, taking me back to the first time she sent me into a hotel suite with a producer.

Fucking agents, man.

"Do you have something for me?" I asked, brushing him off.

With an exaggerated sigh, he stood and went to a desk,

raising a manila folder.

Standing, I grinned and gave him a wink. "Good boy. Let's see that contract."

He had another drink, and then we sat down at the table. I scanned it quickly. Nothing was really needed from me. We just needed his signature to green-light it. Once he signed, everything would get going. Thornton was one of the head producers for the studio. Whatever he said went.

"This looks great." I pushed the contract over to him.

He barely glanced at the paper as he quickly signed. He was too distracted by my exposed abdomen to care. For a moment, I felt a little pride in myself. I'd just gotten a fifty-million-dollar movie budget green-lit. Who knew my cock was worth that much?

"Should we drink to this?" I pushed back my chair and stood, hurrying to the bar. I wasn't mentally ready for this. I wasn't attracted to Thornton. He wasn't necessarily my type. I was drawn to people my own age.

Maybe I should have taken one of his little blue pills.

"Sure. Pour me another, will you?"

Turning my back to him, I prepared our drinks, filling my glass with ice.

"I was honestly a little shocked you wanted to reboot the series. We'd been trying to squash it ever since Lita Reyes fucked things up for everyone."

I froze, my hand on the whiskey bottle.

"What do you mean? She killed herself."

I repeated the lie I'd heard for the last five years. Lita Reyes—dead by suicide on the set of her own movie.

I'd seen her body swinging from the rafters that morning. Death by hanging could not have produced the buckets of blood pooling underneath her.

"We paid a pretty penny to make sure that's what was reported."

My mind went blank.

I'd known. There was no way she could have stabbed and

gutted herself like that. But to hear the confession from someone's lips? My hand, still on the bottle, shook with rage.

"What are you saying, Thornton?"

"I don't know exactly. I'm drunk. I shouldn't be. Those pills don't do great with whiskey." He chuckled.

My gaze drifted to the prescription he'd left on the table, just inches from my hand.

"You killed Lita. What did she do? She was—" I stopped, grabbing the bottle. My breathing grew labored as I did my best to quietly unscrew the cap and dump a few of them into my hand.

"She was a cunt!" he shouted as I set five pills on the counter and crushed a new glass on top of them, turning them into powder. "She always had an opinion on something and could never let bygones be bygones. We couldn't take it anymore."

Putting his glass under the lip of the counter, I quickly brushed the blue powder into his drink and swirled the glass enough to mix it in.

"We?" I asked, turning back to him.

"My friends. I don't know why I'm telling you all this. I guess thinking about that fucking franchise brings out bad memories. She's dead and buried, and that's where she'll stay." He took his drink from me, and we toasted.

I sipped my drink slowly and watched as he downed his quickly, all in one go. His Adam's apple bobbed.

The clock had officially started.

He set the glass down and sighed. "Well, I'm not entirely there yet, but I don't need to be. The contract's signed—take your pants off and put your cock in my mouth." His words slurred together.

Biting my upper lip, I hesitantly stripped down to just my boxers and socks. My cock was devoid of any blood or emotion. Thornton did nothing for me.

Suddenly, a phone began to ring near the bed. The producer swore, stood, and went to the end table.

"It's Glenn, my son. I have to take this," he muttered as he grabbed his phone and went into the other room. Relief washed over me, and I dropped into the chair at the table.

What the fuck had I done?

Once those pills hit his system, his heart was going to fucking explode.

He deserved it, though. I didn't feel any guilt about his impending demise. Just... slight panic.

While he was gone, I hurried to the bathroom and grabbed a hand towel to wipe down everything I'd touched. I cleaned up the pill residue and hand-washed the glasses I'd drunk from. He'd been gone for quite a while, giving me time to do it all. I kept glancing at my watch, knowing that with each minute, he was closer to death.

After half an hour, I felt confident that I wasn't going to be forced into sex tonight. I put my clothes back on and waited. A few minutes later, he appeared, tossing his phone onto the bed.

"Sorry about that. My son is slowly starting to take over things for me, and he's an idiot." He slid off his robe, revealing an unimpressively sized but girthy cock.

Holy fuck.

I stared at his swollen dick in shock. Suddenly, I feared for this man's life. Why was it so... purple?

"Why'd you put your clothes back on?" He scowled and reached for his dick. "Let's do this."

I shook my head, the shock wearing off and being replaced with rage once more.

"We're not doing anything, asshole."

"What do you mean? I signed your stupid contract." He came toward me, but I sidestepped him.

"You killed Lita Reyes. She was like a mother to me. I don't care what she did to you. She didn't deserve that."

His eyes bulged. "This is about that bitch? Jesus Christ, Sebastian, get a grip. You think she's the first person this industry has had to take care of? She was going to ruin us."

"I have a feeling you all deserved it. Who is *us*? How many of you were part of this?"

Sweat lined his brow, and his face was flushed. His breathing grew labored, and he sat down on the bed, clutching his purple dick.

"Like I'd tell you." He snickered through his heavy breaths. "I don't know what's going on."

"What's going on is you took five too many of those precious little pills of yours. You're dying, Thornton. In just a few minutes, I'll be leaving, and you'll be found in a few days, naked and holding your tiny cock for dear life."

"What?" His eyes were struggling to stay open as he fought to breathe. "Why?"

"Lita."

Turning, I went to the table, grabbing the contract. In a few days, I'd mail it anonymously to his office. It would get lost in a sea of paperwork for a bit as people figured everything out, but once they saw the contract had been green-lit, we'd be off to the races.

Simon Says was back.

I slid the contract into my jacket and returned to Thornton, who'd dropped down onto the floor, continuing to clutch himself.

"Now, before you go, want to tell me how many of you took part in her murder?"

I crouched down and waited for him to open his eyes one last time. When he did, he gasped.

"Six."

Six. Six men took the life of a woman I held near and dear. Not only was she the only woman who'd ever treated me kindly, she was the mother of the girl that got away. Lita didn't deserve to go out the way she did, and Evie didn't deserve to lose her mom. I nodded and patted his shoulder, leaving him with some final words.

"One down. Five more to go."

CHAPTER 13

SEBASTIAN

The Prop

"Are you going to help me or what?" Glenn snapped.

I stepped forward but stopped when he turned to look up at Evie.

"You're so fucking finished. And before you even got started. You think you lost the movie gig? Just wait. I'll make sure your little podcast show is gone too. The courts will own your ass." He swung his head to me. "What are you doing? If you don't help me, you'll be an accomplice. Getting blacklisted from Hollywood will be the least of your problems."

"Are you threatening us?"

Glenn's eyes bulged. "Is this a joke? Just because I said her mom was loose? Oh, come on. It's not like I'm the first person to say it out loud."

"I can't." Evie threw up her hands and stormed out of the room.

I followed quickly. She went to her old bedroom, and I shut the door behind us.

"Tell me what happened," I said.

"Everything was fine, we were shelving my books, and then he started telling me about how his dad and my mom had an affair. I told him that wasn't true, but he wouldn't hear it." She paced her room.

"Okay, but why was he bleeding?" I'd noticed blood on the collar of his shirt and the mark on his head. She stopped short, staring at me as if she'd just remembered I was there.

"I threw a book at his head. It was a hardcover. One of my Stephen King."

I pressed my lips together. "I see. And he went down?"

"It was *IT*!"

No wonder he'd been knocked out cold. That was a thick-ass book.

She sighed. "Yes, he went down hard, and I was trying to figure out what to do when you rang the doorbell. I knew the longer I kept you outside, the more suspicious it'd look, so I stuffed him in my closet. But then he woke up, so I had to put him in the chair."

"Why, exactly? What is your plan?"

She shook her head. "I— I don't know. I think he knows more about my mom's murder, and I want him to tell me."

"Has he told you anything?" I asked quickly. Most people knew the details around Lita Reyes's death were odd, but asking questions often got you just where she was.

"No! And now I've got him tied up. What do I do?" She wiped away tears.

I reached for her, pulling her into an embrace.

"Let's find out what he knows. Then we'll figure out how to let him go—without him telling anyone we held him hostage."

"This is such a mess. I'm so sorry, Sebastian. I made you an accessory to a crime."

I kissed the top of her head. "Don't apologize. So, things got a little out of hand. We'll figure it out."

This isn't my first rodeo with a Thornton. If he's anything like his dad, he'll go down easy.

I took her hand and led her back to her mom's room, where Glenn was jerking back and forth in the chair, trying to get free. I dug into my jeans and pulled out my switchblade, flipping it open.

"Let's stay still," I warned.

He stopped moving. "You've gotta be fucking kidding me. What is this?" He looked from me to Evie.

Evie stepped ahead of me. "Five years ago, your dad was part of the group that took my mom to dinner. The next morning, she was found *murdered*, hanging on the set of her latest movie."

"She killed herself," he sneered. "Everyone knows that."

"Lita Reyes would never," I snapped. Flashbacks blinded my vision as I recalled the same argument I'd had with his dad. I shook them away. Lita was like a mother to me. Her death hurt me too. I'd seen the body, just like Evie had.

There was so much blood.

"She had a daughter."

"Has that stopped people before? Just accept that your mom wasn't who you thought she was. Evie, this is ridiculous. You think I want to remember my dad as a scumbag who couldn't keep it in his pants? No, but it is what it is."

"Your dad *was* a scumbag," Evie said. "And you're a liar." Her fists clenched tightly, and her body shook with rage.

"You're fucking sad." He laughed. "And to think, I thought you had potential. If you're not careful, we'll find you hanging next."

"Tell me what you know about what happened to my mom," she demanded.

He stopped laughing and looked at me. "I ain't telling you shit until you let me out. Or get me some water," he ordered. "My mouth is dry as fuck from the tights she stuffed in my mouth."

"I'm not leaving her."

"Sebastian, do as he asks," Evie said quickly. "We'll get you a glass, and you'll tell me the truth?"

Glenn rolled his eyes. "Sure, sweet thing. Whatever. And when I'm done, you're going to let me go, and I'll call the police. The entire *Simon Says* franchise will be tanked. You fucking losers."

"You'll float too." The famous line from Pennywise the clown escaped my lips before I could catch it.

"What did you just fucking say to me?"

"Sebastian!" Evie shouted. Then she took a deep breath, speaking calmly. "It puts the lotion in the basket."

Silence of the Lambs.

I stared at her. Why was she slipping into our code? Her eyes narrowed as she repeated the phrase. What did she want me to do?

My jaw tightened. I nodded and turned toward the door. "It does this whenever it's told," I replied.

Not happy about it, I turned and went downstairs to the kitchen—and paused. She wasn't mocking me. Glenn had wanted water, and she'd said...

She'd get him a glass.

I went to the cupboards and threw them open. There was nothing but drain cleaner, oven cleaner, and bleach. Surely there had to be a glass somewhere. I rushed around, searching, but came up empty. What did she want me to do, then? I had no way to poison him without an open container.

My eyes drifted to the table, where unopened bottles of beer and cans of Red Bull sat. I opened a beer and went upstairs, offering it to him.

"Nice try. There's bottled water in the fridge," he sneered. Having expected him to reject an open container, I feigned annoyance as I went back down and grabbed a sealed bottle. My eyes once more drifted to the table, where the Red Bulls sat, right next to the bottle of bleach I'd pulled from the cupboard.

Everyone knew blue was my favorite. Evie's favorite was yellow. I pushed those aside and started to reach for the watermelon flavor when I remembered there was an unopened one in the movie room. I walked to get it, and when I picked it off the table, I took a large swig, grimacing as the taste hit my tongue. These really were the worst flavored ones. Ignoring the sour taste, I took another drink, knowing I was going to need all the caffeine. I returned to the kitchen and jumped when Evie yelled for me.

"Sebastian?"

Glancing toward the stairs, I grabbed the bleach, poured it

in, then swirled it around, sniffing to see if anything smelled off. The watermelon covered the chemical scent. I hurried back and paused at the foot of the stairs. Putting the plastic water bottle in my jacket, I reached into my jeans pocket and pulled out my switchblade, flipping it open.

Maybe seeing a sharp object pointed in his direction would scare him enough to talk.

Or distract him entirely.

Swirling the concoction in the can some more, I went back up the stairs and handed her the bottle of water, setting my watermelon-bleach-energy drink cocktail on the table nearby. Evie unscrewed the cap, let Glenn drink, then started her interrogation.

"Why did they do it?"

"Do what?" His eyes flicked to the knife I was casually spinning in my hands.

"Kill my mom."

"I don't know what you're talking about." One side of Glenn's lips twitched. He was lying. Just like his dad had. I fucking knew it. I paused with the knife, and his gaze flicked down to my hands then back to my face, and the smirk dropped.

"Maybe she knew something she shouldn't have. Maybe she accused them of rape." Glenn glared at Evie, and the two of them shared some sort of silent exchange. It made me wonder if something had been said while I wasn't around.

Glenn rolled his eyes and turned back to me. "Wouldn't be the first time someone was taken care of."

"You're about to be one of them if you don't cut the shit. We know you know something," I warned.

"I don't know shit about what happened that night. Lita Reyes, just like every other woman—and man." He paused to look directly at me when he said it. "Used her best assets to get what she wanted. Maybe that's what happened. She couldn't live with the guilt. Maybe fucking six men in one go was too much, and she figured she'd rather kill herself than be known for the slut she was."

Evie whipped around and slapped him across his face. He fell back, his chair slamming onto the floor. I rushed to set him upright, grabbing his shirt and yanking toward me. He twisted his body, trying to get out of his restraints as he swore at us.

"Let me the fuck out! Even if I did tell you I know what happened that night, no one would believe you. My dad had a lot of pull in this business. And after he died, all of his good fortune passed down to me. You shouldn't have come back, Evie. Nothing good will come from you asking questions."

The room settled, and we sat there, watching each other.

She'd slept with all six men the night she died? That couldn't be true.

We were all waiting for someone to do something. I raised my knife again, and Glenn's eyes widened.

"I'm thirsty," Glenn said abruptly.

Evie bolted upright and offered him more water.

"I'm sorry, Glenn," she said. "You're right. I shouldn't be digging deeper into things. I need to just let it go. Look at me. I'm a disaster." She brushed her hair back behind her ears. "I don't know what I was thinking. Never getting closure about why she died has made me bitter and overly sensitive. As much as I don't want to admit it, maybe you're right about her. This is such a mess. Let me untie you." She moved behind him to remove his restraints. As she struggled with the knots she'd tied, I studied her. She didn't believe any of that shit. We both knew Lita wasn't the person Glenn described.

I was beginning to think Evie was right. Lita was raped.

Evie continued to struggle and make the knots worse. I stepped forward to help, cutting him out. In a flash, he was standing and straightening his clothes.

"It's all right. Although I think any semblance of a romantic relationship is over. It's for the best." He smirked and looked at me. "She's all yours."

"Are you going to report this?" she asked, twisting her hands. "Us?" She glanced at me.

"Well, I should. Because you're a psycho bitch. But maybe we can work out an old Hollywood deal." A slow, evil grin spread across his face as he reached into his pocket and pulled out his own switchblade. He snickered, taking slow steps toward her. She backed away until the backs of her knees hit the bed, causing him to pause. He turned, waving the knife at me with one hand while pulling his belt out of the loops with the other.

"You can stay, Sebastian. You're not the only one who likes an audience. Watch while I fuck her—maybe then you'll learn your place in this business."

"And what's that?" I asked, just to keep him talking. I clenched the knife so hard my hand trembled.

He tugged off his shirt and unzipped his pants, shoving them down and kicking them away. All while holding his weapon and smirk steady. I forced myself to stay put. One wrong move, and Evie could be hurt.

Glenn strode to the table, snatching up the water bottle.

"The actors are the last to be fed. You are replaceable. No one gives a fuck about you. You're just a pretty face." He downed the rest of the water and crushed the bottle, tossing it to the floor. "This yours?" He grabbed my Red Bull.

My eyes locked in on the can. "Yes."

"Mine now. I'm going to need the energy for what I'm about to do."

"And what is that exactly?" My heart sped up, and my stomach rolled. I needed him to say it. I stepped cautiously toward Evie.

He rolled his eyes. "Split her in half."

He brought the can to his lips and chugged. I watched, my eyes widening with each bob of his Adam's apple. He finished the drink and smacked his lips, grimacing.

"This flavor is shit," he muttered, crushing the can in his fist and tossing it to the ground. He shuddered and turned, hooking his fingers around the hem of his boxers and dragging them down. I averted my gaze from his pale ass to Evie, who was visibly shaking.

Glenn held the knife tight as he walked around the bed, his cock in his other hand. He stroked himself, growing hard.

"You can join too if you really want. A hole is a—" Glenn's crude comment was stopped short by him gagging. His eyes widened as the watermelon-bleach concoction hit his belly. The room was silent as the sound of his stomach in turmoil rattled the walls. He gagged again, dropping to his knees on the other side of the bed. I rushed over, and Evie climbed across the mattress just in time to watch Glenn begin to vomit.

Evie squeaked and covered her face as he choked and fought against the chemicals invading his blood. He clawed at his throat and tried to stand, but he was too far gone. I stared down at him, a different kind of pleasure rolling through my body.

Goodbye, Glenn.

He scrambled, slipping in his own bile as he tried to crawl away, but he only made it a few feet. He stretched, grabbing for the can, and as his fingers tightened around the crushed metal, he collapsed.

Evie jumped off her bed and ran to him, dropping to her knees and pulling his body up.

"Sebastian." She looked up at me. "That wasn't watermelon flavor, was it?"

Slowly, I shook my head and closed my switchblade, slipping it back into my pocket.

"What flavor was it?"

I cleared my throat and looked up at the ceiling, shoving my hands into my pockets and rocking awkwardly on my heels.

"Bleach."

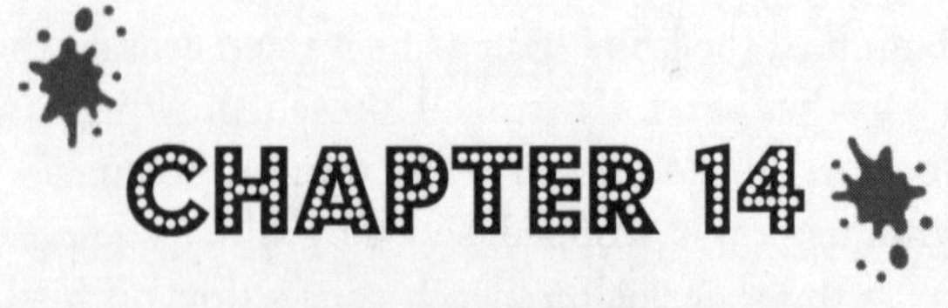

CHAPTER 14
EVIE

The Reset

"This isn't fucking *Heathers*." I stood up, gagging at the vomit that had spilled from Glenn's mouth after he'd consumed a bleach-watermelon-energy-drink cocktail.

"If it were *Heathers*, it would have been Drano, and we'd already have fucked." Sebastian snickered. "I did the best with what was available. I didn't have a handful of little blue pills lying around to give him a heart attack."

I cocked my head. He was smirking as he watched me put two and two together.

How did he know about Glenn's dad?

"That was you?"

He nodded.

"Why?" My chin trembled.

"Because he was involved in killing Lita."

I looked up at him. His eyes were nothing but honest. They held no sympathy for Glenn or his father. Something stirred within me. Suddenly, I wasn't looking at Sebastian Shaw, Hollywood heartthrob. I was looking at...the dreamiest man I'd ever seen.

But the discussion we'd be having about Glenn's father would have to wait.

"We have to hide this. This wasn't part of my plan. This is all wrong." I stormed out of the room to grab carpet cleaner and a rag from the closet. I hurried back and dropped to my knees to begin scrubbing the vomit and pink drink staining my mother's beautiful carpet.

"What do you mean this wasn't part of your plan?" Sebastian sat on the edge of the bed, watching me. "What plan exactly?"

"My revenge plan. He wasn't supposed to die," I said, not looking up from my task. "I needed more time with him. I shouldn't have told you to get the bleach. Now I'll never know how his dad was involved."

Sebastian slid off the bed and dropped to the floor. He put his hand over mine to stop my scrubbing. His other hand went to my chin, raising it to force me to look at him. Tears stung my eyes as I tried not to let the panic set in.

"Hey, it's okay. I can help clean this up."

I stared at him, my mind going blank. How could he be so calm right now? I threw the rag down and fell back against the wall. The curtain over the window spilled across my face. I shoved them back in annoyance. "Fuck!"

Sebastian sat with me while I sobbed into my knees. This was all so fucked. Glenn would have told me what I needed to know, probably, at some point, if we hadn't dumped fucking bleach down his throat.

What had we done?

We were monsters.

I was a monster.

I knew there was something suspicious about that red can and chose not to question it.

"I'm partial to blueberry."

"Evie, is that why you came back? Revenge?"

I looked up, wiping the tears from my face. Pain and disappointment flashed across his expression. It put a pit in my stomach that twisted until painful, but I couldn't lie to him.

"Yes," I murmured. "I'm going to kill every last one of them."

His expression deflated, his Adam's apple bobbed, and he nodded. "All right, then let's do this." He slapped his thighs and stood.

I stared up at him. "What do you mean?"

He offered me his hand and pulled me to my feet. "You're here for revenge. You want to find out the truth about what happened to your mom?"

I nodded, sniffling and continuing to wipe my face.

"Then we're going to do that. Let's find all those fuckers who hurt her."

"And kill them?" I asked, my words hopeful. In my heart, I knew killing was wrong. I was upset about the man on my floor right now. I didn't crave random death. I just craved theirs.

He nodded.

"You're going to help me? You realize that...we will—we could—" I couldn't say it, but his green eyes shone with understanding. We very well might die doing this.

"Yes. But first, let's dispose of this one."

"Where?" I blurted, shaking my head. "This wasn't the plan. If I'd known—"

"Shh..." Sebastian pulled me into his arms. "It's okay. No more tears. Especially not because of that bastard. He was about to rape you. Have you forgotten already?"

My gaze shot to Glenn, wearing only his socks.

Oh, right. How had he phrased it?

He was going to split me in half.

I curled my lip, suddenly less guilty about his murder.

Like father, like son, I supposed.

"Let's get him dressed. We'll figure it out from there."

We worked together to pull his clothes back on. Once we were finished, Sebastian tossed him over his shoulder with a loud groan.

"Do you have a vehicle? I'd rather not put him in mine."

"Just the moving van." I shrugged.

"Perfect."

Sebastian propped him up against a wall in my kitchen as I opened the garage and pulled the van in. Thankfully it was a smaller vehicle and was able to fit, albeit snuggly. I pushed the button to shut the garage and then opened the back of the van.

"Plenty of space." Sebastian groaned as he hoisted Glenn over his shoulder and tossed him like a rag doll into the back. I jumped as his body hit the metal flooring with a loud *thump*!

"Your mom have a shovel?" Sebastian asked, looking around the garage.

"She did!" I hurried to the wall and grabbed it. I'd never been more grateful that I hadn't thrown anything out. Not only did we have materials to help with getting rid of the evidence, but I knew exactly where to find them. I handed him the shovel, and he tossed it into the van.

"Cool. Get in." He flashed the keys and nodded to the other side of the moving van.

"Where are we going?" I asked, sliding into the passenger side.

"Water or desert?" he asked, reaching for my hand and squeezing it. Digging out my own keys, I pushed the button to open the garage, and slowly, he backed out and drove down the long driveway, passing his car as we went.

It took me a moment to understand. "Well, we have the shovel." I shrugged. Was there a correct answer?

"Desert it is. Thankfully, we're close to I-10 East, there's not a lot of cameras. I'll watch for those, you handle the music."

The stereo began to ding, and suddenly my voice assistant on my phone chirped.

"Where would you like to go, Evie?"

Sebastian hit the brakes and turned to look at me.

"Your GPS is on?"

I shrunk in my seat, cringing.

With a low growl of annoyance, Sebastian stopped, drove back into the garage, and handed me his phone. I grabbed it along with mine before heading into the house, tossing them onto the living room couch. Returning, I buckled my seat belt, and we backed out of my drive again but stopped at the end of my driveway.

"Where's his phone?" He looked back and nodded at Glenn. "Grab it and use his finger to unlock it. We'll see what music he's got."

I climbed into the back, grimacing and avoiding touching his lifeless body as much as I could while digging into his pockets. I pressed the button on the side and pushed Glenn's pointer finger onto the glass. I huffed as the phone rejected the attempt.

"It wants his face." I glanced up at Glenn's head, slumped backward. Would it still work with his eyes rolled back and tongue hanging out? Reluctantly, I turned the overhead light on and grabbed Glenn's hair, pulling his head up. My stomach rolled as I stared at the man who had been alive only an hour ago. Steeling myself, I quickly tried the face recognition, and much to my relief, it worked.

Rejoining Sebastian in the front, I pressed the buttons on the radio to connect and then went to Glenn's music.

"He likes country," I muttered, scrolling through his Spotify.

"Liked," Sebastian said firmly.

I looked up into his cold eyes and nodded. "Right. Liked."

I typed emo into the music app's search bar, something I knew he liked.

Sebastian gripped the wheel, and only when My Chemical Romance poured from the speakers did he press on the pedal. A grin spread over his face as his shoulders relaxed, and we drove off the property and onto the road. As soon as we were on the highway, he began to belt the song, and soon, I found myself joining in.

For three hours, it felt like we were kids again—just cruising, goofing around, and singing to MCR and all the other emo bands from the early 2000s. Back then, this was what we listened to on set. The adults in *Simon Says* had been teenagers in the early 2000s. They loved blasting the music they grew up on while in hair and makeup or between takes.

I couldn't wait to be a part of that. This time, I would be in a makeup chair too.

With our turn back in time, I'd all but forgotten the dead

body in the back until we drove past the sign for Joshua Tree National Park.

Oh, right. We'd killed someone.

"You wanted the desert," he said as he parked and got out of the van.

I joined him and gazed out at the dark, moonlit landscape. There was no one for miles. A good thing for disposing bodies.

While it looked peaceful and quite pretty, with its dried foliage, large cacti, and even larger mountains in the distance as our only audience, the silence was deceiving. There was tension in the air—telling us we needed to be on watch, lest a predator sneak up on us.

"Scavengers will take care of him soon enough," Sebastian added. "Honestly, we probably don't even need to bury him."

Together, with Sebastian taking his arms and me taking his legs, we dragged Glenn out of the van. He fell onto the ground, causing dust to blow up into our faces. I coughed and stepped back. Once the dust settled, I continued to help Sebastian drag the body a short distance away from the van. Setting him down, I rubbed my sore shoulders.

"So, we just toss him out here? What if someone finds him before the animals..." A twinge of guilt twisted in my belly as I looked down at the man. Just four hours ago, maybe five, he was alive and well. He'd had his whole life ahead of him—and we'd fed him bleach.

He'd also tried to rape me.

Sometimes dead is better.

"We could speed up the process, but it's not gonna be pretty."

I gulped as a pit began to form in my stomach. "How so?"

Sebastian pulled out his switchblade, popping it open. "We need to give the coyotes something to sniff for." He pulled off his leather jacket then his shirt, handing me both. He stripped down to his boxers, tossing the rest of his clothes to the side, then he dropped to his knees, knife raised.

"Don't look."

I turned away quickly, my stomach rolling, but looked over my shoulder, curious.

"Stay turned that way if you don't want to see this," he warned. "You're gonna fuck around and find out."

Steeling myself, I faced forward again and stepped farther away, snapping my eyes closed. A moment later, I heard the grunt of Sebastian swinging down and the squish of the knife plunging into something wet. A whimper escaped my throat, and I quickly covered my mouth as I continued to hear the sounds of Glenn being...

Curiosity got the best of me, and I turned my head slowly, popping an eye open. It took a moment for my eyes to zero in on the details of the scene, but the moment I saw eyeballs, I spun back around. The movement was too quick, and my body revolted. Dizziness filled my vision, and I dropped to the ground, catching myself on my palms.

"Evie, you okay? Did you look?" Sebastian called, an accusatory tone in his voice.

"I looked," I admitted, keeping my eyes closed to stop the spinning.

"I warned you." He clicked his tongue as he continued working on Glenn. While I couldn't see it, I could hear every little squish of blood releasing, every bone being cracked by force, and every... I wasn't quite sure what, but it was making the sound of Velcro ripping.

"You fucked around, and then what?"

"I found out," I replied miserably as I gagged, trying not to vomit and leave more evidence behind. Taking deep breaths, I steadied myself and stood, making sure to keep my back facing Sebastian and Glenn.

"Is there any water in the van?" Sebastian asked.

I didn't want to turn but forced myself to, keeping my eyes shut as I drifted over to the van to search. I found a half-finished bottle in the back, and bracing myself for the gruesome scene, I brought it to him. My hand trembled as I handed him the bottle.

I stared down at the body as Sebastian stood and slowly poured the water over his hands, chest, and thighs, rinsing off the blood.

Glenn was really gone. He no longer had eyeballs, and his face was crushed to an unrecognizable level.

I could kind of pretend before when he just looked unconscious. But there was no coming back from having your brains peeking out through your eye sockets.

"Have you done this before?" I asked, unable to pull my eyes away.

"No, it was awful. Truly, truly awful. Ready?" Sebastian asked, the crinkling from the empty bottle pulling me from the gruesome sight.

I nodded. "Yeah, let's go. Oh, wait." I grabbed Glenn's phone from the passenger's seat. "Should we leave this here so it doesn't track us back? I don't want it at my house."

Sebastian thought for a moment, wiping sweat off his brow and looked toward the sky.

"How did he get to your place? I didn't see another car."

"It should still be at the studio lot. He rode with me from there."

He rolled his eyes and paced for a moment. "Fuck it. There's no avoiding cameras once we get to the parking lot. Let's wipe it clean from our fingerprints and I'll toss it out the window somewhere between here and home." He returned to the van for his clothes.

"Shouldn't we destroy it? Otherwise they'll see the GPS. What would he have been doing here in the middle of the night?"

"I don't know. That's for the police to figure out, come on." He adjusted his leather jacket and brushed his hair back.

Smart. Sebastian was way better at this murder thing than I was. I wasn't sure if that was comforting or terrifying.

Both.

We climbed back into the moving van and started back. The music wasn't as loud as it was on the way to dispose of Glenn. Instead, the mood was somber, and we discussed what we'd tell the police and what my next moves would be once we knew we were in the clear. Sebastian was confident we wouldn't be linked to Glenn's death, but he was also a professional actor, so I had a hard time believing him. His entire job was to convince his audience.

We pulled the moving van into the lot, right next to Glenn's car, just as the sun was starting to rise. Sebastian took my hand. He smiled down at me and lifted his wrist to flash his watch.

"Would you look at that? It's call time. Let's go play pretend, Final Girl."

CHAPTER 15

EVIE

The Showmance

Having done a quick inspection of the back to make sure there was no evidence of Glenn, we closed the doors, and I left the key for the moving company to come pick the vehicle back up. Utterly exhausted, I leaned on Sebastian, wrapping my arm around him. However, the moment I saw a crew member pass by, I yanked myself away. The guy gave us a tight smile and wave before moving on.

"Ouch." Sebastian whistled. "That's hard not to take personally."

"What?" I cringed. I hadn't meant to have such a visceral reaction. "Sorry. I just—"

"Don't want people seeing us together?"

"Sebastian..." I sighed as we walked toward set.

"No, no, I get it. I understand you don't want us to get serious. I just wish we'd had this talk *before* we ditched a body in the desert."

I leaped in front of him and slapped my hand over his mouth. "Beep beep, Ritchie!"

He grinned under my hand. His eyes lit up, knowing he'd gotten a rise out of me. I looked around and tugged him around the corner, behind a sound stage, before removing my hand.

"What are you doing?" I hissed.

"Apparently, getting shot down."

"What are you talking about?" I shook my head. This was not the time or place to be discussing something that wasn't even a possibility. I leaned against the wall, running a hand through my hair.

"That's why I came to your house last night," he said. "Because we had a moment at the chemistry test, and I thought maybe—"

"Maybe what? That I'd want to date again? That I'd fall back in love with you, and we would run off into the sunset? Sebastian, that's not why I'm here. I can't—"

Dante passed by and caught sight of us. He walked over, and I shut my mouth.

"Beep beep, Ritchie," I whispered.

"*Back*?" Sebastian asked.

I cocked my head, confused. His expression had clouded over. His eyes seemed to be recalling a memory, and his jaw had gone slightly slack. An instant later, he looked down at me, his gaze curious. "Fall *back* in love with me?"

My belly fluttered, and I opened my mouth to tell him this was not the time, but before I could, Dante reached us, and I snapped my mouth shut.

"You're both here! That's great. I have to be on set in a bit for some establishing shots, but I need you to go over to the production office. We've got our PR managers and some lawyers there that want to talk to you."

"Lawyers?" I squeaked.

Sebastian reached over and squeezed my hand. Dante's eyes flickered to them, and he smiled.

"Yeah, it'll be fine. You're not in trouble. Let's go. I'll have my assistant drive you over."

We hopped into a golf cart with a guy named Darryl. He made small talk as he drove us away from set and the trailers, but I was too deep in my own head to join in.

What could they need a lawyer for?

He stopped in front of an unlabeled building and opened

the door for us. We went in and found a handful of people at a midsize table, stacks of papers in front of them. Kate, the intimacy coordinator, was there, along with Antoinette and others I didn't recognize.

"Antoinette?" I went to my agent and sat down across from her. I noticed then that the only seats left were across from the others. Sebastian sat beside me, and we shared a curious look.

"They called me last night. Didn't you get my text?" she asked.

"I... No." I'd left my phone at home—while we dropped Glenn off in the desert to be eaten by predators.

"You look like shit," a man said to Sebastian. "Where did you sleep last night? J-Tree?"

J-Tree.

Joshua Tree National Park.

I forced myself not to react, despite my racing heart.

Sebastian snickered. "Bold of you to assume I slept. You got a Red Bull?"

The man rolled his eyes and stood, going to a mini fridge, pulling out two blue cans. He offered one to both of us. I took mine hesitantly, glancing over at Sebastian—and it was like we shared the same thought.

Thank Anthony C. Hopkins the cans were still sealed.

"So, why are we here?" Sebastian popped the tab and took a long drink.

"Yes, well, hello, Mr. Shaw, Ms. Reyes." An Asian woman with a short pixie cut and a teal blazer stood and offered her hand to shake. "I am Stacey from Pepper-Walsh PR. We handle all the studio's press releases and marketing. My team and I have been working for a while on *Simon Says Six—*"

"*Six Six*," Sebastian interrupted.

She paused for a moment, her forehead lines creased, then with a quick eye roll, she continued. "*Six Six*. We think with the right marketing, this movie could be the next big thing. A pivotal moment in your careers. This could skyrocket you both to fame." She was really selling it—wide eyes, large smile, extended arms.

"What more do you want us to do?" Sebastian leaned back in his seat, pulling his arms up behind his head, and yawned. "I'm already showing off my circumcision scar."

She blushed then cleared her throat. "Yes, exactly." She pointed at Sebastian then went to the front of the room, where a TV was mounted on the wall. Another member of her team turned it on with a remote, and Bradley Cooper and Lady Gaga appeared on screen. Stacey nodded, and a new slide appeared. Vanessa Hudgens and Zac Efron. Then Elizabeth Taylor and a man I didn't recognize.

"These are famous showmances."

"Showmances?" I raised an eyebrow.

The next slide was Robert Pattinson and Kristen Stewart.

Oh.

"We are going to leak rumors of your full-frontal reveal to the media. That is going to get people talking—and selling tickets. But to really sell that this is going to be the hottest movie of the year, hotter than *Step-Devil*." She paused, staring at Sebastian. "We need to ramp this up. We need a showmance."

Sebastian looked at me, then back at her. "What are you proposing exactly?"

"A fake relationship—for the cameras. Evie, we want you to use your channel, *The Body Count Bimbo,* to post behind-the-scenes content."

My channel showed on the TV.

"We will film the content for you, edit it, and post it all. You don't have to do any of the backend work."

"So, acting off screen?" My shoulders fell. I was exhausted. I needed to sleep. "I'm not entirely sure I follow. That's not my usual content."

"We know. We did consider your brand and that your established fanbase likes videos of you relaying information above all else. But if we announce a *temporary takeover* while you film and put the videos and clips into organized playlists, our team of experts think your channel will grow, rather than lose followers."

I scrunched up my nose. I was hesitant to hand over my business. While I didn't need the money, as my mom had left me quite a sizable fortune, *The Body Count Bimbo* was my baby. I'd worked hard to grow my career.

On the other hand, posting new content would keep my channel relevant. The hiatus was slowly killing my account with each day I didn't post.

Stacey continued. "You'll be compensated for all of it. The channel revenue, your working hours, everything. That's why the lawyers and your agents are here."

I glanced at Antoinette. "You like this idea?"

She gave me a tight smile. "Well...it's a smart idea. The algorithm loves active channels."

I looked around the table, and my eyes zeroed in on Kate, the intimacy coordinator. "Wait. Why are you here?"

Her eyes went wide. "Well—I—well..."

"We want to really ham this up. Handholding, embracing, kissing," Stacey interjected. "We want the off-screen chemistry to look so real, so hot— people will feel the need to see you two screwing on camera."

"That's not professional," Kate said softly.

"Sorry." Stacey snickered. "I just wanted to rip off the Band-Aid." She reached for a folder and pulled out two thick packets, offering them to Sebastian and me. "The studio is prepared to pay handsomely for all of it."

"Why?" I asked, skimming the contract. It was all here, kissing, with and without tongue, hand holding, hugging, butt touching. What I'd post on my channel. Who I'd speak to. How much I'd get paid.

Anthony C. Hopkins.

The zeros at the end were...a lot. I looked up, shaking my head. This didn't make sense.

"I'm a nobody."

"You're Lita Reyes's daughter. Your name is gold." Stacey grinned. "It's why you were cast. No offense."

"Not just your name. You performed well in the chemistry test." One of the other PR people stood—a Black man who was dressed as if ready to go golfing. "It's why we wanted the test in the first place. This isn't some sudden idea we had in the middle of the night. We've been waiting for the right pair to take this on. We think you're it."

The room fell silent as they waited for us to speak.

"I'd...like time to look this over." I stood, grabbed the packet, and fled the room.

Antoinette followed, and together, we took a golf cart back to my trailer. Once inside, I tossed the papers aside and paced.

"This is not a good idea. There's too much..."

"Chemistry?" Antoinette crossed her arms.

History.

"Evie, we don't have to do this. But as your agent—who also practices law—the contract is a good one. We can negotiate whatever you'd like. More money, less touching, any of it."

I stopped and stared. She actually thought this was a good idea. I couldn't believe it. In the room with all the PR people pressuring us, sure. But here, one on one, she still wanted to do this?

Even if we took my channel's life out of the equation, there was still Sebastian. If we pretended to be in love, I might just...

There was a loud rap on the trailer door, and we turned.

"Come in!" I shouted.

Sebastian opened the door and hurried up the stairs.

"Can we talk? I have a proposal." He looked from me to Antoinette, who then looked from me to him.

"Yeah, it's fine. Antoinette..."

She raised her hands in surrender and left the trailer.

"What's the proposal? Marriage?" I shot at him the moment the door was closed.

He reached for the contract I'd tossed aside and stepped toward me, waving it inches from my face.

"You have five men left on your list, right? If you sign this contract, I'll get you close enough to kill them."

CHAPTER 16

SEBASTIAN

The Bridge

A loud knock on Evie's trailer door made us both turn our heads.

I looked back at her, raising an eyebrow. "What do you say? How badly do you want those men dead?"

She stared me down, weighing my words. Could I really hold up my end of this deal? The knock came again, followed by a call.

"Ms. Reyes? Mr. Shaw?"

Evie sighed heavily and snatched the contract from me. "I have come here to chew bubblegum and kick ass. And I'm all out of bubblegum."

A large grin spread over my face at the quote from *They Live*. I pulled a pen from my jacket and handed it to her. She signed it quickly and then brushed past me to open the door.

"Yeah?" she snapped at the man on the other side.

I eyed the tall, stocky Black man and the much shorter, heavy-set white woman smiling behind him.

"Sorry. They want Sebastian on the sound stage for stunt training. And they want you for PR training," he said.

"And who are you?" she asked, changing her tone from charged to relaxed as we both exited her trailer.

"Sorry, I should have introduced myself. I'm Connor, Mr. Shaw's production assistant for the film. I'll be making sure you stay on schedule, among other things. If you need anything, I'm your guy." The man built like a linebacker took my hand and shook it.

"And I'm Raissa, Evie's assistant!" The woman popped out from behind Connor, tossing her long brunette hair with purple streaks over her shoulder. "Let's get you over to the right building." She motioned to the set of golf carts beside the trailers.

"Right. Okay." I paused, reaching for Evie's hand. I squeezed and looked into her deep, dark eyes. "I'll catch you after work, okay?"

She nodded, and we went our separate ways. Connor told me all about himself as he drove me over to the sound stage.

"I played pro ball, NFL, but quit two years in. The brain damage wasn't worth it anymore. So, I took all my money and came out here instead. Figured I could use my film degree." He chuckled. He seemed like a decent guy, but I found myself distracted by Evie.

She'd just agreed to fake date me.

The timer had started. I had until she killed the last man on her list to convince her to drop the act and be with me for real.

"Sir?"

I looked around, surprised. We were parked in front of the sound stage. I'd gotten lost in thought again and hadn't noticed how quickly we'd gotten here.

I leaped out. "Thanks, Connor. Call me Sebastian."

I headed into the building and was sent to change and prepare for stunt training.

"Bout damn time!" Bryce, my old friend and co-star for five, soon to be six, *Simon Says* movies, greeted me when I made it to set. He did a double take when I came closer. "You look like hell."

I raked my gaze over him. Bryce had an aloof cowboy style, which made it easy for him to maintain a put-together appearance, even if he wasn't. His blond hair was longer, going to his shoulders, which were broad. His body shape was similar to mine, although he'd gotten his from farm work, and mine came from attending the gym daily. Working with him today was going to be brutal.

"I've been worse." I drank the water Connor had given me, tossed the bottle into the trash, and raised my fists into a fighting stance. "Let's fucking go, big boy."

The morning was spent sparring. At lunch, I checked in on Evie, but she was still in PR training across the lot. I took a quick shower in my trailer, letting the hot water soothe my screaming muscles. Returning to set after, I was rigged with a harness and dragged, tossed, blown back, all the things they'd potentially be shooting in the next two months. This wasn't new to me, and I grew bored fast.

"You all right there, kiddo?" Bryce asked as we wrapped for the day.

Stunt days were typically short so we didn't hurt ourselves. We exited the sound stage and walked to the trailers, rather than drove. "You seemed out of it most of the day."

"It's just been one of those days." I shrugged off his concerns.

Bryce was like an older brother. He was about fifteen years older and had always been protective of me when I was a kid on set. When I grew into an adult, we started hanging out after work on occasion. He was probably the closest person I had in this world, other than Evie.

"I'm just trying to get out of here. I have things to do."

"Things? Or people?" He chuckled, then shuddered. "It's weird seeing Evie back and all grown up. Kinda makes me feel like some deadbeat dad."

I laughed. "What the hell are you talking about?" Bryce was always two thoughts ahead of everyone else. He often had conversations in his head, forgetting to let us in on whatever the topic was.

"Well, I watched you two grow up on set. You were basically toddlers when we met. Considering neither of you had father figures, or well—good ones." He cringed, and I waved him off.

My dad was like the rest of them: money hungry. I hadn't actually spoken to him since I was eight. My mom was long gone by then, having ditched us for a boyfriend when I was a newborn.

That left my dad to raise me, but when I started the *Simon Says* movies, it was clear that he didn't care about me. He just wanted the paycheck. Heather, my agent, ended up taking him to court to get me emancipated. At the time, the courts thought having Heather around in place of my dad would keep me safe. They were wrong.

You can't be a kid and be safe in this town.

"I was eight," I clarified. "Which would have made you what, twenty-three?"

"Yeah, I guess so. Man, how time flies. I'd love to be twenty-three again, although I will say, I make thirty-six look good." Bryce laughed and then stopped, his smile fading. "I kind of took on a protective role. I liked watching over you guys, making sure no one was hurting you. I just... wish I could have done that for Lita too."

Sadness washed over us momentarily as we thought of our lost castmate and friend.

"Anyway, I kind of think of you two as the kids I'll never have. I'm glad she's back."

"Me too." Just as we got to our trailers, I spotted Evie getting off a cart, her assistant in tow. "Hey, I'll catch you later," I said to Bryce as I walked off.

"Maybe we can all get pizza or something soon!" he shouted after me.

I didn't respond, my brain too focused on Evie. Even with tired eyes and slumped shoulders, she was the prettiest woman I'd ever laid eyes on.

"Hey. How was PR training?" I asked when I reached her.

She didn't look my way. Instead, she kept walking.

"You can go get your stuff. I'll be ready soon," she said to Raissa, who quickly fell back and went the opposite direction.

"Evie? Is everything okay?" I reached for her wrist as she made it to her trailer, the one next to mine.

She stopped and turned. "Yes, I'm just tired. I didn't sleep last night," she reminded me.

I nodded. I knew once I got home, I'd crash out myself. Right now, I was energized from the excitement of being near her. "I'm having Raissa take me home in a bit. The moving company picked up the van earlier."

My mood fell slightly. I wanted to be the one to drive her home.

"Do you want company? We could talk about...things. I can come over later."

"Not tonight, Sebastian. I am so mentally drained, it's not funny. And I officially start shooting tomorrow, so I need to rest, learn my lines, and de-stress. We can talk after. I'm just stopping in here to grab my script." I let go of her wrist and she climbed the stairs to her trailer, opening the door.

"Sure, of course. I haven't checked the call sheet. Are we doing scenes together?" I followed her in.

She grabbed the script, and we promptly left her trailer.

"No, it's me and Skye. I think they're saving most of our scenes for last."

I knew all this. This was what they did for *Step-Devil* too. They wanted us to have as much chemistry as possible before we started to film. They were going to stall filming our sex scenes until the very end. Just like I was stalling right now. I was grasping at straws, but I didn't want to let her go just yet.

"Well, maybe we can carve out some time. I wouldn't mind talking about last night," I suggested as we crossed the parking lot.

She spun around, her eyes darting across the lot. "Beep beep, Ritchie!" she hissed and stepped closer to me.

I lifted my shoulders. "What? Are we not supposed to say we were together—"

She cupped her hand over my mouth, and I relished the feel of her soft palm on my stubbled jaw. I inhaled deeply, taking in the scent of sweet pea lotion.

"Look, no one knows about this, and no one needs to," she said carefully. She was talking about both Glenn and our showmance.

I stepped back, dropping her hand. "It puts the lotion in the basket. It does this whenever it's told." I snickered.

She crossed her arms. "You're not funny."

"No? I was told that's why they keep bringing me back," I quipped.

Her shoulders slumped, and she tossed her hands up. She gave me a glare and turned away. "I have to go. Don't call me. I have things to do."

"All right," I shouted as she stormed away. "I'll see you tomorrow, Final Girl!"

She shot me the middle finger. "Good night, Psycho Killer!"

Before she could reach the cars, she made a sharp turn toward an office building. I cocked my head.

"Where are you going?" I shouted before she got out of earshot.

She turned around and shook her head. Even from a distance, I could see the eye roll. She pointed to Glenn's car, then the building.

"I have to break it off with Glenn! Hopefully he takes it well!"

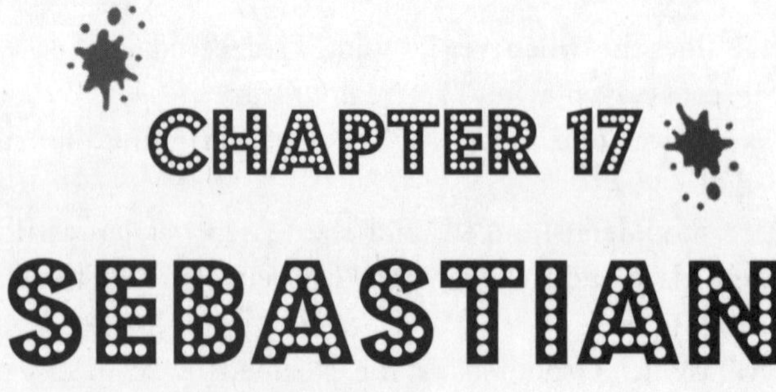

CHAPTER 17 SEBASTIAN

The Sound Bite

One Month Later

"I can't believe it took this long, honestly," Bryce said as we watched Glenn's caår get towed. "They checked the car weeks ago."

"And still nothing?" Skye asked, chewing her nails.

"Not a peep, from what I heard." I snickered.

Evie elbowed me, and I laughed. "What? He tried to get me pulled from the franchise that I've been tied to most of my life. Sorry if I don't feel bad the bastard's mouth finally got him in trouble." I made eye contact with Evie and added, "Someone probably plucked his eyes out and smashed his face in."

She paled as her eyes widened. An odd sensation of satisfaction swelled in my chest. It was almost like our chemistry test, exposing Evie and me in front of unaware people.

Was I developing a new kink?

"How oddly specific," Evie muttered through clenched teeth. "Is that a confession?"

"Like I have the time," I quipped, then rolled my eyes for effect. "It was probably the mob."

"You think it was the mob?" Skye squeaked.

Skye was naïve. Too naïve for a career in this town. She was slowly growing on me, only because Evie had taken a liking to her. They hung out often after work, making it hard to get alone time with Evie. How were we supposed to develop chemistry when we were never alone? Bryce, too, was starting to piss me off with his company, which normally I enjoyed.

We had two days off filming while they reset the stages, but we were still required to report for PR stuff. I'd told myself these two days were my shot at getting some alone time with Evie. But the first moment I got, Glenn's car started getting towed and people came to watch.

Fuck me.

"It was not the mob," Bryce said. "Well, I don't actually know that. It could be. Who knows how the other half lives? He was a cocky asshole, you're right." He nodded at me. "If he's dead or on the run, it was his own fault, I'm sure. Let's go. We've got interviews to rock." He kicked off the wall we'd all been leaning against and motioned for us to follow him into the next building.

"Yay!" Skye squealed.

I glanced at Evie and smirked as we followed a few steps behind. We abandoned the sight of Glenn's car, and I forced the darkness of that night back to the recesses of my mind. I put on a smile, gripped Evie's shoulders, and then jumped into the air.

"Groovy!"

I wrapped my arms around her from behind and nuzzled my face into her neck. I inhaled, reveling in the smell of her sweet perfume. She giggled as my stubble tickled her neck, but the moment she caught Skye and Bryce looking, she shoved me away and mumbled for me to stop.

I huffed but dropped my arms.

This showmance was going at a turtle's pace. Filming had been going on for a month, and all we'd done was some light flirting and hugs for her YouTube channel. She'd given the PR team control over it, with her getting the final say over content. She was very protective of *The Body Count Bimbo* brand. I watched the videos after they were posted and read the comments. I had to admit, Stacey and her team were good at their jobs. The videos really looked like we were trying to fight the attraction, playing it off as just friendly banter.

There was no fighting on my part. I'd fuck her right here if she'd let me.

My gaze drifted to her ass, bouncing as she walked. I squeezed my hands at my sides, wishing she'd stop pushing me away.

We spent the next hour in hair and makeup, getting ready for a group interview led by JoJo Perkins for some horror talk show. She was like every other gossip journalist. I'd been taught how to deal with these types of people, so she didn't faze me, but Evie looked like she was going to be sick from the nerves.

"I saw your interview before we started filming. She was kind of pushy. I'm not going to let her bully you," Skye told her protectively.

Jealousy flared within me. *I* wanted to be the one to protect her from the world.

Maybe in another life.

We were directed to the stage, and when Evie tried to sit by Skye, she was redirected by an assistant to sit on the loveseat with me. I plopped down and pulled her in, causing her to fall onto me and creating a silly moment of her scrambling off my lap. All of which was caught on the cameras.

Groovy.

JoJo came out a moment later. "Welcome back, Ms. Reyes. I am so excited to get another chance to talk. And Sebastian, a pleasure." She grinned and shook all our hands. I put my arm around the back of the couch, and JoJo's dark-brown eyes shot right to it. A slow grin slid over her face as she took her seat across from us.

You're welcome. I snickered. *I just gave her a story.*

The cameras, which I knew had gotten all of this, counted her down, and then she started her greeting.

"Hello, and welcome to *Featured Creatures*, the only show where we keep the female gaze at the forefront as we explore all things horror. I'm your host, JoJo Perkins. Today we have in the studio the cast of *Simon Says Six—*"

"*Six Six*," Evie and I blurted in sync. She remained stiff beside me, wringing her hands in her lap.

JoJo paused and corrected herself with a laugh. "*Simon Says Six: Six Six*. *Simon Says* is one of the few best-selling, long-running franchises in horror history. Known for its iconic killer clown, Simon Says, played by Bryce Oliver, and its tasteful transition from a Final Girl to a Final Boy after they lost a main cast member five years ago. The franchise has five, soon to be six, movies in the series, spanning almost fifteen years and millions of fans worldwide. Let's welcome Bryce Oliver, Sebastian Shaw, Skye Stevens, and Evie Reyes to the set. Hi guys!"

We all said various greetings, and she started in on her interview.

"Let's start with the old guard. Bryce, what's it like to be back in the famous disgraced ringmaster suit?" JoJo asked.

I glanced over. Today, Bryce wore a short-sleeved button-up, opened to reveal a clean, crisp white undershirt, distressed designer jeans, brown boots, and a cowboy hat he brought from his own wardrobe.

"Well, I had to shave my mustache and grow my hair back out for the role. At this point, I should just keep it this length, considering how many times they keep bringing me back." He laughed, and we joined in on autopilot. "But putting the face paint back on and sliding into the suit, it's like greeting an old friend."

"I bet. That costume is so popular with fans. I see it all the time at cons or during Halloween. What about you, Sebastian? Are you glad to be back?"

This went on for a good hour or so. JoJo kept to questions that were on her cards. She made sure to toss us questions evenly, and the longer the interview went, the more comfortable we all grew and the sillier our responses became.

"Now, Evie, I know you're going to hate me, but it's on my cards." JoJo hid behind the papers, concealing her grin, but her brown eyes shone with glee.

Evie stiffened beside me.

"I have to talk about the spicy stuff."

Evie whipped her head toward me, and I inwardly swore. The cameras caught that. The world just caught that.

"Yes! See, okay, here we go. I've been dying to talk about this. Evie, your debut film features an on-screen sex scene with Hollywood's hottest man in horror. How do you feel about it?" JoJo squealed.

"Oh jeez. Well, uh—Intimate scenes are so awkward for actors, but umm... we're professionals. I—I mean we—know it'll be handled with care," Evie said, stumbling over her response.

"Yes, but I'm sure having a good-looking scene partner must make it easier," JoJo pushed.

"It does for me," I interjected.

JoJo grinned, her eyes lighting up. I grinned back at her. This was probably a bad idea, but I was trying to save Evie.

"Have you started filming those scenes yet?" JoJo turned her attention to me since Evie wasn't giving her anything good.

"Not yet. Those are the last scenes scheduled, for obvious reasons." I smiled reassuringly at Evie, but her face had paled, and her eyes had gone glossy. She looked like she was going to vomit.

"Well, it's not obvious to me," JoJo replied with a smirk. "Usually, those are filmed last because the actors don't have chemistry. You two have it in droves. The heat coming off that couch is making me sweat." She fanned herself then leaned forward, as if trying to talk to Evie one on one. "Girl, be real right now. How much time have you guys spent practicing for *that* scene?"

"Hey now—"

Skye began, but the jealous ass in me flared to life. I'd be damned if her bestie came to her rescue. I blurted the first thing that came to mind, forgetting all my years of PR training.

"We don't need to rehearse what's already been done. We're good." I put my arm around her and squeezed, and then it hit me.

I just told the entire world that we'd had sex.

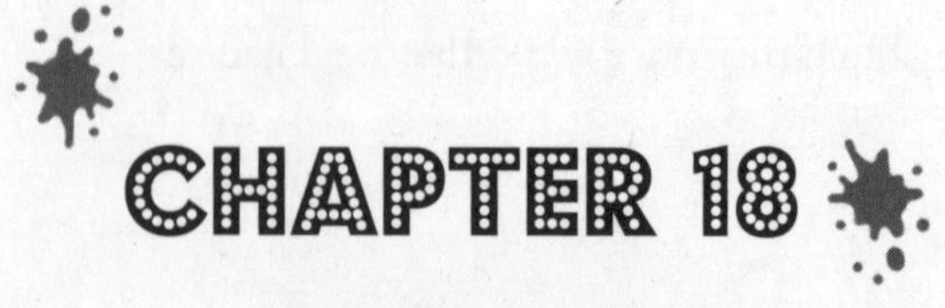

CHAPTER 18

EVIE

The Renegotiation

"Are you mad at me?"

"You just told the world I lost my virginity to you when I was sixteen. Yes, I'm fucking mad at you!" I yelled in front of everyone, storming off the stage and leaving him standing there, looking confused.

How could he? I went straight to the green room. Once the door was shut, I went to the couch, grabbed one of the small pillows, shoved it into my face, and screamed.

There was a knock, and the door creaked open.

"Hey, Evie, it's me. Are you okay?" Skye crept in. I lifted my head from the pillow. She was staring at me with pity. "I'm sorry that happened. Sebastian is an idiot."

"That's an understatement." I threw the pillow down and stomped on it in frustration. The door opened farther, and I turned to see Sebastian standing at the door, his eyes downcast and his mouth stretched tightly. He waved awkwardly then shoved his hands into his jeans.

"Technically, you did."

"Did what?" I snapped.

"Told the world we—did that with each other first. I just said we did it. Not when."

"Oh, Jesus Christ, Sebastian. Fuck off." I shoved past him,

leaving the room and then the building altogether. I took the long way back to my trailer, avoiding all the main paths so that he couldn't follow me.

I couldn't believe him. This was all another ploy to convince me to give him a real chance. As if the world thinking we were together would cause me to rethink my plans. I couldn't be with him romantically even if I wanted to. The moment my revenge was complete, I was leaving this town. I would run before I got caught.

Reaching my trailer, I slammed the door behind me. I went to the bed and tossed myself face first onto it, screaming into the pillows once more. I was going to blow my voice, and I didn't care. I was so fucking mad. I valued my privacy, and Sebastian revealing such an intimate detail about my past felt like I'd been stripped bare in front of the world, and not in the good way. If people knew we'd had sex, they'd want us to be together. The pressure, as it stood, was overwhelming. Now? It'd be downright unbearable.

I can't let my feelings get involved in this.

Sometime later, the trailer door opened, and he called for me.

"Evie, come on. I didn't mean to make you so upset."

I sat up and rolled off the bed. I went to him and poked his hard chest.

"And what exactly did you mean to do? What is your end game here?"

His brow furrowed. "What do you mean?"

"It's been a month. I've done everything that's been asked of me. I let you touch me. I laugh at your jokes. I do everything to sell this stupid showmance, but you act like you forgot your promise."

"Promise?" He frowned, then his expression relaxed as he huffed and fell back, plopping onto my couch. "There was no timeline on that promise. Nor was it ever discussed in detail. I've tried, several times, but I'm always shut down." He put his arms behind his head and crossed his feet at his ankles.

"What do you mean? It's a pretty cut-and-dry deal. I do this stupid pretend-dating, and you help me kill the men who murdered my mother." I crossed my arms and stared at him, making himself at home on my couch.

"Nuh-uh." He shook his head and shifted, putting his legs up onto the couch and stretching. "That's not what I promised. I said I'd get you close to them. Which, while doable, is difficult. I can't just walk next door and pull some *Princess Bride* shit."

I stared at him until he elaborated.

"My name is Inigo Montoya. You killed my father?"

"Prepare to die," I finished with a sigh. I swatted his legs down to the floor and sat where they'd just been. "Fuck. I've been here a month, and only Thornton is crossed off my list. And he was dead before I got here!" I fell backward, and he sat up.

"Hey, don't beat yourself up. Killing isn't easy." He pinched my chin teasingly.

I swatted him away with an eye roll. He made it sound like I'd accidentally spilled paint, not killed a man. The memory of Glenn, naked and covered in vomit on my carpet, flashed across my mind.

He continued. "Did you have a plan when you got here? Knowing might help me keep good on my promise."

I rolled my head to look at him. "Plans? I figured I'd stalk them, learn their schedule or something, and meet them in a dark corner and just—take them out." I pointed my fingers like a handgun and pretended to shoot.

"Have you practiced shooting a gun?"

"Yes," I said through gritted teeth. One time.

"Okay, that's a good start. You know some of them will also have guns. Unless you're locked and loaded, they'd easily draw faster."

"I'm prepared to die for this," I muttered. "You know that, right?"

"Anthony C. Hopkins, Evie," he swore and ran his hand through his hair. "Don't—okay, fuck it. Show me the list."

"I thought you already knew it."

"I'm a visual learner. Hold on. I'll be back." He leaped up and left my trailer, returning a moment later with a whiteboard and a handful of markers. I cocked my head, and he grinned. "Connor writes my schedule on this every day. Here, let's plan." He gave me a marker and set the board on the table.

I stood and went to it, writing down the names of the five men still alive who had murdered my mom.

Jason Dourif

Frederick Castle

Charles Hodder

Arthur Englund

Elliott Bradley

He leaned over me and nodded. "Okay, this was who I thought. Well, not him. I don't know who that is." He pointed at Charles.

I explained that he was a realtor, and he continued.

"You want to meet them?"

"I want to kill them."

He snickered. "Well, you're on your own for that. Murder assistance comes at a much higher price than some public flirting." He gave me a wicked smile.

"What exactly are you proposing?" My heart sped up as his green eyes bored into mine with such intensity, I felt it in my core.

"You seem really insistent on not letting me shoot my shot. I've tried playful flirting, throwing my emotions on the table, I fucking killed a guy for you, and I got nothing. You want help ending these sick fucks? Then I want a real shot for each one."

I straightened and put my hand on my hip. "Okay. And what exactly is a real shot?"

Sebastian followed suit, standing straight and turning to face me. His green eyes were hypnotic as they stared down at me.

"Sex."

The air slid out of my lungs in one quick whoosh. The world grew silent as his word settled around me.

"Huh?" My voice came out small, confused, and...not uninterested.

"I want to fuck you five times."

"Why?" I shook my head, not entirely understanding.

"Because I know the moment this is over, you're going to leave." His Adam's apple bobbed, and he inhaled deeply. "I want five shots to try to change that. One for each man dead."

"You think you can convince me to stay with the power of your dick?" I smirked, despite the very thought making my nipples harden. My breathing was labored as we maintained eye contact.

"Yes."

"And when will this be done? Before or after each kill?" I crossed my arms over my chest, covering my intrigue.

He grimaced. "That makes it sound like work. This isn't a transaction, Evie."

"What is it, then?"

"It's my last-ditch effort to get you to love me as hard as I fucking love you."

Guilt seeped into my gut, causing any feeling of arousal to quickly disappear.

"Sebastian, I—" I looked down at my feet.

"Just...hear me out. Have you heard of free use?"

I looked up, raising an eyebrow.

"Free use?"

"You consent to letting me fuck you five times, whenever, wherever I want. There's no timeline, no strict rules. We could do all five times in one night or throughout our killing spree. Just... let me try."

The desperation in his expression was enough to give me pause. I looked into his pleading eyes, reevaluating my original plan.

Nothing he did would convince me to stay. Even if I survived all this, I'd be on the run. Sebastian Shaw was far too famous to just slip into obscurity somewhere. There were no Mexican beaches in our future. Once this was over, he'd stay here, grow even more famous, and I...would most likely be dead.

I stared at the handsome man I'd once loved deeply. It had hurt to let him go, but I couldn't stay here after my mom died. And he couldn't leave Hollywood. Would this be a cycle for us?

The chemistry test flashed through my mind. Him naked on his knees between my thighs. It'd been the most erotic thing I'd ever experienced. I'd thought about it entirely too often in bed and in the shower. Would agreeing to have that again, even just briefly, be that bad?

"Fine. Five times. Once you use them, that's it. I am not promising I'll change my mind about things. I came here to do one thing and one thing only. Nothing is going to deter me from that."

He put his hand out, and begrudgingly, I shook it.

His goofy, charming smile returned, and he looked back down at my list.

"Talent manager, lawyer, realtor, executive, and a fucking A-list celebrity." He clicked his tongue. "Okay, let's start low. I can get us close to Dourif."

"You can?" My nervousness over Sebastian's *free use* idea disappeared in an instant. I could taste the revenge on my tongue, and it was sweet. "When?"

"Let me make some calls. I might be able to make that happen soon, actually. I had an invite that I blew off. I bet I can get on the list again." He pulled out his phone and began texting.

"What event?" I asked.

He brought the phone to his ear, and it started ringing.

"A movie premiere. You'll need a dress." His gaze slid over my body, going down then slowly back up. "Something tight." The other line picked up, and he turned to leave. "Hey, can I still get into that premiere for *Slice Slice Baby*? I think it'd be a great PR stunt, taking Evie to something public." He opened the door and then paused, turning back. He gave me a thumbs-up and nodded. "Cool, and the after-party?"

The door shut behind him, and air seemed to finally return to my lungs. I replayed the conversation we'd just had in my head.

Five times. Free use.

What had I just agreed to?

CHAPTER 19 EVIE

The Press Shoot

Psycho Killer

We're on for tonight, Final Girl.

My early morning alarm woke me, and I stared at the text on my phone sent an hour ago. How had he gotten up that early? It was four in the morning. I hurried to shower and get to the studio, where Sebastian was already standing at the craft services table, drinking his morning Red Bull and eating a bagel.

"Mornin', Final Girl. Did you get my text?"

I grabbed a water and nodded. "It's early. What are we on for tonight?"

He rolled his eyes. "That movie premiere. You asked me to introduce you to Dourif. He's going to be there."

"Beep beep, Ritchie!" I hissed, looking around.

He smirked and spun on his heel. "I'm heading to makeup."

I waited behind for Skye to get to set, and together, we went to hair and makeup. It took almost two hours in the chair before we were sent over to costumes. Bryce was there, putting on a stylized version of his *Simon Says* costume. It was a sharp, plum-colored ringmaster's suit.

I shook my head. "I don't know how you do this every day." I pointed to the clown makeup on my face. "It's hot."

He laughed. "Well, the pussy I get makes up for it." He made a circle with his finger around his own face, covered in similar makeup. "Bitches love a hot clown."

"That we do," one of the costume designers said, her tone husky.

I turned to see what she was looking at, and my breath caught in my chest. Sebastian had just walked in.

That we do.

Sebastian, like all of us, had his face fully painted in clown makeup. It was equal parts scary and sexy, which was entirely the point of this photoshoot. We had all been painted as hot clowns. Even Bryce's makeup, while still similar to his normal stage makeup, had been given a slight tweak to enhance his handsome features underneath the paint. Sebastian's nose was colored red, and diamond shapes were painted around his eyes with black and glitter. They trailed down his cheeks, drawing attention to his bloodred lips. He was easily the hottest person in the room, and everyone knew it. With the paint down to his shoulder blades, they'd made him take his shirt off, leaving him in just his black jeans and onyx boots. He stood with his hands in his pockets and a loose smirk on his lips, looking so casual. As if he too understood the effect he was having on everyone. Except maybe Skye. She'd given him a glance and had gone back to her own mirror.

I was glad my face was caked with white so that he couldn't see how flushed my cheeks were.

"And you slept with that?" The costume designer sighed dreamily. "I love that for you."

Her words pulled me back to earth. I turned to the clothing rack. "It was five years ago, and it was one time," I told her.

"What was? Oh—us, twisted in each other's naked bodies?" Sebastian asked, coming to join us.

"Beep beep, Ritchie," I snapped, snatching the hanger with my name and hurrying into a dressing room. I returned a few minutes later in my costume for the shoot and swore.

Anthony C. Hopkins. He'd gotten even hotter.

My gaze slid up from his black dress shoes to his face. Wardrobe had put him in all black. Pants, undershirt, and suspenders. Everything was fitted tight where it needed to be, and he stood with his head and shoulders back, so confident, so effortlessly sexy. Reason was giving way to lust the more I stared.

"Looking good, Final Girl." He smirked once our eyes met.

I looked down at myself. I'd been dressed in a comically poofy black babydoll dress. There were five versions of the same dress in various colors, but this was labeled *first change*.

Skye came out of the changing room, breaking the tension between Sebastian and me. "Look at us!"

While I'd been given dark colors to match Sebastian, she'd been given jewel tones to match Bryce. We were called to set, and before any further conversation could be had, the photoshoot started.

"*Featured Creatures* already released the sound bite for the interview," Skye said as we posed together. She sat in a bright-red chair, and I sat on the ground between her legs, with mine splayed out as far as I could stretch them apart. "Guess what they used?" She laughed.

I sighed. "I can't believe he did that."

"I can't believe you never told me. No wonder he fought so hard for you to play opposite him."

"Skye..." Before I could say more, Bryce and Sebastian were brought in for group shots. We stopped talking to do those, and then when I was dismissed for a costume change, she and Bryce took their solo shots.

I came out of the dressing room in a pink dress with blood splatter on it, only to find myself alone with Sebastian. I shoved down the butterflies going mad in my belly.

He was shirtless now, with just the suspenders.

"You look good in a little red." He winked then slipped out of the room before I could respond. Not that I'd know what to say. I fanned my warm face and went to watch Skye and Bryce. When Sebastian showed back up to set, splattered in fake blood to match the splotches on my dress, he somehow looked even hotter. Skye and Bryce handed us bloody axes—Simon Says's weapon of choice—and we took our place in front of the photographer.

"Can you look a little less...distressed?" she asked me as Sebastian put his arms around my waist.

"Distressed?"

"She wants you to relax, Final Girl," Sebastian purred in my ear, sending delicious chills down my spine. "Act like you want me."

There was no acting with him dressed like this. Seeing him in his clown getup set off a chime in my brain.

New kink unlocked.

I inhaled deeply once, twice, and on the third breath, I shook off my nerves, steeled my expression, and posed. The photographer beamed and snapped her camera wildly.

"Yes! Sit on the floor. Sebastian, crawl to her."

I sat down facing sideways, and she directed me to spread my legs. I bit my lip, knowing I was about to flash Sebastian my panties. His green eyes dipped to them the moment I moved, and he grinned. Slowly, he crawled toward me. Just before he reached me, I lifted my leg and placed my stiletto on his forehead. He froze.

"Jesus Christ. You're making me hot," the photographer gushed as her camera went crazy. I met Sebastian's gaze. His eyes narrowed, but I could see the dark desire behind them. We were asked to continue the pose she'd originally requested, and as he crawled between my legs, memories of our chemistry test flashed in my mind, and my breathing grew labored. He dipped his head, placing his lips on my thigh.

A deep chuckle vibrated across my skin, running straight to my center.

"What?" I gasped as he ran his hands along the length of my legs.

"They shouldn't have given you such light-colored panties,"

he murmured, low enough for only me to hear.

My brow furrowed. He raised himself back up and pressed his chest to mine, cocking his head and whispering in my ear, "I can see just how fucking wet you are. You've soaked right through, Final Girl."

A small shriek left my throat, and he pulled back, biting down on his lip as it curved into a taunting smile.

My heart raced so hard and fast in my ears that I couldn't focus on what the photographer was saying, and Sebastian had to help. I was practically a rag doll as he shifted me around to get the right shot. I closed my eyes, trying to steady myself, but his lips on my arms and neck were making my skin hot and tingly. Finally, the photographer lowered the camera, and people began to clap.

"We're going to sell so many fucking copies of this magazine." Stacey, who'd been off to the sides watching us, shook her head, her eyes shining with dollar signs. While we'd been shooting, Bryce and Skye had returned to set, covered in blood for their couple shots. As I walked toward the dressing room, Skye stopped me.

"Evie, that was the hottest thing I've ever seen. Holy crap. You are—"

"It's just work, Skye," I said flatly. She gave me a look then rolled her eyes.

"You are delulu if you don't see how hard he's claiming you. No wonder Glenn backed off. Sebastian basically just wrote *mine* all over you with his tongue."

I shivered and looked over my shoulder. He was coming toward us now. I shook my head. "He didn't claim anything," I said sharply, making sure he was within earshot.

"Are you talking about me?" Sebastian came forward. With his hands behind his back, he leaned on his heels and grinned. He grabbed my waist and pulled me into him, our chests bumping. "Skye's right. I did write *mine* all over you."

I elbowed him and rushed off set, slamming the dressing room door closed. Staking a claim over something that wasn't his wasn't going to change things. I sighed deeply and fell against a wall. How was I supposed to keep this showmance up when I was actively trying to keep away from him?

Letting myself feel something for him wasn't safe. It would only lead to his heart breaking when I was gone, and I never wanted anyone to feel the way I'd felt when it happened the first time. I was steeling myself to tell him this when he entered the green room, blowing the door wide open.

Suddenly, forgetting my vulnerability, I opened my mouth to yell at him for making such a show. Before I could say anything, he crossed the room, crushing his lips on mine. His tongue invaded my mouth, and he placed one hand on my back, forcing our bodies together. Finally, he pulled back, and then he spun me around and shoved me away.

"What are you doing?" I squeaked as he raised my dress, exposing my panties. The rattle of his belt sent a rush of adrenaline through me. I bolted upright.

"You talk a lot of game for someone who has no say in what I make mine." He slid his hand up my thighs, lifting my dress, then spanked me, causing both a pinch of pain and a shiver of pleasure to come from my core. "Now bend over so I can make you come."

The Green Light

"Sebastian..." Evie squirmed under my firm grasp.

"Are you backing out of our deal, Final Girl? We've barely started." I ran my hand over her perfect, round ass, going under her skirt. My fingers slid over her slit, feeling just how damp I'd made her. "If you'd rather kill them all alone..."

I pressed my strained cock against her, letting her feel just what she did to me—just by existing. I started at her feet and slowly drank her in. Stilettos. Tattoos. Legs for days. An ass I wanted to sink my teeth and tongue into... I finally reached her curled hair fanning across her back. I brushed it aside, feeling how soft it was. She turned to look back, her adorable, clown-painted face wide-eyed and innocent looking. My cock wept with precum, begging to defile her.

Slowly, I reached for the edges of her panties, slid them over her ass, and dropped them to her thighs. Nudging them to her ankles, I urged her to lift her feet to step out of them, and I spread her legs. She let out a sharp cry of surprise and her legs buckled, but my hands flew to her waist. I pulled her back up.

"Now, now, Final Girl...We have such sights to show you.."

Our secret language caught her attention. I dropped to my knees and dragged my hands down her smooth, tanned legs. I stood slowly and took in the sight of her beautifully bare pussy from behind, and my mouth watered.

"We can't, someone can come in..." Her voice was so soft, it took me a moment to rip my gaze from her to register the tension in her tone.

I went to the door, locking it. For good measure, I dug through my backpack and found my phone. I clicked on my music and turned the volume up.

"Okay, that feels kind of obvious, don't you think?" Evie stood, panties on the floor, arms crossed.

"What?" I shrugged, feigning innocence—but the grin tugging at my lips gave me away. "I like this song."

"Doja Cat and a locked door. We basically just shouted what is going on."

I tossed my phone onto a chair and returned to her. I dipped down and scooped her up, taking her to the couch against the wall.

"Sebastian!" she squealed, giggling as I set her down and dropped to my knees. I pushed her legs apart and dove between them, smearing my makeup against her thighs. I spread her lips and ran my tongue along her wet and wanting slit. She inhaled sharply, and her hips shifted up encouragingly.

Good girl.

I spread her farther and, feeling bold, slid a finger inside. We were beyond rehearsing scenes. We weren't seeing if we could handle this. We were completely consenting and lusting for each other. My soaked finger inside her pulsing pussy was proof. I ran my thumb over her clit in slow circles, teasing her, coaxing an orgasm from her slowly. I needed her to ask for it, to scream for it.

I needed her to beg.

She grew close, and I shifted to my mouth, and when she tightened again, I stopped and changed movements.

"Sebastian..."

"Nuh-uh, Final Girl." I came up for air, my gaze flicking to her thighs, now covered in white, red, and black face paint. I looked up into her eyes then back down. "I'm not letting you come this easily. I've never been so fucking turned on by a clown in my life." I groaned as I reached for my cock and rubbed through my pants.

She giggled. "You're psycho."

I cocked an eyebrow. "Is that what you call me when I'm not around?"

"What if I did?" She turned her head, hiding the flush in her face, but I could see it through the white makeup. I ran my fingers up her pussy slowly, teasing. Spreading her lips just a fraction then pulling back with her arousal on them.

"Do you want more, Final Girl?" I asked, licking her juices off my digits.

"Yes," she panted, pushing her backside out.

"Then tell me what my nickname is."

"Psycho Killer," she whispered.

"Glorious." I dove back in, pushing two fingers inside her and curving them, now eager to make her scream. "I'm only answering to that when we're doing this. Understand?"

"Yes," she panted as she closed her eyes and threw her head back, unraveling in my hands. Her pussy gushed and tensed around my fingers, and I leaned in, lapping up every drop of her cum.

"Fucking beautiful." I pulled my fingers out and stood, grabbing her hand and pulling her to her feet. She buckled, and I caught her in my arms. She let out a nervous laugh.

"These stilettos are a bit much."

"I think they make your legs look even sexier." Using the finger that had just been inside her, I made a circle motion in the air. "Spin back around and hold on to the couch."

Her lips parted, and I repeated myself.

"Okay."

"Okay what? Say my name." I turned her and bent her over.

She reached for the back and gripped it as I raised her dress over her ass. I ran my hand across it, and my cock pulsed. Letting her go, I quickly unbuttoned and shoved my pants down my thighs, freeing my cock. Gripping it, I directed the tip between her glistening pussy lips. She gasped and squirmed as my head entered her.

"Okay, Psycho Killer."

"Good girl." I finished pushing myself inside her tight walls. I bit my lip, taking a steady breath so I didn't come fast. She was clutching me so tightly I was seeing stars.

"Oh! Condom," she said.

I slid out of her pussy and thrust back into her, eliciting a small cry.

"You're the only one I've ever been bare with, and I've got a clean bill of health. Do you?"

"Yes," she groaned as I began a slow, torturous rhythm, thrusting in and out, as if we weren't at work and had all the time in the world.

"Good. I need to feel you completely," I said, reaching around and tugging on the collar of her dress. It stretched easily, and I pulled it down, along with her bra. Her nipple was already hard. I pinched it between my thumb and forefinger, and she moaned harder, pushing against me.

"Faster, please. Harder," she pleaded.

I did as requested. Her pussy clenched around me. My balls tightened in anticipation. I was so close, but I needed to wait for her.

"Come on, Final Girl. Come for your Psycho Killer."

She let out a sharp cry, and her head dropped, grazing the couch as she came, pulsing wildly around me. Her orgasm was my undoing. I came harder than I had in years. I pumped every last drop inside her, needing to mark her as mine.

When I was finished, I stepped back and pulled my pants up, leaving them unbuttoned. I reached for my Final Girl and spun her around. She'd collapsed headfirst when she came. I grinned as I caught sight of my makeup covering her thighs. The evidence of our tryst made my cock jump again.

I could go again.

"Sebastian—" Evie's face was flushed, her chest rose and fell as she shook her head. "What..."

"Did we just do?" I snickered. "Took one of my shots. Have I convinced you yet?" I stepped back to properly adjust myself in my pants and button back up. I went to the mirror and found my disheveled look quite amusing. The makeup around my mouth and cheeks had been completely rubbed off.

I'd painted her pussy and thighs. If someone were to walk in, it would be obvious what had just occurred between her and I.

"Convinced me of what?" she asked.

I stared at my reflection, still undecided. Would it be better to keep our relationship a secret or let it be known?

"To stay. You know, in Hollywood. With me." I turned back to her, and she laughed.

"What? Hell no. A—" She stopped herself and looked away from me, suddenly bashful.

Oh, Final Girl, I just had my tongue and cock deep inside you. Why are you shy now?

"We had an agreement. Five for five. You just used one of yours. Now I get one."

There was a knock on the door, interrupting our imminent argument.

"Shit. Shit, shit, shit. Sebastian! We need to clean up," Evie hissed, scrambling to pick her panties off the floor.

I rolled my eyes and turned to look for a towel.

"Afraid people will know you're attracted to me?" I sighed as I began to clean the evidence of the best sex I'd ever had from my face.

"No..."

The knock echoed louder, and Evie hurried to open the door, letting Bryce and Skye in. The pair took one look at us, and despite Evie's poor attempt at hiding, they exchanged knowing looks and stepped inside to change.

Skye passed by Evie and giggled as she glanced my way.

"I told you. *Mine*," she teased.

I smirked, deciding not to say anything as I left to splash

water on my face to get the rest of the paint off.

She was right.

Evie was *mine.*

CHAPTER 21 SEBASTIAN

The Soft Launch

As I got ready for the movie premiere later that night, I jerked off to the memory of Evie. I'd missed her so goddamn much. It wasn't just my balls that ached for her.

I dressed in relative silence, my thoughts keeping me company. She'd laughed when I asked her to stay here. What was her plan then, exactly? To kill all these men and then run back to Michigan? Or did she have some wild plan to flee to another country, or worse—was I a pawn in all this? What if she had someone waiting for her? A lover, a partner, a legal spouse even. Was that the guilt she showed every time I pursued her?

No, it had to be something else.

I would know if there were someone waiting for her.

She wouldn't have agreed to my little free use idea.

Just the words sent my cock pulsing again, calling for me to rub one more out before the event. I forced myself to stop thinking about her, bent over and dripping with need in that dressing room, as I slid my shoes on and slicked my hair back with gel like an old-time Hollywood star.

The limousine came for me and started toward Evie's home. The drive was about twenty minutes, and I took the time to have a glass of whiskey and slam another Red Bull.

How could we have had such an incredible moment in that

dressing room, and she just laugh at me for wanting more? How could you not want that over and over again?

But the real question was—the one I feared the answer to—was she running from this town or from me?

I didn't have time to dive deeper inward before the limo stopped and the door opened. I climbed out and stared up at her house. So many of my childhood memories were from this place. It felt like a lifetime ago that Lita was serving us cola and popcorn, introducing us to the classics, and teaching us who was who in horror—and why it was important to recognize their achievements.

What I'd give to have those moments back.

I inhaled as I walked up to her door and knocked. It opened a moment later, and all my reservations about seeing Evie so soon after our tryst washed away. She was stunning.

"Why hello, Final Girl." My gaze trailed down, pausing at her full, cupid's-bow red lips before catching sight of her breasts. She wore a strapless light-pink gown that hugged her waist and dipped low to show off her cleavage. I saw a high slit at her thighs, and my cock stirred imagining pushing her dress up and using another one of my times before we went to the premiere.

I forced the thoughts down. I couldn't be wasteful. I only had four shots left.

She grinned at me. "Hello, Psycho Killer. You clean up well." She offered me her arm, and I looped mine through hers and escorted her to the car.

"I'm a little nervous," she admitted after the door was closed and we'd started off. "I haven't done one of these since I was a kid, and I didn't look like this." She laughed nervously.

No, she had not. I admired her—and had to force the thoughts back down. This was literal hell. Being so close and yet so far away. I'd been given access to her body, but it was her heart I wanted. Hell, I'd be celibate for the rest of my life if she just agreed to stay here with me.

"That was the *Simon Says* premiere, wasn't it?" I remembered that one. It was my first movie. I was eight years old. Heather didn't want me to attend—she had lined me up for another audition the next day and didn't want me to be tired. However, Lita Reyes, the powerhouse she was, insisted and offered to be my chaperone.

I'll bring my daughter too. They're the same age. They can keep each other company.

"It was! You remember that?" Evie asked.

"How could I forget?" I looked down at my whiskey and stirred it once before taking a large gulp and looking out the window with a sigh.

She'd looked beautiful then, too.

"You've done tons of these now. It's going to be interesting watching you do your thing in real time," she added.

I turned, raising an eyebrow. "It's just a job." I shrugged. "Nothing I find entirely thrilling."

The general population thought that red carpet events were nothing but fun and excitement. One big party. But these things were far from that. I'd spent years learning how to behave in front of paparazzi. I couldn't have fun—not when all I could think about was where the cameras were, how to pose, and what I could say out loud. Anyone could be listening, and they'd sell you out in a second for a cover story.

"We are getting paid for this, by the way," I added. "Not sure if they told you. The PR team loved the idea of us going out in public together."

The vehicle slowed, and we began to hear noise from outside. I sat back and closed my eyes, knowing we were now in line. Suddenly, I felt the warmth of her hand reaching for mine. I turned and opened an eye. I took her hand and squeezed. Soon, the door opened, and I let her out first, following behind. She clung to my side, and I wrapped an arm around her, making sure my hand didn't dip too low.

We were still just friends, officially, after all.

"Sebastian! Over here! Who are you with?" Paparazzi went crazy with their cameras, the flashes blinding.

I forced a smile and turned to face them. Evie stepped aside. Hating the instant feeling of loss, I did my standard poses quickly then returned to her side.

"Who are you?" several people asked Evie.

Not liking their arrogant tones, I answered for her. "This is Evie Reyes, daughter of the legendary Lita Reyes. She is my co-star in *Simon Says Six*."

"*Six Six*," Evie muttered under her breath just for me.

There was a moment of hushed whispers before it hit them, and then the frenzy erupted.

"Evie! Tell us about your mom!"

"Evie! Are you wearing pink as an homage to Lita?"

"Evie! Are you and Sebastian dating?"

Questions were thrown at her, and I felt a twinge of guilt for not giving her any coaching in the car. Although the PR team had given her some, she seemed to have forgotten it all. Her body was stiff, and I had to force her along.

I leaned in and whispered, "You don't have to answer anything you don't want to. Just breathe, Final Girl."

The paparazzi must have taken a moment to do a quick internet search, because as we continued down the red carpet, the questions became more specific.

"Are you here to promote the new *Simon Says* movie?"

"Did you get cast because of your history with the franchise?"

"What about your YouTube channel?"

"Is this a stunt to gain more followers for *The Body Count Bimbo*?"

I moved her along as fast as I could, but the line ahead of us was slow.

"I'm going to go blind with all this flashing." Evie smirked. "They cannot be this interested in me."

"I don't think you realize the pull you have," I mumbled, a sly grin sliding over my lips. I slid my hand down her back, squeezing her ass. The paparazzi went wild, screaming, calling out, snapping photos.

Evie's eyes widened, and she glared at me.

I rolled my eyes and murmured low. "It's showmance, baby. PR is going to love us."

Her mouth fell into an O shape. The rumor mill was going to go wild. Our names would be everywhere tomorrow.

Finally, we reached the doors to the theater and slipped inside. Once we were away from the cameras, I let out a breath.

"Okay, let's see..." I scanned the room, recognizing most of the people here. The premiere was for a midlist horror film. I got invites for these all the time, as did everyone else. The horror community was very tight-knit.

"What are you looking for?" Evie asked, keeping close to me.

"Not what, but who," I said, weaving through the crowd. "You said I wasn't holding up my end of our deal, remember?" I stopped short and pointed discreetly to a middle-aged man with a tan so dark his skin looked like leather and stark-white hair styled like a news anchor. He wore rose-colored sunglasses and a worn, oversized, baby-blue suit. He looked entirely out of place here, which I knew he would. It made him easy to find and easy to stand out.

"That is your next target, Jason Dourif, the talent manager."

CHAPTER 22

EVIE

The Talent Manager

Jason Dourif.

He sat a few rows ahead of us, off to the side. The movie had started, but instead of watching, I found myself staring at the back of Jason's head. He couldn't be more than midfifties, yet his hair was ghost-white, and his fake tanned skin had gone leathery, aging him up. Having given the paparazzi what they wanted outside, Sebastian left me alone to stew in my thoughts during the film. He sat beside me politely, making no moves that suggested intimacy beyond colleagues.

Halfway through the movie, Mr. Dourif stood and climbed over the other guests. Thankfully, I'd taken an aisle seat. I stood quickly, excusing myself, and followed him out of the theater. He didn't notice me at first, so I pretended to go to the other bathroom and then waited. When I saw the men's room door open, I came out of mine and bumped into him.

"Oh!" I feigned surprise.

"Why, hello there," Dourif chuckled, his hand instantly finding my waist to steady me. He had a Southern accent I couldn't quite place. He let me go and stepped back. "I know you."

I fought back a grimace. "You do?"

He looked me up and down, lowering his glasses to leer better. "Sure do. You're Lita Reyes's daughter. Evelyn."

"Evie," I corrected.

"Right, Evie. I remember when you were just a little thing." He chuckled. "I used to come over to visit with Lita. You remember your ol' Uncle Jason?"

I chuckled uncomfortably. I did not.

"My mom had lots of friends."

"That she did..." The way he said that, paired with how he was looking at my chest, made me squirm. He tore his eyes from my dress and looked back up at my face. "Well, consider me just plain ol' Jason Dourif, talent manager." He offered his hand, and after I shook it, he stuffed his hands into his pockets and rocked on his heels.

"You know, while I love my clients, I wasn't a huge fan of this movie. It's why I excused myself halfway. Didn't want to fall asleep!" He laughed loudly.

I glanced at the doors, glad they'd been shut before the film started. He was a loud speaker.

"You do pictures?" he asked.

"I'm starring in my first one currently." I looked down, playing the bashful, new-to-town actress.

"Is that right? I saw you with ol' Sebastian Shaw. You doing a *Simon Says* film? What are they on now, *Simon Says Six*?"

"*Six Six*."

He didn't catch the joke. I suspected he wasn't actually listening to me. He just wanted to keep me here.

"You two together?" He licked his dry lips and wiggled his white eyebrows.

I forced back a grimace. "No, we're just friends."

"Good! It's never good to mingle with your coworkers. Smart girl, just like your momma. She did her minglin' outside of work hours." He tapped his temple and pinched his lips together, seemingly in thought. "Where you going after this?"

"Home, presumably."

He laughed and reached for me, patting my shoulder when I moved away.

"Nonsense. I'm having an after-party. You and Sebastian-boy come on over. It's an open bar, and we got some good music. Drugs? I got all of 'em. We have a whole lotta fun at my parties." He dug into his pocket and pulled a card from his wallet.

I held back an eye roll. A business card? Who still used those? He handed it to me, and I read it quickly.

"Come around sometime tonight. We can catch up, now that you're grown. I'd love to get to know how little Lita grew up." He winked and grabbed the door handle, opening it and stumbling back inside.

I stayed out for a moment, taking in what had just happened. I was disgusted but...excited. I'd just got an invite to my next kill's house. I tucked the card into my cleavage and hurried back to the movie. I squeezed Sebastian's hand and was finally able to focus on the film, which wasn't half bad.

After the movie, I remained by Sebastian's side as he networked. He introduced me to everyone, and while my mind was elsewhere, I probably made some connections.

"You okay?" Sebastian asked as we finally got into the limousine. "You've been glossy eyed for hours."

"I got invited to an after-party at Jason Dourif's house," I blurted, producing the card from my dress.

Sebastian's eyes widened then darkened. He nodded solemnly. "I see. And you're going?"

"Well, yeah. What is the proper etiquette for these things? Do I change? When do they start? Do I bring something?" I leaned forward, my excitement bubbling over.

"For what? A murder, or a party?" He snickered. "Yeah, you bring me," he grumbled. Tugging on his bowtie, he loosened it and sat back with a huff.

"You don't have to come. I've got this."

He gave me a stern look. "You're not going to this dude's house alone. He's a creep."

"They're all creeps." I crossed my arms. "I can do this. You upheld your part of the bargain. You got me close enough to...do what I have to do." I hesitated to speak about it with a driver up front, even with the privacy screen shut.

"I have no doubt in your...determination. But your plans have a way of going awry. I'm coming, end of discussion," he said, pushing the remote to open the screen to speak with the driver. "Anton, I have an after-party to go to."

He instructed the driver to stop by his house to grab clothes. He ran in and out, planning to change at my place. He came back out with a backpack. When I asked about it, he grinned.

"We might be out late again, like last time."

Last time being when we killed Glenn.

I looked away and let the driver take us to my place. Sebastian followed me inside and up to my room.

"What do I wear?" I walked into my closet, looking for something comfortable but nice enough to fit in with the other partygoers.

"Well, if you're going for dramatics, I'd look over here." Sebastian pointed to the other side of my closet, where all of my mother's clothes sat on hangers. I hadn't been able to throw them out. "What did he call you again? Little Lita?" He stuck his tongue out and shuddered.

"He did." I drifted to her clothes and began yanking hangers to the side, searching for the right outfit.

"Ooh." I pulled a red-and-black blazer off the rack. It had pants to match. Perfect. I pushed Sebastian out of the closet and climbed out of my dress, sliding on the pants and jacket. I came out and gave him a mini runway walk. "What do you think?"

His Adam's apple bobbed. "I vaguely remember Lita wearing that, but...she had a shirt underneath." He looked away quickly.

"Well, this is more my style. Plus, Dourif was wanting Lita, but new. I'd say this fits the bill."

"You're nothing like her," Sebastian muttered. When I didn't reply, he continued. "She was great, but...not you."

I didn't have time to dissect his statement. My mind was elsewhere, already halfway to the party.

"What's that?" I asked after I came out of the bathroom, ready to go. Sebastian was adjusting a long blond wig on top of his head. It looked rather good. He shoved a beanie on his head and slid thick-framed glasses over his nose.

"*This* is Ash Wilkes. My disguise for whenever I don't want to be noticed."

"Ash Wilkes, as in..."

"*Evil Dead* and *Misery*." He grinned.

I pursed my lips and looked toward the closet.

"Should I put on a wig too?" My mom had a dozen of them, probably for the same reason.

"Sure. Let's find one."

We dug through the boxes, and I found a long, straight, ruby-colored wig. I had to pin back my bangs, but I tugged it on and tied a scarf around my head, pairing it with large sunglasses with pink frames. I stared at my reflection, trying to think of a name.

"I'm Beverly Bradford," I decided.

"As in?"

"*IT* and *Black Christmas*."

"Great choices," Sebastian complimented.

I beamed at him.

We hurried back into the limo, where we were taken across town to a large house. It was nice but only half the size of my mother's small mansion. Cars lined the street and driveway. Music poured from the house, and as we walked inside, it was just as Dourif had described. Alcohol, music, and whatever drugs I wanted. People were dancing with abandon—and having sex with even more. I took Sebastian's hand, and he led me through the house in search of the man of the manor, Mr. Jason Dourif himself.

When our self-guided tour came up short, we had to resort to asking. That was something neither of us had wanted to do. Asking someone gave the police a possible witness. However, Sebastian found the drunkest person at the party—someone who wouldn't remember us—and they pointed and slurred something. Whatever was said had been correct, because Sebastian returned to me, grabbed my hand, and took me to a back room I hadn't noticed before. He pushed the door open, and I turned my head in disgust as I caught a young redhead giving the midlist talent manager a deep-throated blowjob. He looked up, and when she paused, he shoved her head back down.

"Who's there?" he called.

I slid my glasses off, and he instantly recognized me.

"Hey! Little Lita! Come in. Close the door behind ya. She's almost done," he said, letting his head fall back.

Sebastian snickered and gave me a look. "You going in?" he asked.

I scowled. He found this entirely too amusing.

"Or you gonna wait outside?"

The question was layered. Sebastian wasn't referring to waiting for the blowjob to finish. I'd watched him put a knife in his pocket when we were at my house. If I didn't kill Jason, he would. So what was I going to do?

Do what I came to Hollywood for, or continue being part of the audience?

CHAPTER 23 EVIE

The Exposition Scene

"Come on in, Little Lita. Take off those disguises. Who you got there with you?" Dourif waved us in as the redhead lifted her head from his lap and wiped her mouth.

I cringed as he stood, flashing his spent cock before stuffing himself back into his pants.

"Sorry, friends. She's sloppy." He patted her head and pushed her away.

Urging me farther into the room with a hand on my back, Sebastian greeted him. "Jason, it's been a while."

"Ah, it's you—Sebastian Shaw." Dourif smiled wide. "Welcome to my humble abode. Valerie, get out of here. I'll call and get you that audition tomorrow, first thing."

The pretty redhead stood and turned to us. Her eyes widened when she saw Sebastian, but she quickly dipped her head and scurried out.

I grimaced. She had to be close to my age, if not younger.

Sadness dripped from me as I watched the desperate woman flee. I handed Sebastian my disguise, and he set it down.

"Come. Sit, you two. You do cocaine?" Dourif asked me, plopping back down onto the couch. A large white pile of powder sat on the coffee table in front of him. He pointed to Sebastian. "I know you do. Come get some of this before I go through it all myself."

"We're good," Sebastian answered for both of us.

Something about his tone irritated me. He didn't speak for me. Dourif caught the look I gave Sebastian and licked his lips.

"Come on, Little Lita. Do a line. It's just a little coke. Come sit with Uncle Jason." He rubbed the spot beside him, and I was eternally grateful that I didn't need his *skills* to advance my career. I sat down and watched as he prepared three lines. "You sure you don't want in on this? It's good stuff." He looked up at Sebastian, who simply shook his head.

"I think I'll pass too. I just...wanted to catch up," I said, looking at Sebastian.

"Catch up? Girl, I barely knew you. Unless you're here to suck my cock, do my drugs, or hire me as your manager, you can leave." As he spoke, he picked up a pre-rolled five-dollar bill and offered it to me.

I licked my lips. Would I get a second chance to be so close to this southern, leather-bag monster?

"Evie..." Sebastian warned. "Don't."

"Aw, is he your daddy now? He tell you what to do and where to go? I bet he picked those clothes too, didn't he?" Dourif mocked, bending down to do a line.

"Shut the hell up, Jason." Sebastian rolled his eyes.

Jason came back up, grinning. "I'm just calling it as I see it." He put his hands up. "Feel free to prove me wrong. Does he own you, darlin'?" Once again, he offered me the bill.

This was a test, I just wasn't sure what the question was. This had nothing to do with Sebastian ordering me around.

"I don't do drugs alone," Jason whined. "So one of you better take this bill from me or get the fuck out and don't come back."

Sebastian started to lean forward, but fear caused me to shove Jason's hand away and dig into my own wallet. I pulled out a twenty and rolled it up, leaning toward the drugs. Sebastian's hands turned into fists at his sides as he understood what was happening. If one of us was going to keep our wits, it needed to be him.

"That's right. Go on now. Plug one nostril and just snort." Jason put his hand on my back encouragingly. Keeping eye contact with Sebastian, I did as instructed, hoping he'd read my mind. My stomach tightened with nerves as I bent down and snorted. I'd never done cocaine before. The powder stung. I fell back, stunned. My heart sped up, and warmth spread through me—everywhere but my face, which had gone numb.

Then...

There was a beat where my mind was blank, and then—everything hit at once. I looked around and inhaled deeply. Everything was so...sharp! I could smell every note of the cigar on the table. I could feel every beat of the music reverberating through my body. My fingertips vibrated. I could think clearly! And fast. I could do anything I wanted to. I leaped up, and Dourif took his two lines and joined me.

"Atta girl. I knew you weren't no cop. Come on. Dance with me like your momma used to." He turned the music up with a remote. Club music bumped in my ears, making the euphoria that had taken over my blood even better. I didn't consider myself a dancer, but when he reached out and started swaying, I found myself joining in. Sebastian, a few paces away, turned and went around a bar, where he ducked and came up holding a Red Bull. He popped the tab and strolled over.

"Those things are so bad for you!" I shouted over the music.

He froze, the can on his lips. "Bitch, you just did cocaine."

The words sounded silly when he said them, causing me to burst into laughter. I spun around and danced with Dourif. When my high wore off, I was a bit tired. I plopped back down onto the couch, and when Dourif went for another bump, I forced myself not to partake. I'd passed the test. I needed to get back on task. There would be other opportunities for fun. This was Hollywood, after all.

Sebastian's eyes were glued to the ceiling in annoyance.

Dourif snorted another line and sat back, turning his head

to look at me.

"Now, why are you here, Little Lita?"

"Here? I—you invited me."

"No, why are you back in Hollywood?" He snickered. "I'm not fucking stupid. We heard they shipped you off to some aunt in the Midwest. Why come back? This ain't no place for a girl like you."

"Like me?"

He reached out, running a long finger down my cheek. I shuddered and clenched my fists to keep from smacking him away.

"Innocent."

I fought back a smirk. My gaze drifted to Sebastian, who was shaking his head and sipping his Red Bull. He caught my eye and tilted the can, encouraging me to go off. I turned back to the man on the couch.

"I know you killed my mom!" I blurted then widened my eyes, wondering if I was still feeling the effects of the cocaine. My eyes shot to the clock on the wall. It'd been close to an hour.

"Whoa now." He threw his hands up in the air. "I didn't take part in no killin'."

For a second, guilt poured into me, but then he continued.

"I was just there for the rapin'."

Without a second to think, I reached forward and grabbed him by his white hair and yanked him down, smashing him face first into the coffee table. Cocaine flew everywhere, and when I let go, he lifted his face and gasped, looking very much like Mrs. Doubtfire. He shook his head and sniffled loudly, inhaling what cocaine was near his nostrils.

"Now, Little Lita, if my face wasn't so fucking numb, I'd be a lot angrier." He stumbled up and shook the attack off, turning his back to me. I jumped onto the couch and then launched myself at his back.

"You raped her?" I screamed. From the corner of my eye, I saw Sebastian standing off to the side, drinking his Red Bull and watching me go crazy.

"I don't know why you're mad at me!" Dourif twisted, trying to get me off him. "It's not like it was just me there. She took all our cocks that night."

"And who exactly is *all*?" Sebastian stepped forward, shoving him.

Dourif stumbled back but stopped struggling and stared at him. "Like I'd tell you. You smug fuck. Just because you got a pretty face and know who to blow, you think you've got some weight to throw around. Nice try, you stupid, naïve piece of shit."

Dourif spun hard, causing me to lose my grip and fall to the ground. He glared down at me. "I think it's time you left, Little Lita. Leave this town before something bad happens."

My brain malfunctioned for a moment, going back to my bedroom with Glenn. He'd said the same things shortly before drinking his bleach cocktail.

The sound of a click made us turn. Sebastian had his knife open at his side. "Is that a threat?"

"It's a promise. Maybe not by me, but you're digging up shit that's better buried. Lita Reyes..." He paused, looking up at the ceiling. "She was something, but she's dead now. Let her soul rest. God knows she didn't get to while alive."

He started toward the door, but Sebastian blocked him, thrusting his arm out and keeping the door closed.

"Go sit back down and give us some answers, old man."

"Old man?" When Sebastian raised his knife, Dourif lifted his hands again and started back my way. "All right, all right. I doubt I have the answers you want, but sure. Ask away."

"Why? Why did you rape her?" I asked, my voice cracking.

"Oh, hell." He sighed. "This was years ago. I can hardly remember two weeks ago—I'm fucking high." He groaned and looked down at the table riddled with cocaine. He was quiet for a moment and then burst out in laughter, startling us. "You're just like your momma, you know that? She always asked questions too." He reached into his jacket pocket and pulled out a cigarette case. Plucking out a smoke, he lit it and smirked. "And that's why they killed her."

"What questions? Why would they need to kill her?" I pushed. "Why did she go to dinner alone with you all?"

That was the question that kept me up at night. Why did she go with them?

He took a long drag, and I watched as the cherry at the end burned bright red. Without warning, he pulled it from his lips and leaned forward, putting it out on my arm and pressing it deep into my skin.

I screamed and shot to my feet.

"You bastard!" I brushed the ash off and winced at the burn.

He stood and rolled his eyes. "You really think I'd tell you shit? I'm not trying to have ol' Elliott Bradley on my ass. *Girl*, get out of here. And you." He turned to Sebastian.

While he wasn't facing me, I looked around and picked up the metal tray. Gripping it tightly, I raised it and pulled back.

"I'd suggest you forget you were ever here. I'll do the same. If people find out you're snooping around—"

I swung.

When I hit the side of his face as hard as I could, he spun and dropped to the ground. I leaped on top of him and raised it again.

"Why did you rape my mother? And why did they kill her? Why was she there that night?" I screamed, lifting the tray again.

"Evie." Sebastian's voice pulled me from Dourif. I turned and saw him extending his knife to me. I took it, and slowly, my eyes returned to the man I was sitting on.

"I suggest you answer *something*," I said.

"Pick one, then," he spat.

"The rape. Why did you rape her?"

"It wasn't my idea. We were told to. She was making a lot of demands, and he—they wanted to teach her a lesson."

"What lesson?"

"To let dead dogs lie." His eyes narrowed. "Sound familiar?"

"Anthony C. Hopkins, Evie. You're bad at this," Sebastian muttered and leaned over, snatching the knife back. He swung the knife down quickly, stabbing Dourif in the shoulder. He yanked it out and then handed it back to me.

Dourif screamed and tried to buck me off.

Sebastian yelled over him. "Come on, Final Girl. Let's finish this."

"What was she demanding?" I asked, watching the blood spill out from his shoulder.

He snickered. "Money, of course. What everyone in this fucking town wants."

"My mother had money. Why would she want more?" I asked through gritted teeth.

Suddenly, he lifted his head and grinned. "For you. She wanted your daddy to cough up some child support. Give you an inheritance. There was only one problem."

I shook my head. That didn't sound like her.

"What was the issue?" Sebastian asked.

Dourif laughed dryly. "She didn't know which one of us it was."

What?

No.

"Do it," Sebastian muttered.

I looked at the knife in my hands.

One of the men on my list was my father?

I fell to the side, and looking at the man who may potentially share half my DNA, I grew sick. I scurried back until I hit the coffee table.

My stomach rolled hard. Bolting over on all fours, I gagged and promptly vomited all over the floor.

"Oh, Jesus H. Christ, girl, get ahold of yourself." Jason stumbled to his feet, holding his open wound. He wheezed as he dragged himself to the bar, grabbing a rag to stuff the hole in his shoulder. "Having me for your daddy wouldn't be that bad."

"You were just trying to fuck her a few minutes ago," Sebastian said, rolling his eyes.

Jason pointed sternly at him with his empty hand. "I don't

want to hear from you right now. You've made my shit list. You're lucky you've already made a name for yourself. Otherwise, I'd make sure you never got work again."

I stared at the two men sparring with their words. Sebastian didn't look the least bit fazed.

This man could be my father? I wiped the vomit from my mouth and climbed to my feet. I joined him at the bar, going behind it to pour some water from the small sink underneath. I swished the liquid in my mouth and spit, and then looked back at Jason.

"There's no fucking way she'd do that to her child."

Jason scoffed. "What do you mean? I come from a long line of Southern gentlemen. You'd be lucky to get these genes. Unfortunately, I doubt it was me. You're a bit too tan to be my baby, darlin'. I had to get this at a salon." He lifted his orange, leathery hand.

My stomach rolled again. I inhaled deeply, trying to shove the nausea away. Out of the corner of my eye, I caught sight of Sebastian quietly picking up the knife I'd discarded when I scurried away from Jason. He saw me looking and put a finger to his lips to silence me.

"If you're not my dad, then which one of you is it? It'll save me a whole lot of time if I can just go right to the bastard." I came around the bar to stand beside him, leaning my elbows on the counter.

Jason was struggling to breathe. While Sebastian hadn't hit a lung, it was still painful, I was sure. He turned his head toward me and smirked.

"Now, why would I tell you that? It'd ruin the surprise." A slow grin spread across his face as Sebastian came over, finishing his can.

Using it as an excuse, he went around the bar to toss the can in the trash, and as he did, he slid the knife into my hand behind my back. Jason didn't notice. He kept on talking.

"You missed your chance. I knew you were too chickenshit

to end my life, Little Lita. Just like—" Dourif was cut off by me swinging my arm and plunging the knife straight into his neck. The puncture made a sickening wet sound, and I could feel the veins and muscles I'd hit as the knife went in. I yanked the knife out, and blood sprayed my front, going into my mouth and eyes. He tripped forward, grabbing for me. I leaped out of his reach, and his eyes widened as he stared ahead. His body hit the ground with a thud. The sound of his throat gurgling was low under the music still pumping through the speakers.

He twitched and a moment later fell limp. Wiping my face, I spit out the blood that had gotten in my mouth, and I inhaled deeply and looked over at Sebastian.

"I really hope this fucking creep wasn't my dad."

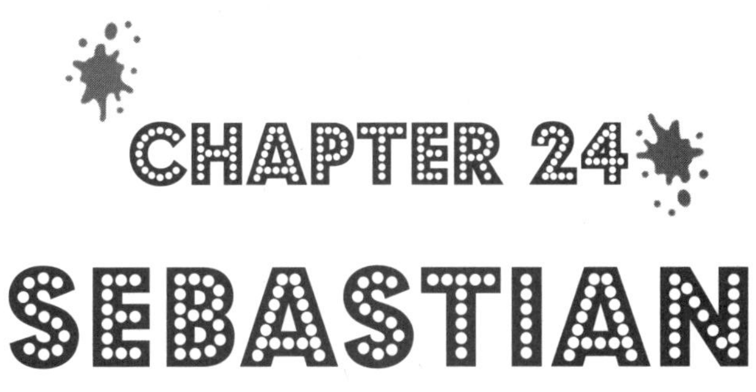

CHAPTER 24
SEBASTIAN

The Set Tour

"I did it. Holy shit, Sebastian—I did it." Her face was a mixture of shock and excitement. She was smiling, but her eyes kept drifting off. I didn't blame her. Dourif had dropped some major information.

"You did. Good job, Final Girl." I reached for her hand across the bar. "You're a natural. You ready to get out of here?"

"What? Shouldn't we take care of his body or something?" Her brows knitted together.

"Look around the room. He's got a table full of coke and the reputation as a slimeball fuck of a manager. No one's going to give a shit about him. They're going to assume he got into some trouble. It's fine. We just gotta wash the blood off ourselves." I grabbed the can I'd discarded and came around the bar, stepping carefully to not stomp in the blood. I went to the coffee table, where the cocaine was scattered all over. Bending down, I grabbed the tray with Evie's prints and took my shirt to it, wiping it clean. I set it back down carefully without touching it with my own hands.

"Where do we do that? We can't go back the way we came." Evie's eyes grew wide as panic began to take over.

"There's a back door. Look, he's got a pool. Let's go out that way and jump in real quick. We'll be fine." I grabbed our wigs and headed to the back door.

Exiting, we walked over and stood by the pool.

"Will this work? With DNA and stuff?" Evie asked, squeezing my hand. I dropped the wigs and sighed.

"I think it will do well enough. Dourif is so low on the totem pole, no one's going to look that hard for who did it."

"Sometimes dead is better," she muttered.

"Exactly. Let's do this, quick." With my free hand I plugged my nose. Bending my knees, I counted down. "One, two, three!"

Together, we jumped into the pool, fully clothed. The water stung momentarily, but I popped back up a moment later and blinked away the chlorine. Evie followed a second later, wiping her face.

All around us, Dourif's blood mixed with the water. I wagged my hands under the surface, and soon, the red was gone. Paddling to the ladder, we pulled ourselves up, now significantly waterlogged.

Picking our wigs back up, I glanced back at the house. The party was still in full swing, thankfully. He wouldn't be found until morning at the earliest. I called for our driver, and as we waited, we wrung our clothes out.

"You think he'll notice?" Evie asked nervously as she squeezed her hair out into a bush.

"Yeah, but let's play it off." A few moments later, he pulled up, and we got in, leaving the scene.

"Are you wet on my seat?" The driver asked, scowling. I snickered.

"Yeah, things were crazy over there. We fell into the pool. Sorry, bill me for the damage."

He huffed and rolled the window up, then clicked on the intercom to ask where we needed to go.

I looked over at Evie. She yawned and slumped in her seat. Between her coming down from the coke, the fight with Dourif, and the jump in the pool, she looked like hell.

"What time is it?" Evie asked. "We have to be at the studio at six."

I looked at my watch. It was just past midnight. She needed rest, but I'd just slammed a Red Bull and was wide awake.

"Take us back to my place," I told Anton and then turned to her. "You can sleep in a guest room."

"I'm tired, but I'm not at the same time," she sighed.

I knew the feeling.

She closed her eyes as I got out my phone and started to text Anderson, asking for a later call time, but I hesitated then deleted the message. It would look bad if we didn't show up to work on time and had been seen at the party. We'd just have to power through tomorrow and take naps in our trailers when we could.

Evie fell onto my shoulder, and I looked down, taking her in. She looked even more beautiful covered in blood. I sighed. She didn't realize it, and I wasn't sure I'd ever tell her, but her enemies were my enemies. She'd just killed a man and was sleeping like a baby. I imagined I'd sleep well, too, once this was all over.

When we reached my house, I woke her up.

Her eyes fluttered open, and she sat up. "Where are we?"

"My house. I have dogs. Just a heads-up."

She rubbed her eyes. "Dogs?"

"You good?" I asked with a chuckle as I helped her out of the car.

"I'm great. That little nap was actually really refreshing."

"Good, because it's going to be a late night." I unlocked the door and pushed it open.

"Late? But our call time is early."

"Yes, but we need an alibi."

I let her go in first and flicked the hallway light on as I shut the door. A second later, there was a scratching sound, followed by panting. My tiny white Bichon Frise ran into the hall, followed by my Saint Bernard.

"Is that..." Evie stared down the hall as they paused then bounded our way.

"Precious and Cujo?" I squatted for my babies to greet me. "Yes, ma'am. Although you wouldn't guess who's who." I lifted the smaller dog and waved his little paws. “Meet Cujo.”

“And that’s Precious?” Evie laughed, dropping down to pet the giant Saint Bernard.

“I got Precious first. Cujo seemed like the low-hanging fruit, but I wanted another name from horror.” I explained how the big one got the name of the dog from *Silence of the Lambs*. “But then I was gifted this little guy, and I thought it was funny to give them reversed names.”

“It’s cute. I love it. I would have never guessed you’d own a poodle dog.”

“Bichon Frise,” I corrected and stood, taking Cujo with us. “And he was a gift.”

“That’s wild. Who gifts people pets?” she asked.

I bit back the truth of who exactly had given me Cujo and instead made a joke. “That’s Hollywood.”

She didn’t need to know that Cujo came from a producer I’d spent the night with to get a gig I’d wanted. The producer felt guilty about the bruising she’d left me with and thought Cujo would make up for it, even though I’d told her a role in her movie was enough. But she’d insisted, and in a way, it did help. I’d always wanted a dog growing up, and I also got the part in her movie.

Taking our wet socks and shoes off at the door, I took Evie into the living room. She’d never been inside. Suddenly, I felt a little exposed, which was ironic, considering my career. I looked around, hoping the furniture and decor weren’t too cringe.

“So, what were you saying about needing an alibi?” she asked.

Right, the alibi.

“Yeah, well, if people were to investigate, which again, I don’t think they will, they might remember we were at the premiere. We need to make it look like we’ve been here all night.”

“How do we do that?”

“The internet.”

She cocked her head.

Cujo squirmed in my arms. I let him down gently and followed him to the kitchen, where both dogs demanded snacks.

I offered them treats and then looked up at Evie. "We should do a livestream, where we casually drop that we've been hanging out at my place all night."

Her lips formed an O, and then she looked down at herself, drenched still, and shivered.

"I...need to change."

"You can have one of my shirts," I offered, taking her upstairs. I went to my closet, and as I stripped out of my own wet clothes, I tossed her a band tee. "Take everything off. I'll wash them."

"Everything?"

I walked out of my closet in nothing but a clean pair of boxers. "Everything."

She blushed as she turned away.

I stood and watched as she pulled off her jacket and pants then put on my shirt. It was so large on her, it covered her ass, but just barely. My cock pulsed as she unhooked her bra and slid her panties down her shapely legs. She turned and gave me the clothes.

"Can I borrow some boxers?" she asked.

"These were my last pair," I lied, smirking.

The giant eye roll and twitch of her lips told me she knew I was lying, but didn't call me on it. I wondered if she was remembering the dressing room, where I fucked her dressed as a clown. I was.

"Well, how am I supposed to go live almost naked?" she asked as I took her back downstairs, tossing our clothes into the wash. My laundry room faced the backyard. I gazed out the window.

"Let's get in the hot tub." I flicked on the outside lights, revealing my backyard. "Our hair is already wet, so it'll look like we've been in the pool all night. Oh, you'll love this." I went to the control box and pushed the button to retract the tarp.

"Whoa. Why is it red?" She stepped toward the pool, her wide eyes and even wider smile giving me joy.

I grinned. "Neat, ain't it? Cost me a fucking fortune. It's the liner. The water is normal." I took her down to the pool. Due to the reflection of the liner, the water resembled blood, which was the point.

"I'm obsessed," she muttered.

I moved behind her, sliding my arms around her and cradling my chin on her neck. "Me too."

Silence fell between us as we took in my confession. She gently stepped out of my arms and turned.

"Okay, I'd like a few hours of sleep at least, so let's get this livestream over."

"Right, yeah."

I went inside and grabbed my phone and a stand. On my way back, I turned the hot tub on. I looked around but didn't see Evie anywhere. A shred of panic settled around me, and I called her name. Her head popped up from inside the pool, and I jumped. She laughed as she swam over to the ledge and climbed out. My shirt clung to her curves, sending my mind to depraved places.

"I had to see for myself."

"How's the burn?" I asked, reaching for her arm. He'd landed the cherry on one of her tattoos.

"It stings, but I'll be fine." She winced.

I held up my phone and nodded toward the bubbling hot tub. "Get in. I'll set this up."

I watched as she climbed into the hot tub, dressed in just my shirt. My cock wept, but the idea of fucking her in a place that wasn't entirely special for me felt...wrong. I wasn't going to waste one of my times in the fucking hot tub.

She was worth more than that. Evie wasn't some cheap lay.

I set the stand at the edge and climbed in with her. The hot water felt great on my sore muscles. I sank low and then popped back up.

"Okay, so we'll get on camera for a bit, do some flirty Q&A stuff, and we need to mention that we're so tired because after the premiere, we came here and have been hanging out all night. Got it?" I turned back to her.

She gave me a thumbs-up, and I pushed the timer to go live. I leaned back to rest on the seat next to her.

"Okay, Final Girl, convince them you love me."

CHAPTER 25 SEBASTIAN

The Misdirection

"What?"

"Huh?" I attempted to correct with more playful energy, but I was stumbling over my words and thoughts, and she was scowling at me. There wasn't time to say anything else. The timer on the screen dropped to one then went live. I put my arm around her and forced a smile that just moments before had been real. Under the water, I pinched my thigh for being so fucking stupid.

"*Convince them you love me.*" I'd tried to be playful, but I'd fallen on my face.

"I should get drinks," I muttered and hopped out, flashing the viewers my boxers. My heart was going wild with embarrassment as I dug through my fridge for beer. I pulled out two brown bottles and hurried back. I relaxed in an instant when I saw Evie bobbing in front of the camera, talking excitedly to the viewers.

"Oh, good, you're back!" She turned, slurring her words some. I cocked my head and matched her energy. Acting drunk was easy.

"Yeah, babe, of course." I handed her a beer and slid back into the hot tub.

"I was just telling them all about the movie," she said.

"What movie?" I raised an eyebrow.

"*Slice Slice Baby*, the one we just went and saw tonight!" She laughed. "Have you forgotten already?"

"Baby." I took a long sip of my beer. "I think imma have a hard time remembering anything tomorrow."

She fell back against me, and I caught her, wrapping my arms around her waist. "You should remember...some stuff, I would think."

My cock hardened under the water, and I shifted to press it against her thigh. The knowledge that she wasn't wearing any panties was not lost on either of us. She stiffened when she felt me then shifted away.

"Anyway, I wanted to give my review of the movie and tell everyone they need to go watch it. It was *so* good," she said, facing the live feed again. "I told Sebastian I wanted to do it earlier, right after the movie, but then he—"

"I'd do it with you anytime." I nuzzled my nose into her neck.

She giggled and fought to get away. "Stop! You're tickling me! I meant talk about the movie!" She escaped my grasp for just a moment. Her beautiful smile was sending me places I shouldn't go. Less sexy places. More...

I pulled her back onto my lap. She kicked and giggled, and I nuzzled her neck, softer this time, careful not to brush my stubble too hard against her skin.

"There were more pressing things," I said, raising my eyes like I'd been trained to do in order to look smoldering. Hearts, stars, and crowns flooded the screen as people gave us gifts and wrote comments.

"Stop, you goof!" Evie pushed me back and went to the phone. "People are asking about *our* movie. Should we do a little Q&A about *Simon Says Six*?"

"*Six Six*," I replied and then shrugged. "I have come here to chew bubblegum and kick ass."

She turned to look back at me and stuck her tongue out playfully. "And we're all out of bubblegum. Okay, let's answer some questions. Ask away."

I leaned forward to read the comments that were popping up

at lightning speed. I glanced at the viewer counter: 250k.

"Someone wants to know if we're done filming," she asked.

I looked at her. "We haven't even gotten to the spicy stuff yet."

She giggled and swatted me.

I picked the next question. "They want to know where our castmates are."

"Bryce and Skye? Well—uh..." She blushed, and I wasn't sure if it was fake or not. I found my hand drifting to her hair, pushing the damp strands behind her ear, showing off her beautiful face to the camera.

"It was a private party," I told the fans.

"Maybe we should have gone to one of the after-parties," she said.

"Nah, those are always boring. I prefer a more..." I smirked at the camera "Intimate gathering."

Oh, people were going to eat this up. Between the red-carpet ass squeeze and this livestream, the rumors were going to go wild. I bet I could get the PR team to give us bonuses.

"Are we dating? No. Sorry, guys, Sebastian just needed a date, and I had nothing to do tonight, so I agreed to go with him. We're just friends," Evie said.

The comments turned from the constant questions to skepticism.

"I know, I know, it's not what you want to hear," I added, wrapping my arms around her from behind. "But, like she said, just friends." I gave an exaggerated pout, then, when she wasn't looking directly at the screen, I winked at the stream.

"Who's the best person to work with on set?" she read off.

We continued answering questions about the movie from true horror fans, and between those, we answered a few flirty ones. We made sure to keep denying any relationship outside of work, all the while touching and flirting.

Finally, she complained about wrinkles from being in the water too long, and we got ready to shut the livestream off.

"We've got an early call time, so we should attempt an hour or so of sleep." She yawned. There was a barrage of comments with various forms of *sleep isn't going to happen if you share a bed.*

"She's staying in my guest room, guys. I'm a gentleman, I swear," I joked.

But just as Evie was about to shut off the stream, she froze.

"What is it?" I asked.

She didn't say anything for a long moment, but then, seeming to come to, she shut the stream off and sat back, her eyes blank and unfocused. I checked the phone to make sure it was off then turned to her.

"Evie, what's wrong? Did someone comment something gross? You just gotta ignore them. They're just trolls."

She was stiff, and despite being in the boiling water, she had goose bumps. "I murdered someone today. On purpose."

I narrowed my gaze. "How does that make you feel?" I asked.

A slow smile parted her lips, and a thrilling chill slid up my spine. The question seemed to pull her from the daze she'd been under.

"Good. Scared, but...also good. Sebastian, I need them to know it's me coming after them. I want them to be scared. I know we just established an alibi, but I kind of hope the men on my list start to realize they're being targeted."

We dried off, and I gave her another shirt to wear. I directed her up the stairs and down the hall to one of the guest rooms, but she insisted she sleep in the living room instead. The couch was apparently too comfy to move from. The dogs loved it, and the moment she lay down, they joined her, Precious at her feet and Cujo near her head.

I stood and stared, watching her sleep. She wasn't quite at peace yet, but she'd gotten one step closer tonight. She was practically glowing.

I hoped one day, after all those names were crossed off, being with me would have the same effect.

Maybe I could be her peace.

In time, I said to myself as I left her to snag a few hours of sleep. *In time.*

CHAPTER 26

EVIE

The Production Hold

"Is there anything I can help you with?" Skye, dressed as Riley, glanced up at me from the reception desk, an annoyed look on her face.

I shifted my purse on my shoulder and looked behind her. "I'm here to have lunch with my boyfriend."

"Boyfriend?" She cocked an eyebrow then looked me up and down, her distaste for my appearance clear. We were total opposites, with my all-black ensemble and her orange dress reminiscent of something from the sixties' sunshine era. "Are you sure you have the right business? This is—"

"Amity Incorporated?" I turned my body and pointed to the large sign behind me. "I'm positive I'm in the right place."

"Well, I don't think—" She rose slowly, preparing to ask me to leave.

"Lucy! You're here!" Sebastian, as Ronny McCoy, entered through a glass door, wearing a dark-gray suit, his hair slicked back. He strode over and put an arm over my shoulder, pulling me close. "Riley, this is my girlfriend. I told you she was coming this morning. Did you forget?" He laughed, not catching the tense energy between us.

Skye scowled and then looked down at the stack of papers on her desk. "Must have. Oops."

"Cut!" Dante called, and we all instantly relaxed.

I stepped out of Sebastian's hold and turned to Skye. The moment our eyes locked, we burst into laughter. She gave me a fake scowl, scrunching up her nose and pursing her lips.

"Lay off my man, you bitch."

I raised my fist and shook it like an old man trying to get kids off his lawn. "You'll have to fight me first."

Dante came over and gave us notes so we could run the scene again. "Let's try one with less shade and more...denial. Skye, you're shocked that Lucy is here and hurt when Sebastian reminds you he has a girlfriend."

We reset and ran the scene again, and then two more times, changing little things here or there so that Dante and the editors would have things to work with.

We shot until noon and then cut for lunch. I hurried to my trailer to take a quick nap. After the livestream last night—and the murder of another man on my list—I'd tried to sleep but overall had been unsuccessful. By the look of the bags under Sebastian's eyes when he drove us here a few hours later, I thought he was in the same boat. I closed my eyes and fell into a deep sleep, waking up to my alarm an hour later. I rolled over and stretched, feeling refreshed and prepared for the next six hours. It wasn't a full sleep but manageable.

I stepped out of my trailer and went to hair and makeup for touch-ups. I was still in my chair, thinking about how it was technically my first murder, but it was the second man off my list, when Dante's assistant came in, wringing their hands.

"Evie, uh, there are police here. They want to talk to you?"

The breath escaped my lungs, and I raised my eyebrows. Forcing myself to react minimally, I looked at him through the mirror. "What about?"

"They wouldn't say. Dante said to call your agent."

"Right, okay." I pulled out my phone and texted Antoinette, then started to text Sebastian, but I realized that could be incriminating if they wanted to look through my phone at any point.

The makeup artist finished touching up my hair, and I got up, following the assistant to one of the offices, where two policemen in uniform were waiting. One was a tall Black man with a mustache, the other a short but muscular Hispanic man with thick eyebrows. Their faces were grim.

Had someone ratted us out about Dourif? My stomach rolled with nerves as I stared at their serious expressions.

"Hello. I was told you wanted to talk to me?"

"Yes, Miss Reyes. Please sit." They motioned to the seat on my side of the table.

We sat down. I kept the look of confusion and boredom plastered on my face. I refused to give them anything.

The Hispanic officer, whose name tag said Reyna, spoke first. "We wanted to speak to you today because we are investigating a missing person's case. Glenn Thornton."

I raised my brows. Glenn? He'd been dead for over a month now. What had they found?

"Glenn? Did you find him?" I leaned forward.

They exchanged glances. "I'm sorry to inform you that Glenn is dead."

My mouth fell open, and I covered my face with my hand. "No!"

"Some of his remains were recovered by hikers. He'd been... scattered by scavengers."

"Scattered?" I gaped. While my surprise was false, my nerves were real. My insides were twisting so tightly it hurt.

"Do you need water?" asked the Black officer with the tag June, offering me a plastic bottle on the table.

Water meant fingerprints.

I shook my head and inhaled deeply. "So, Glenn is gone."

"Yes," Officer June said. "And we were told by some of the staff that you two had been dating shortly before he went missing."

"Dating is an overexaggeration." I rolled my eyes. "We had drinks one time because he saw me at a bar, and then we flirted and texted some. We had plans to go for dinner, but he went missing before we could."

Reyna scribbled it all down. "I see. So, you never saw him the day he went missing?"

"What day was that? The last time we spoke, he was helping me move back into my mother's home. He was going to stay and help me unpack, but then we fought on the way there, so I pulled over and let him out. That was like...over a month ago."

"You fought? About what?" Officer June leaned over the table. "Where did you leave him?"

They were eating this shit up.

"A few blocks from my house." I shrugged. "I'd just been cast opposite Sebastian, and he didn't like that Sebastian was making his...feelings clear. He wanted me to turn the role down, and I said no."

"Feelings?"

I sighed and sat back, crossing my arms. "I'm sure you'll see it soon if you haven't already. Sebastian and I dated briefly a few years ago, and there were some residual feelings on his side when he saw me on set the first time. He made that known, and Glenn felt like Sebastian wasn't respecting him, as Glenn and I had just started talking. Honestly, it was just one big pissing match between the two. It was dumb."

"And was Sebastian happy when Glenn went missing?"

"Of course," I said, pausing. "Just like most of the production team. Honestly, I hate to speak ill of the dead, but it sounds like I dodged a bullet. I've never heard anyone say anything pleasant about Glenn, other than his good looks."

They nodded in unison, as if that was what they'd heard too.

"So, you know Sebastian. Do you think he's a violent man?"

I laughed. "Sebastian? Maybe to himself. He talks a big game, but I don't think he did anything to Glenn, if that's what you're asking. He didn't seem to care that he was gone. Just like everyone else. It's sad he's dead, but I don't think Sebastian had anything to do with it."

"I see. Well, thank you for speaking with us. We'll let you get back to work."

I stood and shook their hands. "Of course. I'm sorry I can't be more helpful. I barely knew the guy." I started out but then paused at the door. "Am I allowed to tell people?"

They looked at each other then nodded.

"That's fine. Maybe one of them will know something." Officer Reyna pulled a business card from his pocket and leaned over to give it to me. "If you hear something, give us a call."

"Sure thing," I said. Turning slowly, I slid the card into my pocket and did my best to walk out the door with my shoulders high but not cocky. I needed to look aloof, but also confident. I passed Skye on the way and gave her a sympathetic smile.

Her fixed grin fell off her face. "What happened? Is someone dead?"

I nodded. "Glenn."

"Glenn!" She slapped her hands over her mouth. "Oh, my God."

"Yep. Good luck." I patted her on the shoulder.

"Good luck? What does that mean? Am I being investigated? I didn't do anything."

"I know that. I didn't mean anything by it. Just good luck not crying in front of the officers." I forced a laugh, and she wiped at the tears that had already started.

"Right, I know. I'm a baby sometimes. I didn't even know the guy. It's just so sad."

I left her and returned to set. We needed Skye for the scene, so we shot other things, including some behind-the-scenes videos to post on my channel. Skye's interview took longer, presumably because they let her sit there and cry. She returned with a puffy face and red eyes. Bryce was next, but we were able to film without him, so we finished our scenes for the day and started toward our trailers to undress and go home.

Word about Glenn had spread fast. Everyone was talking about it in hushed tones.

Bryce caught me as I was leaving. Sebastian was with me. Since he'd driven me here, he had to give me a ride home. "That's crazy about Glenn, ain't it? Ripped apart by vultures."

"Is that what happened?" I leaned over to look at him, feigning shock.

"Well, that's what I heard."

We reached the parking lot and stopped in front of our cars.

Bryce took a long drag of his cigarette then winked at Sebastian and me. "Sounds like they bought it. I say, whoever did it? Good for her."

CHAPTER 27 EVIE

The Alliance

I stared at Bryce, my mouth hanging open.

He tipped his cowboy hat at us before hurrying to his car, snickering.

"Bryce, wait—" I called after him.

"I've had a long day. How about dinner Friday?"

Friday was five days away.

I bit back a protest and nodded.

"Sure, sounds good."

If it were anyone else, the prolonged wait would've eaten at me, but I knew that whatever Bryce knew, or thought he knew, was safe with him. When we were younger, he was always the first person to help us on set. He would even go toe-to-toe with my mom on occasion, when he felt she was being too harsh. He'd known many a secret of mine during my childhood. He was the brother I'd never had.

I got into the car, and Sebastian drove me home, where I crashed the moment my head hit the pillow.

THE WEEK WENT fast, just like the interest in Glenn's death. By Wednesday, they were officially looking to replace his position.

Friday came, and after we wrapped for the day, Skye asked if she could come over and watch movies.

"*Reptilicus* on the big screen? Fresh popcorn, Buncha Crunches? Just you and me?" she pleaded. She loved my mini theater.

"Ooh, I do love *Reptilicus*. It's tempting, but I can't tonight. I have a...date."

"A date?" she hissed, eyes growing wide. "With Sebastian?"

She and I had only briefly talked about the dressing room incident. She wanted more details, but I wasn't much of a kiss-and-tell person.

"No—well, he might be there. I don't know."

I didn't think her eyes could get any larger, but somehow, they did.

"Evelyn Reyes, are you in a triad?"

"What? No. It's nothing. Just some friends. Sorry. I'll catch up with you a different night."

She pouted her lip and crossed her arms, but I promised to make it up to her later. I hurried home to shower and change. I put on a pair of ripped jeans and my black hoodie I'd gotten from a movie festival I'd gone to last year. They'd given them out with the early screening ticket I'd purchased. On the front, the title of the movie, *Slash or Pass 2: More Blood More Titties*, was written on it in a creepy font. It was my favorite.

I hurried out the door, off to Bryce's bar.

This was the first time I'd been to my friend's business. He talked about it often, but usually when we went out after work, we visited other places. I was excited to see it all, so I was the first one there. Sebastian sauntered in moments later. Bryce came out from the back after we'd already had our first drinks. He was carrying a small pink box with a red bow. He set it on the side of the table.

It looked like something my mother would have put under the Christmas tree.

"Sorry I'm tardy. I had to run home, and when I tried to leave, I had some lady fans that needed my attention." He gave us a knowing smile, and I shook my head. "They love *Simon Says.*"

"That they do." Sebastian snickered.

I wondered for a moment if he too used his fame to pursue sex. I had to stop myself from rolling my eyes. He absolutely did. I'd seen the tabloids. He'd been featured with many men and women in rather intimate, candid photos.

"Let's get some menus over here." Bryce waved our waitress down and ordered some appetizers and a round of beer for the table. Once she was gone, he turned back to us. "Now, let's talk."

"Right," I started, then paused to look around the bar. It was quite full, but the backs of the booths were high, and no one seemed to be paying us any mind. "You said, 'Sounds like they bought it.' What did you mean?"

Sebastian reached for my hand under the table, reassuring me.

"Oh, just that we all know he didn't die being eaten by buzzards." He cackled. "Or whatever else is out there."

"Do we?" Sebastian asked.

"Oh, we do." Bryce leaned forward. "How'd you do it?"

"What do you mean?" I feigned innocence.

He looked between us and rolled his eyes. "I know it was you. The day he went missing, you both came to set with dust all over your clothes and tangles in your hair. You smelled like dirt and iron and—" he paused, leaning in "—desert."

"I had to bury my cat," Sebastian said smoothly.

"Oh, you buried something. Although not that well since they found the pieces." Bryce snickered and fell back against the booth. "I didn't think you two had it in you. Killing in cold blood. Like I said, good for you. Since you couldn't get his daddy, it was nice to hear his little bloodsucking asshole of a son got his comeuppance."

I sat there, watching him go on. The waitress brought us soft pretzels and beer, and we waited patiently for her to disappear before continuing. Bryce reached for the food and dipped a bite into the cheese. "Now, curiosity has gotten the best of me. How'd you do it exactly?"

"Bryce..." I sighed.

"Come on. I'm not telling anyone. I know what they did to your mom. If I wasn't afraid for my own life, I would have killed them a long time ago. I can't tell you how hard I laughed when I heard about Mike Thornton." His gaze flicked to Sebastian. "You hear how he died? Face purple, hand gripping his cock—the same color. The hooker he'd been with robbed his ass on the way out."

"I'd heard," Sebastian said, tone clipped.

I eyed him curiously. He'd told me that he'd killed Mike Thornton, but for some reason I hadn't put two and two together. Was Sebastian the sex worker Bryce was talking about? Returning my attention to the table, I relented under Bryce's poking about Glenn.

"He drank bleach out of Sebastian's energy drink," I said, ripping off the Band-Aid.

Bryce flinched, then laughed. "Jesus, I bet that burned like a motherfucker. Good. He was just as bad as his dad." He gulped down his beer and raised his arm for another.

"When did you put things together?" I asked, reaching for a pretzel bite.

"Oh, I don't know. About a week after he went missing? Someone on set mentioned Glenn, and you got all nervous, and Sebastian said"—he pushed out his chest and put on a serious face—"'Isn't he irrelevant now? Let's talk about how good my line delivery was today.'"

I glared at Sebastian. His ego was the tell, not anything I did.

"Not to mention that little fight you had before the interview. Skye may not have given it two thoughts, but I did." Bryce laughed again. "Really, don't worry about it, guys. I don't give two flying fucks about those bastards. After what they did to Lita? It's all karma."

I straightened. "What do you know about that?"

"Too much," he muttered and took the drink the waitress set down. "They did her dirty. You too, by default."

"I heard they..." I couldn't say the words. Memories of

Dourif's last moments flashed in my mind.

"They sexually assaulted her. All of them," Sebastian told him.

Bryce took his hat off and set it on the table, the smile falling from his face. "I wish I could say I'm surprised, but I'm not. Those men are depraved. They couldn't just kill someone and walk away. Was it before or after?"

My jaw dropped, and my eyes widened at his question.

Anthony C. Hopkins.

The very idea that they could have raped her *after* they'd murdered her... I was going to be sick.

Bryce retracted his question quickly. "Evie, I'm sorry. I didn't mean to be crude. It just came out. I—"

I put my hand up to stop him as I closed my eyes, forcing the idea that men would rape a dead woman out of my mind. "It's fine. Honestly, I wouldn't put it past them, but I think it was before."

"To use another man's words, they wanted to teach her a lesson," Sebastian said, taking my hand again. The warmth was comforting, and I relaxed.

"I see. I'd ask what lesson, but it doesn't matter. No one deserves what they did to her."

Silence followed briefly, but Bryce was good at pushing the darkness away. "Anyway, I just wanted to talk to you guys and see what your plans were. Not too many people have heard—or care—but I got word that talent manager Jason Dourif was found in his house, face covered in cocaine, and he'd been stabbed to death. Now, to anyone else, he's just another dumb talent manager who didn't pay his dealer. But to me, knowing what I know..." He tapped his temple. "I have a feeling you two made a guest appearance at his house that night. Didn't you?"

Sebastian and I looked at each other. His expression softened, his eyes comforting me. We turned back to Bryce. What was his endgame? This little cat-and-mouse situation wasn't his MO. Finally, I just asked.

"What do you want? Money?"

"Money?" Bryce's mouth fell open, as if truly shocked I'd ask such a thing. Leaning over the table so that we had to do the same, a slow grin spread over our friend's face. Out of the corner of my eye, I saw him reach for the pink box with the red ribbon and slide it across to me. "I'm not here to take. I'm here to give. I've been waiting five long fucking years for this moment. She gave this to me the day before she died."

I straightened and took it, lifting the lid. Right on top sat a note with handwriting I hadn't seen in years. My breath caught in my throat as I lifted the small piece of paper.

James Dean once said, "Live fast, die young, and leave a good-looking corpse." I have a strong feeling that I might be doing that tonight. If I didn't come home and Bryce has given you my last parting gift, please, learn how to use them.

Don't let them take you alive.

Love,

Mom

Tears flooded my vision as I read the words over and over again. The men at the table sat silently, letting me take things in. Setting the note down gently, I peered into the box.

Inside were two small push daggers. I lifted the one on the left and ran a finger along the sharp edge. Slowly spinning it in my hands, I admired the short, smooth, four-inch light-pink blades with red handles that had *Good For Her* engraved in a pink cursive font. A chill went down my spine, and I looked back up at Bryce.

Red and bubblegum pink were her signature colors. They matched the box they came in. She'd given them to him to give to me because she knew there was a chance I'd need them.

Don't let them take you alive.

She'd known she wasn't coming home.

Bryce reached for his beer, pulling my attention from the gift. "Evie, I don't want money. I want to help."

CHAPTER 28

SEBASTIAN

The Signature Weapon

"I can't imagine her carrying knives." Evie sat between Cujo and Precious on my couch a week later, twirling the daggers between her fingers. "But she clearly had them specially made. They look new."

"Maybe they were," I suggested, coming from the kitchen with a Red Bull in my hand. I offered her a bottle of water and sat down on the other side of the couch. I'd tried to sit with her, but my dogs seemed to prefer Evie to me. They'd never liked a sexual partner I brought home before, but with her, it was like she'd been their original owner, not me. I tried not to get jealous of the amount of cuddles they were giving her, but this side of the couch was quite lonely.

"Maybe they weren't hers but made for you. They don't say Lita on them."

"True," she mumbled as she studied them. They were pretty nice push daggers. "Good for her. That's kind of iconic, don't you think?"

"They are very Lita-coded," I agreed.

"And that theory makes more sense. If they'd been hers, why didn't she have them on her that night? Why give them to Bryce before she died? She knew that one day I'd have to take down this fucking town."

Evie grew quiet, and her eyes glazed over. Bryce knowing what we were doing, and being willing to help, had been a lot for her. After dinner that night, I'd taken her home and left her to think. I was surprised when she asked me to hang out after work the following Friday. She'd been hanging out with Skye most of the week.

"Who's next?" I asked.

"Frederick Castle," she said without looking up from her weapons.

"I see..." I scrunched up my nose and quickly looked away. I'd been really dreading this one.

"When I first made the decision to come back, I did some research. I contacted a few true crime channels. You know, those amateur sleuth ones? They found so much information on my mom's case that I didn't know existed. I made the list in order from easiest to hardest. I think, anyway."

"Right. That's the list you showed me before."

She nodded. "Frederick Castle is an entertainment lawyer. He hangs out in his office most of the time, and it's a nice one with lots of security. I can't even get a meeting with him."

"I know Fred. That sounds right." I rolled my eyes. Fred Castle was a royal dick.

"So, should we give it a bit of time? Dourif has barely been dead two weeks. And now that they've found Glenn..."

"Maybe. Are you thinking of using those going forward?" I pointed to the knives in her lap. Her brown eyes lit up, and her lips turned upward.

"Yes! The note that came with them? She wanted me to do this. Avenge her death."

Lita Reyes was a confusing creature. She had a lot of secrets but was always two steps ahead of everyone, until that night. The more I thought about it, Evie's theory was probably correct. Lita had given the engraved knives to Bryce in the event something happened to her and her daughter needed to fight back.

But why even go to dinner in the first place?

"You need to learn how to use them, then."

Evie pushed the dogs off her lap and leaped up. Handling the knives, handles between her fingers, she hunched down, taking a fighting stance, and then punched the air. I raised an eyebrow, and when she saw the skepticism on my face, she stood straight.

"What? I've got this. I took a class." She swung again, haphazardly. Her arm was not steady, and the landing was weak. There was no way she'd be able to take on someone alone.

"Your instructor was shit, then." I snickered and stood.

Once she stopped swinging, I faced her front and reached up, snagged her wrist, and yanked her arm down. I grabbed the other and forced them to her sides, squeezing until she whimpered.

"Drop them," I demanded.

Her eyes watered as she tried to fight against me. She pressed her lips together, and I squeezed harder. That seemed to trigger something in her. Her brow furrowed, her eyes darkened, and she sneered at me.

"Fuck you," she spat. Her eyes glazed over—I had a feeling she wasn't speaking to me, but one of the men on her list.

I squeezed harder, hating myself for it but needing to prove my point.

"You think they'll hesitate to snap your bones in half?" I asked, finally letting her go.

She stumbled back, dropping the daggers to the floor so she could rub her wrists.

I bent down to retrieve her weapons. "I'm sorry, Final Girl. These men will fight for their lives. You've gotta be prepared for that."

"Maybe I can't do this." She dropped her body onto the floor in defeat. "Sometimes dead is better," she huffed the line from *Pet Sematary*, expressing her frustration.

"Not in my movie." Replying with the quote from *Scream*. I crouched down and lifted her chin to meet my gaze. "You can do this. And you will. We've already killed two out of six, remember? You got Dourif no problem. But we know they aren't all going to be that easy, so we have to prepare. I actually bought you something to help with this."

Her eyes, having gone shiny with tears, now showed...hope. She sat up straight, putting her hands on the floor to steady herself.

"You did?"

I stood and hurried to the kitchen, where I'd left the box. I wasn't entirely great at giving gifts. All the people I knew had everything they'd ever wanted. Not that Evie was lacking for anything, but I wanted...

I wasn't even sure what I'd wanted when I made the order. I was excited yet nervous to show her. Would she like it? Or was I just copying Bryce?

I handed her the box wrapped in paper that was meant to look like TV static, accented with a bow that was a sickly shade of green. "Forgive me for the wrapping job. Normally my assistant does this stuff, but considering the sensitive nature, I thought it best we keep this to ourselves."

"These are the logo colors for my channel!" Evie laughed as she tore through the paper and lifted the box. Dipping her hand inside, she pulled out a small leather belt and paused, cocking her head and furrowing her brows in confusion.

"What is this?" she asked, pulling out a second belt and eyeing them curiously. Setting them down beside her, she dug back into the box.

"Those are straps. They go inside your—"

"Boots! Anthony C. Hopkins, these are so cute." She pulled out the matte black leather combat boots and turned them in her hands. "I'm obsessed."

"Check out the soles."

A gasp came from her throat as she turned them upside down. Etched into the rubber were the words:

Good For Her.

Scrambling up, she unzipped them and slid them over her feet. The boots went to midcalf. Grabbing the straps she'd abandoned on the floor, I had her take the boots back off to try the belts. Pulling her pants up to secure the belts, she slid the daggers into place before putting the boots back on. She zipped the boots up again and tightened the laces then bounced on the balls of her feet and did a few kicks and poses. Reaching down, she drew both blades in a fluid motion.

"Fucking groovy."

"I thought you'd like them." I grinned as I watched her pretend to fight. Honestly, it was a little sexy, watching her brows knit in concentration. She doubted herself, but I never did for even an instant.

"Every villain needs an iconic outfit," I told her. She paused midkick and turned.

"I'm a villain?"

I shrugged. "Some people would probably classify you as such. Definitely the men on your list." I laughed.

She tapped her chin with her forefinger and nodded.

"True. What is it they say? Everyone is a villain to someone?"

"And every villain has a tragic backstory. I'd say yours fits the bill."

"Yeah, but it's not really..." She pursed her lips and relaxed from her fighting stance, sliding the knives back into her boots before sitting back on the couch. The dogs lifted their heads in interest and then dropped back down. She sighed. "It wasn't me who was brutally raped and murdered."

"No, but someone close to you was. They murdered your mother, Evie. Your reasons for revenge are valid." I watched the dogs to make sure I wasn't attacked as I moved to sit behind her and pull her into my arms. She relaxed into my chest, and my heart soared. I wanted this every night. Every time she let me in, I reveled in it.

How long could I make this last?

"There's a reason revenge horror is so popular," I said, resting my head in the crook of her neck. "*I Spit on Your Grave, The Crow, Midsommar*," I listed.

"*Slash or Pass, American Mary, Jennifer's Body*," Evie added, the sadness in her voice lifting with each title. "So many women hurt in so many different ways. Sometimes the screen gets a little too real."

"Exactly. It doesn't matter how they were hurt. It's the revenge we like to see. We want to see the bad guys lose. And when you leave the theater, you find yourself saying—"

"Good for her," she finished, a deep sigh leaving her body.

"Exactly." I shifted my head to kiss her salty cheek. For the first time since she'd come back into my life, my affection wasn't given with lust in mind, but comfort. When she was hurting, so was I. I wanted revenge just as much as she did, and I had every intention of helping her get it. She settled deeper into me, and I wrapped my arms tighter.

"If it's with my last dying breath, I'm going to do everything in my power to make sure you get your *good for her* moment, Final Girl," I whispered into her ear, following it with another kiss.

We relaxed into the couch, and I took a deep, heavy breath.

Well, fuck.

She wanted to go for Fred Castle next. I knew this day would come, but I wasn't entirely prepared for it. After all, he lived next door.

CHAPTER 29

SEBASTIAN

The Unreliable Narrator

"So, I've been dying to know. I don't know why I haven't asked yet. What happened with Michael Thornton?" She dropped back onto the couch, handing me the bowl of popcorn, then took it back once she'd settled in. I turned the TV on and started to peruse my movies.

"You heard Bryce. Heart attack," I said, reaching for my Red Bull. I sipped it while not taking my eyes off the TV. "Monster, shark, found footage, clowns?" I asked.

"Clowns. Oh, come on, don't be like this. I already know bits and pieces." She tossed a piece of buttery goodness at me, and I opened my mouth to catch it. I failed, and when it rolled onto the couch, I plucked it up and ate it.

"Sometimes dead is better," I muttered, asking her to back off. I picked the remote back up to keep scrolling.

"Not in my movie," she protested with a loud guffaw.

With an exaggerated eye roll, I set the remote down and turned to face her. I put my hands up and made a cross with my fingers. "The power of Christ compels you. Begone, Satan!" A smile slid over my lips, and her expression went from pouty to shocked. She set the bowl aside and launched herself at me. We rolled to the floor, laughing as she demanded I spill the details of my first kill.

I playfully pushed her away, but she swung her leg over my body and pushed me onto my back, straddling me. I inhaled deeply as I took her in, biting down on my own lip. What was she doing?

With a devilish grin, she wiggled her ass on my crotch. My cock rose instantly, pressing and straining against my PJs.

"We could use one of your five times, right now, if you tell me what happened," she teased.

It was tempting. I had to look away from her in my oversized shirt and boxers. It would take nothing to slide them to the side... Evie ran her hands under my shirt, her fingers exploring my muscles. I dropped my head back and closed my eyes, savoring her touch.

Would it be so bad to use one?

"I'll let you do whatever you want..." she encouraged, grinding harder. Her words bolted me out of my hypnotic state. I sat up abruptly and pushed her away.

"First of all, that's not how free use works. It's when I want you and how I want you. I don't need your permission to do what you've already consented to." My cock relaxed, now that I was irritated. I tugged my shirt back down and stood. "Now, are we watching a movie or what?"

I plopped down onto the couch and grabbed the popcorn, silently cursing myself. We'd had sex once since she'd come back, and she hadn't stopped me when I'd licked her pussy during the chemistry test. But we hadn't really spoken about either of those moments. They'd happened, and then, it was as if they hadn't the moment we were done. This was the first time she'd even mentioned fucking, and I'd said no.

She rolled her eyes and climbed back onto the couch with me, reaching over and grabbing a handful of popcorn. She nodded at the TV.

"*Killer Klowns From Outer Space*, please."

Oh, so now she wants to watch the movie. Two can play at that game.

I started the movie, and as the iconic opening song blared

through my surround sound speakers, I turned to look at her.

"I'll tell you what happened if you tell me some stuff about you."

"Like what?" she asked, knitting her brows.

"I want to know about the in-between. What happened during the five years we didn't talk?"

"You already know that. I finished high school and started my influencer career. Which, by the way, the studio made an offer for my channel. I'm tempted to take it."

"Stop changing the subject," I said. "What about your love life?"

She shut her mouth and pursed her lips. "Fine. I'll talk, but we take turns."

"You go first."

The dogs suddenly remembered we were here and came barreling in, running straight to Evie and shoving me to the edge of the couch.

"Oh, come on, Precious!" I swatted his large backside playfully as he stuck his tail in my face. He sat down and snuggled in with Evie. We stared at each other from across the couch, and she smiled.

All complaints slipped from my mind.

I'd do anything for that curve of her lips.

"They just wanted to catch family movie night." She laughed.

Family movie night?

She turned to watch the movie, and for a bit, we forgot all about Thornton—and all the men she fucked that I didn't want to know about but, as a glutton for punishment, eventually needed to hear about.

"Did he really die from a heart attack?" she asked as Mike and Debbie ran from the alien circus tent and toward the police station.

I pulled my eyes from the screen. "He did. How long did you wait before you started dating again?" I shot back quickly.

I thought the rapidness of my reply surprised her. She pursed her lips. "I didn't date until I was out of high school, so...about two years. You?"

"Dating isn't something I've ever really done," I answered truthfully.

"What do you mean?" She laughed dryly. "I've seen tons of photos of you with people."

"Sex. I wouldn't consider any of them my exes or anything."

She grew quiet and returned to the movie.

"Glenn and Bryce said he'd taken too many erection pills? Is that part true?"

I pursed my lips. I didn't particularly like to remember that day. He was a real bastard, and I had no regrets, but he'd made me feel so low, I still hated him for it.

"Yes, but not voluntarily. I tossed a handful of Viagra into his drink. Too many, and your body goes into shock. Who was he?"

"Who was who?"

"The man you dated after me. Did you guys sleep together?"

"What makes you think it was a man?"

I raised my eyebrows. "Are you..."

I was openly bisexual—had been for years. I'd never thought to ask Evie about her sexual preferences in a partner. That stuff never interested me. Sexuality was a spectrum; we were all on it somewhere. She shrugged and motioned for me to hand her the popcorn. I had to raise it over the dogs and stretch to pass it.

"I tried dating women, but it wasn't for me."

"Okay, so stop avoiding the question. Who was he, and did you guys sleep together?"

Her jaw tensed. She didn't want to tell me.

"His name is Trenton. He's a programmer at Western Michigan."

"Trenton?"

"He's super nice, but it wasn't a love connection. Just fun." She shrugged, then returned to the movie.

I begrudgingly turned to the screen and watched the killer klowns from outer space terrorize Crescent Cove. I couldn't focus and enjoy the movie, though.

How many people had she had *fun* with? I knew it didn't matter. I'd slept with so many men and women I'd lost count. But the thought of Evie dating, touching, or loving another man was making me spiral.

"Glenn said he'd been having an affair when he was found, but Bryce said it was a sex worker. Do you know anything about that?" she asked.

I snickered.

Yes.

"That's not exactly unheard of in this town," I said.

"Which one?"

"Either."

"But you said you were there."

I rolled my eyes to the ceiling. She was dancing around the question. "Just ask me."

She squinted and then relaxed. "Do you do sex work?"

"That's literally my job. Or have you forgotten about *Simon Says Six—*"

"*Six Six*," she added.

"*Six Six*, already?"

"No, not that kind of sex work. Like..."

My patience was wearing thin. This was a tennis match, both of us going hard, back and forth at each other.

"I was not paid to be there," I finally told her. Well, not in cash anyway. I'd made sure he signed a contract before mixing his drink.

"So, it was a love affair."

I choked and began to laugh. "Love affair is bold. I'd say more of an...agreement. I had something he wanted, and he had something I wanted. No money was ever exchanged. If he was having a love affair, it wasn't with me."

"What was the thing you wanted?"

"*Simon Says Six: Six Six* green-lit. That's a few questions. Shouldn't I get one now?" I asked. As if they understood me, Cujo and Precious lifted their heads and shot me looks. I glared right back at them. Cujo gave me a low growl, and Evie stroked his coat until he snuggled back into her.

"Okay, but ask something less *which ex of yours do I murder first,* yeah?"

"Have you loved any of them?" A pit formed in my stomach, making me uncomfortable. I wasn't sure if I was ready to hear the answer.

Her smile fell, and her eyes glossed over.

"Love isn't really in the cards for me."

"Why not?"

She sighed deeply. "Why let someone fall for you and grow attached if you're just... Did he know it was you who dosed him?" she asked.

"He did. I was looking dead in his eyes as his heart stopped. I told him I'd done it for Lita. He knew, in the end, that karma had finally caught up with him."

My words settled around us, grounding us back to earth. I reached for her hand and squeezed.

"Thank you," she whispered, and I simply nodded.

The movie continued, and we didn't speak until it was almost over. It was as if we both had so much to ask still and so much we were holding back. She didn't want to tell me about her past, and I didn't want to tell her about mine.

After the movie, I took the popcorn to the kitchen and dumped the leftovers in the trash. Spinning back, I locked eyes with Evie and jumped. She'd startled me.

"I just don't want anyone to hurt or grieve for me when I'm gone," she blurted.

Pain and heartache slowly tugged at my chest. I shook my head and tossed the bowl into the sink. Leaning my back against the counter, I crossed my arms and shook my head.

"I think you're too late for that, Final Girl. I grieve every time."

CHAPTER 30

EVIE

The Liability

"Simon says sit the fuck down, bitch." I swung my fist, and Skye's harness jerked her backward.

In character as Riley, she fell onto the mat and caught herself on her elbows. She swung her head back up, hair fanning her face, breathing heavily, her filthy white undershirt stretched across her chest so tightly it was nearly transparent. She glared at me.

"This isn't over. It's never over."

I stalked over to her slowly, and she raised her leg, kicking. My harness tugged me hard, and I flew through the air. When I landed, I rolled onto all fours—and promptly vomited all over the set.

"Cut!" Dante groaned. "Evie, you okay?" He hopped off his chair and hurried over, along with the medical personnel, Skye, and a handful of others. I closed my eyes and fought back tears as my body kept forcing me to throw up.

"Oh jeez, she's gonna need a shower. Someone help her out of her harness while we clean and reset. Everyone else take lunch!"

Someone reached for my hair and held it back. Eventually, the retching stopped, and I sat back. A medic and Raissa, my assistant, lifted me gently off the ground and into a golf cart to take me back to my trailer.

"I just need my nausea meds," I told Dante as I passed him.

"Right. We'll talk with medical and see how we can prevent this next time. Go rest up, and I'll have wardrobe bring new clothes to your trailer."

I took my medicine as soon as I got to my trailer. They worked quickly, and I showered without assistance. My muscles screamed with overexertion from the full day of stunts. We'd been shooting the epic fight between Skye and my character for about six hours before I got sick.

I fell asleep in my towel and woke up to my phone ringing, indicating that lunch hour was done. I stood, pulling on the new clothes wardrobe had brought, and headed back to hair and makeup.

The rest of the day had changed to ensure I wouldn't get sick again. I wasn't on a rig anymore, and they even offered me a stunt double, but I politely declined.

"I'll keep my meds handy. Guys, it's really no big deal," I assured them. But it was nice to have them so concerned and willing to accommodate. "I've had chronic nausea forever. I just wasn't as prepared as I thought I'd be," I said after we wrapped for the day and was asked once again if I was okay. The moment Raissa arrived with the golf cart to drive me back to my trailer, I bolted for her.

"Speaking of prepared, tomorrow's schedule changed. We can't shoot any of Ronny and Lucy's scenes." Dante came over, a scowl on his face.

I stopped just short of my assistant and turned. "What? Why?" I hadn't had time to hang with Sebastian all week, so I'd been looking forward to tomorrow—despite it being our bedroom scenes. Those, I was nervous about.

"The intimacy coordinator got fired. Apparently, she lied on her résumé, and the studio lawyers aren't happy. They actually want to talk to you about it, if you're feeling up to it." His eyes narrowed, and he placed a polite hand on my upper arm.

"Sure. Take me over?" I asked Raissa. She nodded, and as I got into the golf cart, I called Antoinette. I gave her the rundown and asked her to come. Already on the lot, she agreed to meet me there. I was taken to the same offices I'd been interviewed by the police in when they'd found Glenn. Once inside, I was directed to a room filled with men I didn't recognize—and one I did.

Frederick Castle.

Lawyer to the stars.

"Evie Reyes, welcome. How are you? We heard about your sick spell this afternoon." They greeted me and attempted small talk about my filming experience while we waited for Antoinette to arrive. I tried not to stare directly at the next man on my kill list, but curiosity was getting the best of me. He was a conventionally attractive middle-aged man—trim, tan, dark hair full and styled. He wore an expensive, tailor-fitted suit and a look of total power. He exuded the energy of someone in charge, and the way everyone in the room looked to him every time someone spoke, I was right. He was the top dog here. Antoinette finally arrived and sat down beside me.

Frederick sat up straighter in his seat and cleared his throat. "Ms. Reyes, Ms. Gaines. As you may have heard, we were unfortunately forced to let go of our intimacy coordinator. The studio already has interviews lined up and should have her replacement by the end of the week," Frederick said. "We know it's an inconvenience to everyone involved in production, so we wanted to check in and make sure you were satisfied with your experience on set so far."

Antoinette crossed her arms and snorted loudly. "He wants to know if we are going to sue them for letting someone unqualified do your intimacy coaching—because of their lack of due diligence."

"Sue?" I did a double take.

"W-Well—" One of the men flanking Frederick started to stumble over his words.

"Do you want to sue them, Evie? If so, we need to walk out right now," Antoinette, ever my strongest advocate, spoke over him.

I shook my head. "No, I don't think so. We didn't really do

anything yet."

You know, except that one time during our chemistry test when Sebastian went too far, and I let him eat me out in front of everyone in the room.

I wondered for a moment if they had all known we weren't faking. Had they all gotten off on it? I shuddered at the thought.

"Well then, if that's settled, we'd like to get your signature." Frederick pulled his briefcase onto the table and popped it open, bringing out a packet. "This just confirms that you are aware of what was discovered, how it was handled, and that you are not pursuing legal action."

They had us both sign the papers, and then we were released. We stood, and the rest of the room joined us. Arms were thrust out, and one by one we started down the line, shaking hands. When I reached Frederick, he gripped me tight, holding me in place.

"I've been waiting a long time to formally meet you, Ms. Reyes." He grinned, but the smile didn't reach his cold, dead eyes.

I stared, memorizing every line in his face.

Was this the man who fathered me?

"You have?" I forced back my nerves.

He continued to grip my hand. "Oh yes. I was close to your mother. Many of us were. She was a legend, a real Final Girl. And it's lovely to see you following in her footsteps. Good for you."

My smile fell. *Why did that feel like a threat?*

"Right." I ripped my hand back. "Thanks. She was great."

"She really was. We all used to hang out back in the day. We had a card game once a month. Mike Thornton, Jason Dourif, and Lita, of course. Do you remember any of them?"

He didn't take his eyes off me, and it was then, in that moment, I knew he knew. Everything he'd said was calculated. He was goading me. I was missing something. How much did he know? I gave him a tight smile and lifted my shoulders.

"Sorry, I don't."

"But didn't you date Glenn, Mike's son?" he pushed.

I cocked my head to the side. "Oh, not really. We just flirted some. He went missing before we could—"

"Evie, let's go." Antoinette, her agent hat on, put her hands on my shoulders and directed me to the door. "If there's anything else you'd like to say to my client, email me," she said firmly.

Frederick's gaze bounced from Antoinette to me.

"You're very protective of your client. That's the sign of a good agent." He smiled tightly.

"Yes, well, it's my job to keep her safe," Antoinette snapped back.

"Sure, of course." He smirked, and his eyes grew distant for a moment before snapping his attention back to me. "Maybe we'll see you at a card game sometime!" Frederick called as she shoved me out the door.

"What a creep," Antoinette muttered. "He must have had the hots for your mom back in the day. He was looking at you like he wanted to eat you." She shuddered. "Don't be alone with him, ever," she warned.

"You don't have to tell me twice," I muttered.

Returning to my trailer, I got a text from Sebastian.

Psycho Killer

Did you hear about the schedule change?

I did. Bummer. I wanted to hang.

What are you doing tonight?

He typed, stopped, and then started typing again.

Psycho Killer

I was voluntold to come to a poker game.

A chill went down my spine, and I stared at the phone, reading the words multiple times before replying.

Poker game? With who?

Psycho Killer

Guess.

Fear sank deep into my belly, and I steeled myself. There was no way he was going alone. Antoinette's warning flashed in my brain, and I huffed, realizing how quickly I'd abandoned the advice. I typed a reply.

I'm coming with.

She said not to be alone with him. Technically, I wasn't.

CHAPTER 31 SEBASTIAN

The Deal

The poker table.

"Sit down, Shaw." Fred stared me down from across the table, his friends snickering and hiding grins behind their cards. "Let's play a game."

Steeling my nerves, I pulled the chair out and took my seat at the table. A server in a tuxedo came to take my drink order.

"Whiskey on ice, please," I told him.

"Whiskey on ice." Fred whistled. "I'll take one of those too, Tobin."

I cleared my throat and reached forward, grabbing a cigar from the mahogany box in the center, next to the pot of chips. I glanced around the circle, taking in all my opponents. I recognized most of them because they worked in film.

Ben Willis, Seth Brundle, Jack Sawyer. All bastards. There were two men I didn't recognize but was introduced to quickly. I nodded and mumbled hello to them.

"Frank Cotton, legal," the man beside me with hair plugs said, offering me a lighter.

"Thanks, and I don't think we've ever met," I said to the man whose hair was styled with a giant wave and a smile too fake and too large.

"Christian Hughes, News Channel 9."

I put the lit cigar in my mouth and tried to focus on my breathing. I could not let them see how fucking nervous I was.

"Now!" Frederick clapped his hands. "Let's get back to the game. Sebastian, what's your buy-in?"

"What's the minimum for the table?" I asked, not looking him in the eye.

The table chuckled. Fred snickered. "Five, but each game is one."

Five thousand dollars? I'd been to these before, and each table was different, but they were never this high. I usually stuck to the lower tables because I was a shit poker player. I looked up and saw the men staring at me, daring me to object. I pulled the cigar from my mouth, licked my lips, and rolled my eyes.

"Give me twenty."

Twenty thousand was no drop in the bucket for me. I lived comfortably, and with each film I made, I was paid more than the last. Once I got paid for *Simon Says Six: Six Six*, twenty thousand would be nothing. There were murmurs around the table as Fred smirked and counted the chips, sliding them over.

"Good luck, kid."

I'd need it. I hardly remembered the rules. But I hadn't really been invited to play cards. I was here for them to see what I knew. And I was here to do the same. Tobin brought us our drinks, and Fred grabbed the deck to shuffle and deal.

Every few seconds, I fought the urge to flick my gaze back to where Evie sat on the other side of the room. I hadn't wanted her to come, but she'd insisted. She didn't realize what she'd done by coming, and I couldn't tell her otherwise.

"So, who's the hottie?" Brundle, a special effects guy, asked. "Your sister?" He raised his eyebrows in a hopeful way.

One by one, everyone put their chips in. I tossed chips totaling one thousand into the pile. Fred then dealt us our hands.

"No. She's my girlfriend." I shot him a glare as I lifted my cards. Seven of diamonds and two of spades.

Fuck. These cards were bad. I stretched my neck to see the three cards in front of Fred. I was going to lose real fucking quick.

I folded the first round, watching as Ben Willis, a boat handler for one of the studios, took the pot. We went again. This time I got the three of hearts and the eight of diamonds.

"You look like you're starting to sweat over there, Shaw," Fred mocked as he flipped over his three cards. I checked, and the game continued—with me losing.

"I'm a little rusty," I admitted. "It's not often I have free time to sit and relax with people like yourselves."

"Yes, you are a busy guy, aren't you?" he muttered, his lip curling in the beginnings of a snarl.

"You're working on the newest *Simon Says*, aren't you?" Christian asked.

I glanced over at the blond-haired, blue-eyed man. I remembered him. We were often up for similar roles, but I always managed to land them over him. Seeing as he'd landed a gig on the news, he must have given up on stardom. He was playing nice now, but I knew just how much of a bitter ass he was.

"*Six Six Six*," I responded. "They're paying me very well for it."

"Good. That means you can stay here all night," Fred quipped, and the table laughed. "Although if you run out of cash, we can make arrangements for other forms of payment."

The circle quieted as they looked at me. I chewed the inside of my cheek in annoyance. Word had spread about me, it seemed.

I shrugged and knocked the cherry off my cigar into an ashtray. "That's when the real fun starts, doesn't it? You'd been playing for a while before I got here—is this money just to humor me?"

A standoff was happening between Fred and me. I stared at him across the table, waiting for him to expose the real thing they gambled with. Everyone knew what these games were. Fred Castle didn't play for money. He played for information.

"Fair enough. You want to bet something else? What do you have? Any suggestions for what Sebastian Shaw could offer the table?" Fred sat back, putting his hands behind his head.

"What about a recommendation?" Christian leaned in. "I know you're friends with Susan McAlester. She's starting auditions for her next shark movie. Can you get me an audition?"

I shrugged. That was easy. "Sure, next game."

I lost the second round of poker, and the real game began with the third. I wagered a call to my friend, and everyone else made similar bets, along with a few who just offered money. I lost for the third time. But then, as the familiarity of the game came back to me, I had a stroke of good luck. I'd also stopped drinking after my first glass, while the others kept pounding their alcohol and offering each other various unmarked pills. Everyone was having a damn good time—except Fred and me.

He was only drinking when I was.

"This is getting kind of boring, don't you think?" Fred asked after a solid half hour of me winning.

I glanced at my watch. It'd been about two hours since we got here. I'd glanced over at Evie a time or two. She was relaxing and looked all right, with her lemon drop martini.

"How so? I could go all night."

"I'm sure you could. You've collected quite a few things tonight, haven't you, Shaw? Three months with a dietician, a custom costume from Brundle, how much money?"

"I haven't counted." I lifted my drink, and he did the same. I set it down without drinking, and so did he.

"Tell me why you're really here."

The table grew quiet. All eyes were on me, then Fred, then me.

"Do you really want me to tell the table?" I raised an eyebrow.

"We're all friends here." Fred grinned. "If you want something, just ask."

I cocked my head to the side. Did I dare? It was what I'd come for in the first place. However, just saying it aloud could get me killed. I glanced back at Evie.

I had to try. For her.

Clearing my throat, I looked back at Fred. "I want to know what you know about Lita Reyes's murder."

The table stopped all noise.

A slow, forced smile slid over Frederick's lips. "Lita Reyes wasn't murdered. That's a pretty bold statement."

"What's bold is you saying she wasn't."

I had him cornered.

"Fine. But I want something from you. If you want details about something you clearly know nothing about, you're going to have to bet something worth it. No phone calls, no autographs, no fucking charity appearances. I want something good."

The blood drained from my face as an evil, unsettling smile curled upward on his.

"You want Lita? I want Evie."

I shoved my chair back, jumping up. The two men beside me grabbed my arms, holding me back from launching over the table.

"What do you say? Care to place a bet? If you win, I'll tell you everything I know about Lita Reyes's untimely end. If I win, I want a night with your girlfriend. How confident are you in your poker skills?"

I wasn't at all.

But I'd had a good streak.

"Just you and me." I shrugged the men off and sat back down.

Fred offered the cards to Christian beside him and nodded. Christian took the cards and began to shuffle them to deal.

"Just you and me."

I sat there in stony silence as the cards were dealt. I lifted my cards—nine and ten of spades. Relief tried to creep in, but I wasn't out of the water yet. Christian flipped over a jack, queen, and king.

Holy shit. I forced myself not to react to my luck. I glanced at Fred and only saw the same irritated look on his face.

Christian flipped the next card, a two of diamonds.

And then, the fifth. An ace.

I had a flush.

I had a fucking flush.

I set my cards down and lifted my head to look at Fred. He saw my cards, and then he laughed.

He laughed.

Instantly, all confidence and hope disappeared. Fred laid his cards down, revealing his royal flush.

No. No, this couldn't be happening.

I stood up again, my chair clattering to the floor.

The table cheered and laughed at my misfortune. What had I done? Evie—I couldn't. Oh no.

Fred stood, straightening his suit. Reaching behind him, he removed a gun from his belt, handing it to Christian.

"Good game, Shaw. I see you didn't expect to lose. I didn't really expect to win, either. And for that, I'm feeling a little... compassionate. Clearly, you were just trying to help a grieving daughter. I'll give you a choice."

I clenched my fists, chest heaving. There were no real choices here.

Fred smiled. "I can take her upstairs now and fuck her in the privacy of my bedroom. Or you can bring her over to the table and force her onto her knees in front of this crowd."

"Fuck you!" I spat. "She's not blowing you or fucking you."

"Fine, I don't care. I fucked my maid before my guests arrived tonight. This isn't about sex. It's about knowing your place. Bring her over, Sebastian. Now that I think about it, it's best you show her just where her place is. On her knees."

CHAPTER 32

EVIE

The Power Mixer

"I'd really rather you not." Sebastian groaned when he opened his front door and saw me on the porch, bouncing on the heels of my boots.

I pushed inside and was welcomed by the dogs. I crouched down to soak in their affection.

"I don't care. I need to see who he hangs out with—AKA, who is guarding him."

"Do you plan on killing them too?" he scoffed, walking past me after shutting the door. "This isn't *Kill Bill*."

"If I have to. Following orders isn't a valid excuse to do bad things." I stood and followed him through the house. He went right up to his room and began removing his clothes.

"If you're coming, you can't wear that." He looked me up and down as he stood in his tight boxers and socks.

"I didn't bring anything else." I raised my arms and looked in the wall mirror behind him. I didn't think I looked terrible. I was in my best jeans, a black blouse, and a leather jacket. "This will have to work."

"Yeah, it won't, though. I've been to these. There's a dress code. Call your assistant and ask her to bring you a short dress with a low neckline and tight waist." He walked into his closet, and I—slightly salty—reached for my phone and shot a text to

Raissa with my size, Sebastian's address, and told her to bill me.

He came out a moment later in an all-black suit. He'd styled back his hair with gel, creating a look that had me clenching my thighs and focusing on my breathing. He was stunningly handsome.

"I see. This is just for a simple poker night?"

He turned to look at himself in a nearby mirror and adjusted his jacket. "There's no such thing as a simple poker night in Hollywood, Final Girl. You'll see. Just know, you're not going to like it."

I tried to get more out of him, but he didn't want to elaborate. Anytime he replied to a question, it was purposefully vague.

Raissa was at the door in an hour with three different dress options and heels. I thanked her and brought them in for Sebastian to assist me in deciding.

"The puffy one and get rid of the boots." He pointed to the shortest dress with the deepest neckline.

I reluctantly put it on, along with the heels that went with it. The neckline plunged nearly to my belly button, and the skirt barely covered my ass. I wasn't thrilled, but it was all black and the softest material of the three. I joined Sebastian downstairs and looped my arm through his.

"Let's go. How far away does he live?" I asked as we stepped outside.

Sebastian rubbed the back of his neck and scrunched up his nose. We walked down the driveway and took a left.

"Here." He pointed to the estate right next door. I stopped short and looked up at the grand, three-story mansion. It was smaller than Sebastian's but was farther back from the street, and his front yard was full of bushes shaped like animals. In the dark, the cute little bunny rabbit trees were almost menacing.

"Are you serious? Why didn't you tell me?" I demanded. "I could have already killed him!"

"Beep beep, Ritchie!" he hissed. "I didn't tell you because I don't want my property value to go down. Now, I'm not going to let you go in there fisting your fucking knives like you're in *Planet Terror* or something. You need to keep your shit together. Our time will come. You cannot go in there knives drawn. Understand?"

I rolled my eyes. While I had put my knives in the bralette of my dress in case the situation came up, I knew something like that wasn't reasonable for survival. I still had four men on my list.

"Fine."

"Groovy." He took my arm, and we finished the brief journey to the house next door.

We were greeted by a woman in a short French maid costume. Sebastian shot me an eye roll as she took us through Frederick's house and down to the basement, where a party was already underway. It was designed as a modern speakeasy. There was an impressive bar on the back wall with a bartender in a tuxedo. To the right were several poker tables, with games already underway. Closer to the bar was a lounge area, where women dressed like me were sitting with drinks, socializing. The lighting was dim, and the music was loud enough to be heard, but not so loud that you had to yell. Smoke filled the room, creating a thick fog. I breathed in the familiar scent of cigars, unable to get away from it. A waiter greeted us, offering drinks and an escort to the poker table.

"Shaw!" Frederick—now in a suit similar to Sebastian's, only light gray—stood and greeted us. "Take a seat," he said, the cigar in his mouth bobbing as he spoke.

Sebastian let go of my arm. A slither of panic came up my throat as I realized there was only one seat at the table.

"Evie, go socialize with the other women," Sebastian said softly, resting his hand on my lower back, urging me forward.

"What?" My gaze shot to the women on the other side of the room. Panic shot up my spine at the thought of being pulled from him. "No. I want to stay with you."

"Go. I'll be back after a few rounds." He gently pushed me away, and reluctantly, I nodded and stormed off.

The women barely looked up from their drinks and conversation when I joined them, and when I finished my blueberry lemon drop, I was given another one right away. They were strong. After I'd drained the second, I felt a little dizzy.

I glanced over at the table. There was so much smoke, I couldn't see them well. The only indication that we were all still in the same room was the laughter and occasional cheers of wins and groans of losses coming from the poker tables. I wasn't sure how much time had passed before Sebastian came for me, his face grim.

Something wasn't right.

I stood and wobbled on my heels.

"What's wrong?" I asked as he practically dragged me to the table.

"Welcome back, Evelyn Reyes, our guest of honor!" Frederick greeted me again, warmly.

Guest of honor? I looked at Sebastian, but he refused to meet my eyes.

"What's going on?"

"Well, you see, sweetie, we invited your boyfriend here because we have reason to believe he knows something about our late friends, Mike and Jason. He swears he doesn't."

"It puts the lotion in the basket," Sebastian murmured so low I almost didn't hear.

I flicked my gaze back to the table, where Frederick was staring at us, his eyes lowered to slits.

"What was that, Shaw?"

"I said I was sorry," he said loudly.

Sorry? For what? I was confused and growing scared. I tried to back away, but Sebastian gripped my wrist tightly.

"I warned you that sitting at my table was a risky game. Take your loss," Frederick demanded.

A bolt of unadulterated terror ran through me as I realized all the men at the table were looking at me with wide, hungry eyes.

"It does this whenever it's told," Sebastian finished the quote. In our secret language, he was telling me to follow along with whatever he was about to do. But something in my gut said it wasn't going to be good. He cleared his throat and spoke louder.

"Get on your knees, slut."

For a moment, my mind went blank, and I looked up at him. What the fuck?

"Did you not hear me?" Sebastian gripped my shoulder and shoved me to my knees.

The table erupted in laughter.

"Sebastian." I fought to stand back up, but he held my head firmly in his palms. My face flamed in embarrassment. What the hell was going on?

"Consider this number two," he said as his hands went to his belt buckle.

I tried to pull back, but he reached out and fisted my hair, holding me in place. "I'm your number-one fan," he murmured.

I looked up at him. His eyes were shiny and full of shame as he pulled his erect cock out of his jeans. Hot, heavy tears spilled from my eyes as I realized what he wanted me to do. He'd been giving me signs the whole time.

"*It puts the lotion in the basket.*" Just go with it.

"*Consider this number two.*" He was going to use his second free use.

"*I'm your number-one fan.*" A line from *Misery*. It was his apology.

I started hyperventilating as he shoved me toward his groin. I reached my hands out and pushed against him, trying to get away, but he slid his hand down and gripped my neck, squeezing to the point of pain. I cried out, and he shoved his cock into my mouth. I gagged, which elicited laughter and cheers from the men at the table. My attention shifted to them briefly, and that's when I saw the gun pointing at Sebastian's back.

He wasn't doing this to be cruel. He'd been given no choice.

Sebastian forcefully moved my head back and forth, and I realized that the more I fought, the worse it would be for both of us. It was clear that Sebastian wasn't jumping to do this. He'd been told to. Was it for Fred to prove his dominance? Was it meant to degrade me and shame Sebastian?

I closed my eyes and focused on Sebastian's erection plunging in and out of my mouth, pushing the loud room out of my mind.

I wasn't going to let Frederick Castle win whatever game he was playing.

I shifted my thoughts as I worked my tongue, the heat slowly fading from my face. Instead of this room of laughing men, we were somewhere else, somewhere better, and I was enjoying this. I had volunteered to give him pleasure, and soon my mouth relaxed enough to perform a blowjob worth having. I ran my tongue along his length, sucking and using my teeth ever so lightly.

This was a test, and it very well could be life or death. They needed to trust Sebastian, and if degrading me like they'd done my mother was the way to gain their trust, so be it. I didn't know why, but I had a feeling this wasn't Sebastian's first time in this scenario either. That's why he knew just what to do to get it over with.

He'd tried warning me, but I hadn't wanted to listen.

As I continued to suck and lick his cock, I felt my body reacting to it all. I fought the urge to reach down and satisfy myself. I was almost sure the alcohol I'd been fed all night had assisted in this, and once it was over, I'd spend the night replaying it all, wondering who this person enjoying having an audience was. But for now, in this moment, I let myself revel in the fact that I was sucking Sebastian's cock, and I was sure the men watching were jealous.

In another lifetime, I would have loved for this to be our life. We could be married, with our dogs, and every night would be filled with carnal pleasures, finished with horror movies and cuddling. But that wasn't the life I had. The life I had now was one where I was sucking him off in front of a room of perverted, middle-aged men who wanted to kill him. One of which might be my father.

Suddenly his breathing hitched, and he pushed my head closer until my lips touched his base and he found the back of my throat. With a loud groan, he came, shooting hot jets of cum into my throat. I took every drop and then fell back onto my ass.

Frederick came around the table and petted my hair. I jumped away, but that only made him laugh. He patted my shoulder and walked back to his men.

"Good girl. Just like your mother."

CHAPTER 33 SEBASTIAN

Special Consideration

"Don't fucking touch her."

Frederick pulled back, a look of surprise on his face. "What, now you've got a spine? Zip your pants up and get back to the fucking table."

I looked from him to Evie. She didn't know what had gone down just a few minutes before. I wished I could tell her. I'd tried to get information for us, but I was a shit gambler. Shaking my head, I leaned down and lifted Evie off her knees.

"I need to take her to the bathroom."

I was directed to the toilets and stood outside while Evie cleaned herself up. This part of the basement was down a short hall and relatively quiet. The air was cold and cleaner, not having the smoke directly around.

I—I couldn't believe it. I was shocked I'd remained hard the entire time. I'd been so nervous and disgusted and horrified and... I hadn't wanted to do it, but my body betrayed me. Having Evie's full, rosy lips around me was heaven, but the circumstances around it were pure hell. Fred was right. I was just like them. I was a fucking asshole.

I should have known better than to be so cocky at the table. If it weren't for the gun pointed at me from behind, I would have taken Evie and run. But I hadn't been able to communicate the entirety of our situation, and guilt was twisting my insides.

A figure came down the hall toward me, but I didn't look up. I was too ashamed.

"Good job, Shaw." Fred nodded. "Tame that bitch now before she gets out of hand like her fucking whore mother."

I clenched my fists at my sides, forcing myself not to turn and swing on him.

"There's a hierarchy in Hollywood. You've got your executives, your producers, your heads of casting and marketing and whatever else. And then, at the very bottom, is you. You're just a pretty face that can read a fucking script, Sebastian.

"You learned that early. We tried to teach Lita. She thought she was higher on the food chain than she was. She thought her voice had weight and she could make decisions and calls on things she had no knowledge of. She wanted to be in charge, but no matter how many times she was warned, it never got through her head. Pretty people don't control this place. We do." He pointed at himself.

"The sooner Evie learns, the better things will be. You did good, kid." He slapped my shoulder and turned to go back to the main room. "Oh, and Sebastian."

I straightened and turned to face him. "What?" I said through gritted teeth.

"We know." He didn't need to finish the statement. I heard him loud and clear. "And we'll make sure the police can't even identify that little bitch's body if she tries anything else. I'll rip her fucking throat open with how hard I use it before her body gets dumped."

"Is that a real threat?" I snarled, leaning toward him.

Fred stopped smirking and nodded. He furrowed his brow, and his lips settled into a grim line. "Yes, Sebastian, it is."

I shook my head, grimacing. "You'd make your possible daughter fuck you? You're sicker than I thought."

Castle's brows rose, the surprise that I knew this nugget of knowledge evident on his face. "You don't know what you're talking about."

"Oh, I think I do. Your friend Dourif sang like a bird before Evie slit his throat." I stepped forward. "He told us everything. The gang rape, the murder, that one of you is Evie's biological father. All of it. Evie doesn't care. She wants you all dead."

Fred's eyes had widened, but the more I continued, the more relaxed his face grew, returning to its cold, demanding expression. "Is that so? I see why you went all in. Well, she better watch herself. She already knows what we can do. She's lucky you were here tonight to fight for her. None of us would have been so nice." He pointed at me, and I almost snatched his finger and snapped it in half.

"Why don't you come over this weekend? We can talk all about this possible paternity and all that. I just redid my hot tub. Bring your girl again," he said, his eyes darting to the bathroom door behind me.

"Why? If you think you know something, why not end it now?"

He snickered. "I like a good back-and-forth."

He left, and I continued waiting patiently for Evie. After another five minutes, I grew concerned and walked into the bathroom. My gaze went straight to the open window above a small table.

I hurried to climb the table and crawl out to find her.

"Evie!" I called as I got to my feet in the grass. Looking around, I found myself on the side of Frederick's yard. I yelled her name again and hurried to the front. I found her stumbling back to my house, wobbling on her heels, hair knotted and wild from where I'd yanked on it.

"Evie!"

She didn't look back.

"Evie, please! Talk to me."

"The power of Christ compels you," she groaned as I caught up to her.

"Evie..." I sighed. "I was watching *The Exorcist*," I tried, but she sniffled loudly.

"Don't. Sebastian, you—" She put her hand up, and I stopped trying to talk.

I reached her as she made it to my door, and I grabbed her shoulders, spinning her around and gripping her tightly.

"Evie, I'm so sorry. I had to. They were going to..." I didn't want to tell her what happened at the table. I didn't want to scare her worse than I was sure she already was.

"To what? Force me to—"

"Yes!" I shouted over her.

She flinched. Sighing, I reached into my pocket and unlocked the door, pushing her gently inside and locking it behind us. I turned to her. "It was either me or one of them. They forced me to place you as my bet."

"Why?"

The ins and outs of this world, the politics of it all, were so disgusting and vile that I struggled to get the words out. If I told her that I'd tried to get more information about Lita out of them, would she feel guilty? I couldn't make her feel worse than she already felt, so I shoved it down.

Evie saw my struggle and shook her head. She sniffled again and wiped her tears. "It doesn't matter. It's done. Like you said, you used your second free use...whatever. I just want to go to bed. Where's my phone?" she asked, patting her dress.

"You're not spending the night alone," I insisted. "Stay here."

"Why, so you can do it again?" she snapped.

It was like I'd been punched in the stomach. Did she really think I'd wanted to do that?

I'd been a part of three murders and felt nothing, but the very idea that I'd take glee in what just happened next door? I wasn't a fucking monster. Those men had deserved it. Evie didn't.

"Evie, I would never..." I gulped. Maybe I was a monster. My defenses disintegrated, and guilt swarmed me. What I'd done to her in that basement hadn't been by choice, but I couldn't explain that to her in a way that would paint me as the hero. I was no hero.

I was a fucking coward. "Please, it's not safe for you to go."

Her shoulders fell in defeat. "Fine, but I need to be alone, please."

I nodded and left her in the foyer, going upstairs to retrieve one of my shirts for her to sleep in. I left it on the bed in the guest room across from mine, then went to my room, where I cried into my hands.

What had I done?

And why had I found some of it so hot?

There was deep shame in my soul for having come. I should have pretended, forced my cock flaccid. Something. My body was all-too willing to let her suck me off in front of that room.

I was trapped inside my head until I heard the shower turn on in the guest room. There was a moment or two of water pouring onto the tile—then came a tortured cry.

I bolted across the hall, my feet moving faster than my brain. I threw the bathroom door open and found Evie naked, crumped at the bottom of the shower. I stepped inside, fully clothed, and sat down with her. Pulling her into my arms, I rocked as she sobbed against me. I didn't speak or try to soothe her in any way past holding her. What could I say? Sorry for forcing myself on her wasn't going to cut it. But the fact that she didn't push me away now told me more than any words could.

The hot water eventually turned cold, and only when her teeth began to chatter did I lean up and turn the faucet off. I helped her to her feet, then scooped her into my arms, cradling her out of the shower. I took her to the bed and rushed to cover her with a towel. She didn't look my way as she moved into the fetal position. I peeled off my wet clothes, leaving briefly to get dry boxers, and then lay beside her, pulling her into my embrace.

"Evie..."

"Beep beep, Ritchie." The words came out strained and cracked from the sobs in the shower.

I did as told and shut my mouth, holding her until she fell asleep. Eventually, my conscience let me do the same, but before I did, I vowed that now, this wasn't just revenge for her mother. I was on a path to avenge Evie as well, and maybe, in the deepest roots of my psyche that I'd pushed down for no one to ever uncover, I was going to do this for me as well.

Lita wasn't the only one who'd been used and abused by Hollywood. There was a price for fame, and day by day, I was realizing that it wasn't worth it. I'd do anything to simply live a quiet life with Evie. Maybe, after this was over, I'd leave all of this behind with her.

But not yet. We had a task to finish.

This weekend, at Fred's little hot tub party, he was as good as dead. Property values be damned.

CHAPTER 34 SEBASTIAN

The Lawyer

Bryce stopped by my trailer after we wrapped for the day. "What are you doing tonight? Skye wants us all to hang out."

I looked up from my phone.

"Actually, I was *invited*," I said, using air quotes, "to my neighbor's place."

"Invited?"

"Yeah, I can't say no. You know how it goes."

I'd just gotten a reminder text from Frederick Castle, in fact. He'd made it clear that my attendance wasn't an option.

"Who's your neighbor? A new director?" Bryce raised an eyebrow.

While he didn't know exact details, he knew some about how I'd made my way in this town.

I shook my head. "Nothing like that. I think those days are behind me now."

Evie, smiling and laughing on my couch, flashed through my mind briefly, warming my chest.

"He's a lawyer for the studio. He just wants to push his foot on my neck a little. Make sure I know my place."

Bryce leaned on the counter in my mini-kitchen and crossed his arms. "That's what they all say, ain't it? Know your place?"

"You're not wrong," I admitted. "But I can't miss this."

"Fine, Skye and I will go with you. Bring Evie too."

"I don't think this is a good idea," I warned.

He rolled his eyes, so I clarified. "This is a man on Evie's list. I'm going to take care of it."

He took in my words, nodding and pursing his lips. "Even more reason to have company. Let me cancel on Skye." Pulling out his phone, he shot off a text to her. However, whatever he sent her must not have been clear enough, because when I pulled up to Evie's to pick her up, Skye was there.

"What are you doing here?" I said, sharper than I'd meant to.

"Bryce canceled on me, so I drove over to see what Evie was doing." She shrugged. I turned to Evie, but she was looking away guiltily. She always had a hard time telling Skye no. Sighing heavily, I tried to work out everything in my head as we drove back to my place, but there really was no good way to do this.

It was looking like the lawyer would live to fight another day.

By evening, the four of us were walking to Fred's, swimsuits on and towels slung over our arms. I held Evie's hand firmly, making sure she knew I would not allow a repeat of last time we'd come here. All week, our chemistry had been off. We hardly spoke, until our emotions exploded on set at the end of the week, and we talked about what had happened at the poker game. Our conversation continued after work and well into the night. We talked about body betrayal, both hers and mine. I explained how everything transpired that night and how it led to me pushing her to her knees. While I wasn't entirely sure what was going on in her head, she seemed to welcome me back into her orbit, but at a distance.

Fred's French maid welcomed us in, confusion on her face as she saw my party. She took us around back, and Fred gave us all the same look as he eyed us in a line. "Evie, Bryce..."

"Skye," I said when he didn't recognize the last person in our little group. "You said in your text you wanted to see the star of the movie. Well, it's a collective effort. All of us, I'd say, are the stars."

"Your paychecks would say otherwise," Fred muttered but

invited us farther into his backyard. "I'd only planned for you and me, but luckily I always keep my bar stocked. Welcome to my home. Gwen, drinks!" he shouted at his housemaid. Stripping off his robe, he dropped it where he stood and strode to the pool, where he dove into the water and popped back up. He climbed out and went straight to the hot tub. "Come on, join me!" He smiled.

I raked my gaze across his yard, comparing it to my own. It was pretty average for this neighborhood. A large pool with a hot tub nearby, very little grass, with concrete covering most of the property. To the right was a large outdoor bar decorated like a cheesy tiki shack.

I squeezed Evie's hand and dropped it so that I could set our towels down and slide my shoes off. I wore loose black shorts that went to my knees. Bryce kept the cowboy hat and had chosen navy shorts that were so tight, I saw his frank and both beans. Skye had on a pink-and-green bikini that could be undone with one tug of a string, apparently she kept one in her car just in case. Evie had unintentionally matched me, with a black two-piece. Her swimsuit had bikini bottoms, but the top was a skin-tight long-sleeved crop top that I found ten times sexier than the bikini Skye wore. We joined Fred, and a moment later, music began playing from speakers around the yard.

"So, how is everyone? Did you work hard this week making the biggest movie of next year?" Fred asked warmly, but his eye twitched as he forced the small talk. He'd been thrown off by all of us, and it showed.

We chatted, and Bryce, ever the entertainer, took charge of the conversation. If I didn't know exactly why I'd been brought here, I would think Fred was a decent guy.

An hour into our evening, Fred climbed out of the hot tub and called for me to join him at the bar. He went around the counter and prepared us all fresh cocktails.

"I think your plan backfired, Shaw," he said with a smile.

"What plan?" I glanced back at my friends. They'd climbed out of the hot tub too, and the girls were lounging on the beach chairs. Bryce popped up behind me, dropping his hand on my shoulder and leaning over the bar.

"Where's your can, Castle?"

"My bathroom? It's inside, right past the kitchen. My maid went home for the night, but just turn on the lights. You'll find it," Fred told him, then he turned back to me after Bryce had disappeared into the house.

"Your plan to surround yourself with witnesses. Did you think I'd kill you tonight?"

I hadn't ruled it out. Why else would he have wanted to get me and Evie here alone? I'd confessed that I knew what he and his friends had done to Lita. He couldn't just let that information get out.

My thoughts must have shown on my face, because he snickered and slid my drink to me.

"I did consider it, but this movie is costing a lot, and your death would make many of my friends, and myself, lose quite a bit of money. So, for now, you live another day." He lifted his drink, expecting me to toast.

I did so, bitterly.

He laughed after taking a sip. "Consider this a probation period. You have until the movie wraps. After that, we'll decide what we want to do with you."

He took the rest of the drinks, put them on a tray, and carried them to the girls. Leaving his drink by the hot tub, he dove into the pool. I joined him this time, and soon Evie and Skye left their chairs and stepped into the cooler water.

Just as night started to fall, Bryce returned and cannonballed.

"'Bout fucking time," Fred muttered when Bryce's head popped out of the water. "You clog my toilet or something?"

Bryce snickered. "Got a little lost is all. I like the farmhouse look you've got going in your kitchen."

"I actually need to redecorate. That kitchen was my second wife's doing. She was all about that live, laugh, love bullshit."

As the night went on, I noticed Bryce was really schmoozing

him, and I wondered if he had an ulterior motive for coming tonight. He was feeding Fred drink after drink and matching him sip for sip. Only, something was off. I knew Bryce almost as well as I knew myself, and he could hold his liquor.

He was faking being drunk.

Unsure and uneasy, I drifted to the pool chairs, and Skye and Evie joined me. We drank and enjoyed the music, while Bryce and Fred hung out loudly in the hot tub.

"Why don't you join us, Evie, Sebastian?" Bryce called out.

Fred, completely shit-faced, huffed.

"She's not coming anywhere near me. She's mad at me for fucking her mother." Fred reached for his drink and laughed. "And if that's the case, she's got to be mad at half this fucking town."

Evie sat up, and I reached for her hand, squeezing it tight.

"Beep beep, Ritchie," I muttered.

She inhaled deeply and sat back, forcing herself not to engage.

"Sorry, it's just a fact. Lita Reyes was Hollywood's mattress. She kept kneepads in her purse."

"Evie, Skye!" Bryce snapped his fingers and looked directly at me. All pretense of drunkenness was gone from his eyes.

I sat up, curious.

"Go make us a couple of drinks, will ya?"

"Fuck you, Bryce," Skye said, settling back in her seat.

"Fine, fine." Bryce climbed out of the hot tub, puffed his chest, and strode over to the bar. He ducked down and came back up. "You got an extension cord, Castle?"

"Yeah, here!" Fred popped out of the hot tub just long enough to grab an extension cord and toss it to Bryce.

Bryce came back over, took it, and tugged it all the way to the bar, plugging in a blender.

"Oh, shit, I gotta go piss," Bryce said suddenly, then ran inside.

Fred turned his attention to us again. "I think you're just a little out of your depth, sweetie. Sure, you got Mike and Jason. They were easy to pick off. Jason was a dumb fuck, and Mike—

well, you knew Mike, didn't you, Shaw?" He snickered.

I remained silent, but I couldn't control my expression. My nostrils flared as I shot daggers with my eyes. Fred glanced from me to Evie. And when I did as well, I saw a look of confusion on Evie's face.

"I guess Lita wasn't the only one keeping secrets from you, then," he said to Evie.

He kept talking, and out of the corner of my eye, I saw Bryce slip back outside, something in his hands.

"What do you mean, secrets? I know one of you might be my father." Evie sat up.

"Is that what she told you? She was always so full of it. She knew who'd knocked her up. It sure as hell wasn't me. I got snipped two weeks after moving to this godforsaken town. She knew that. Let me guess, was she raped, too? That bitch was a willing participant every single time, of which there were many. Many, many times." He sat back against the wall of the hot tub. "Lita had a magic pussy—kind of like your boyfriend, Evie. They call it something different in that community..."

A shadow caught my eye, and I flicked my gaze behind Fred, who was still rambling. I tried not to react as Bryce slowly walked toward the hot tub, a toaster in his hands.

It was plugged into the extension cord.

"Pick up your feet." I kept my voice calm but firm.

Skye and Evie looked at me, confused, but quickly pulled their knees up to their chests.

"What was that saying all over your kitchen again?" Bryce asked.

Fred spun around, startled. "Live, laugh—"

Bryce lifted the appliance over his head and threw it into the tub, cutting him off.

There was a loud pop, a bright flash of electricity, and Fred stiffened as the shock ran through his body. He cried out, but it was cut off in an instant. His eyes rolled into the back of his head, and then slowly, he fell face-first into the water. I leaned over to get a better look. It had only been moments, but his body was already ashen. The bubbles from the hot tub continued to roll around him, the electricity flickering under the water.

Silence fell over the yard as we stared in horror at Bryce—who was beaming proudly.

"Toaster bath."

CHAPTER 35 EVIE

The Patch Job

The sound of Skye drawing in a deep breath caused me to bolt upright and throw myself in her direction. I slapped my hand over her mouth just as a bloodcurdling scream came from her throat.

"Shh... it's okay. Everything's fine. It's—" I tried to say but she slapped me away.

"Fine? Bryce just murdered someone!" she wailed. "Evie, we need to get out of here." She pulled back and looked around frantically.

"Actually, that's probably a good idea," Sebastian said, rising from the pool chair. "Evie, take Skye back to my house. We'll deal with this."

"Deal with it?" Skye's eyes were so wide and red with tears. She was losing it. Would she call the police?

Suddenly I was more scared of her than Bryce—and the dead lawyer floating in the hot tub. I knew how Bryce and Sebastian felt about my mission, but I had no clue what Skye was thinking.

I stood and grabbed her hands, tugging her up. "Let's go. I'll explain everything."

Skye shook like a tiny dog, sobbing all the way through Fred's house. I paused at the front door and placed my hands on her shoulders. "Skye," I warned. "All of these houses have cameras and security and neighbors watching. You cannot walk out looking like this. I'm going to give you a moment to fix yourself, and when we step through that door, we're going to be laughing and acting like nothing is wrong. Do you understand me?"

"But, Bryce, he—he—"

I put a finger to her lips. "We're not going to talk about that. I don't know if there are cameras watching us right now."

Her head whipped around, looking up to find cameras.

"Skye, focus on me," I said, keeping my voice calm and steady. "Don't look around."

She looked up, blinking tears away rapidly, then nodded. "Okay. And you'll explain everything?" she asked, her eyes shiny and pleading.

I threaded my arm through hers and plastered a smile on my face.

"Of course, bestie. Now, let's do the best acting of our lives. Act drunk."

We strode out the door, pretending to be tipsy and giggly. We stumbled over each other until we made it back to Sebastian's. I typed in the code on his front door and pushed her inside, instantly dropping the act.

The dogs came running in, and I bent down to greet them.

"Explain. Now, please," Skye pushed.

I looked up and stood, patting my thighs.

"Come," I called to the dogs, heading to the living room. My suit was still damp, but it was the least of my concerns right now. I sat down on the couch, surrounded by Cujo and Precious, with Skye sitting on the edge, her body turned away from me.

"My mom didn't kill herself. She was murdered," I started. "I've known this whole time, and I came here to get my revenge."

"Revenge?" She cocked her head, and then turned all the way to face me.

"Yes. There were six of them that night. They raped her, stabbed her in the stomach repeatedly, and then hung her from the ceiling. Then they paid people to cover it up."

"Why would they—"

“Because they can.” I shrugged. There really was no other reason for these people to hurt others this way—except that no one was stopping them.

Until me.

“So... Bryce knew? And Sebastian?”

“They do. They are helping me get through my list.”

“And Fred...”

I looked away in shame, having gotten more people roped into this. “He was one of the six.”

“Oh, my God. Evie, I am so sorry.” She scooted closer to me, causing the dogs to scurry back. She threw her arms around me and hugged me tightly. “Fuck him so hard.”

I patted her back and hugged her. Skye never let go of a hug first, and tonight, I needed that. When I let her go, she sat back and crisscrossed her legs. Suddenly she was back to her bubbly self.

“Okay, so go back. Tell me everything. When did Bryce find out?”

I explained the timeline starting with day one of seeing Sebastian.

“That’s where Glenn went?” she gasped. “You tried cocaine?” she added as I continued with my story.

Her commentary was oddly charming, and it relaxed me. I confessed everything easily, and when I was done, it not only felt freeing, but I didn’t feel judged or like she was going to turn me in.

“This is literally the most bonkers story I’ve ever heard, but I am loving all of this for you,” she exclaimed when I was done. “And Bryce and Sebastian are helping you?”

“Well, you too, I guess.” I cringed. “By not telling anyone.”

“Oh, boo.” Her eyes softened as she used the endearment. She reached for my hands. “Your fight is my fight. Let’s kill some bastards.”

“Really?”

“Really. I mean, I don’t know if I could actually stab someone, or poison, or like—” she shuddered “—do what Bryce did, but I’m in.”

We hugged, and just then, Sebastian and Bryce came in. The dogs lifted their heads but remained in place as they walked into the room carrying all the pool gear we'd left behind.

I stood, and so did the dogs.

"What did you end up doing with the body?" I asked.

Sebastian shook his head. "Nothing. We're leaving it there."

"What?" I shook my head. "You can't. They'll—"

"Think it was suicide," Bryce interrupted. He pulled out his cell phone and then another. "We were trying to figure out what to do but didn't want to get electrocuted."

"That and the fucking maid saw us come in earlier," Sebastian pointed out. "We tried to write a note but couldn't get the handwriting right. Then Bryce suggested—"

"AI voices," he said with a smirk.

Bryce turned one of the phones on, unlocked it, and tapped something on the screen. Fred's voice suddenly filled the room, startling me.

> *"This is the last will and testament of Frederick Castle. I've been thinking about this for a long time. There are things that have been weighing on my conscience that I can't move past. I'm sorry. I leave everything to my ex-wife. I leave no children behind. Goodbye, and I'm sorry."*

The room fell silent as we listened to what sounded exactly like the deceased man.

"How the..." Skye frowned.

"That's unethical," I shook my head. "And coming from artists—do better."

Sebastian scrunched up his nose.

"Now, I've never used the stuff, and I probably never will again, because fuck AI. But I needed to cover up a murder, and this was the best idea we had. Can we all agree that *none* of this is exactly ethical?"

"Okay, but the AI use might be worse than the murder." I smirked. Skye crossed her arms across her chest and stayed close to me, keeping a united front.

Sebastian's shoulders slumped, and he threw his hands up. "Well, by all means. Any better ideas?"

"We could try the note again." Bryce shrugged. "My handwriting is shit."

The room erupted into a small fight as we discussed other alternatives to covering up Fred's untimely end.

It was oddly difficult to make the decision. AI stole from people like us. Artists. We kept going back to the ethics of AI use, and the more time that slipped away, the louder our voices grew.

"Do you know how bad it is for the environment, Sebastian?" Skye yelled.

"Okay, we're not going with the AI!" I shouted over them.

They all turned to look at me.

"It's too...icky. Let's do something else. Actually... Come on. We're going back."

Returning to the scene of the crime, putting on the drunk act once more.

"Did it have to be a toaster?" I asked Bryce.

"It rhymed," he protested. "Live, laugh...toaster bath." The last bit drifted off in a whisper.

"Since when are you a poet?" Sebastian smirked.

"Hey, I'm more than just an ex-cowboy turned movie star. I have other interests."

"Guys," Skye warned. "We need to finish this. People probably saw us come in and out of the front. We need a good reason for it."

"Right." I nodded. Suddenly, Skye was the levelheaded one, and it was throwing me off.

"So, let's fish the toaster out, and..." I looked around.

"Toss the blender in instead?" Sebastian suggested.

I started to say no, but then Skye interrupted.

"Actually, that would make sense. We make some margaritas,

toss the blender in, then call the police. When they come, we'll say we were drinking, having fun, and started to run low on margarita mix. Evie and I went back to Sebastian's to look for some, but we took too long, and you two came to get us. We returned, empty-handed, only to find that he'd been so drunk, he'd tried to make the drinks while sitting on the ledge of the hot tub and slipped."

We all stared at each other. Bryce lifted the phone with the AI voice recording again, waving it in the air.

I rolled my eyes.

"It's the best we've got." I sighed.

I reached for the phone and tossed it into the hot tub. As it hit the charged water, there was a quick flash, telling me it was fried. I went to the bar and watched as Sebastian and Bryce carefully unplugged the toaster and fished it out. Fred's body floated lazily in the tub, his head still underwater.

Good.

Skye joined me behind the bar and pulled out the blender. Humming a tune, she ducked down and popped back up with a bottle of tequila and a nearly empty jug of margarita mix. She gathered everything and took it over to the men, who plugged in the appliance. Sebastian held it while she poured the cocktail into the blender. Bryce then took it from her and warned us to stand back as he tossed it into the water. Another pop and zap of lightning came upon impact with the water.

We stared in silence as the cord ripped from the extension and slipped beneath the water, disappearing under the bubbles. No one said anything until some time later, when Skye cocked her head.

"Which do you think Fred would have preferred? Sugar or salt on the rim?"

CHAPTER 36 EVIE

The On-Screen Kiss

Fire crackled in the background from burn barrels and an overturned car. I hauled myself to my feet, limping as I did. My hair hung down, wild and untamed, making me even hotter than I already was. Reflex made me want to shove it back, but they liked my hair like this, so I forced myself not to reach up and adjust it. I clutched the jagged breakaway glass in my hand and narrowed my gaze into slits.

"Looking for me?" Skye called from behind me.

I spun around. She looked just as beaten as I did. Her clothes were torn, her skin covered in grease.

She clicked her tongue. "Tsk, tsk. Simon didn't say turn around, bitch." With a scream, she raised her arm, wielding Simon Says's signature axe. She charged toward me, ready to kill.

"Cut!" Dante shouted. "Reset!"

Skye stopped inches from me, and we stared at each other before bursting into giggles. We ran the scene again and then a third time. Then we started the close-up fight. She tore my shirt, exposing my low-cut bra. I was less than impressed by wardrobe, but this movie was intentionally sexy and built for the male gaze.

Although, I'd argue that Sebastian's full-frontal scene was for the girls, the gays, and the theys. Even if I hadn't experienced him firsthand, I wouldn't have denied that Sebastian Shaw's naked form was otherworldly. My mind drifted to the last time I'd experienced that form, and my heart sank. Our bodies had betrayed us both. We'd been forced into a position where we had to perform for people. It was degrading and made me rethink the excitement from the chemistry test. I wasn't even sure I'd be able to do the sex scenes for the movie now.

I wiped the sweat from my brow and put my hair up in a ponytail as I walked off set in the direction of my trailer.

"Popcorn for your thoughts?"

Sebastian seemed to come from nowhere. I shoved my sad thoughts back when I caught sight of his smile. He felt the same as me about it all, and that was helping me work through my feelings. He was holding a brown bag of popcorn from craft services. He tilted the top to me—there were M&M's in it.

"Nothing. Just that today has been super fun. I love the days Skye and I film together."

He leaned against my trailer next to me and popped a few pieces into his mouth. "That's how I feel with Bryce. You know it's gonna be a good day when we're both called. What are you up to tonight?"

"I'm starting with a shower to get this off." I lifted my greasy arms. "Then a hot bath to soothe my muscles. Pretending to fight is exhausting!" I laughed.

Skye walked past, looking like hell, and waved eagerly, wiggling her fingers as she went to her trailer.

"She's been shockingly cool about it all," Sebastian said. "I really thought we fucked up, her being there with Fred..."

"Yeah, me too. Bryce must have known something we didn't. I never thought I'd have a friend other than you to help, but...now I have three of you?" I shook my head in disbelief. I hated that I kind of liked it.

How did this even happen? Friendship wasn't part of the plan.

After my mom died, I closed myself off from everyone—even my aunt Yvonne, who'd taken me in. Thankfully, she wasn't around much, so it didn't seem to bother her. I had a feeling that when I was eventually gunned down in front of the Hollywood sign, she wouldn't even come for the funeral. But these three? They would be the ones carrying my casket.

"Friend?" Sebastian frowned. "Is that what you're calling me?"

I looked up at him in confusion. "What else would I call you?"

He stared, his green eyes boring into me, a strand of his black hair falling over his eyes. I knew I'd touched a sensitive button. His obsession with keeping me here was ever-present whenever he was around. He was obvious with his interest in me, but I couldn't offer the same to him, even if a tiny part of me wanted to stay. Every day that I stayed here was another day the police had to put evidence together and send me away forever. Or worse, for some big executive shark to find out and do to me what they did to my mom. Once I was no longer in their direct line of sight daily, my crimes would be forgotten and the cases abandoned. I needed to leave when it was all over, but Sebastian would make it so hard to go.

"Someday, Final Girl." He pushed off the trailer and tossed a handful of popcorn into his mouth. Spinning around, he began to walk backward. "Someday, I'm going to win you over."

"Sure, Psycho Killer," I teased. "Someday."

Raissa came by to take me to set to finish the fight scene. Skye took her own cart but wasn't far behind me. We got onto set, spoke to the stunt coordinator then began practicing. We sparred for a while and then started shooting.

"You ruined everything!" Skye, as Riley, screamed as she swung her axe. While it looked menacing, with its metal-looking decals and crusted-on fake blood, it was hollow plastic. Strong enough not to bend on impact, but not hard enough to hurt if I was accidently hit. "You should have left town when I told you to!"

"Simon didn't say leave!" I mocked.

She snarled and whacked the back of my calves, sending me to my knees. I crawled forward, rolling and dodging her axe.

"I tried to save you. This could have been peaceful. You didn't have to die."

I turned and glared up at her.

"I could say the same for you." I lifted my leg and shot it forward.

"Cut!" Dante reset us and got close-ups of my sneakers coming into contact with her shin, then of her flying through the air in a harness.

Before filming the final bit for the day—the close-up, roll-around scene designed for the male gaze, where we have even skimpier clothing and do lots of whimpers and moans as we fight—they gave us a small break. Skye bounded over. I downed a bottle of water and reached for another. Despite having hardly any clothes on, it was hot as hell on set, and I was struggling not to overheat.

"This has been so much fun!" Skye squealed, dropping into a chair. She reached for a bottle and beamed at me as she took a small drink.

I fought the urge to slap her or roll my eyes. She did everything so effortlessly. Normally, I loved that about her, but right at this moment, as I was struggling to breathe, I needed her to choke on that water she was sipping.

"What are you doing after we wrap? I kind of want to go out, just you and me. Drinks? Dancing?" She bumped my hip playfully.

I scrunched up my nose. "I don't know how you can even think of dancing. I am dying over here. I groaned and slumped against the craft services table, fanning myself.

"It is kinda hot," she agreed, which only annoyed me more. There was no *kinda* about it.

"So, I have to ask. Last weekend..." She bit down on her lip, and I stiffened. Was she really about to talk about Fred Castle and his live, laugh, toaster bath right here, where people could overhear?

"You and Sebastian..." she finished, and relief washed over me.

I snickered and grabbed another water. I started to tell her what I'd told Sebastian earlier this afternoon but stopped short. We were still pretending to date for the movie.

"It's complicated," I said lamely.

"He's like, fallen head over heels for you," she said.

I eyed her curiously. Had he put her up to this?

"I don't really want to talk about him. We're...complicated," I repeated and stepped away, returning to set.

Everyone else made their way back slowly, and we went through the final choreography.

"Hands on each other's arms. We want to see your chests. Sorry. I know it's crass," Dante said. "But lots of over-the-top moans, whimpers, gasps, stuff like that."

"Like a mediocre porno."

He grinned. "Exactly."

He stepped back, and we got into position. Skye swept her foot under mine, causing me to fall. I grabbed her ankle and took her with me. In a flash, she was on top of me, pretending to punch and slap me. My head went back and forth as directed. I arched my back to make my breasts stick out farther and groaned as Skye ground her pelvis into mine.

I overpowered her and rolled on top, trading places. I tore at her hair and smeared her lipstick with a stage smack. She rolled me over again, and I pretended to struggle to regain power.

"Nice try, Lucy," she crooned, dipping low, our noses touching.

I looked into her eyes, my own going cross-eyed. I closed them as she said, "Simon didn't say escape."

Suddenly, her lips were on mine, and it took me a moment to fully register what was happening.

My eyes fluttered open as uncertainty washed over me. Skye closed her eyes, her tongue darting out, probing through my lips that had parted more from surprise than eagerness. This wasn't scripted.

I looked to the side frantically, waiting for someone to yell cut.

Finally, realizing no one was going to stop this, I moved my head and pushed her away. I sat up and scooted her off completely. I stood, raising my arms in frustration and confusion. Tears flooded my vision as I looked around and saw more excited faces than angry ones. I scanned the crowd and realized who was missing, making my stomach sink. Heat flamed my face as embarrassment took over.

What the hell?

I looked back at Skye, who couldn't look me in the eyes.

"I'm sorry. I-I—"

"I've got to go." I stormed away, my heart beating furiously, the sweat pouring from my face no longer from exertion but from something else. Something...terrifying.

I wasn't upset that Skye kissed me, as unprofessional as it was. I was upset because it felt like I'd just cheated on Sebastian, and I didn't know how to feel about that.

CHAPTER 37

SEBASTIAN

The Character Moment

I stood with Bryce, Dante, and the rest of the crew as Evie and Skye filmed their epic fight scene. There'd been a silent call for anyone interested in watching two hot girls roll around to come out of their trailers, so naturally, almost a little disgustingly, the room filled fast. I hung near the back but still saw everything.

"Bro, what the fuck just happened?" Dante asked the room as Evie stormed off, leaving Skye on the ground, tears in her eyes and swollen lips pouting.

"The hottest fucking thing on this set," a cameraman snickered, and Bryce leaned over and slapped him on the arm.

"Have some class, man. Obviously there were some blurred lines."

Skye stood and called out to Evie, apologizing. Remembering she had an audience, her face flamed red and she began to blubber.

"I-I'm sorry. I don't know why I..." Stumbling over her words, she put her face in her hands and fled the set, choking back tears.

"Blurred lines? I think there was a pretty cut and dry line," I muttered, then hurried off to find Evie. Something was off.

I didn't bother with a cart and instead jogged to the trailers. When I knocked and got no answer, I tried the handle and found the door locked. I sighed and looked around.

"I shouldn't have done that." Skye sniffled from behind me.

I turned and found her with red-rimmed eyes and puffy cheeks.

"Can... Can we talk?"

I cringed, looking from Evie's trailer then back to Skye. I didn't want to abandon Evie if she needed me, but looking at Skye about to have a complete meltdown had me nodding and following her to the trailer beside Evie's, where she wailed so loudly, I jumped back, startled.

She collapsed onto the couch, and I stood there for a long moment, watching her cry, before eventually sitting beside her. In a flash, she was lying on my lap like a cat, crying.

"I can't believe I did that!" she exclaimed.

Not sure where to place my hands, I settled on her ankles. I patted her politely.

"I just— I thought we were having a moment, and—oh God!"

I sat back and let her cry it out. The whole time, all I could think about was Evie. She'd run off so fast. What was going through her mind? It was just a kiss. But they hadn't rehearsed that. Sometimes it was okay to improv, but if it didn't land...

"I bet she's disgusted with me, being...like that."

"Being like what?"

There was a pause, and then she whispered, "Gay."

"Why would you think that?" I asked, although we'd all seen Evie's reaction to Skye's kiss. But I knew Evie wasn't homophobic.

"I— I shouldn't like her." She sniffled.

"You like her? Like, like-like her?"

The more Skye spoke, the more confusing yet clear things became. It was as if the pieces of a puzzle were all coming together. The playful flirting with Evie. Her trying to be with Evie outside of work almost every night. Small touches here or there.

Skye sat up and wiped her face. "Can I tell you something?"

I wasn't entirely sure where this conversation was going. Would I have to compete for Evie with Skye? Of all the people I thought I'd have to worry about, I hadn't considered her best friend.

"Yeah, of course. I'm here for you." The words sounded fake coming from my lips. I wasn't any good at any of this stuff—I wasn't someone people came to for comfort.

"It's about my past. My parents. They..."

The blood drained from my face. Parental trauma was not good. I had it in droves.

"Skye—"

"They are hyper-religious. They saw me kissing a girl and told me to never come home," she blurted before I could stop her.

"Fuck your parents so hard. You don't need them. You've got us."

She rolled her eyes and sniffled. "Hardly. Evie hates me now."

"That's not true. She was just surprised."

Eventually she calmed down. I stood and went to her mini fridge, pulling out water for both of us.

She threw her arms up and huffed. "Sebastian, I don't think I like men very much!"

I fought back a laugh. "Is that so?" I recalled her going on a date with me in place of Evie the first day we met. However, looking back, she wasn't all that interested in me, speaking mostly about getting the lead part alongside me. She'd been trying to schmooze, not seduce.

I could see the weight coming off her shoulders. She smiled and fell back against the couch, and I followed suit.

"Yeah. I mean, I've slept with guys. I went through a phase in high school. My parents were always trying to get me involved with the boys in youth group."

I let her vent. She told me about her past. She'd grown up in a religious household, and after her parents caught her giving a chaste kiss to a neighbor girl, they disowned her. She spent the next few years trying to make it in Hollywood and then landed this gig.

"Evie..." She sighed and rubbed her face. "That was so dumb. I don't know what I was thinking. I thought maybe we..."

"I'm sure she's not as upset as you think," I assured her.

"What if she hates me for being..."

The religion they'd shoved into her for years continued to return, and I wanted to murder both her parents and their church for what they said to her.

"Gay?"

"Maybe bi." She scrunched up her nose in thought. "Sex with men isn't terrible. I can appreciate the male form. I think I definitely like women more, though. God, that feels so good to say!"

I laughed. "Sexuality's a spectrum. Everyone just falls somewhere on it. And Evie can't hate you for being gay because then she'd have to hate me too, Skye."

"You're..." Her mouth fell open.

"I've had sex with both men and women. I prefer women." I shrugged. "I came out publicly a few years ago. You didn't know?"

"No! I had no clue. And it didn't affect your career at all?" Her eyes widened as I told her a bit about my experience of coming out in Hollywood.

"Maybe ten years ago it would have been a bigger deal, but now? The only people making sexuality a big deal are the bigots, and no one listens to them here," I assured her. "Honestly, I think making it public helped my career more than not."

"Really?"

"Oh yeah. Horror is the gayest genre of film. I was welcomed by the fanbase with open arms."

"So you think I should just..."

"Be yourself? Yeah, I do." I gave her a half smile. I meant what I'd said. "But, like, if you could try to not steal my girl anymore, that would be great."

"Oh, my God." Her eyes widened. "Sebastian, I am so sorry! I was so worried about myself, I just realized I kissed your girlfriend. Fuck, I'm a mess! She didn't kiss me back, I swear."

I laughed and waved off her worry. "I know. You're fine. Evie isn't..." I'd had a heart-to-heart with her, sure. But I wasn't going to spill about the PR deal. That was a lot of money to lose if it got out.

"I'm not entirely sure she feels as strongly about me as I do about her," I confessed.

That, I could say.

"Oh, Sebastian." She threw herself at me, and I patted her awkwardly on the back. I was glad I could help her, but her exuberant energy was still a bit much for me.

There was a loud knock on the door, and I glanced at my watch. It'd been almost a full hour. Shit.

"Let's get out there. Hopefully, you can finish the scene and go home. You want to get dinner or something?" I asked her. I had a feeling now that she'd come out, at least to me, she needed a friend tonight.

"I'd like that," she said, and we exited her trailer, only to be greeted by a blinding flash that made us fall back.

"Sebastian! Have you moved on from Evie Reyes? Is your other co-star your new girlfriend? How does Evie feel about the relationship?"

A paparazzi, dressed in a security uniform was instantly tackled by an actual member of security. I groaned as they ripped the camera away from him, but it didn't matter. As he fought them, I noticed a second one snapping photos with his phone. He scurried away before I could chase after him. I pointed security in his direction, but I knew it was too late.

A photo of Skye and me coming out of her trailer looking secretive was about to be on the internet in just a few hours.

Fuck.

CHAPTER 38 SEBASTIAN

The Turn

One of our camera guys stopped me on my way to set the next day. "Did you not get a phone call? Schedule changed. You're off today."

"What?" I glanced at the Red Bull in my hand. "No, no one told me. What the hell?" Irritation swelled in my chest. It was five in the morning. I could have slept in.

"Sorry." He shrugged. "Evie called off. Emergency or something."

"When's she coming back?" I was already pulling out my phone. I hadn't talked to her last night—I'd been preoccupied with Skye. We had made plans to have dinner, but after the paparazzi snapped photos of us leaving her trailer, we'd canceled the plans, and instead, she'd spent the evening on the phone, telling me how much of a relief it was to finally say out loud that she preferred the company of women over men.

"No idea. Dante isn't thrilled, but the executives are giving us all the time we need so long as we deliver on those scenes, so, it is what it is." He smacked my back and gave me a tight smile. "Go home, head to the gym early, take a nap, enjoy the day off. Lucky."

He left me staring after him, fuming.

She just called off?

I spun around and stormed back to my car. I slammed my

Red Bull on the way home, and when I got back to the house, I took Cujo and Precious for a light jog. I went past Frederick's house and paused, staring at it. He'd died a week ago. His maid had found him the next morning. Unlike the people on Evie's list before him, he'd actually made the news.

Death by Margarita: Hollywood lawyer dead in hot tub, blender at the bottom.

There was talk among the studio. *Could anyone believe it? He was just here a few days ago! He was a big name. Who knew he was such an alcoholic?* On and on it went, as more seemed to come out with their own stories, although with each passing day, the stories grew taller and more fantastical. In some iterations, he'd been found naked, with the blender around his crotch and his dick floating in the water. Others said his maid and ex-wife had conspired to do it. Rumor had it, the maid had already found employment at the woman's house across town.

Every new nugget was more entertaining and shocking than the last, and not one mentioned any of us having been there that night. It was as if no one had really cared that he was dead. The police hadn't even come by after that first day. No one asked for video footage from me or any of my neighbors. No door cams, no security, nothing.

After our walk, I tried calling Evie but only got her voicemail. I sent a text instead, but I suspected I wouldn't be getting a reply. She couldn't really be mad at me for the paparazzi photos. She knew I wasn't interested in Skye. How could I be, when my heart and mind were so wrapped up in her? Her ignoring me made no sense. Something had to be wrong.

Unsure about what to do on my day off, I opted to work out, shower, and then, with the dogs surrounding me, I fell asleep on the couch watching *The Blair Witch Project*.

I woke sometime later and checked my phone. I had a bunch

of texts and calls from Skye, but nothing from Evie. With a groan, I wiped the sleep from my eyes and read the messages.

Skye

I am so sorry, Seb! I've been trying to call Evie.

Skye

Please don't be mad. My manager said she'd speak with the press.

Skye

Are you mad at me?

Skye

I'll fix this.

She was typing.

Anthony C. Hopkins. Calm down.

I pushed the call button. She answered on the first ring and spoke quickly, not even letting me say hello.

"Sebastian! Oh, my God, are you mad at me?"

"Well, I'm not entirely thrilled to see you blowing up my inbox," I grumbled. "What is going on?"

"I think we've gone viral."

"We?"

"All of us. Someone took a photo of me kissing Evie and then the photo of you leaving my trailer. You haven't seen it? I'm pretty sure it's why Evie isn't taking my calls," she sighed.

I tried to absorb all the information she was throwing at me, but I was still half asleep. I ran my hand through my hair and pushed the dogs away as they tried to climb onto my lap.

"I haven't seen anything. What are they saying?"

"They're saying we kissed, you got jealous, then you cheated on her with me. I'm the movie slut, you're the vindictive asshole, and poor Evie," she sighed mournfully. "She's the brokenhearted woman. Sebastian, I'm so sorry."

I took a deep breath. "It's fine. Thanks for the heads-up. I've got to go." I hung up and grabbed my keys.

I had to see Evie. If she wouldn't answer her phone, then I would go see her in person. I gave the dogs dinner and left, doing my best not to speed over there. When I reached her place, the lights were all off, but her vehicle was in the driveway. I went up the drive and knocked, but there was no answer, which I knew would happen. I looked up at her camera and spoke to it.

"Evie, come on. I know you're here. Can we talk? Obviously, we both know there's nothing happening between me and Skye. People just love a good scandal." I looked behind me, suddenly paranoid. "I wouldn't be surprised if someone was taking photos now, actually." I sneered. Maybe I shouldn't have come. I stuffed my hands into my pockets and turned back to the road. "Call me, please!"

I abandoned my plans to storm in, grab her face, and smother her mouth with mine until she promised to never ghost me again. Tomorrow, when she was back at work, we'd be starting our sex scenes, and things would fall into place. It was going to be so hot and heavy on that set, she wouldn't need to be convinced. My cock was getting hard just thinking about when we were on set for the chemistry test.

I'd do it again if I could.

I went back to my car and stared at the house. Maybe she wasn't home. Did something happen? A home invasion? A kidnapping? I hurried to get in the car and plan my next steps. Worry and panic were setting in. I knew Evie like the back of my hand. Something wasn't right.

Just as I'd turned the key in my car, I got two texts. One from an unknown number with a video attached, and the other from Dante. I ignored the unknown number and clicked on Dante's text. Maybe he knew what was going on with Evie.

Dante

All the sex scenes are off. Evie just pulled out.

CHAPTER 39

EVIE

The Recast

Raissa, this is Evie. Tell Dante I have to go. I won't be filming anymore

Raissa

What?

this week. Sorry, hit send early. I've got to go.

With shaky hands, I turned off the cheap burner phone I'd bought on the way to the airport and shoved it into my pocket.

They'd warned me about being tracked.

I stared ahead, watching people come and go through the lobby. I pressed my lips together, trying to hold in my fear and emotions.

The video I'd been sent hours ago had rattled me to the core. My hands were still shaking from the initial text, and my heart rate refused to slow. Someone had kidnapped Antoinette. They'd tied her to a chair and gagged her with a handkerchief. I'd watched the video a dozen times, memorizing everything I could about the brick background, the noises the floor made, and the lighting coming from the windows.

"This industry only works if everyone falls in line. We have been given no choice but to teach those who need it a lesson. If you don't learn your place, this will end in a bloodbath."

Following the video came a text message with an address in Detroit, along with a timer for ten hours.

I'd already burned two just getting here and waiting.

There was a chance that following the sender's instructions—to come alone and leave my phone at home—would get me killed too, but I couldn't ignore the video. Antoinette had been taken, and if I were lucky, she'd be alive when I found her.

And if I wasn't lucky...then I hoped they'd bury us together.

ANTOINETTE'S BODY HAD been left tied up and slumped in a chair in an old, abandoned restaurant. I'd slowly walked over, although it was obvious from the hole in her temple, the blood on the walls and down her body, that she was dead.

This will end in a bloodbath.

I untied Antoinette and used all my strength to drag her body out. Adrenaline powered me, and once we were out, I dropped to the sidewalk and sobbed, holding her body to my chest. Antoinette had been more than just an agent. She was my friend. She'd helped me start my career and encouraged me to come back to Hollywood. To sit there with her body, waiting for the police to come, it rivaled the pain of the day my mom died.

I screamed, I sobbed, I fought for air as I clutched her to my chest, soaking her hair with my tears. It was as if I'd been torn in two, my entire heart shredded, as the realization that she was gone, and it was my fault hit me, wave after wave, harder and harder each time. With each moment that passed while I waited for the disinterested police to show, the pain grew. The anger grew.

How could they take so long? She was human. Antoinette did nothing but shine light out into the world, and when flashing lights finally came and they pulled her body from my arms, my grief shifted to fury.

"Well, I doubt we'll find much. There're no cameras in this area, and she's been dead a while."

They weren't even going to look. I knew how people like this worked. They didn't care because they knew it was too dangerous to go digging. It was what happened to my mother. No one dared investigate deeper, because they knew whatever they found wouldn't be worth their own lives.

That's what separated them from me. I didn't care. I was going to get my revenge. But now, it was more than Lita Reyes. I was doing it for Antoinette as well.

"Would you like a ride, miss?" An officer asked. I turned to him, stone faced, and nodded at the ambulance taking my friend away, covered in a sheet. He saw my pained expression and attempted to offer sympathy. "There's nothing you can do for her."

Oh, I could think of a few things.

RETURNING HOME A week later, I turned my phone on. It had died while I was away. I felt numb. One day, we were making deals and talking about the future. The next, I had been sent a clip of her snuff video and an address to retrieve her body. I found out later that day that I'd only seen the first half of the video. The full-length version had been sent to news outlets, where, right after the man gave his speech, he put the gun to her head and pulled the trigger.

They'd never intended to let me save her. They'd been trying to draw me out, and it had worked. I was lucky to be alive, having left everything behind the way I did—with no phone and without telling anyone where I was going. But I didn't feel all that fortunate.

Once the phone powered on, it pinged for almost three minutes straight with notifications. I'd expected this, as I'd dropped everything right in the middle of filming the biggest horror movie of the year with no notice or explanation. I was sure they'd gotten word of Antoinette's murder by now. It was everywhere. The flowers on my doorstep confirmed it.

The dings eventually stopped, and I picked up the phone to sort through them all. I gave up a moment later, feeling so overwhelmed by the names, numbers, and messages on the screen. Setting an alarm, I lay down in bed and decided to show up to the studio tomorrow morning and hope I could plead for my job back.

Even though I fell asleep the instant my head hit the pillows, my alarm came too soon. I pulled myself up and almost fell back down. I ached from a week's worth of tears and strain on my brain and body.

I braced myself for the looks of pity and awkward apologies for my loss on my way to set, but there weren't as many as I'd been prepared for. Instead, there were a lot of confused stares. I reached my trailer and stopped short when I saw a dent in the door. *What the hell?*

"Evie!" Dante rushed over. "I heard you were on set. I...didn't know you were coming. We haven't cleaned your trailer yet. I wouldn't go in there. Let's get you right to hair and makeup. I gotta figure out some things."

"Clean it? It wasn't dirty when I left."

"Yeah, but then Sebastian threw a fit and... Ah, let's just move on. Don't even think about it." He grabbed my shoulders from behind and directed me toward makeup. I wasn't happy, but I was tossed into a chair before I could investigate further. The stylists made small talk as they curled my hair. They asked about Antoinette and offered their condolences, but then we moved on to the normal things we'd chat about, and I felt a sense of relief. While my heart would never go back to how it was before they'd killed her, I could pretend for a little bit that it hadn't been my fault.

I was sent to wardrobe, where they seemed unsure of what to put me in. I stood around awkwardly until finally someone handed me a set of black lace lingerie and a red silk robe. I'd forgotten that last week we were supposed to start the sex scenes. I slipped them on, but as I started out of the room, I heard commotion nearby and stopped.

"If she's here, change it back." Sebastian's voice. He was mad at something or someone.

"We can't. I just spent an hour on the phone with producers trying—"

Cautiously, I scooted forward to peek around a column. He was standing with Dante, waving his arms furiously. Dante looked utterly exhausted with his lead star.

"Sebastian—"

Sebastian turned and kicked a mop bucket. It went flying as he continued his tantrum. Dante saw me, and his eyes widened. He shook his head slightly, and I backed up, attempting to hide. However, Sebastian had seen Dante and spun around, catching sight of me immediately. His expression was...

Like a psycho killer's.

He stormed over to me, stopping inches from my face, his boots nearly on my toes.

"What are you doing here?" he demanded.

I took a step back, putting my hands up in innocence. "What do you mean? I'm— I'm—"

"Last time I heard, you dropped out, left town, ghosted me again."

His words boiled my blood. I straightened my spine, narrowing my gaze at him.

"My agent was murdered, you asshole. I was her only family. I had to get her body. That's where I was," I spat.

He shook his head.

"Yes. You just *had* to run to her. Take off, no warning, no explanation, into a potential trap. You're so naïve, Evie."

He spun around and pointed to Dante.

"Don't make me do this." He shot a glare my way. "I'll walk out of this studio and never fucking return again. Bye-bye, millions."

"Sebastian," Dante sighed. "We don't have a choice."

My jaw dropped. What was going on? Did he not want to do the scenes anymore?

"You signed a contract. It's happening," Dante said firmly.

I stood back and watched the director and his star fight.

I didn't fully understand why Sebastian was so mad, other than the fact that I didn't call him. I had no obligation to tell him where I was going or what I was doing. I'd told my work, and of course, the video had been all over the news. I just didn't get it. His anger felt entirely selfish.

Maybe it was.

I realized, as I watched the pair scream at each other, that I purposely hadn't tried to find alternate ways to contact him. The day before I left, I'd had some major emotional changes I was struggling to come to terms with, and the idea of being near Sebastian was difficult for me. If I saw him while in active grief and dealing with such a traumatic event, there was a chance I'd confess my growing feelings, and he'd convince me to stop my quest for revenge and simply stay with him and his dogs forever.

I couldn't do that.

If I did, Antoinette would have died for nothing. I didn't know who had taken and murdered her in cold blood, but it was clear they were connected to the six men on my list. Now, I wasn't just killing to avenge my mom. I was killing for Antoinette as well.

My attention came back to reality when Sebastian turned toward me. I looked over, and he shook his head.

"We are paying you to flash your cock and pretend to fuck someone. Nowhere in your contract does it say who that person will be. Do your fucking job, Sebastian!" Dante screamed.

My heart sank. What was going on?

"Get Skye to set," Dante ordered an assistant and stormed off. "We're filming these goddamn scenes. I'm not losing my job over this."

My lower lip trembled.

They didn't want me anymore. I'd been recast.

I pressed my lips together tightly and lowered my shoulders. "I'll go change to leave, then," I mumbled. Why had they even bothered to dress me? All those confused looks throughout the lot now made sense. I wasn't supposed to be here.

Sebastian turned and glared daggers at me. "Are you happy now? They thought you were gone for good, so now I have to film with her."

"I'm sorry," I said softly. "I had to."

"Had to what? Not tell me?" Sebastian strode over, putting his hands on my upper arms. "I would have gone with you. That was dumb, Evie. You could have been killed."

"I know that, but—" But what?

A moment later, Skye came in from behind Sebastian, already in her robe. Her normal smile was gone, replaced with a grim look of despair. Her eyes were always so reflective of her moods, and today, there was sadness in them.

"Evie, I'm so sorry."

I pulled away from Sebastian and put a hand up. "It's fine. It's just a job. And...you wanted it more than me, anyway." I took a deep breath and lied through my teeth. "I'm so happy for you."

Dante came over, his eyes tired and his hair a mess from pulling on it. He did that often when stressed.

"We'll talk about this later, Evie. This was out of my hands. I'm fighting to get you back in. Stick around and—"

Sebastian snorted, cutting him off.

"Well, Evie, what are you gonna do? Run back and hide in your trailer, or stay and watch me fuck someone else?"

CHAPTER 40 SEBASTIAN

The Actor's Notes

"What would you like me to do?"

Her question was a loaded one. We stared each other down, not saying a word. There wasn't a movie quote out there to express what I wanted in that moment.

She wasn't asking about the scene I was about to film with Skye. She was asking about us.

"Stay."

The world around us seemed to disappear for a moment, and I thought briefly that she'd tell me what I'd been begging to hear since the day she'd returned to Hollywood.

Instead, tears welled in her eyes, and she backed away.

"No." Spinning on her heels, Evie fled the set.

I started to go after her, but Dante grabbed my shoulder and pulled me back.

"I know you're going through some shit right now, but we have to give the producers something. They'll fire us both."

I stared at the door Evie had just left through. If I walked off this set right now, I could lose my job, my reputation-- the movie could get scrapped. The billionaires running the show watched their bottom line, but they also had no issue tossing money out the window on a whim. I could lose everything by leaving.

Or I could lose Evie by staying.

I locked my jaw, steeling myself for what could be a big mistake, and shrugged Dante off me.

"I've got to go. I'll be back." I took off out the door.

"Where are you going? Sebastian!" Dante shouted after me.

I ignored him and stormed after Evie. When I caught up with her, she'd just run into her trailer. I went to it, ripping the door open so hard that I was shocked it was still on its hinges. Slamming it shut, I locked it behind me.

"Get the hell out, Sebastian. You have work to do." Evie's words came out in a choked sob. She'd flopped onto her bed and lifted her head to glare at me. My gaze trailed the length of her body.

"Round three," I said, tugging at the string on my robe.

She sat up and wiped her face. "What?"

I parted my robe and let it fall to the floor, exposing myself completely. "I told you to stay."

She rolled her eyes, making my cock weep with need. I loved her bratty side. She turned her back to me and crossed her arms.

"Yeah? Well, we both know me staying anywhere is a long shot at best. You shouldn't get your hopes up. It's probably easier if you just leave now. Go use that thing with Skye." She turned and flopped onto the bed, burying her face in her pillow.

Inhaling deeply, I strode to the bed and straddled her thighs. I caressed her ass above the robe. The silk was soft against my fingers. She lifted her head, attempting to buck me off. I put more weight on her.

"Sebastian, get off me. Are you hard? You are such a pig!"

I stroked my swollen cock and then leaned my hips forward, pressing against her beautiful ass. The silk of her robe sent chills through my cock as I rubbed against it. I moved slowly, enjoying the low waves of pleasure.

"I took a small dose of those pills I gave Thornton to prepare for today's shoot. I'm not going down until I'm inside pussy." I raised myself up on my knees and reached for the bottom of her robe, sliding it slowly up her thighs.

"Why would you do that?"

"Because I knew I wouldn't be able to keep it up for anyone but you." I drifted the fabric up past her ass, revealing her beautiful, tanned flesh. My cock wept, wanting to be between her cheeks.

"You need to leave." A gaspy moan escaped her lips, contradicting her words.

I reached around and lifted her head, turning it to capture her mouth with mine. Our tongues teased each other's deliciously, and her body relaxed underneath me. I moved to rest beside her, and as soon as I was off her thighs, she spun around and attempted to adjust her clothes, but while trying to cover her bottom half, the belt loosened and her robe fell open just enough to tease me with a peek of her breasts. My desire turned into a hungry need. I reached out, pressing on her shoulder until she was on her back. She kicked and rolled, trying to get out of my grasp.

"You can't really think this is an appropriate time," she spat, trying to push me back as I undid her robe farther, pushing the silk away and revealing the most beautiful, tattooed, hourglass figure I'd ever laid eyes on. She was a true work of art, with movie tickets on her ribcage, Vincent Price's head on one thigh, Jaws on the other. Everywhere that had ink, there was another piece of horror history.

I nudged her legs apart and moved between them, our bodies parallel with each other.

"What is an appropriate time, Evie? Before or after you're dead? You gave me five times free use. I'm not letting you go to the grave without having used each and every one. I will prove to you why your life is worth keeping. We made a deal. You don't get to tell me no."

My lips crashed down onto hers. She bucked me with her hips, but I only pressed against her harder. Her face was puffy from crying, and I could taste the salt from her tears on her lips.

"Evie," I pleaded. *Kiss me back.*

"There's no point. You're right. I have a death wish."

She opened her eyes fully, and I stared into them, memorizing the rich brown. So beautiful, so deep, so...mine.

"It's probably better that I was recast. I can finish what I started and disappear completely."

"Enough about the fucking movie," I snarled. "Why do you have to go through with this? Why not just—" As I pleaded for her to let me into her heart, I unhooked her bra and tugged her panties off. She tried to grab them, but I tossed them across the trailer. She covered her breasts with her palms quickly.

"Stay with you and live happily ever after in a world that chews people up and spits them out, leaving them for dead? Sebastian, I came here with a mission. You weren't meant to get involved."

"And yet, here I am. I'm not going anywhere. I just wish you'd understand that."

I repositioned myself, taking hold of my cock and lining it up with her pussy. Despite the anger on her face, she was soaked. "I'm taking my third shot," I said as I slowly entered her.

"You know, I can revoke consent at any time. Dubcon only exists in fiction."

Her words contradicted her body. As I sank into her, she arched her hips to assist me.

"Fine. Stop me, then, Final Girl." I thrust, eliciting a cry so loud I almost came just from the sound. I molded her breasts under my palms and leaned down, taking a pebbled nipple between my lips, grazing it with my teeth. Slowly, I began to fuck her. I wanted to take this painfully slow. We weren't finished until I decided I'd fully proved my point—despite this being a temporary thing, she didn't want it to end. I needed her to come again and again and beg for me, like I'd been begging for her.

"Sebastian," she moaned. "You're the devil."

Her hands went to my shoulders, running down my back. Her fingers sent shivers through me as she pushed me closer against her and wrapped her legs around my hips.

"Maybe, but you don't seem to be upset about it. I'd almost say you're enjoying all this sin."

Our tongues intertwined in a dance so delicious I never

wanted it to stop. Out of the corner of my eye, I noticed a small throw pillow. Reluctantly, I pulled my face from hers and, remaining inside her, sat up and leaned over to grab it.

"What are you doing?" she asked as I encouraged her to lift her hips. I moved the pillow into place, and she eyed me curiously until I began thrusting again. Her eyes widened at the new position. Her lips fell open in a soft O, and her pussy clenched around me, preparing to explode.

I ran my hands down her body, stopping at her lower belly. Gently, I pushed.

"Seb—oh my... Oh, my God."

Her eyes slid up, and then...

Her body gave way to pleasure. Her eyes rolled into the back of her head as her release soaked the pillow underneath her. A slow grin spread over my face as she unraveled around me, drenching my cock, her sheets, and my soul.

"There we go, Final Girl. See, it can be like that every night. All you have to do is stay."

I let her come down and then resumed my rhythm.

"You make it sound so easy." She sighed, wrapping her arms around me and pulling me to her. Her body was eager for more, and I was more than willing to get her to a second orgasm.

"Isn't it?" I asked.

"I wish it were, Psycho Killer."

Evie was rocked by another sudden orgasm, and it gave me chills. I wasn't lying. I always wanted it to be like this with us. And it could be. With every thrust inside her, I planned a part of our lives.

Red carpet events.

Move in together.

Family photos with the pups.

Family movie nights.

My brain froze, and my balls tightened. Her pussy was contracting with another orgasm, finally sending me into mine. I pumped into her, giving her every drop of my seed. It felt glorious—marking her, claiming her, making her mine.

Even for just a little bit.

Rolling over, I pulled her into my arms and stared up at the ceiling. I listened to our heavy breathing, steading myself.

How had this happened? One moment I was on top of the world, having gotten a movie green-lit and about to make millions. The next, I was planning my wedding and what to name our future children. Children? Where the fuck did that come from? I tried to push the thoughts away, but suddenly, the idea of a family with Evie didn't sound too bad. Could I be a true family man? Did I want that?

With her I did.

Which meant if I wanted that future, I needed to do everything in my power to make sure we had that opportunity. She was my forever Final Girl.

It was getting harder to cover things up. And now, her agent had been killed? Fred had known what we were doing before he died, so I was sure he'd told the others. Hodder, Englund, and Bradley. The guy who owned every good property around here, the studio executive, and the man who was basically Oprah.

Fuck.

"What?" she asked me. I started to say the phrase that I'd longed to say to her every day since she showed back up. The phrase I said in my head every time she walked by. The very thing that would make her pull away from me, but I forced the iconic movie line away from my lips and replaced it with a more melancholy, more singular quote. The line from *Scream* would just have to wait. For now, I quoted *The Bride of Frankenstein*.

"I'll make sure we're together forever."

CHAPTER 41 SEBASTIAN

The Celebrity Sighting

"This will end in a bloodbath," the masked figure said to the camera before stepping to the side and putting a bullet into Antoinette's brain. I'd watched the video over a hundred times, analyzing each and every frame. Who had done such a heinous thing, and why had they done it the way they had?

I spent my day off thinking of every possible scenario. This kill order had to have come from Elliott Bradley—the top dog in all of Hollywood. But there was no way it was him, or any of the others on Evie's list, in this video. They'd hired the masked man. They were smarter than Evie gave them credit for. Sure, we'd taken out the first three relatively easily, but that was only because they were glorified frat bros. But the next three? They were going to be much harder.

I gave up trying to figure out who the masked man was. Instead, I focused on the one thing I couldn't make heads or tails of. Why had they taken her all the way to Michigan? You'd think if they were driving Evie to run to Antoinette, they'd have done something once she got there, but they let her take Antoinette's body with no issues. She'd returned unharmed, albeit emotionally destroyed. Needing her to finish the movie was a bullshit excuse for keeping her alive. Everyone was replaceable.

They'd tried to replace her. They gave me the ultimatum:

stay on set and keep my job, or walk away and be fired from the franchise I helped build. I walked out, fucked my Final Girl until she saw stars, then came back to set to take my punishment. Only, there was none. Dante and Skye had both fought with the producers to cut the scenes with Skye and me, and much to my shock, it worked.

The movie wasn't canceled, I still had a job, and Evie remained my Final Girl.

Since Antoinette's murder, she'd spent a lot of time with Skye and me, alternating evenings. When she was with me, she cried a lot. I gave her the space to do so. I only wished I'd been able to do the same when Lita was killed. She'd left so fast, I hadn't had time to even say goodbye. We'd left the funeral, and the next day she'd blocked my number. I had to hear through the grapevine that she'd moved to Michigan to live with an aunt. It was all so odd and hurtful.

I didn't tell anyone, even Evie, that I was doing my own little investigation into the video. I looked into who owned the building Antoinette was found in, along with where she'd been when she was taken. I wasn't sure if I was getting anywhere, but I had to try, for Evie's sake.

The next day, I was on set, lunch was called, and I went out to take my break. While on my way to my trailer, I bumped into someone unexpected.

"Sebastian Shaw, what a surprise!" Elliott Bradley, of all people, saw me from across the lot and started over, outstretching his hand when he grew close.

I stood there awkwardly and let him come to me. When our hands touched, he squeezed hard before letting go.

"Hello... How do you know who I am?" I asked, surprised. While it was safe to assume Fred had told him before he died, it was still odd for an A-lister to recognize a working actor like me.

"*Step-Devil*? How could I not? You were great in that. I told my agent we should get you on one of my shows. Maybe *What Movie is That?* The fans would love that."

I scanned through my mind, trying to recall the show he was talking about. He hosted or judged so many of them. It was hard to keep track. "Yeah, sure. Sounds fun. Have your agent call mine." I tried to move on, but he put his hand on my shoulder and squeezed. He kept his smile plastered on his face, but his eyes turned ice cold.

"Hold on. We're not done here. I've seen you in the tabloids. You and Lita Reyes's daughter, huh?"

I nodded. "Yes, we're dating."

"Right, dating." He winked. PR relationships were no new thing, although most, like mine and Evie's, were secret. "I've *dated* a time or two during a film. How's that going?"

"It's great, actually. I think she's a wonderful person."

"Good boy. Your PR coaching was worth the money." There was an awkward silence, and then he pursed his lips. "She's something, ain't she? She reminds me of her mother—feisty, smart, sexy."

I cringed. This man might possibly be her father. Hopefully he wasn't, but he could be. I scanned his face, searching for traces of Evie in him. It was difficult, as Evie resembled so much of her mother. Elliott was traditional Hollywood handsome with a Latin edge. Strong facial structure, eyes and hair the same dark shade of brown that was almost black. He had a tall build and broad shoulders, presumably washboard abs. I wasn't all that different from him. I just came in a different style. It was on the tip of my tongue to mention that he shouldn't be calling his potential daughter sexy, but then it hit me. He'd been testing me. He wanted me to react.

He wanted to see what I knew.

I bit back the words and nodded.

"She's talented. It's been an honor working with her."

"Oh, I'm sure. A legacy? Lita was an extraordinary actress. She could tell a story so convincingly, she would have everyone enraptured and hanging onto every word as if it were the truth. She once told us a story so well, she had tears streaming down her face, and the men at the table with their wallets out, ready to give her the world, only to find out she'd just told us the plot of *Evil Dead*."

He clicked his tongue and shook his head.

"Women like Lita, like Evie, know the kind of power they hold. They see the light in a man's eyes when they look upon them and know how to use it to their advantage. It was fun with Lita—for a while. But when she got too pushy and her requests turned into demands, well..."

"She committed suicide?" I said.

He smiled. "Exactly." He stared me down, refusing to look away.

"Well, it was nice meeting you, Mr. Bradley." I tried to step out of his way, but he mirrored my movements so that we stayed parallel.

"I'm not done. I heard about your neighbor, Fred Castle. He was a good friend of mine."

I nodded and pursed my lips. "Suicide. His house is already for sale if you're interested. Might be a bit small for you." I played it aloof.

"Suicide, that word gets thrown around a lot here. It's easy for rumors to spread. Do you think he killed himself?"

The cold stare told me he was prepared for me to lie.

"It's hard to say. He was divorced. Wife took everything." I shrugged. "Wasn't he an alcoholic? I'm sorry for your loss."

"No, you're not," he snapped, then looked around to see if anyone was watching. He'd stopped me in broad daylight. He seemed to remember this, and stepped back, removing his hand from my shoulder. "I'm not stupid. Fred wasn't either. You just caught him with his pants down. That girl of yours better behave."

"I have no idea what you're talking about," I lied. "Now, if you'll excuse me, I need to get lunch."

I started to walk away, and finally, he let me go with no resistance, but then he called out.

"I know you were there that night with Mike Thornton."

I stopped and turned. He stormed over to me and brought his hand up, pinching my chin. I clenched my fists at my sides, fighting the urge to swat him away. Catching a charge for the assault of America's sweetheart? That would have longer damage than any bruise I might have dealt him.

"I know all about what went on. Mike and I were close, which you know. I read the report, and I get why you did it. He was an ass when he was drunk. I can only imagine what he did that day with you. But it was a mistake on your part. You should have stayed in your lane. That's what's going to get you in trouble. It's what got Lita Reyes in trouble too, and by the sounds of it, her stupid kid isn't far behind. This is your warning, Shaw. Sit back down."

"Or what? Evie deserves to know what happened to her mom." I slapped his hand away, then I plastered on a large smile, as if this were all some sort of game between us. I wasn't going to admit to anything, especially not here. If he were anyone else, I would have already swung my fist into his jaw, but this man had his hands in every pot. He had shows, films, book deals, clothing lines—even cookware, I was pretty sure, at some point. If a photo or video of us was captured with me looking anything but perfectly pleasant around him, my career would be dead by midnight.

"What happened to her mother is public record. She killed herself for being a whore." Elliott laughed loudly, as if he'd just told me the best joke known to man.

People passed by and smiled when they saw Elliott, but no one caught on that we were arguing. We were just two friends catching up.

His smile fell, and he grew serious again. "Let's not keep going with this. It doesn't have to be so messy. I'd hate for that man from that video to be telling the truth."

My mouth opened partially. "What?"

Elliott leaned in, that chilling smile returning as he whispered in my ear, sending fear slithering down my spine with each word. "This will end in a bloodbath."

CHAPTER 42

EVIE

The Boon

"It's a trap. Don't move!" my mother, as Lana Westcott, yelled to a young Sebastian dressed in his Ronny costume. She stood in the middle of a gymnasium, hands on her head. Bryce, as Simon Says, stared at her from across the room—an axe in his bloodied hands—preparing to sever a rope that would trigger a Rube Goldberg machine designed to slice Sebastian's character in half.

"But he said Simon Says!" Sebastian, in his tiny eight-year-old voice, cried out in a panic.

I watched the first *Simon Says* movie from the comfort of my home theater. I was at the start of a movie marathon. None of these movies were well-written or shot, but that was what made them great. The budgets were nonexistent, but the passion of everyone involved showed on the screen. It didn't matter if the movie was "good." It didn't have to be. It just had to be fun.

Even at such a young age, Sebastian was a natural. He stepped onto set and transformed into the character. He held his own with the adult cast. It was no surprise that when my mother died, they didn't bother replacing her with another female but let Sebastian step into the lead role.

My phone chirped with a text, interrupting the ending. I set my bowl of popcorn down and reached for it.

Psycho Killer

Can I come over?

I looked at the clock. It wasn't terribly late. My stomach rumbled.

Only if you bring dinner.

Psycho Killer

Deal. See you soon.

I finished *Simon Says* and immediately started *Simon Says 2: Simon Didn't Say.*

My vision blurred, and I began to zone out, remembering the last time we'd had sex. It felt like the dynamic between us had shifted. It wasn't just bodies colliding with a mutual goal. Instead, it was...

No, it was wrong to start catching feelings now. It was selfish to love him, only to keep putting myself into situations where I could be killed. I couldn't let him watch me die. Or get hurt trying to save me. That would be cruel. I'd already given him the false hope that I might change my mind. That was bad enough. Shame filled my chest, realizing how I'd been all too willing to let him have this false hope so I could get what I wanted. Pulling my knees up to my chin, I contemplated it all.

But was it false hope? Maybe Sebastian was right. Would it be so bad to stop my quest for revenge and live a peaceful life with him and his dogs?

An hour later, Sebastian was at my door—takeout in one hand, blue and yellow Red Bulls in the other, and a backpack slung over his shoulder.

"Up for a marathon?" I asked as he followed me into the house and toward the theater room.

"Sure—oh, really?" He cringed when he saw the screen, his ten-year-old self frozen in terror where I'd paused the movie. "Please, can we not?"

I grabbed the boxes of food and plopped down on the couch. "What? They're good! This is the one where Simon Says uses an axe as a peg leg for half the movie."

"I was there. I remember," he grumbled, sitting down beside me and popping his can open. He set the backpack on the floor, and I pointed to it with my fork as I opened the takeout, revealing Chinese.

"What's that?" The bag was faded pink and worn to hell.

Sebastian shifted in his seat and looked down, reaching for a different food container and fork.

"Let's eat first."

I pushed play, and when we finished *Simon Says 2*, I went to find *Simon Says 3: Old Games, New Rules*—but hesitated to push play. This was the last movie my mom ever filmed.

"We can skip this one," Sebastian offered, rubbing my back. "The fourth is easily the worst one in the franchise. I could use a good laugh."

With only a slight twinge of guilt on my part, we skipped *Simon Says 3* and went into *Simon Says 4: Summer Camp*. He was right. It was the worst one. The dialogue was choppy, they'd given Sebastian's character a dog that was always licking itself, and there was more unnecessary nudity than ever. I commented on all the topless women, and Sebastian shrugged.

"As a freshly eighteen-year-old sneaking onto set to watch them, I wasn't entirely mad about it." He smirked and then grew serious. "But really, those women were lovely."

An odd sensation of jealousy ran through me, and I asked, "You never joined in?"

He gaped and then burst out in laughter. "Balls don't sell cheap slashers. Tits do. They weren't interested in my dick until they saw how much money *Step-Devil* brought in. This film was completely shot with the male gaze in mind." He nodded to the screen.

I gasped dramatically. "What?" I pressed a hand to my chest. "I'm shocked," I said.

"I know, right?" He snickered, and just like that, we were back to our silly, goofy, relaxed selves.

My belly now full and my heart happy after how much fun the evening had been watching movies with Sebastian, I sank deeper into the couch and slid my legs over his lap. I nodded to the backpack again. "Okay, what's up with that?"

His smile soured. "Right... Well, right." He sighed and leaned forward, reaching for the bag. "This was on my doorstep when I got home."

I pushed myself up, pulling my legs from his lap. "And you just brought it here? Did you check inside it?" Slight unease slid into my belly as I stared at the bag.

"No, it's nothing like that. I did go through it," he said, unzipping it.

"Well, if it's not something scary, then what's in it? Some crazy fan's underwear or something?"

"I almost wish."

He set it on top of my legs, and I grunted—it was heavier and harder than I'd expected. I sat up, pulling my legs back. Sebastian unzipped the bag and pulled out a large photo album. I was surprised it had fit at all. He offered it to me, and I took it gingerly, running my hands over the cracked pink leather. There was a gold trim around it, and tiny little heart stickers had been placed in the bottom left corner. Something about all of this felt like...

My mom.

"I feel like whatever is inside this is going to change things," I whispered.

"Yeah, probably. Maybe," Sebastian said, being entirely unhelpful. He nodded for me to open it.

Slowly, I cracked the first page—and my breath caught in my throat.

Photos of my mother as a young woman with a handsome

man her age were in each slot. I stared at each one carefully, flipping to the next page, finding more of the two.

"I've never seen these before," I said in disbelief. "She looks... in love."

Photos of them at the beach, skiing in the snow, camping, smiling, and laughing.

"Who is this guy?" I asked, pulling out a photo of just him. He was a handsome, tan man with thick auburn hair and a full beard to match. He had hazel eyes and a chiseled jawline. It was easy to understand why she was in love with him. I put the photo back in its slot and kept looking through the book.

My mom had to have been in her twenties when these were taken. It was hard to judge her age because she took great care of herself until the very end, but the fashion choices made it easier to put a time stamp on things.

Sebastian finished his energy drink and sat up, his shoulders bouncing excitedly. "I had the same question, so I pulled one out to see if there was anything written on the back."

I stopped on a page of them at a picnic and pulled a photo out. It stuck to the plastic, and I worried I'd tear it, but I finally managed to ease it out, flipping it over and reading aloud.

"*Lita and Charles, summer 2000.* This was before I was born. She was..." I shook my head. "Who is this?"

"Keep going," he urged.

I continued flipping through the book, viewing a timeline of their love.

Lita and Charles—Paris

Lita and Charles—Hawaii

Lita and Charles—on location

Charles's first sale

The last set of photos was of Charles standing in front of various houses and buildings, beaming.

We reached the last page, and Sebastian leaned in, putting his finger on one of the photos. I squinted at the sign he was pointing to, and when it registered, my heart stopped.

It was a real estate sign.

"My mom was in love with Charles Hodder," I gasped.

"Seems that way."

Charles was on my list. He was the next one, in fact.

The real estate tycoon. I couldn't believe I hadn't recognized him.

I shoved the book away. It fell to the floor, and Sebastian leaned down to pick it up.

"How could he—he led her to the fucking slaughter," I snarled. "I can't believe this!" I was at a loss for words. It was clear that at one time they'd been in love, and yet, he was one of the men who'd killed her. What had happened in the time between these photos and that night she died?

"I know. I had no idea she was ever romantically involved with any of those men. Whoever dropped it at my house knew it wasn't well known but wanted us to see it. Why?"

"I don't give a shit why," I snarled, standing up. I paced in front of the screen. "Maybe it was Charles himself, trying to get some sympathy before we come for him. It doesn't matter. He loved her and still murdered her. He's going down."

"Evie." Sebastian stood and came to me, wrapping his arms around me and fighting to keep me in place. "I know you're angry, but we can't go into this guns blazing. We need to think."

"Why? I want to go to his house right now, wherever that is, and stab him straight in the throat."

"You can't do that."

"Why not?"

"Because...what if he's your dad?"

CHAPTER 43

EVIE

The Unauthorized Shot

"You've reached the offices of Hodder Real Estate. We're unable to take your call right now, so leave your details, and we'll be in touch. Have a great day, and we look forward to helping with all your real estate needs." The voicemail was taunting me now. I'd called about thirty times this morning. I needed answers.

How could Charles look so deeply in love and yet go on to rape and murder my mother?

I knew it wasn't uncommon for people to murder their partners. But it still didn't make sense to me. Regardless of what I discovered from that backpack, or who left it for us, I was still planning to end Charles's life.

In the privacy of my trailer, I watched tutorials and practiced with my daggers, preparing for a battle. I wanted to be ready. Standing in a defensive stance, I counted down. When I hit zero, I snatched the blades from my boots and lunged forward, slicing invisible Hodder's belly open with one hand and plunging into his jugular with the other.

I paused when there was a knock on my trailer, and Skye popped her head in.

"Hey, what are you up to—whoa, intense." Her eyes widened when she saw the knives in my hands.

I relaxed and set them on the counter. "Come in. What's up?"

I shut the video off and grabbed my water.

She came in and leaned against the counter. "Nothing much. I just wanted to see if you wanted to come out with us tonight. Sebastian is taking me to his favorite gay bar. It'll be my first time." She beamed.

"Sounds fun! I'm excited for you, but I'll pass tonight. I'm tired."

She pouted. "Are you sure? You'll miss me taking my first real steps toward lesbianism."

"I can't. I'm still trying to get a handle on using these things."

I picked up a dagger and spun it between my fingers—then fumbled and dropped it onto the floor.

"Evie..." she sighed.

I picked it up swiftly. "Hey, you have your plans, I have mine. Go, get laid, or kissed or whatever you're looking for tonight. I want you guys to have fun. Let me be my loser self."

"Fine, but once your whole *revenge era* is done, you're going out with me." She wagged her finger at me and left my trailer.

I picked up both knives and examined them, reading the engraving.

Good For Her.

My mother had left these for me. She knew I'd need them. She knew about the monsters in this town, and that someday, they'd get her. There'd be time for nights out after.

Or probably not. But I'd always known that.

I ignored Sebastian's texts and dodged him as I left the studio after we wrapped for the day. He knew about my evening plans and wasn't happy about me ditching him and Skye for sitting alone and plotting my next kill.

He'd mentioned stopping my quest for revenge, but until I could sleep peacefully—with no nightmares of my mother's feet dangling in the air, her blood pooling on the floor, my screams echoing until I woke up—I wouldn't stop planning their deaths.

If they wanted a bloodbath, I'd give them one.

CHAPTER 44

SEBASTIAN

The Extra

"I fucking knew it."

At the club, I stared at the live feed on my phone of Evie's front door. She'd just left the house with her hood up, looking overly suspicious. I dropped my head back in frustration.

"She's going to find Hodder."

"Should we go stop her?" Skye scrunched up her nose and sipped her cocktail.

I looked around the large room. This club was one of my favorite places. Tall, secluded booths lined the walls, and there was a large dance floor in the center. The bar had a giant blue backlight, matching the lights that danced under the flooring. They pulsed to the loud club music.

I wasn't being a great wingman. I'd promised I'd help her meet people tonight, but so far I'd only managed to help her talk to a cocktail waitress.

"No, I'm texting Bryce to go stop her. She'll think it's just a coincidence if they bump into each other." I shut off the feed and texted Bryce where Evie was going and to go catch her. He responded with a thumbs up, and reluctantly, I put my phone in my pocket.

"You know, putting your own cameras at someone else's house is creepy, right?" Skye said.

I rolled my eyes. "I think she'll forgive me later."

I'd done it when she left to help Antoinette. I'd wanted to know when she got home. I figured once this was all over, I'd mention it. For now, it was helpful in keeping her safe.

"Evie is too impulsive. If she's not careful, she's going to end up dead."

"I don't think she really cares," Skye said.

Despite the music pounding and the dance floor crowded, it felt like silence had fallen over the room. I hated that she was right. So instead, I slapped the wood and hopped off my stool.

"Let's dance!" I held out my hand to help her up.

She tugged on her short teal sequined cocktail dress, trying to cover her thighs better. She looked around, wincing as she stepped out with heels that made her almost taller than me. Plenty of eyes were on her, but she was too nervous to notice.

"Won't that make us look like a couple?" she asked as we went onto the dance floor. "I don't want people to think—"

"It's fine!"

As we danced, I looked around and found a pretty redheaded girl close by. I danced over to her and politely nudged her. She turned and stared, as if trying to place me.

"Hi. You're pretty. Want to meet my pretty friend? She's new to town!" I pointed to Skye—who was dancing alone, swinging her hips with her eyes closed.

"That's your friend?" The girl followed where I pointed, raising an eyebrow. She grinned and followed me over to Skye.

I introduced them, and Skye seemed to freeze, her eyes wide like a deer in headlights.

The redhead noticed her nervousness and took charge. "Do you have a drink? Can I buy you one?"

And just like that, Skye forgot I was there. She nodded eagerly and followed the girl to the bar. I chuckled and danced my way off the floor, pulling my phone back out as I slid into a booth in the back of the club. I shot a text to Bryce to check on things.

Bryce

I called her. We're going back to her house so she can spar with me.

I took a breath, and when a waitress came by, I ordered a beer and sat back, attempting to relax. A few guys stopped and chatted with me, but once they realized it was going nowhere, they ditched to try another table. I had to explain I wasn't on the market tonight and was simply here to support a friend. After the fourth or fifth look of disbelief, I was tempted to leave and let Skye do her thing unaccompanied, but that would be a douchey move. While she'd barely waved at me in the last hour, I'd promised to stay with her.

I was deep in my phone, looking at Charles Hodder's professional website, when there was a loud slap on the table, causing me to jump.

Skye plopped into the seat across from me, pushing her damp hair off her cheeks. Her face was flushed, and she seemed to relax.

"Oh my gosh, it's so much fun out there! I know you're not looking tonight, but you need to go dance—the DJ is everything!" she screamed.

I flinched at her volume.

"Yeah?" I yelled back. "You're having fun, then?"

She nodded, her eyes sparkling. "So much fun. Thanks for getting me in!"

This was a higher-end club—one you had to know someone to get into. I probably should have taken her to a place more accessible for when I wasn't with her, but I wanted her to have a good time tonight, and this was the best place.

I'd been here quite a few times. Most of the men here were others in the industry. Dancers, lower-level actors, reality stars. While I didn't date, almost all my one-night stands were met here. I found myself drawn to stuntmen, usually. I'd hooked up exclusively with stuntmen, now that I thought about it.

What could I say? I loved a good drink and a guy who liked

being told what to do.

"Of course. For you, anything," I told Skye.

"What are Evie and Bryce up to?" she asked.

A moment later, a waitress came by with a bright-blue cocktail for Skye, courtesy of a gorgeous Black woman in a tiny green dress, all legs and long, black hair. She gave a cute little wave to Skye from the bar. Skye beamed and waved back.

She turned to me, her mouth agape. "That is the most beautiful woman I've ever seen."

"Go say hi," I suggested.

Skye smirked. "In a bit. I want to check in with you for a flash. Are you okay? Is Evie all right?"

"She's fine. I'm just..."

"Madly in love with her?" She smiled and reached for my hand over the table, squeezing it briefly.

"Something like that," I admitted.

"I love her too," Skye said. "In a different way, of course. But she's not just yours to protect. Bryce and I want her to stay alive after all this too. She's not just your Final Girl. She's all of ours."

I raised my eyebrows. "Oh yeah?" I didn't think she realized just how determined Evie was to see her revenge to the finish line.

"Absolutely. Okay, I'll be back. I don't want that girl to run off before I say thank you for the drink." She scooted off the bench and took her drink with her.

I smiled as she chatted with the woman at the bar, and I must have zoned out because suddenly they were approaching the table, arms threaded together.

"Sebastian, this is Chloe. Chloe, this is my friend Sebastian."

I shook the woman's hand, and they moved into the booth.

"How's it going? You look like a whole bundle of fun." Chloe laughed.

"He's just missing his girlfriend a little tonight," Skye explained.

"Ah, and a gay bar is the perfect place to sulk."

This wasn't the first comment about my attitude tonight, so I flashed a smile and set my phone down.

"How's it going out there? Still having a good time?"

"Such a good time. Chloe is a model and a DJ! She's taking me to one of her gigs next week!"

I bit back a joke about everyone being a DJ in this town and sipped my drink. Neither woman seemed to notice or care that I didn't have much to say. I suspected they'd only joined me to get relief from the tall heels they both wore.

"What were you looking at?" Skye pointed to my phone.

I glanced at Chloe and shook my head. "Nothing important."

"Oh, come on," Chloe said. "You don't have to hide things. I don't really care. I'm just here to relax before I go back to dance."

Reluctantly, I flashed them my screen. Charles Hodder's headshot from his website was on display.

Chloe squinted at the photo, then her face lit up. "Oh, my God. I know that guy."

"You do?" Skye asked.

"Yeah, he tried to match with me the other day, but when I told him I was more gay than not, he got totally homophobic, and that is not the vibe in this town."

She pulled out her phone, began clicking, then turned her screen to show me Charles's dating profile.

"What app is that?" Skye said, pulling out her phone. She glanced at me briefly as she downloaded the app Chloe told her to. "Is that your guy?"

I peered over and, upon a quick glance, nodded. In five minutes' time, Skye had downloaded the app, made an account under a fake name, and matched with Charles. She set her phone down, gave Chloe a triumphant look, then directed her attention to me.

"There we go. Once he messages me, I'll get details." She put her arm around Chloe and pulled her in, kissing the new woman.

I looked away as they shoved their tongues into each other's mouths. When she pulled away for a breath, she looked at Chloe and gave her a lame excuse as to why we needed to see Charles.

"Charles backed into my friend's car and won't answer his calls now."

"Girl, I don't care. Let's go dance."

The two scooted out of the booth, and before Chloe could pull her away, Skye leaned down to wink at me.

"Sebastian, you go in my place, or I'll go with you, and then you can ambush him. I told you, Evie is *our* Final Girl, and she's not going anywhere."

CHAPTER 45

SEBASTIAN

The Photo Op

"Are you sure you're okay with this? We're going to be close by the whole time."

I checked in with Skye for the umpteenth time before we took separate cars to the restaurant.

"Yes." She rolled her eyes. "We purposely chose a public place, remember? Charles can't do anything without having a hundred eyes on him at any given time. I'm just gathering intel today."

"And if he tries anything, sock him in the nose." Evie put her fists up and punched the air a few times. She'd spent the night before with Bryce, learning better ways to punch and kick and swing her knives. Bryce had a slice running up his arm—that makeup wasn't going to be happy with—to prove that she was still working on her craft.

"I'm a lover, Evie, not a fighter. But I'll use my strengths to make sure you get to use yours."

"I'd hardly call them strengths." Tonight made me nervous. Evie had been warned to slow down, but she didn't seem to be listening. It wasn't safe to just rush through things, and I hadn't told her about my encounter with Elliott Bradley—it would only serve to piss her off further. She was hellbent on revenge, not only for Lita but Antoinette now too. And while I understood the rage, I knew this was a long game. Rushing was only going to make us sloppy. Sloppy was what got you caught.

Evie didn't care.

"You don't have to be involved," Evie pointed out. "No one is forcing you to come tonight."

I smirked and reached for her, threading my arm through hers and directing her to my car. "And miss the opportunity to take you on a real, certifiable date? Fat chance, Final Girl."

A small smile teased the edges of her mouth as I opened the door. She slid inside, and I waved to Skye and went to my side.

"We'll see you there." I got into the car and drove off toward the semi-upscale restaurant Charles had picked, most likely to impress Skye. As someone who'd gone to many very exclusive and expensive restaurants in this town, I knew this place was mediocre. This was where rich men took their hookups to look like they were putting in effort...without shelling out enough money to mean anything.

Our reservation was thirty minutes before Skye and Charles's. We walked in and looked around. The walls were dark green, with black curtains draped over the window. Standing candelabras were placed between the windows, along with dozens of fake white roses. String music played lightly over the speakers, giving it an upscale Olive Garden appeal. The hostess recognized me and offered us a seat in the back.

"There's privacy, if you'd prefer to dine alone." She gave us a knowing look.

"No, thank you. A booth is fine."

She nodded and took us to a booth. We sat down, and a waitress came by to take our drink orders. I made sure to sit facing the room so I could see when Skye walked in. The waitress returned with a beer for me and a lemon drop martini for Evie, along with complementary appetizers.

"The waitstaff are really big fans," she gushed, setting down a plate of mini lobster rolls.

I fought back an eye roll in Evie's direction and forced a smile at the woman. "Oh yeah? Which movie is your favorite?"

The waitress's face went blank, and she stepped back, her face flushing. "Oh, I'm sorry. We were..." She looked over at Evie and smiled. "We love *The Body Count Bimbo.* We watch every week and talk about the episodes. We've been having to go back and rewatch old content while you film that movie. I have your merch... Would you...sign something for us?" The waitress looked over her shoulder. There was a gaggle of waitresses huddled together by the bussing station. When they saw us looking, they waved excitedly.

Evie laughed and waved back. "Sure. I don't have any of my merch on me, but—"

"Oh, that's fine. If it's okay, we all live together and have Amy running back to our house to get everyone's stuff. We are huge fans."

Evie reached for a roll. "Sure. Just make sure she gets back before dessert!"

"Of course. Thank you, Evie!"

The waitress went back to her friends, squealing excitedly, and I stared across the table in awe. Evie was shoving the food into her mouth, looking beautifully... silly.

"You caused a staff trained not to react around celebrities to break. Congrats." I raised my beer and toasted her. "Interesting."

"What, you doubt my influence?" She arched an eyebrow.

"No, I just didn't realize how large your fanbase was. When you're wrapped up in Hollywood, you don't always see what the rest of the world is up to. They keep you so busy with training, fitness, and public events, you don't have a whole lot of opportunity for recreational things."

Her eyes narrowed, and she pursed her lips as if in thought. "What do you watch or listen to when you're working out? Or on your days off?"

I looked away, trying to think. That was a good question. "Honestly, I mostly enjoy the silence. I listen to music sometimes too, but I'm always having someone talk at me. I enjoy the solitude when I get it. I don't feel a need to fill it."

"Must be nice," she murmured, reaching for her drink.

"Silence makes me bonkers."

Her dark eyes turned darker, and I could hear her unspoken words. Silence made her think about all she'd lost and why she was here in front of me tonight.

"Anyway, it's nice to see that I still have fans, even though I haven't made any new content other than stuff for the movie since coming out here. I'm still on the fence about selling it or not. It's been nice not having to work so hard to get videos out every week, but I put so much work into growing it. That, and I genuinely love talking about movies. I can't really imagine not doing that, you know?"

"I thought your plan was to die in a blaze of glory in front of the Hollywood sign?" I snickered. Her face fell, and I instantly regretted my smart remark. While she'd told me numerous times she'd finish out her mission—life or death, it wasn't something to joke about. However, her considering not selling was a little slip into her subconscious. Was she thinking about... staying alive?

"You're right," she said, her voice cold and distant. "My future doesn't really matter. Maybe I'll sell and donate the money. Do something good."

I started to apologize, but my attention shifted when I caught sight of Skye and Charles walking in. The hostess took them to a table right in the middle. I held back an eye roll. That table was for attention, and those who needed to be seen there were people not worth watching.

"Are they here?" Evie hissed.

I nodded slightly, then returned my eyes to her and reached across the table to take her hand. "Yes. Now let's act like we enjoy each other's company. My fans might not be watching, but yours definitely are. I'm sure a picture or two will be taken. You're really thinking about selling your business?"

"Maybe. I don't really need the money, and..." She scrunched her nose as she trailed off. "Is this our first real date?" she asked.

"I think so. Group dates and hanging out at your house hardly count."

We ordered our food and, while still glancing at the couple in the center from time to time, enjoyed our first date.

"This is where we get to know each other, right?" I teased.

"Don't you know enough?"

"I don't think I know anything."

She smirked. "What do you mean? You know more about me than anyone else."

I looked at her, truly looked at her, for the first time in a while. She was always so closed off, even when she wasn't trying to be.

"I know."

My words fell over the table. There was an awkward beat that was fixed when the waitress came with our food and a bunch of merch for Evie to sign. As her food cooled, she signed shirts, totes, and notebooks with her logo all over them.

"Thank you again, BCB. This is so cool."

"Anytime." Evie smiled kindly at the woman and even stood for a photo and hug. When she sat back down, the smile remained on her face.

After the waitress left, we started to eat, and I used the excitement Evie still showed on her face to bring back the conversation.

"So, *if* we make it out alive, what is your plan? Sell your business, then what?"

Evie lifted her drink and swirled the liquid around. "I don't know. I kind of like doing this. It's hard but also easy. When you do what you love, you know?"

"You love acting?" Excitement filled me. Ideas of movies we could audition for began flooding my mind as she blushed and looked away.

"Kind of. Is that bad?"

"No, I just..." Suddenly, I felt a bit exposed. "I'd love to do more movies with you." I might as well have just thrown my heart on the table.

She stared at me for a beat and nodded. "Yeah, maybe," she said vaguely. "We'll see how all this goes. Whether I need to go on the run or not. It'd be nice to have time to sell the house if it's not safe to stay here."

She focused on the table, and the conversation died. Right as I was starting to change topics, Skye stood, catching my attention. I followed her with my eyes as she went to the bathroom. A moment later, Evie pulled out her phone. Her face turned grim as she read the screen.

"He wants to take her to one of his properties. This wasn't the plan. Why is he leaving so fast?" she hissed. "We need to go now, before she's alone with him. She shared her location. Let's follow." She started to scoot out of her seat, and I grabbed her wrist.

"No, we need to wait. Let them go, and in five minutes, we'll leave."

She wasn't happy, but I paid for our meal and forced her to sit and fake small talk. Once I felt like we were enough of a distance apart, we took our leave.

"We barely got our food. How did they leave so fast?" she huffed when we got in the car.

"Maybe it was just drinks and appetizers. This place is notorious for being where you take your hookups."

"Have you been there a lot?" She peered over.

I smirked. Was that jealousy in her eyes?

"Would it be worse to say that I rarely took my hookups out?"

She laughed and swatted me playfully. "Maybe. Is that them?" Evie had been watching Skye's location on her phone. We drove past a large, unoccupied house with a truck in the driveway. A sign with Charles's face stood proudly in the yard.

"Where are you going?" she hissed.

"I'm parking a block away," I told her, slightly annoyed. For someone who was so insistent on going on a murder spree, she had no clue how to not get caught.

We parked and walked over to the house. Thankfully, it was already dark out, so it was easier to sneak right up to the front door, which had been left unlocked.

I opened the door and, making sure the coast was clear,

stepped inside before letting Evie in. However, three steps in, there was a loud click, and something hard and cold was pressed to my shoulder blade.

"Beep beep, Ritchie."

CHAPTER 46

EVIE

The Backlot

My knives were missing. I could feel the empty space in my boots from where they'd been. I raised my aching head and stared into the darkness. The air was chilly, and it smelled of dirt and rain. I tried to move, but I found myself tied to a chair with thick rope. I glanced around, trying to focus my vision in the low light. I was near water, and a single streetlight lit up the area.

"You used it wrong," I groaned, closing my eyes again. I racked my brain. The last thing I remembered was—

"What?"

Charles—the realtor, my mother's ex-lover, and one of her murderers—stepped out of the darkness with Skye in tow. He was different in person from the man in the photos. He'd obviously aged, gaining a beer belly and a grayed beard, but up close, he wasn't as attractive as the photos made him appear. His eyes were beady, and he was shorter than I realized. He was stocky, like an elderly lumberjack.

He appeared calm and collected under the streetlight.

"You said 'Beep beep, Ritchie' before hitting me over the head. That's not some catchphrase. It means shut the fuck up."

"Well, it worked, didn't it?"

My head drifted backward into nothing, and I righted myself again. Maybe he had used it correctly. I didn't know. *Had he given me a concussion?*

"You're lucky my date thought to move you off the property. I'm showing it in the morning. Wouldn't look good to have two dead bodies in the foyer."

My eyes drifted to Skye.

She stood behind him, eyes wide with fear.

"Who are you?" I asked, keeping her cover.

"Don't worry about her," Charles muttered. "She's gonna be rewarded after this is over, and that's all that needs to be said. Riley, sweetie, go back to the car. I'll be there in a bit. Twenty minutes, tops."

I fought back a snicker. She'd used her character name from the movie. Locking eyes with me, she backed away, into the shadows.

A groan came from beside me, and I turned my head to see Sebastian, looking like I felt. His head hung low, his shoulders were slumped, and he too had been tied and bound to a chair. I wiggled my arms, but I wasn't going anywhere.

"You used it wrong," he muttered. "The quote."

"This again? Jesus, you guys are like one brain. No wonder it was so easy to hit you over the head."

"Where did you bring us? I know this place..." Sebastian groaned.

"I'm sure you do, Mr. Hollywood. I took you to one of my favorite places to toss garbage."

"I know this set..." Sebastian turned his head from side to side.

I did too, and that's when I noticed a plane, a cabin, a lake...

"Are we at Falls Lake?" I blurted. Dread pooled in my belly as I remembered stories my mom had told me about the lake.

"Stay far, far away from there, Evie Reyes."

"Good job. You know your movie trivia."

He'd taken us to the studio lot where some of the most famous movies were filmed...but why?

"After I'm done with you, I'm just gonna throw your bodies in the water. I own some shares in the lake. They won't be changing the water for another month or so," he said, as if reading my mind.

"Just fucking do it, then," Sebastian muttered. "Get it over with."

"I can't. Elliott wants information."

"So do I," I piped up. "You were in love with my mom. Why did you help kill her?"

He paused, his brows furrowing, face contorting in pain. Eventually, he just shook his head.

"She hurt me long before I ever hurt her. If she hadn't broken my heart, I probably could have saved her."

"You could have saved her at any time," I snapped. "What you and the rest of your friends did was a choice. Every step of the way, you could have pulled back and helped her, but you didn't. You murdered her."

"That we did. I'd say I regret it, but I'm not entirely sure I do. I finally got sleep after she was gone."

That bastard.

I yanked at my restraints. I no longer cared if I didn't have my knives. I was going to strangle him with my bare hands.

Charles reached into his jacket pocket, pulling out a worn, leather-bound journal. "I keep records. I used to say that if I wasn't into real estate, I would have liked to be a writer. Your mother always encouraged that. She got me my first journal. This one. Thought it was only right to bury it with her daughter."

I stared at it, then at him. He really was going to kill me.

"How many people have you put at the bottom of this lake?" I asked, interrupting his ramblings.

"You'll be my first," he admitted. "But not the lake's first."

My blood chilled. He was so calm about all of this. It was deeply unsettling. For the first time since I'd started my revenge tour, the danger felt real.

Suddenly, he pivoted the conversation. "What's your favorite horror movie with a lake, Evelyn?"

I licked my lips and darted my gaze around, looking for

something that could help me escape this. I was realizing this man liked to play with his food before eating it. I'd have to play with him.

"*Cabin Fever*," I answered.

"Never heard of it. I can't remember the title of my favorite, but it was about an author who would bring women to his cabin. After he was done with them, he tied bricks to their feet and took them out on his boat, dropping them into a lake to create his own little garden under the water. You ever see that one?"

It was then that I spotted the boat just offshore and the cinderblocks beside it about twenty feet behind him. My stomach dropped. He wasn't going to shoot us and toss us overboard. He was going to drown us.

"No, I haven't." I answered.

"I'd forgotten about it until I found this journal and started to reread it." Charles opened the book and began flipping through the pages. "Lots of interesting stuff in here."

"Sebastian," I whispered when Charles stuffed the journal back into his pocket and headed to get the cinderblocks.

"It's okay, Final Girl," he whispered. "Don't panic."

It would have been the perfect time to panic.

"I had to cut my date short for this," Charles grumbled, bringing one of the concrete blocks over, dropping it in front of me. "She's a cutie, very eager to please. Blonde, young, stupid. After Lita, I couldn't be with brunettes."

"Why did you break up?" I wanted to keep him talking, but I was also genuinely curious. Sebastian had brought up a good point the other night. Charles was the man most likely to be my biological father out of the six. He paused, squatting down near my feet.

"She cheated on me. Right after I took her to Paris."

Silence followed his confession. It was on the tip of my tongue to ask when that was. Had it been nine months before I was born? I searched his face, looking for signs of myself. Did we share a nose, dimples, maybe a special freckle? I saw nothing that would indicate blood relation, and it made me a little sad. He was the one who'd loved her.

"I'm sorry." I wasn't sure why, but I felt bad for the man who'd tied us up and was planning on tossing our bodies into the lake.

My apology seemed to pull him back from his memories. He'd gone quiet. He wrapped a rope around my ankle and tightened the knots. I winced. Sebastian and I shared a look, and I shrank in my seat.

"Elliott told me. He's the only true friend I've ever had. She deserved what she got in the end. And you will too."

Did he really consider an affair deserving of rape and murder?

"Wait, did she cheat on you with Elliott?" I blurted. I wasn't entirely sure where it came from, but something about the way he spoke of his friend made me curious.

He shot me a look that said to stop asking—but also, yes. Charles bent down in front of me, pushing the cinderblock under my feet.

"You said Elliott wants information. What information does he want?" Sebastian asked as Charles tied a rope around my other ankle and then again attached it to the concrete block.

"He wants to know your plans," he muttered.

"I don't have any," I finally admitted. "I did some digging, found out she'd had dinner plans with some important men that night, and I knew it was them that had killed her." I glanced at Sebastian. "I paid some internet sleuths to help me figure out who they were, and you guys came up. So, I packed my bags and came out here to start with Thornton. That's it. That's the plan."

Shame filled my belly as I felt Sebastian's presence beside me. I'd tried to pretend I had plans or some semblance of organized thought, but there were none. My brain didn't work that way. I had too many ideas and nuggets of information and no clue how to use them to execute things.

"Hm. Guess I don't need to wait, then. Let's do this," Charles said. His face was blank, and my blood ran cold. He wasn't lying, I realized. He was going to drown us in that lake.

He stood and walked over to Sebastian, tying cinderblocks to him as well.

"Wait! I—I have to know. Did you guys kill Antoinette, my agent?"

Charles cocked his head. "I don't know anything about that. See, you're just like her. Digging into things you shouldn't. If it hadn't been us that night, it would have been another group of men. Lita was no stranger to getting herself into trouble," Charles told us as he worked.

"What trouble?" I pushed.

Charles looked up, raising an eyebrow. "She threatened to expose us, to lie about us. She was going to tell everyone we raped her. She was going to ruin us."

"So you killed her because she was going to tell the truth?" I gaped. When he didn't immediately reply, I began to wiggle in my seat, attempting to loosen my restraints.

"Because she was going to ruin our lives. We had wives, kids, important jobs. She didn't care. She was just upset that no one was interested in sharing those things with her. She was a deeply unhappy woman. We had to protect ourselves."

I shook my head. He was a liar. My mother was happy with her life. She'd had it all. They took that from her.

"You're pathetic," Sebastian snarled. "Your friends don't care about you. You think Elliott Bradley will care if you die?"

Charles didn't respond, but his jaw ticked, and I could see in his eyes that Sebastian had struck a nerve. Just then, we saw a shadow move. Sebastian's head shot up, and my attention flicked to it. Hope washed over me.

Skye.

She was creeping up slowly. Arms raised. My heart soared as the knives—my knives—caught the light as she clenched them high in the air.

"We were told to put an end to all of this. Elliott doesn't like to be played with. Picking us off one by one has only pissed him off." He stood, shaking his head and rubbing his jawline. Was he having second thoughts? Could we stop this?

"Are you my father?" I blurted.

He did a double take. "What?"

"My dad. One of you is my biological father. Which one is it?"

Charles took in my words—then laughed. It started as a chuckle and turned into a full, wholehearted belly laugh.

"You really think she'd have wanted me to father her child? Lita Reyes, the most beautiful woman in Hollywood, creating a child with someone less than her? Sorry, sweetie, I'm not the guy you're looking for. I wasn't good enough. Now let me go get Riley so we can haul your asses onto the boat. She's such a good girl."

"I'm not your good girl."

Charles turned and gasped as Skye swung her arms down, plunging both knives into the sides of his neck. The blades pierced his flesh, making the sound of a juice box being punctured. Blood sprayed everywhere as she pulled them back out. She leaped back as he fell forward, almost landing on her shoes.

The gurgling sound of him choking on his blood filled the silence, and only when he stopped breathing did we look away. It all happened so fast, it didn't feel satisfying at all. In fact, I felt a little bad. He wasn't innocent by any means. He had plans to murder me and Sebastian. I just...

What a way to go.

Skye inhaled rapidly, her face sprayed with blood, a smile slowly formed on her lips. "Did I do good?"

CHAPTER 47 EVIE

Strike

"Do you think he was telling the truth?" I asked as Skye untied us. I rubbed my sore wrists and glanced down at Charles's lifeless body. He'd claimed in his last moments that he didn't know who my father was. I wasn't entirely sure I believed him.

With each name crossed off my list, the chances of figuring out the mystery I hadn't known I cared about were growing slimmer and slimmer.

As long as it wasn't Jason, I supposed. Or Mike Thornton, considering I'd almost dated his son. If he were my father... I brushed the gross thought away. It wasn't Mike or Jason. If what Charles said was true—that my mom hadn't deemed Charles handsome enough—then she certainly hadn't picked Dourif or Thornton.

"No," Sebastian answered, kicking the body. "I think he was too entangled in Elliott Bradley's web. He was going to defend him till the death."

"Was that too messy?" Skye cringed, handing my daggers back to me after wiping Charles's blood and gore off them.

"Jason was worse," I told her.

"Oh, phew," she sighed in relief. "I thought it was too much. God, I'm an actress, but pretending to be on board with knocking you two out and stuffing you into his car was too much."

Sebastian bent down and put his hands under Charles's arms, lifting. "Let's get him to the boat. He gave us the tools. Might as well use them."

"The boat?" Skye asked, heading toward Charles's feet.

I joined her, and we each took a leg as Sebastian lifted his torso. Together, we took his body over to the rowboat and rolled him over the top, dropping him inside with a loud *thump*. We followed Sebastian back to the wooden chairs we'd been tied to and grabbed the cinderblocks, returning them to the boat.

"Will this float?" I asked. "With all of us in it?"

Sebastian's brow furrowed as he stared at the boat. Skye put her hands up and stepped away. "You guys go. I'll stay on land and try to clean up. I saw which building he grabbed the chairs from. There was a hose inside."

"Are you sure? I mean, this is your kill." I felt guilty leaving her on shore while we disposed of Charles's body, almost as if I were stealing this from her. "If you want to go, you totally can."

"No, for real, you go," she insisted, but the smile she had on didn't meet her eyes.

"I'll stay," Sebastian blurted. "You guys take the body. I'll make sure there's not a single trace of what happened. Skye, can you row a boat?"

Skye's face lit up, and she threw her arms around Sebastian. "Oh, yeah. We used to go out on boats at Bible camp. Let's go."

We climbed into the boat, and as Sebastian pushed us off the shore, I realized that arguing over who got to dump the body was such an odd thing to fight over. I smiled, holding in my laughter. *What was my life these days?*

"What's so funny?" Skye asked as she rowed us toward the center of the lake.

"Nothing. Just...this entire night. One moment I was signing autographs. The next I was watching a guy turn into a human juice box."

"Oh my God, okay, so you heard that too!" Skye said. "I swore it sounded like Sebastian had popped the tab open on one of his energy drinks. I got a little thirsty," she giggled.

I stared at her, so bubbly and unconcerned over our current situation. She'd been so upset over Jason's death. She'd claimed to be a lover, not a fighter, and yet here she was, having fought for me.

"I love you so much," I laughed.

"Right back at you." She winked, and a moment later, she stopped rowing. Falls Lake was a set, so it wasn't very big. It'd only taken us about two minutes to get to the center. "Okay, let's weigh him down like he'd planned to do to you," she said in such a chipper tone, it was as if she were talking about hauling groceries instead of a dead man.

"Wait. I want that journal," I said. I searched inside his jacket, retrieving the leather notebook. Then, curiosity getting the best of me, I dug through the rest of his pockets, finding his keys and wallet. I tossed the journal onto the floor of the boat, then Skye and I started the process of rolling him over the side and into the water.

"Holy shit. This is harder than I realized," she groaned as we lifted. We'd tried headfirst but barely managed to get his head out of the boat.

"Do the cinderblocks first!" Sebastian called from the shore. We turned to stare at him. His hands were cupped around his mouth as he called to us again.

Skye and I looked at each other and nodded.

We pivoted, hauling the cinderblocks over the side. Charles's body practically flew out of the boat and down into the water. It happened so fast, I let out a small yelp as water splashed into the boat and onto our faces.

"Whoa..." Skye said. "How did he know that would happen?" She gripped the sides of the boat, trying to steady us.

I looked back at the shore. Sebastian was giving us a thumbs-up. As we took our seats and Skye rowed us to shore, I pondered her question.

How did he know how to do all this stuff? He'd been entirely too eager to help me. He'd killed Thornton before I arrived in Hollywood. I'd spent these last few months thinking he was helping me with my quest for revenge, but had I been manipulated this whole time? Did I run into him while he was in the middle of his own murder spree?

"I kind of want to look for that movie he was talking about."

"What movie?" I shoved my thoughts to the back of my mind with the plan of returning to them later.

"The one with the rose garden in the lake? Charles was rambling about it on the way here. I kind of want to look it up."

"I've never seen it either, actually. Which is weird, considering my mom told him about it, apparently." I picked up the notebook, tracing the faded gold lettering on the front with Charles's name. The further I got along this journey, the more I was discovering I didn't know Lita Reyes as much as I wished. I hated these men more and more for taking her from me. Now, I would never know these things. She hadn't been given the opportunity to show me that movie. I flipped through the pages. Maybe this book would tell me something.

"We should just do a cabin horror movie marathon. *Cabin Fever*, *Cabin in the Woods*, *Evil Dead*, *Evil Dead II*, *Camera Stays On*. Iconic," Skye rattled off as we returned to shore.

Sebastian assisted us out of the boat once we got there. The chairs were gone, as were all traces of Charles's blood.

He was too good at taking care of crime scenes.

Red flags were being waved, but I couldn't figure out what exactly they were. I was just as bad as he was, right?

I looked back at Skye. "That sounds great. I actually love *Cabin Fever*. It's so bad, it's good. Can we get out of here now?"

"We're not that far from our lot, and my trailer has hot water. I need to shower. My call time is in a few hours. I'm going to be really sad once this is all over," Skye said.

"What do you mean?" I asked, stuffing the notebook into my pocket.

"*Simon Says*."

"*Six*," I added.

"*Six Six*," Sebastian continued.

Skye rolled her eyes.

"See! This! You guys have made filming so much fun. Bryce too. These last few months have been so amazing, life changing in so many ways. But I won't be coming back for another one because I'm being killed off." She paused, her eyes widening. "I just don't want it to end and stop hanging out all the time."

"Oh, Skye." I threw my arms around her and hugged her tightly. "That will not happen. You're my friend for life. We're so fucking trauma bonded, we're friends until the end."

I chose my words carefully. I didn't want to make promises I couldn't keep. I wasn't lying, though, when I said we'd be friends for life. Whether that was sixty more years or sixty more days.

"You want to walk with me?" Skye asked.

"Actually..." Sebastian stepped over to us, reaching for my hand. He tugged me to him, and I shivered from his sudden warmth. "I was thinking Evie and I could take the scenic route. What do you think?"

He nodded to Skye, and we started in the opposite direction at a lazy pace.

"Scenic route?" I glanced around. I'd never actually been in this part of the studio before.

"You ever see the *Psycho* house?"

"As in...Norman Bates?" I asked, my eyes growing wide with excitement.

He pointed off in the distance, and I turned, exhaling. "Groovy."

He chuckled, and we started off in the direction of the infamous house.

"Groovy."

CHAPTER 48

SEBASTIAN

The Studio Tour

I didn't look back after we split ways with Skye. I was on a mission—and a timer. My call time was just as early as hers. But...a small detour wouldn't hurt.

"I feel like a tourist," Evie giggled, her head whipping from side to side, admiring all the old, infamous movie sets.

"Well, consider this an exclusive tour. No cameras, please."

Everything was so close together, we reached the Bates Motel in minutes. I'd been here more than a dozen times, but I still enjoyed seeing it just as much as I had the first time. It was part of movie history, and I got to see it up close. I got to stand where my fucking heroes stood.

"Can we go in?" Evie's eyes lit up, pleading for me to let her go wild.

I gestured her forward.

She let go of my hand and rushed ahead.

"I mean, if you find one that works, sure." I shrugged, doubting that any of the handles would turn.

Evie flew down the line, trying all the doors but finding none of them functioning the way she'd hoped. "Boo," she moaned as she made it to the last door.

"You can peek through the windows," I offered, feeling a little bad she didn't get what she'd wanted. She cupped her hands over her eyes like binoculars and peered into a window.

"Just a lot of scaffolding." She pulled back and shook her head. "Never meet your heroes, friends." Her shoulders fell. "Where to now?"

"Well..." I gave her an impish smile. This had been my plan—kind of. "There's still the house."

Her eyes lit up again, and when I offered my hand, she took it eagerly. "Let's go!" She ran ahead, and I gladly let her drag me along. We climbed the iconic stairs and hurried up to the large house.

"I can't be disappointed twice in one night. I need to see the inside of Norman Bates's house," Evie said, a determined scowl on her face.

"I'll do my best not to let that happen. I hate seeing you sad," I said as we got to the top of the stairs. She stopped short and stared up at the piece of horror history.

"This is..."

I licked my lips, my heart rate climbing. I opened my mouth to speak—

Crack.

"What was that?" We both jumped, and she gripped me tightly.

Looking around, I saw no one, but that didn't mean much. I wasn't taking any chances. If someone had followed us, we weren't going to stand out in the open and let them take us down.

"Come on. Let's go exploring." I tightened my jaw and squeezed her hand. I reached for the door handle. Much to my surprise, it opened. I pulled her inside quickly, shutting the door in case someone was watching. We turned, facing away from the door, and I looked down at Evie.

Watching her take it all in was so much more exciting than looking at it myself.

"This is..." Her eyes widened as she stepped deeper inside.

"Careful," I warned, reaching for her. "This place isn't kept up to code. They never filmed inside." I looked around at the scaffolding holding this large mansion up. It wasn't a real house, like people imagined. It was just a pretty box that was held up by tons of wood.

"I never would have imagined it looked like this," she said, her voice small.

"I know. A bit disappointing, huh?"

"Not at all!" She spun around and grinned. "It's so cool! Like, I know a secret. Oh, if I were still making content, this would make me so much money." She scrunched up her nose. "But I don't want to do that. I'm tired of this mindset that everything I do should be caught on camera for views. I... I think I'm going to sell."

"Really?" The selfish part of my heart pitter-pattered. Selling meant she'd be considering her acting career more.

"Maybe. I like not being attached to a camera at all times. Stuff like this? Exploring without having to take photos or make a video would never happen if I had to keep making daily content. I want this every day."

Once we were done exploring, we circled back to the front of the house. Evie reached for the door, and I took her hand, pulling it away from the knob. Turning to face me, she gasped when I pressed her against the door, enveloping her in a kiss. I grinned, placing my hand on her hip.

"I want this too," I told her.

"Want what?" Her voice came out breathy, her chest rising and falling fast.

"To have you all to myself with no cameras, every day. And you know what else I want?" I whispered in her ear.

"What?"

"I want to fuck you in the *Psycho* house." I pulled back, and she grabbed my face, yanking me down, our lips colliding.

"Oh, Sebastian..." she moaned. "You're..."

"What?" I asked, sliding my hands down her body.

"A psycho, but you're also so sweet. I—I don't know what to do."

"Sweet?"

"You helped me kill three men, and yet you still take me to dinner, and introduced me to your dogs, and now you want me to..."

"Stay here forever. Are you really ready to give this up?"

"Hollywood?"

"Me."

My lips crushed back down on hers, and I didn't pull away until we were both struggling for air. Taking in a breath, I grinned and reached for her jacket, tugging it off and tossing it onto the floor. She yanked at my clothes, and together, we helped each other undress. I kicked off my boots and grabbed Evie by the waist. Dropping to my knees and keeping her standing, I pushed her against the door. Spreading her thighs, I dove between her legs and ran my tongue along her slit.

"Sebastian, what if someone was out there?"

"Let them watch," I snarled. "It's too late for them to tell us we can't be here. Anthony C.—Evie, you're so fucking wet."

"What can I say? Something about defiling my followers' holy grounds gets me hot."

"That's an episode I can't wait to watch. Make it your goodbye video—go out with a bang." I chuckled and inserted a finger inside her, continuing to make her squirm with my tongue. Closing my eyes, I shifted closer to her, reaching around to squeeze her ass. Cupping her cheeks, I lifted her off the ground, putting her thighs on my shoulders and pressing her against the door, settling into a more comfortable position for us both.

"What if they catch us?" she asked, closing her eyes and letting her head fall back.

"What if they don't? What if we kill all those motherfuckers and get away with it? Wouldn't that be one helluva story?"

Taking her clit into my mouth, I sucked and flicked my tongue, doing what I knew would get her to gush. In less than a minute, she was yanking on my hair and pleading to a higher power. My mouth was filled with her orgasm, and I lapped up every drop before pulling back and lowering her feet to the floor.

"You're a fucking psycho." She laughed as we kissed.

I slid my tongue between her lips, allowing her to taste herself.

"Only for you, Final Girl." I chuckled. "I don't know what it is about you that makes me feral, but I'm not ready to let it go, Evie." I teased her nipple with my thumb, running the pad over her sensitive nub.

"This wasn't part of the plan." She sighed, arching her back. She closed her eyes and melted against me.

Wrapping my other arm around her, I held her tight, resting my forehead on hers.

"I don't care if I wasn't part of your plan. You were always a part of mine, Evie. I finally got you back. I'm not giving you up. I'll literally let go of everything else to show you how much you mean to me."

"You don't mean that."

"If you go, I go," I declared.

"What do you mean?"

"If you leave Hollywood, I'm going with you. And if you die—I die."

"Don't say things that aren't true."

"I don't think you realize how fucking crazy I am for you, Evie."

"I— I'm scared, Sebastian," she confessed.

I knew her words were layered. It wasn't about getting caught right here, right now. It wasn't about dying in a shower of bullets on her revenge quest. It was about me. Her and me. What our futures could be once this was over.

"Me too, but that's the business we're in, baby. Scared is what we do best."

I tilted her chin up, and the moment our eyes locked, I crashed my lips down onto hers. Lifting her again, she wrapped her legs around my waist, and I sank my cock into her, pushing her against the door.

I nipped her neck with my teeth and began to move, pushing her harder against the door. It was such a fragile set, the wood rattled with each thrust of my hips. I kissed her again, and our tongues began a slow, passionate dance devoid of rhythm. It felt like we were both trying to absorb into the other. As I ran my thumb over her nipple and pinched, I decided her leaving me was no longer an option. Before, I was going to simply ask her to stay—beg, even. But now... There was no choice for her.

I wasn't losing her a second time.

"Sebastian..." She trailed off as her body tightened and then unraveled. Her muscles convulsed around my cock, milking me as she came. I ran my tongue down her neck as she cried out, relishing in what I'd done to her. Could I coax a third? I slowed as she savored her second, and then I started the hunt for my own release.

I worked her body, softening her, then winding her back up. Sweat poured from her brow, and the scent of her perfume blending with the look on her face as she was building up to come again was doing something to my senses. I was wild for her.

"Come on, Final Girl. Come for me one more time."

"I—I can't..." she whimpered, her eyes shut tight.

"Oh, I think you can. I'm not done until you are." I ground into her, my cock pressing against her G-spot. She was struggling to breathe, which I found amusing, as she was constantly doing the same to me.

How I craved this.

She gasped as she came again. Her fluids drenched me, running down my legs as I pumped harder into her, searching for my release, finishing right alongside her. We fell against the door, limp, sweating, and trying to catch our breath.

"I—" The words were caught in my throat, but I needed to say it. I was vulnerable and needed to tell her how I felt.

"I was watching *The Exorcist*," I said into her shoulder, afraid to see the rejection in her eyes, but I changed my mind. I pulled back to look at her, and before I could speak more, she yanked me to her.

"Beep beep, Ritchie," she said before bringing her lips to mine.

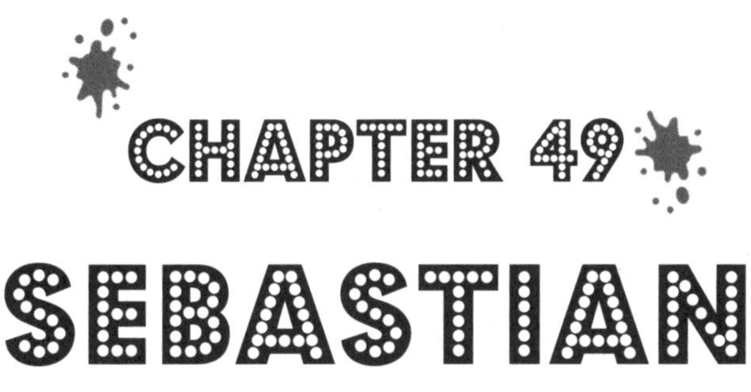

CHAPTER 49 SEBASTIAN

The Modesty Patch

Yesterday's tryst was on replay in my mind as I prepared for today's workday. Getting waxed and groomed for a day of sex scenes was awkward as hell—especially when my dick kept getting hard every time I thought about Evie. And it was interesting because I wasn't just thinking about sex with her. I was thinking about the future. Movie nights with her and the dogs, vacations to Scotland or Australia, making more movies with her, marriage.

It was never really about sex with Evie Reyes. It was all the stuff in-between that had my mind going haywire.

After I was fully waxed, I admired myself in the full-length mirror in my trailer. I'd put a lot of work into maintaining the Hollywood physique. I hoped Evie liked how I looked. Before my mind could take me on a montage daydream of all the things I'd like to do with Evie, again, there was a knock on my trailer. Connor came in and said they were ready for me.

As my assistant drove me over to set, I noticed how protected things were for today's scenes. This wasn't any different from sex scenes I'd done before, but for some reason, I felt overly protective toward Evie's and I's privacy. A sense of comfort came over me as I spotted all the signs reading *Closed Set*.

"Thanks, Connor," I said as he handed me a Red Bull and dropped me off.

"Anytime, Sebastian."

I went inside and flinched at the harsh lighting. Filming sex scenes was one of the least sexy things to do in filmmaking. The bright lights, the shouting of directions, the constant awareness of not only the people in the room, but your scene partner. I suddenly felt self-conscious as I stared down at my limp cock. Could I... perform?

"That's, uh—not what I was hoping to see." Dante caught me staring at my doll-like groin and walked over. "What happened to full mast? You'd think you'd be excited to be filming with your Final Girl today."

"I am," I assured him. "Thrilled, actually. I'm just a little nervous, I guess. This is what's going to be in the movie?"

"Yes, sir. Do you need a little help? Your agent negotiated for a fluffer. We can call one."

I shook my head. "No, I think I'll be fine once Evie gets here." The amusement on Dante's face made my face flame, and I rephrased. "I mean, once we start acting, I'll be able to focus. Fuck off," I muttered and went to find a corner to drink my Red Bull in peace. I found the chair with my name on it and plopped down, mentally preparing myself.

As if my soul were connected to hers, I knew the moment Evie walked onto set. My breathing hitched, and my thoughts disappeared for a flash as I turned my head to see her. She was... beautiful.

They'd curled and styled her hair. Her makeup looked perfect, her red lips were fuller, her lashes longer, and when she batted them, her eyes shone. Suddenly, my cock rose from the dead beneath my robe.

"There we go," Dante said, seeming to come from nowhere.

Glaring at him, I placed a hand over my lap. "Can you not monitor my erections, please?" I asked.

He put his hands up. "Fair enough. Let's just keep that energy going for the shoot today. Once we get these shots, I don't care if you ever get hard again."

He left me, and I stood to go see Evie. There was a bit of fanfare to her arrival. She'd been swarmed by the production team the instant she came through the door. I waited until they'd moved on before going to her. She was standing at craft services, grabbing a yellow Red Bull.

"Ready?" I asked.

She took a deep breath and nodded. "They set my modesty patches already. I made them double some up," she said with a laugh.

She blushed and looked down at her feet. I licked my lips. She seemed to worry about a repeat of our chemistry test, while I was *hoping* for a repeat.

"I hope they used superglue, because I'm putting my all into this today."

She crossed her arms under her chest, causing my eyes to shoot to her breasts then back up to her eyes. Before she could say something smart back, they were shouting for everyone that wasn't necessary to leave set. They filed out and with them, all the relaxed energy. Suddenly, everything felt very serious.

Dante came over and explained the scene. It felt pointless, as I'd read the script a hundred times. I knew what was going on. Which was good because I couldn't focus on Dante's words. All I could think about was Evie and how she was feeling right now.

I was a seasoned actor, used to being a piece of meat to this industry. My place in all of this was to look attractive and read my lines. Once the movie was released into the world, all sorts of trolls would come out online to critique every little thing about us. I could turn my feelings on and off. Could she do that? Would she be able to set aside everything to bare her body for art?

"Got it?" Dante asked us. Giving him a thumbs-up in agreement, he left to sit near the monitors.

I turned to Evie. "What did he say?"

"To make it look good, basically," she said. "He's letting us improvise, and he'll just film and cut it later."

"Got it."

I let her take the lead. She untied her robe, and I did the same. I went to hand it to Connor, but I remembered he wasn't here. I rolled my eyes and smirked as I took it to my chair.

This wasn't my first rodeo. What was I doing?

I tried not to be obvious as I glanced to the side to see what Evie was doing. I was always respectful of my scene partners, but today I was hyper-aware of all my actions.

She was wearing her bra and panties, so I kept my boxers on. I stood there until she reached for my hand and pulled me onto the set.

"Are we ready?" Dante shouted.

Evie wrapped her arms around me, and any anxiety I had about her preparedness for the future, my body's performance, and everything else washed away. She turned to Dante and squinted. "Actually, I think I've changed my mind. Could we do the music?"

"Music?" I asked.

Dante raised his arm and made a circular gesture with his finger, and a moment later, low music poured from speakers I couldn't see.

"It won't be in the final cut, obviously, but he said it might help me focus less on the cameras," she explained. "He let me make a playlist."

I grinned, recognizing the song. It was "Is This Love" by Whitesnake. "Is this your personal bang list, Final Girl?"

She blushed. "Maybe."

"Countdown!" someone shouted, and I straightened, getting into the character of Ronny McCoy—the charming, not-all-there boy next door. You'd think after five murder sprees in which he was a major target, he'd have left town completely—but no, Ronny was still living in Simon Says's proximity.

But it was all paying off, because finally, he was getting laid.

The cameras rolled, and Evie and I were replaced by Ronny and Lucy, the lovers. We made out while standing up, taking direction from Dante. While he had told us he'd let us improvise, his director's soul couldn't help but bark too frequently for my taste. We filmed an hour of making out and heavy petting, then they called for Evie to take a small break so they could get the money shot.

We got the full-frontal scenes of me stalking naked to the bed. I kept my mind solely on Evie and me in the *Psycho* house to stay hard. I'd do it again and again if we could. I wanted to fuck her on every set on this lot. Making a mental list of all the places we could fuck kept my mind off the camera that was inches away from my dick, catching every pore, wrinkle, and drop of precum falling from the tip.

By the time we got to the bed, I was getting a little lightheaded from the lack of blood in my brain. It'd been going to my groin for hours now, and I needed release.

"You okay?" she asked me as we took lunch.

I bit back the urge to invite her into the bathroom to get this handled before we returned to set, but the thought of hearing Dante complain about my limp cock for the rest of the day kept my fantasies at bay.

"Yeah. I just...need a minute."

I was pretty sure my frustration was clear on my face every moment the cameras were off. People stopped checking in on me, and I found Red Bulls and water left on my chair instead. We returned from break, and I almost growled when I got onto the bed and discovered exactly how strong her modesty patch was. I closed out everything around us and zeroed in on trying to make her as sexually frustrated as me. I kissed her thighs, licking up and down her body. I planted kisses on her bare breasts and pinched her nipples.

She groaned and threw her head back. Dante was shouting words of praise about her acting skills, but only I knew she wasn't performing for anyone but me.

I ground my palm against her mound, and she thrust her hips up into me. Was she...

I moved between her thighs and pressed my erection against her modesty patch. If I wanted to, I could rip the fucking tape off and take her. The idea was so tempting, my mouth watered, and my cock pleaded for more against the patch. My hand drifted down, running along the seam of the modesty patch... I scraped the edges with my nails, daring myself to rip it off.

Leaning in, I whispered in her ear for only us to hear. "We could have number four, right here, right now. What do you say, Final Girl?"

CHAPTER 50

EVIE

Crisis Management

"Cut!" Dante shouted and ran onto the set, shoving Sebastian off me. "What the fuck is your problem?" he shouted, just as the modesty patch Sebastian had torn from my body fluttered to the floor.

Crew members pushed Sebastian so hard he fell to the ground with a loud thump. He scrambled to his feet and glanced around, blinking rapidly, as if he was just as shocked as everyone else. Realizing everyone was looking at him, Sebastian stormed toward his chair, grabbing his robe, and slid it on.

"Oh, now you give a shit about modesty. Get the hell off my set." Dante swung his arm toward the door and pointed at the exit. He then turned back to me. "Evie, are you okay? Fuck..." he hissed.

The new intimacy coordinator rushed over with my robe and helped me off the bed. I covered myself quickly, just as embarrassed as Sebastian.

"I'm going to get so fucking sued," Dante groaned.

Putting their hands on my shoulders, the coordinator led me off the set and shot questions at me, asking if I was okay, if Sebastian hurt me, if I wanted to cancel the shoot. So many voices were being thrown in my direction, I couldn't focus. It was so hot I was dizzy. My vision got spotty, and then suddenly, everything went black.

I WOKE IN my trailer with a cold rag on my forehead. Raissa and a plump young Black woman with long braids in a medic uniform sat a short distance away. I sat up, and the room started to spin. Laying back down, the two ran to my side.

"How are you feeling, Ms. Reyes?" the medic asked, pulling out a blood pressure cuff.

"Just dizzy. What happened?"

"Sebastian... "

Suddenly, it all came back to me. We'd gotten too into the moment. Everything around us had disappeared, leaving only our lust. He'd ripped off my modesty patch and was just about to...

"Where is he?" I asked.

"Um, I think with legal? They are trying to figure out if..." Raissa grimaced, giving me the familiar face of "I don't want to tell you" that I'd grown to recognize.

"Do you want to press sexual assault charges, Ms. Reyes?" the medic asked matter-of-factly.

"What?" My mind went completely blank. Sexual assault?

"He tried to rape you."

Rape? My mouth dropped open. That was a startling accusation. I wasn't sure what everyone else in that room had seen, but it was far from rape.

I shook my head vehemently. "No, no, that's not what happened. This is all a mistake." I pushed them away and shifted, putting my feet on the floor. "I need to fix this. He shouldn't be punished. We just got too—"

"Oh jeez, let me get Dante." Raissa rushed down the stairs and out of my trailer.

The medic stepped aside and turned to give me privacy as I grabbed my clothes and began to change. I had just finished pulling on my shoes when there was a knock.

"Come in!" I called.

Dante came in, followed by a group of men and women I didn't recognize. They all wore business suits, causing a ball of dread to form and drop into my belly. He excused the medic kindly, and after she closed the door on her way out, he turned back to me.

"Evie, this is our legal team. We... How are you feeling?"

"I'm okay. You guys can sit if you want."

I put my hands in my lap and watched them eye the couch with uncertainty, then sit.

"Should I have my lawyer?" I asked. Although now that Antoinette was gone, I wasn't sure I had one. She'd been my agent and my lawyer.

"Do you want one?" Dante asked quickly. "We can get you one if you need. Sebastian has already called his. Jesus Christ, this—we shouldn't have—" His lawyers gave him a stern look, shutting him up. "Fuck!"

He put his head between his hands, tugging on his hair and rubbing his short beard.

"Well, I think if you're going to fire me, it's fair I have representation," I shot at him.

"Fired?" Dante stopped rubbing his face and looked up. "We're not firing you, Evie. We're worried you're going to sue us."

"Why would I sue you?" I looked around, trying to understand.

"Sebastian was *not* supposed to do what he did."

"And neither was I," I reminded him. "I was just as complicit as he was in that room."

They stared at me as if I wasn't getting it.

I clapped and brought my hands to my temples. "Look, I'm not suing anyone. I just want to keep my job."

They exchanged looks and nodded. "Fair. No one is losing their job unless you want Sebastian off the project."

I sighed deeply. "No, I do not. Can we finish the day out? What time is it?" I looked for my clock. "How much time did we lose because of this?"

Dante scoffed. "We can't go back to set today. Even if I wanted to, all the studio executives are losing their minds. We'll be lucky to get on set tomorrow. Take the rest of the day off. Get some rest."

I sat there for a moment, replaying everything that had happened today and how it led to this moment. I was keeping my job—but was Sebastian going to be punished?

"Do you have any questions or concerns for us?" one of the lawyers asked.

I pressed my lips together, my belly churning with nerves. "Actually, yes. Sebastian mentioned simulated and unsimulated sex scenes... What if we tried unsimulated..."

"Oh, fuck me." Dante stood and began to pace the trailer. "I'm so fucked. I'll never work again. This is bad. This is so goddamn bad. Did Sebastian tell you to ask?"

One of the lawyers jumped up and went to him while the others stayed seated.

"No!" I swore. "I just..." I drifted off as my face began to flush. How could I tell them that I'd been just as eager to remove my tape on that set?

"Well, Ms. Reyes, unsimulated sex scenes come with a lot more restrictions and rules, and that would—"

"We'd get an NC-17 rating for starters. Then I'd have to worry about one of you revoking consent at any moment, which would cause a myriad of issues. They'll call me the fucking porn king. You can't really be thinking about this, Evie. What the hell."

I lifted my shoulders. "I don't know, Sebastian just—"

"Please don't say he convinced you of this." The lawyers looked at each other. I could practically hear the collective scream—if I said Sebastian had told me to say this, they could be sued out the ass.

"No. I just... I don't know. You wanted the movie to look real."

"Oh, I think it looks pretty fucking real, Evie." Dante sighed. "It's only been a few hours, and already we're getting phone calls."

"Phone calls?"

"Yeah, whoever leaked what happened on set is getting fired,"

Dante muttered. "This is so bad."

I stood slowly to keep from making myself dizzy. "I'm so sorry. I—"

There was a knock on the door, and when I called for them to come in, Stacey, the woman from the PR company, came into the trailer. Suddenly, I felt overwhelmed by so many people in my private space.

"Hey, Evie, how are you feeling? We heard you had a little spill."

"I'm fine." I crossed my arms. "What are you doing here?" Whenever she and her team showed up, it wasn't great. She always had a new scheme.

"Well, word is slowly spreading about the little moment on set, and we wanted to discuss our angle for this. Is legal action being taken?" She directed the question to the lawyers. They shook their heads, and she sighed in relief. "Oh good. So, we'll get contracts stating this, then?"

They nodded, and one of them opened a briefcase and pulled out a standard NDA. I wasn't enthused about not having a lawyer to consult, but I'd signed more than one of these, and it didn't look like anything scary. I signed it quickly, and they left, thanking me as they went. Dante stayed behind and sat beside Stacey as she turned to me.

I was so sick of this fake relationship. I had to be "on" at all times, and I was ready to be "off." It was exactly why I planned on letting go of *The Body Count Bimbo* channel. I wanted to live a real life.

If I never saw Stacey or her team again, it'd be too soon.

"So, let's figure this out, shall we?" She smiled tightly. "Sebastian is still talking with his legal counsel, right?" She looked to Dante.

"I think so, yeah."

"Can we bring him in on this?"

"Probably not." Dante shook his head. "They aren't going to want him anywhere near Evie."

"Fair. Okay, let's sort out details and then get with him."

"Details?"

I was beginning to wonder if I'd gotten a concussion when I collapsed, because none of this made any sense. Who was in trouble and why? Maybe I needed to get the medic back in here.

Stacey leaned over and put her hand gently on my knee. "Evie, sweetie, we have the story that is going to make this movie a whole lot of money, so long as we spin it right. This evening, the media is going to hear about Sebastian removing your modesty patch during filming today, and we are going to tell them that not only is it true, but you two can't keep your hands off each other. The world is going to love you."

CHAPTER 51

EVIE

The Prop Run

"I don't know how you plan to do this. We can't go anywhere without a fucking camera trailing us," Sebastian muttered when I suggested we go to Charles Hodder's house and try to find out what we could about his relationship with my mother.

"So, we lose them." I waved my hand dismissively, despite the growing knot in my belly. Ever since the PR team leaked word of what happened on set, we'd become the shiniest, newest, most exciting toy for the people who got paid to take photos and make up stories about us. I couldn't go anywhere without having someone with a camera take photos or ask me questions. Sebastian, after being cleared from the rape accusations—started by who knows who—and both of us agreeing that no legal action would be taken, had to start escorting me home, driving behind me every night and then going to his place twenty minutes in the other direction. It was exhausting, hiding from the paparazzi while also trying to plan murders.

Tonight, I'd gone to his house. We were going to watch the *IT* TV mini-series that starred Tim Curry.

"You really think we can take a few fast turns and they won't find us? That's the most ridiculous idea I've ever heard, and living in Hollywood, I've heard some doozies." Sebastian pushed the dogs off him and walked over to where I'd been pacing, twirling my knives like batons through my fingers. I still hadn't had a chance to use them. It felt like such a waste after all the trouble my mom went through to get them to me. Even Skye got to use them before I did, and that didn't sit right with me.

I needed to stab someone.

Sebastian caught my wrists mid-twirl and pulled them to my sides. "Evie, I'm not opposed to this idea, but we've gotta be smart about it. Come sit, and let's think."

I pouted slightly as he took my knives, setting them on the coffee table. He dragged me to the couch and onto his lap as he plopped down. I wrapped my arms around his neck and snuggled into his chest. I knew the position was intimate, far too intimate for a casual hookup relationship, but it was comfortable. While I'd fought it for so long, I couldn't deny there was comfort in our history.

That night in the *Psycho* house changed things. It wasn't just a silly deal anymore, where he got sex in exchange for a little murder. He'd made it clear from the start that he wanted more, and then somewhere along the way, I'd started to consider it.

But it wasn't fair to lead him on and make him think we could have a future after this. It wasn't for lack of interest in the future, but lack of a future at all. I would die to make sure I got my revenge, but...he didn't need to witness it. I'd tried to have that conversation with him, but every time I started, it ended in an argument. He couldn't even consider how real the chances of me dying were.

Sebastian pushed a strand of hair back behind my ear, pulling me from my thoughts.

"Let's see... Maybe if we plan this around a bigger event, something that will take attention off us, we could sneak over." He pulled out his phone, wrangling it so that he could keep a hand around my waist while scrolling. "There's a movie premiere next week. It's the studio's summer blockbuster."

"Which one?"

"*Mind to Bend*," he read from the screen. "Let's plan for that night. But if I think someone's following us, it's off."

I snuggled deeper into him and focused on the TV. Pennywise the Clown was straddling a banister and making a crude joke to the adult Losers Club below. "Let's see who can quote this movie the most, and we'll figure out how to get into Charles's house tomorrow."

A WEEK LATER, I dressed in all black, and Sebastian wore his normal clothes to drive over to Charles's now abandoned mansion. He'd been stupid enough to give out his real address to Skye on their date, so we had her drive by it a few times to make sure it was empty. We'd been on alert all week, watching for paparazzi. Seeing exactly which ones were dedicated to catching us, and which were simply bored. Sebastian was close to calling off the mission entirely, especially once he picked me up and saw my outfit, but I insisted the coast was clear.

"You're dressed like a burglar from *The Sims*." He shook his head as I climbed into his car.

"I want to be hidden in the dark," I argued. "They'll see *you* from a mile away."

"Yeah, and I'll be able to play it off like I was at a friend's house or taking a walk. How are you going to explain why you're in the area, dressed like the Hamburgler?"

I stopped talking, seeing his point. I looked down at my hoodie.

Well, shit.

"It's fine. Just take off the hat, and you should be fine. We can make it work," he said, and I did as suggested.

Charles had lived in Bel-Air. For a real estate tycoon, I'd expected nothing less.

"There's gonna be a code for the gate," Sebastian said as we drove into the estate. It was easily twice the size of the house my mother left behind. Which, I'd discovered while digging through her things, he'd been her real estate agent for the purchase.

I rattled off the four digits, 0510, without missing a beat.

We reached the tall wrought-iron gate, and he rolled the window down to punch in the code. It beeped in acceptance, and the metal gates opened.

"How did you know that?" He glanced over, raising an eyebrow.

I pulled Charles's journal out of my hoodie pocket and waved it. "His anniversary with my mother. He talks about it being his secret lucky number."

I'd learned a lot about the man who could possibly be my father through the journal I'd taken before dumping him into the lake. He was clearly neurodivergent, although possibly undiagnosed. At the time he wrote it, I don't think he had gotten help for his obsessive-compulsive tendencies. He never mentioned them outright, but it was clear on the page he was neurospicy of some flavor. With his paranoia and extensive record-keeping of... everything, I was curious to see his home and any further evidence of his eccentricities.

"I hope he didn't have any pets," Sebastian muttered as we drove around the back of his house.

"I doubt that," I said. "He didn't like animals."

"He must have put a lot in that notebook," he commented as we used the same code to unlock the back door and waltz right inside. Sebastian used the flashlight on his phone to reveal a bright-blue kitchen.

"He filled every page, front and back," I said as we walked single file through the house, using his flashlight to guide us. Everything was various shades of blue—the floors, the ceiling, the furniture, all blue. I wondered if he had guests often, and if it gave them the same unsettling feeling it was giving me. It was all decorated stylishly, so it didn't look unnatural, but having read his innermost thoughts, I knew it wasn't just a design choice.

He needed the blue.

Just like my mother had needed the pink.

My mother had hidden behind the color pink. She'd made it part of her personality, something everyone who knew her used to identify her. She'd told me once that she'd grown up in a poor household, where they didn't have luxury items. But on her fifteenth birthday, her father, unable to afford a full, traditional quinceañera party, had a dress made and gifted it to her. It was pink, and despite having nowhere to wear it, she wore it in her room every day, dreaming of the day she'd have a closet full of dresses and a million places to wear them. That soft shade of pink was what she surrounded herself with to protect herself from the harsh reality of life.

I wondered if that was why Charles chose blue, because it was the opposite of my mother's house.

"Why is everything blue?" Sebastian asked as we started up the stairs. "You notice that?"

"I did."

"Must be his favorite color."

Actually, I was pretty sure it was pink. After the breakup with my mother, though...

We reached a room where another code was needed. When 0510 didn't work, I tried it backwards, and it unlocked.

Sebastian went first and froze. "Holy shit."

"What?" Flicking a light on, despite the risk of being seen, I peered past him. And then I saw why he'd frozen.

This was the only room we'd seen that wasn't blue. It was pink.

"This is..."

"An exact replica of the room I sleep in?" I stepped inside, looking around in a mix of surprise and unease. The bedding, the walls, the furniture—all of it was a double of my mother's room.

"This is creepy. Maybe he *was* psycho."

"No, I don't think so." I shook my head and went to the closet, mildly surprised to find his clothes inside and not hers. "I think he was neurodivergent of some kind and his friends took advantage of it. He was smart and talented, obviously. Just..."

"Fascinating," Sebastian muttered, pulling open drawers on the vanity table. "Are these her makeup and creams too?"

I joined him on the other side of the room and scanned the table. They were all the same ones sitting on the table at home. It was like he never left that relationship.

"How did he explain this when he brought partners home?" Sebastian shook his head.

"I doubt he did. This was a shrine to my mom." I shuddered. "He wouldn't dare let anyone in here."

As we explored the room, I began to have doubts. If he was this obsessed with her, could he have been a willing participant in her rape and murder? Or was there more to the story that we didn't know?

"Evie, I think I found something," Sebastian called from the closet.

I hurried over and found him crouched on the floor, pulling out a cardboard box from the back.

"What is it?" I asked, squatting down beside him.

He opened the top, and my heart dropped. There were stacks and stacks of notebooks, just like the one I had left in the car.

"Holy shit," I said under my breath.

A loud crash that sounded like splintering wood came from downstairs. We froze and looked at each other with wide eyes.

What the fuck was that?

Heavy footsteps and angry voices carried up the stairs, and terror slid up my spine.

We weren't the only intruders tonight.

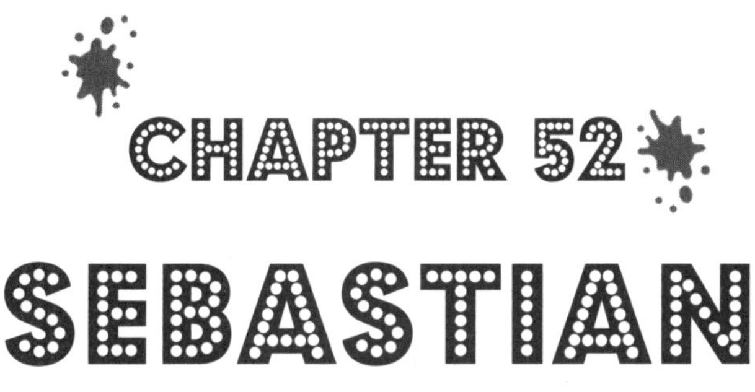

CHAPTER 52 SEBASTIAN

The Near Miss

"Sebastian, I'm scared."

The words from Evie's perfect lips sent my world spiraling. I stared at her as the world around me crumbled into darkness. Evie, the one who had told me time and time again she was ready to die for her revenge, was scared. I reached for her hand and squeezed.

"It's okay. We need to hide." I stood and looked around for a place to put her. She was short. We could make this work.

"Who is it you think?" she whispered as we crept into Charles's bedroom.

"It's probably a looter who's been scoping the house. Shh..." I put a finger to my lips and urged her toward the bed. I lifted the bedding that hung over the side of the mattress. "Get under here."

"Under the bed?" she asked me, incredulous.

"You got any better ideas?" I hissed as I went to the door, shutting and locking it. "They don't know the code, obviously. They broke in. Get under the bed and hide."

"What about you?" she asked as she dropped down and scooted under the large pink bed.

I reached into my back pocket and pulled out my knife. I popped it open and reached for the door handle. "New plan. Lock this behind me." Quietly, I slid out of the room.

"Seb—" Her angry whisper was cut off as I shut the door.

I waited until I heard the click of the lock behind me.

I went to the edge of the stairs and listened.

"Where do you think they'd be?" a man said. He was speaking at a normal volume, implying he wasn't afraid of being caught.

"With how many he's got, I wouldn't be surprised if they're all over. Charles wouldn't be stupid enough to put them all in one place."

My blood chilled. I recognized that voice—Elliott Bradley.

This was serious—Elliott had come out himself.

He was looking for the notebooks.

The notebooks that were currently locked inside the room Evie was in.

I gripped my knife and looked up and down the hall for somewhere to go. I couldn't let them get to Charles's bedroom.

"Open every cabinet and drawer. Check under pillows, cushions, everything. I don't give a fuck. We need those books. I'm afraid Charles grew a heart and told her about them," Elliott said.

Soon, the sounds of glass breaking, wood splintering, things crashing to the floor, and fabrics being ripped drifted up the stairs as he and his partner began trashing Charles's home, looking for something they weren't going to find.

"Are we even sure they're here?" the other man asked. "What if he put them in a safety deposit box or something?"

"He might have," Elliott agreed. "But we need to check here first. I guarantee we're not the only ones looking for them."

Elliott was smart—which made him more dangerous than anyone with a knife.

"Yeah, well, with the paparazzi up their asses, they can't go anywhere without being tailed."

I tried to place the voice of the other man. He spoke to Elliott like an equal, a friend. Was that Arthur Englund, the other remaining person on Evie's list? I was convinced, as I continued to listen to them, that it had to be.

"He called me the night before he died. I told you that, right? He wanted to negotiate a deal for a new *Simon Says*. I'd made a joke about Shaw putting him up to it, then he laughed and told me not to worry about who he was talking to. Mike always did do business with his dick."

"You think Shaw did something?" Elliott asked.

They were talking about Mike Thornton. I gulped. Did someone know my secret?

"I doubt it was on purpose. Mike was always popping those Viagras like candy. If anything, Shaw just watched him die and ran scared. He's too chickenshit to actually kill someone."

I took mild offense at Arthur's assessment. Not only had Thornton's death been intentional; I'd also killed Thornton's son and helped with two other murders.

"I don't know how she wrapped Shaw into this. We're about to lose our biggest investment," he groaned. I'd never met the man, but I knew he was one of our studio executives, and they were all about the bottom line.

"You really don't know?" Elliott snickered. "Like mother, like daughter. I think you underestimate the power of pussy, friend. Shaw got fucked just like the rest of us. What happens, happens."

Were they implying that Evie had manipulated me with sex? Or her mind? Either way, it couldn't be further from the truth. As I rolled my eyes at their crude words, I continued to listen.

"Well, when this is over, the movie is out, and the promotion has wrapped, we'll deal with him. Sebastian Shaw will trip down some stairs or something."

My blood chilled.

They were planning my murder.

I wanted to go down and fight them right here, right now. But I was one man with one knife. They were two, and who knew what weapons they had. Elliott seemed like the handgun type. Instead, I stood at the top of the stairs, waiting for them to come up. I leaned on the banister, almost bored but still listening.

"What do you think happened to Charles?" Arthur asked.

"Well, what have we seen so far? Heart attack, slit throat, and electrocution. Your guess is as good as mine," Elliott said.

"What about Mike's son?"

"I knew the boy. I'm not sold that it wasn't an outside job. He had a smart mouth. Plus, I know the game. Lita's daughter is on a mission."

"Do we know he's dead, for sure?"

"Would Charles ignore us this long? They got him. I just don't know how yet. His body will turn up. These things always do. Are we done down here? Let's start on the upstairs."

Afraid they'd catch me listening, I ran back to the master bedroom. I typed in the code, hurried inside, and locked the door. The lock wouldn't stop them if they really wanted to get in.

"Evie!" I hissed. "We need to get out of here." I went to the bed and crouched down. The space underneath was clear of anything. Fuck. *Where had she gone?* I called out to her again, but she didn't respond. I hurried to the closet, pulling back clothes and pushing boxes out of the way. "We have to go!"

Coming up empty, I turned back to the room, and my eyes zeroed in on the open window on the other side. Fuck. She'd jumped. We were on the third floor. I went to the window and stuck my head out.

"Evie!"

"Shh! Come on!" Her voice was so close to my face I nearly pissed myself.

I turned. She was just a foot away from me, standing on a ledge.

"Be careful, but I think we can get down this way."

There was a loud thump against the door. I turned and heard their muffled, frustrated voices on the other side.

"Sebastián, come on." Evie sidled away to let me climb out the window.

I gripped her arm and slid next to her just as the door burst open. Evie let out a tiny cry, and I threw my arm out, slapping my hand across her mouth. We shared a look, and she nodded. I knew it was an accident, but that little whimper could be what got us caught. I dropped my hand and nudged her to move. She was slow as she sidestepped. Clutching the wall, I tried not to look down. I'd done stunts before, but I had a feeling that if I slipped, I might try to grab her for help and end up taking her with me.

"Finally, a different color," Elliott muttered as the two men began destroying Charles's bedroom. I prayed they didn't notice the open window.

My upper arms burned from holding myself to the wall. We turned the corner and climbed over a railing, landing on a balcony. We fell over each other and breathed in relief when we saw a large oak tree not too far from it. Scrambling, we hurried onto a thick branch and then climbed down to the ground.

As soon as her feet touched the ground, Evie bolted back around the house, toward where we'd exited. I followed quickly, only to stop short when she dove into a large bush, removing a backpack.

"What is that?" I hissed as she slung it over her back and put her arms through the straps.

"I couldn't leave the notebooks, so when I heard people coming, I stuffed them in a bag I found in the closet and threw them out the window," she explained, adjusting the straps and hauling forward. With a sigh, I stopped her and took the bag. I grabbed it, and the bag hit the ground. I wasn't prepared for the weight of all the notebooks.

"Jesus, Evie," I said, lifting it and tossing it over my shoulder.

"I had to get them all!" she exclaimed as I took her hand, and we ran to my car.

Thankfully, I'd had the foresight to park it a distance away and under another oak tree, so it was hidden in the dark. I shoved the bag into the back and started the car, zooming off down the drive. As we reached the gates, we found them destroyed. Someone, presumably Arthur, had taken industrial strength bolt cutters to the bars, hacking them to pieces, creating a large hole for a car to drive through. It looked like the Kool-Aid Man had ripped through the metal.

"Who were they?" Evie asked as we drove through.

I cringed, praying the twisted bars didn't scrape the sides of my car. Once we were safe, I slowed down and answered.

"The monsters you've been looking for. They're on to us."

"What does that mean?"

"It means this isn't just us tracking them down anymore." I gripped the wheel tighter, getting angrier the more I thought about it. "We're being hunted now too. And it's going to come down to who's faster."

"Faster at what?"

I turned my head to look at Evie. Her eyes were large and full of worry. Something had changed in that house. She'd spent so long putting on a brave face, acting as if she didn't care if she died. But now, it was clear she did. She was scared, and so was I.

Elliott Bradley knew we were coming for him, and he wasn't going to let us just run up and catch him unaware. There was a reason he was powerful. Lita Reyes wasn't the first person he'd gotten rid of, and we certainly wouldn't be the last. I looked back at the road and turned toward home.

"Drawing their gun."

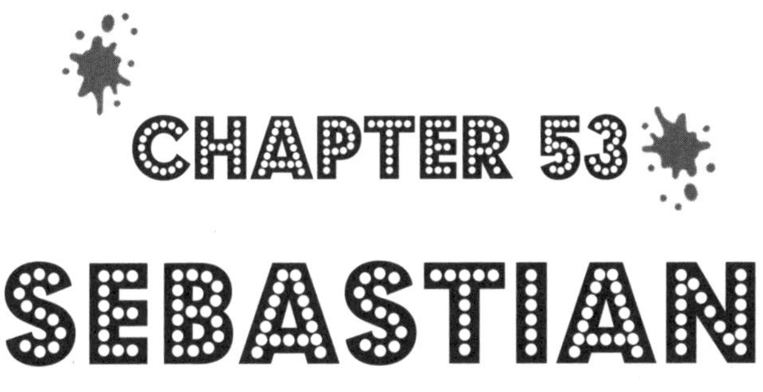

CHAPTER 53 SEBASTIAN

The Quiet Beat

"Do you want to be my date to the Roses event?"

"The what?" I asked, walking into the living room with a towel wrapped around my hips and nothing else. Evie and I had come back to my place after leaving Charles's all-blue mansion, and I'd gone right upstairs to take a scalding hot shower to soothe my muscles. I needed an evening to relax and not worry about Evie's murder list.

She lifted her gaze from the journals she was going through and trailed it up my frame, pausing at my middle, before continuing to my eyes. I went to the couch and plopped down.

"My mom's charity? We Become Roses. I've told you about this." She sighed with annoyance.

I squinted. "Right. Sorry, I remember."

"They help Latine women who are victims of sexual assault. I've never been involved. This is the first time I've ever been in town for their annual awards night, and I want to go. It's basically one giant PR op. All the big donors dress up, have their red carpet moment, and eat a fancy dinner while listening to speeches, awards, and requests for donations."

"When is the event?" I put my feet up on my coffee table, and my towel opened slightly, causing me to quickly grab it and wrap it back around me.

Evie's cheeks took on a pink flush as she flicked her eyes away from where I'd accidentally flashed her.

I bit back a smirk.

"This Saturday."

"Sounds boring, but I'll always take the chance to go on a date with you." I grinned.

She rolled her eyes.

"It's for a good cause. They do good work over there. They give voices to people who had theirs taken away."

"It's great, really. I'll have one of my tuxedos steamed. What color is your dress?"

"Red."

She looked ravishing in red.

She perked up and grabbed one of the notebooks from the pile on the floor. "I don't know what to do with these."

Evie sat on my living room floor, fighting off the dogs trying to slobber her with their love. She tossed another one of Charles's notebooks into the large pile.

"We should probably burn them now that they've drained the lake," I told her. They'd drained Falls Lake for regular maintenance a few days ago, finding Charles's wrinkled, water-logged body. Since then, security had been tighter than ever, and police were rampant all over the studio lots. It was a bitch going anywhere now.

"I—what if I missed something?" She furrowed her brow. "This can't be all of their relationship. It makes no sense. Every page is written on, but it feels like entire pieces are missing. One day, they are in love in Paris. The next they've been fighting in Austria."

She huffed and fell back onto the carpet. The dogs attacked her, breaking the tension. Her giggle filled the room as they licked her face. "Stop, you two!" She laughed, pushing them away and sitting back up. She brushed her hair out of her face and inhaled deeply. "Okay, I need to focus. What do we do now?"

"What can we do?" I shrugged. "Right now, one wrong move

and we'll be caught. I can't take a piss without security standing outside waiting for me."

"It's awful. I feel like they aren't there to protect us, but to watch us," she groaned.

Bingo.

"What do we know from the journals?" I redirected the conversation. I didn't really feel like talking about work right now.

"Charles had a few interesting quirks, including an eidetic memory. I think what he said was true. He's not my dad. The time doesn't match up." She scrunched up her face.

I knew she'd been hoping out of all six possible candidates, her father would be the one who actually loved her mom.

"So, who do you think it is?"

"Your guess is as good as mine." She shrugged. "I don't know if I even care anymore."

The notebooks revealed more about Lita Reyes than we ever knew. She'd come to Hollywood when she was eighteen and was an instant hit with small projects. However, she learned quickly that sex sold, and if you wanted something, you had to use whatever you had in your arsenal to get it.

I'd been taught the same lesson.

Charles recorded every verbal and physical abuse she had suffered at the hands of Hollywood while dating him. He'd written it down matter-of-factly, almost like an impartial third party. It read like a news article, not her lover confessing about the crimes he witnessed. It was all very odd, and it was all in his handwriting, with every entry signed by him at the end.

Lita had been chewed up and spit back out by the industry she claimed to love. She'd told Charles about being molested by directors offering her minor roles—she was barely an adult. She got her start on casting couches, eventually working her way up in a male-dominated industry by shutting her mouth and taking what scraps they gave her—until she finally landed a break-out role and didn't have to take the abuse anymore.

However, from Charles's recounts, it sounded like her mind

had been altered by it all. She'd become jaded, hating most men, which made Charles special.

He was everything Lita needed in a partner. He was kind and took things slow. He took her career seriously and was never jealous of the attention she got. For a while, anyway.

She loved him.

That was what made Lita's betrayal so hard. Evie wasn't Charles's child, because Lita had gotten pregnant while on location filming a movie. Charles had been here in California the entire time.

It made sense now why she started the charity to help women like her. Manipulated by an industry built on taking advantage of people's desire for fame. Sure, she was never required to sleep with any of the men listed in Charles's journals, but she wouldn't have had the career opportunities otherwise.

That was one of the sleazy underbelly secrets everyone knew in Hollywood but would never admit to. It was either who you knew or who you blew. And Lita and I shared that in common. We didn't know anyone.

Having experienced the casting couches firsthand, Charles's accounts of her being a completely willing participant were doubtful. I was sure some, maybe even most, were what both parties had agreed to. But, I'd been in a number of rooms where choices were taken and consent was murky.

It was why she'd left the knives for Evie with Bryce and started the charity. You couldn't trust anyone in this industry except yourself. Evie was right. We were missing a piece of the puzzle. Who was her father?

"I want them all dead for what they did."

"I want that too, but we have to keep lying low for a while," I reminded her. She still wanted to rush this, but Elliott Bradley and now Arthur Englund were watching us closely. I'd spotted them both more than once in the two weeks since we broke into Charles's house. They hadn't approached me, but they'd made sure to let me know they'd seen me.

Evie stood and stretched before coming to cuddle with me, the dogs joining us. I raised my arm and let her crawl into the crook of it. She snuggled into my still-damp bare chest. She'd been more touchy-feely since our morning at the *Psycho* house. Before, she'd been hesitant to be close to me. Now she went out of her way to do so.

"I just want to be done with all of this," she said, her voice breathy.

I kissed the top of her head.

"Whenever you want to be done, we can be," I reminded her.

"I know, but... I swore I'd see it through." She sat back up, and I felt her absence instantly. She took all the warmth with her.

I bit my tongue, choking down the words I wanted to throw at her. *What if she did survive? What if we didn't get caught? What if we could live normal lives? Would she be interested in being more than just partners in crime?*

Would she stay?

These questions ran through my mind day after day, and it took everything in me not to vomit them out. If I thought it'd do anything, I'd get on my knees right now and beg for her to stop this quest for vengeance, this death sentence. Instead, I nodded and pulled her back into my embrace. She didn't argue and instead snuggled tighter.

"Are you staying over tonight?" I asked.

"Is that okay?"

"Always."

She'd been staying over a lot under the guise of convenience. We could drive to work together. It saved gas, she'd tell me. I never called her on the lame excuses. She was always welcome here.

"I'll go home tomorrow," she promised, and I really wished she wouldn't. I wanted her to stay here forever. "I just don't want to be alone tonight. Reading Charles's journals is taking a toll on me," she sighed.

"I know." I kissed her hair again and let her vent.

"Why didn't she tell him?"

If Charles's recollections were to be believed, Evie was the product of an affair. This was the puzzle piece we were missing. Lita had told Charles everything. She gave up every single producer, executive, director, or casting agent she'd slept with to grow her career. She told him about every single lover and act she'd performed before him, but she never told him who impregnated her. Something wasn't right. Why hadn't he written it down?

My gut told me that, whoever her father was, he was still alive.

I wasn't ready to express my theory, but I was pretty sure her father was Elliott Bradley, the worst of them all. And Charles knew. They all knew.

CHAPTER 54

EVIE

The Philanthropist

"You think a journal is missing?" Sebastian looked at me, skeptical.

"There has to be. One moment she's planning their wedding. The next she's six months pregnant."

I knew spending my evenings poring over Charles's journals bothered him. He wanted to let this all go, but we were so close, I could taste the blood of the two men I had left. Arthur Englund and Elliott Bradley.

We spotted them walking together a few days ago. I wasn't paying much attention to my surroundings while I snacked at the craft services table, but Sebastian nudged me. Grabbing a small bundle of grapes, I turned to see two handsome middle-aged men walking by, smiling and chatting with each other.

I recognized their faces from simple internet searches and the many TV appearances Elliott made, but seeing them in person was chilling. I dropped the grape in my hand, my mouth falling open. "Was that—"

"Arthur and Elliott? Yep. I'm surprised this is the first time you've seen them. They've been walking around a lot this week."

"Really? I wonder why," I asked, and when Sebastian gave me a pointed look, my face flushed. Right. They were sending a message as a united front. A warning. We knew they had been the ones inside Charles's house that night. We'd narrowly escaped getting caught by them, but they knew we'd been there.

All of this was suspicion, until later that day, I found a gift in my trailer.

The lost journal.

I ran out of my trailer, waving it in the air as I went to look for Sebastian. Finding him in his trailer, I urged him to leave, so we could go back to his place and read the book. I found myself staying at his house more often than not these days. It was just easier with the filming schedule and the constant fear of someone breaking into my house and murdering me. That and we were supposed to be dating. It really sold the story to our coworkers.

"I told you there was a book missing!" I squealed as we drove home. I flipped through the pages, scanning Charles's tight, clean handwriting. "This is going to fill in the blanks. I know it."

I wasn't sure if I was saying it to Sebastian or myself, but I felt it in my bones, this journal would tell me everything I needed to know, and how to proceed.

Hours later, Sebastian found me on the couch, curled up with his dogs.

"You fell asleep to *The Blob*?" He glanced at the TV, where Steve McQueen was fighting a giant, gelatinous...well, blob.

I rubbed the sleep from my eyes and sat up, disturbing Cujo and Precious. "I had to finish this journal. I fell asleep right as I finished the last page." I patted the empty spot beside me for him to sit. He did, pulling me across his lap to snuggle. "This... Something isn't right," I confessed with a large sigh.

"How so?" He ran his fingers through my hair, and I closed my eyes, savoring the closeness.

I breathed in, inhaling the scent of soap from his shower.

"So, it starts by saying there were six men who could be my father. But we know that's not true because Charles wasn't even in the country. The journal claims she was having affairs with all six of them at once, and when she got pregnant, she claimed rape and tried to blackmail them for money." I shook my head. "None of this matches the other journals."

My twisted nerves told me that this was a dupe. Someone had found the same type of journal and paid someone who could mimic his handwriting to write this.

"When was it written?" he asked.

"The dates are from before she died. According to him, they'd been discussing getting back together, and while they were talking, she told him about all the affairs. At which time, the friend group got together and planned their revenge. I just—" I sat up and turned around to look at him. "This doesn't make sense."

He reached for the journal, flipping through the pages.

"I mean...maybe it's a fake?" he offered.

So he thought it too.

"But how could we tell?"

"I'm not sure. We believed all the other journals, and this has his handwriting, but that doesn't mean much. Wait, who left this for you?"

I shook my head. "I don't know. It was in my trailer. It could have been anyone."

"So, let's do some digging before we take this lead. It might be a trap. Come to bed."

I looked back at the dogs. They seemed to have understood him, because they began to whine. Sebastian didn't allow them to sleep in his bed, so they loved cuddling with me on the couch.

"Evie..." Sebastian started, knowing the guilty look on my face all too well.

"They're so sad," I pouted.

"And so am I. I couldn't sleep. That's why I came to find you."

With a sigh, I followed him to bed and had another restful night of sleep wrapped in his large, warm arms.

"WHAT ARE YOUR plans for your mom's house? Are you still considering selling it once this is all over?" Sebastian asked as we walked through the studio lot the next morning.

"What do you mean?" I scanned the area, seeing all the people heading to their jobs, not paying us any attention. We were never really alone at the studio, but some ears were more curious than others.

"Well, you haven't been spending much time there."

"We've talked about this," I said. "It's not safe for me to be alone there right now. And you have your dogs. It makes sense for me to sleep on your couch," I teased him. The dogs did make me feel safer, but it was Sebastian's presence in the house that helped me sleep.

"Yes, but you're not staying on my couch a whole lot, are you?" He stopped walking and reached for my wrist.

I looked up and caught his gaze. Those glorious greens were blazing, daring me to confess my true intentions and feelings for him. My heart raced, and my breathing quickened. He was right. I said I was sleeping with the dogs, but more often than not, I was slipping into his room and enjoying the comfort of his soft mattress, thick blankets, and warm arms.

"It's strictly platonic." I pulled away, feeling entirely too warm under his gaze, and started walking again.

"I've never cuddled my platonic friends to sleep. Is that what you do?" he called loudly for others to hear.

My mouth fell open, and I turned back around to argue, when my gaze flicked to someone behind him.

"Here's Johnny," I muttered, letting Sebastian know we had guests.

"Sebastian!" Arthur Englund strode over, hand out and a smile on his face.

Sebastian shook his hand, his jaw ticking as he glared at the blond man in the mustard-yellow suit.

He turned to me. "Evelyn, how are things going?"

"Great, thanks. We're actually late for our morning call."

"Oh, I'm sure you have a minute." Arthur glanced at me and winked.

I cringed, but he ignored it.

"I actually wanted to ask if you were attending the Roses Charity Gala."

The blood drained from my face. My heart dropped into my stomach. How did he know about that?

"Roses?" Sebastian said, feigning ignorance.

"We Become Roses. It's the charity Lita Reyes founded, before her passing. I've been a major donor since its creation. We were hoping you'd both attend."

"Who is we?" I demanded. How fucking ironic.

He chuckled. "The board of directors, of course."

Board of directors?

My mother's rapist was helping run the charity she'd started to help other victims. *How had I missed this?*

My head was spinning. I needed to sit down. I was so out of my league with all of this. I'd told myself when I came back to Hollywood that I was prepared for anything, but I was realizing I couldn't be further from prepared. How had I missed that one of my mother's killers was working to keep her charity running?

"So, you're coming? We plan to honor Lita this year for the anniversary."

"What anniversary?" I asked, more and more confused.

"It's the ten-year anniversary of the creation of WBR. It's a big deal. Do you not get our newsletters?"

Our?

Anger seethed under my skin.

"I'm going," I snapped. "It sounds like I've missed a lot. As my mother's proxy, I should probably sit in on a meeting and see exactly who is running her charity and what they are doing. Thanks." I spun around and stormed off in the other direction, deciding on the long way to hair and makeup.

"We'd love to hear you give a speech!" Arthur called out.

I clenched my fists and kept going, refusing to look back. Sebastian caught up with me a minute later, just as I turned a corner.

"Hey, it's okay, Final Girl. Calm down." Sebastian put his hands on my shoulders, spinning me and pulling me into his embrace. He kissed the top of my head as I sobbed into his arms. "It's okay, Final Girl. He's not going anywhere near you."

"It's not just him," I sobbed. "It's everything. It's too much, and I can't keep up. Every day, it's something else, and—"

I felt like I was drowning. I wanted to be organized and do things the proper way, piece by piece, but every time I got one thing done, another three things popped up, pushing me down further.

"Evie!" Sebastian shouted, and I paused, taking a deep breath to steady myself. He sighed deeply and shook his head. "This town is just a lot worse than you or anyone else realizes. The people in power make sure they weave themselves into as many things as they can so they can't lose. The game is rigged, Evie. We just gotta figure out how to cheat right there with them."

Sebastian held me until I stopped crying, and when I stepped back and wiped my face, he took my hand and directed me back toward hair and makeup.

"Don't worry, Final Girl. There will come a payday, and when that day comes, we're gonna be fucking rich."

I could only hope.

CHAPTER 55

EVIE

The Benefit Speech

I admired myself in the full-length mirror, running my hands down the red gown I'd borrowed for the event. I'd mentioned to Stacey that I was attending, and she'd insisted they bring in a designer for Sebastian and me. The designer had dressed me in a deep, burgundy gown with a sweetheart neckline and white ropes of pearls draping across my breasts, hips, and ribs. The sleeves were black, puffed, and off-the-shoulder. The dress hugged my body and flared at the knees, creating a goth-mermaid look that I was living for.

They'd brought in a professional hair and makeup artist to do the rest, and by the time Sebastian pulled up in a limo, I felt like a true Hollywood movie star. This was how my mother would dress for these things, I recalled as I walked through her house. I sighed, wishing I'd spent more time here. Not as a child, but as an adult. I'd returned, but had I really come back? I spent more time at Sebastian's than my own house, and I wasn't sure if I preferred that or wanted to have him come here instead.

Maybe it was time to let go.

Or alternatively, he could move in with me...

The doorbell rang, pulling me from my thoughts. I went to it, welcoming Sebastian inside.

"You're stunning, Final Girl." He lifted my hand, kissing the top of it, sending butterflies through my belly. "I have something for you."

"You do?" I raised an eyebrow, stepping back as he reached into his pocket and pulled out a thin red velvet box.

My heart stopped and restarted at a fierce pace.

He held it up and opened it. I peered inside and gasped as he pulled out a gold necklace. It was a beautiful thin chain with the words *Final Girl* on a single charm, the words separated by a ruby in-between.

"What do you say? Will you be my Final Girl?"

I laughed, staring at the necklace in disbelief. "I don't have any movie quotes for this."

He removed the necklace from its box, and I turned around, lifting my hair so he could clasp it. I admired it in the small mirror by my front door. It was stunning.

"I had it custom made."

"When?" I asked, turning back to him.

His eyes were distant, pained, but also... something else. "The first day I saw you on set."

"Really?" I gaped.

He snorted. "No. I did it two weeks ago. Jeez, you're so easy sometimes."

"And difficult other times?" I quipped, letting him take my arm and lead me outside to the limousine.

"More than you know," he muttered. "Come on, Final Girl. Let's put Arthur in his place."

I stared out the window, my hand on Sebastian's as the driver took us to the venue.

"It's odd they're doing a red carpet for a charity event," I commented as the limo got in line to be announced.

"Everything is an opportunity to tell a story," Sebastian muttered.

Before I could ask what he meant, the door opened, and we climbed out to an explosion of bright lights and loud popping sounds as paparazzi took our photos.

"Sebastian! Over here!"

"Evie! Who are you wearing!"

Sebastian took my waist and escorted me up the stairs and down the red carpet, pausing when appropriate. We went inside as quickly as possible. The room was decorated in pink and deep red. Circular tables with pink tablecloths and red roses filled the room, seating eight people at each. Lining the walls were large banners of my mother and other famous women I didn't recognize. We sat at the table with our names on place cards in the middle of the room and made small talk as the rest of the guests filed in.

"You're our guest of honor, Ms. Reyes," the hostess told us as we sat down and quickly poured water and wine.

I opened my mouth to ask what she meant by that, but Sebastian spoke, distracting me.

"Watch the cameras," Sebastian whispered. His lips brushed against my ear, sending shivers down to my collarbone. "There's one right there and one to your left." He pointed discreetly.

I turned my head as subtly as I could to see. In the corners, cameramen stood with large video cameras, their red lights on.

"Is this live?" I asked.

Sebastian reached for his drink and nodded. He was staying silent on purpose. Why? He knew something I didn't. Then, I watched Arthur come in, shaking hands and greeting people as he did so.

My blood boiled instantly.

"Easy, Final Girl," Sebastian muttered a low warning.

"I—"

"Beep beep, Ritchie," he said in a sharper tone.

My mouth snapped shut. I forced a smile and scanned the room as everyone settled into their seats and dinner was served. While we ate, there were various music acts on stage, and in-between, Arthur hosted. Putting on a charming face, he talked about We Become Roses and what good it had done over the past ten years. He introduced speakers, asked for donations, and presented other non-musical acts. After we finished eating, there was a small intermission, during which I sat solemnly with Sebastian.

Guests came to our table to talk, but we kept the conversations brief and polite, and they got the hint. When the short break was over and the cameras began filming again, Arthur decided it was time to highlight my appearance.

"We have a very special guest here tonight. Lita Reyes left behind a legacy through her movies and WBR, but she also left behind loved ones, and we have one special family member of hers with us tonight. Evelyn Reyes, her daughter."

Applause erupted as the audience and cameras turned toward me. My face flamed, and I waved politely at the cameras. They shifted to the front of the room just as a woman, dressed in a volunteer uniform, walked from behind the curtains, bringing Arthur a gold and pink plaque.

"We at We Become Roses wanted to honor Lita Reyes with an award tonight. Lita gave so much back to the Latine community without asking anything in return. Her kindness has helped countless women take back their freedom, while also educating the community about sexual violence in an effort to save others. The world is a better place because of Lita Reyes, and Evie, we'd like you to accept this glass rose on her behalf."

I stared at Arthur, frozen until Sebastian pinched me on the thigh. My mind came to, and I stood, confused as to what was going on. I made my way to the stage, the room around me one big blur. I took the rose statue from Arthur and stared blankly at the audience, still clapping. Arthur's hand went to the small of my back and urged me toward the microphone. I flinched away from his touch and leaned into the mic.

"Wow, this is...great, really great," I started, my mind drawing a blank. They'd asked me to prepare a speech, but I'd declined. I should have known this was why. I raised the statue. "My mom always loved roses. This is going to go great on her awards shelf."

There was polite laughter, which gave me a little strength. I stood up straight and cleared my throat.

"Helping Latine women who have been victims of sexual assault was important to my mother, as she knew all too well what it was like. Since she's been gone, she's helped a lot of people, and with her money, name, and help from everyone in this room, she'll continue to do so. Thank you all for taking care of my mother's legacy while I was gone. I hope to play a bigger part now that I've returned."

I stepped away from the mic as a standing ovation followed by music played me off. What was I saying? Play a bigger part? Why was I making promises I never intended to keep? I was directed backstage, and the moment I was hidden behind the curtains, I was yanked into a dark corner.

"You better fucking watch yourself, bitch." I couldn't see him, but the voice I'd been listening to all night was instantly recognizable. Arthur squeezed my upper arms.

I let out a sharp cry as I tried wrenching my arm free of his grasp.

"You're trying to play games with players much more advanced. You're as good as dead already."

Suddenly, he let me go, and an instant later, a sharp pinch in my belly turned into a white- hot pain. Or was it cold? I couldn't tell, but I knew what had caused it. I gasped as Arthur pulled the knife from my belly and disappeared into the curtains, fleeing. I dropped against the wall, holding on to my wound.

Fuck.

Fuck fuck fuck.

The pain was blindingly hot. I could barely breathe. I wanted to scream, but alerting someone would only make it harder to exact my revenge later. Gritting my teeth, I stumbled forward, hurrying to the nearest door. I found myself in a green room. I collapsed to the ground, closing my eyes.

Sometime later—I wasn't entirely sure how much time had passed—there was a knock on the door. I was drenched in sweat and could barely breathe. Biting a scream back, I called out.

"Who is it?"

"Sebastian! Evie, are you okay? Arthur said you came in here."

Forcing myself up, I grabbed the doorknob and turned it, collapsing into his arms.

"Help me."

CHAPTER 56

SEBASTIAN

The Third Act Fuckup

"Are you taking me to a hospital?" Evie's face was pale as I brushed her damp hair away from her forehead. I'd managed to sneak her out the back and into the limo with minimal people seeing us.

Luan, my driver, tossed me a look. His eyes drifted to where I was holding Evie's stomach. I shook my head and put a finger to my lips. I bit down, trying to figure out a plan, and then quickly made a decision.

"Take us home."

Luan had been my driver for a year or so now, and he was paid handsomely not to ask questions. Nodding, he put the divider up, separating us from him, and shifted out of drive.

"No. I'm taking you back to my house. I'm going to clean you up. I told you to watch the cameras," I groaned. When she got the award, she went behind the curtains, just out of sight of the audience and cameras. Alarm bells had been ringing, but it wasn't until Arthur returned, flushed and with blown pupils, like he'd just done the best coke of his life, that I knew I had to go check on her. She'd only been gone ten minutes, if that, but in that time, he'd managed to stab her and leave her to bleed out.

I pressed harder on her wound, doing my best to stop the bleeding. Blood soaked through her dress and onto my fingers. I bit my lip. The warm liquid wetting my skin made the reality of the situation hit me. I had no idea how to treat a stab wound, but I'd seen enough movies to know this much blood loss was bad. Both my hands and hers were covered now.

Evie closed her eyes, and I reached for my phone with my empty hand, quickly searching how to sew up a stab wound.

This was going to get me on a watchlist.

It seemed simple enough—clean it, stop the bleeding, sew it up—as long as I had needle and thread, which I was pretty sure I didn't. Laun dropped us at my house, and I lifted her out of the limo, carrying her like my dead bride up the steps.

I shoved the dark thoughts out of my mind. She wasn't dead. She was breathing. She was going to be okay. I opened the door, and the dogs ran into the foyer from the other room, hitting the walls as they slid.

"Guys, not now! Go to your kennels!"

For once, they understood my tone and words and went to their rarely used crates. I ran up the stairs with her still in my arms and into my bedroom. Tenderly, I placed her on the bed and went to my bathroom, searching for alcohol, bandages, and the needle and thread I knew weren't there. I returned with what I had and then got to work. Carefully, I rolled her over and unzipped her dress. Evie's eyes fluttered open, and she screamed.

"Evie! It's okay. It's fine."

I cringed as I tried to calm her, failing miserably. I dropped to my knees beside the bed, reaching for her hand. It wasn't fine, but me losing it wouldn't help the situation. Her entire body was shaking and sweating. The wound in her middle oozed through the dress and onto my sheets, the deep red staining them.

"I got fucking stabbed!" she sobbed. She squirmed as she clenched her jaw tight to hold in the screams.

"Was it Arthur?" I demanded. I needed to know just how desperate they were getting. Were they still using hired help for their dirty work? Or had they started doing it themselves? Either way, he was going to pay painfully.

"Yes, it was him," she hissed, leaning up to help me peel the dress down her torso, revealing the full wound. I flinched. It was larger than I'd expected.

"Is it bad?" she asked.

I stared into the wet, mushy gash in her side. The knife had left a good-sized hole in her. Skin had peeled back, leaving muscle exposed and pulsing as she breathed. The wound was deep.

"No," I lied. I had no idea if it was good or bad. "I mean, it's not good."

"Can you sew it up?" she asked. Her breath grew ragged, and her eyes fluttered closed.

"I'm going to try. You ready?"

She licked her lips and then nodded, replying with a quote from *Hellraiser*. "We have such sights to show you."

"Stay with me, Final Girl," I whispered as I took a rag and dumped alcohol on it.

Bracing for the scream, I placed it gently on her open wound. She lunged forward with a cry so shrill that I ducked as her arms came swinging forward. I braced myself as I tried to push her back down. "It's okay! We're just cleaning it!"

Tears poured from her eyes as she squirmed and tried to push me away.

"Evie, please, we need to do this!" I finished cleaning her wound, taking care of the muscle and other exposed pieces. Once the bleeding had slowed and the area was clean, I was able to better assess the damage. It wasn't as horrible as I originally thought, but she wasn't going to be walking around in a few hours. I needed to get the wound closed so she could rest.

Pulling out my phone again, I tapped the screen, smearing blood on the glass as I searched for at-home options to close the wound.

"It hurts, Sebastian."

"I know, Final Girl. Let me get you some pain pills, and I'll work on closing you up." I went to my bathroom again, returning with some low-dose aspirin and a small plastic cup I'd filled from the tap.

"How are you going to close it?" she asked after taking the pills with the water.

"Superglue or staples. Whichever I have in my office." I hurried to my office, right next to my bedroom, looking for either item. I found a stapler and grimaced, knowing what I was going to have to do next. *Would these things even hold?* I returned to Evie, offering her one of the clean hand towels I'd grabbed. "Put this in your mouth."

"You are not fucking stapling me together." She growled with such ferocity, I jumped.

"It's not that bad," I argued. "Look." Swallowing, I pulled up my sleeve and opened it, pressing it against my arm. Taking a deep breath and bracing myself, I slammed down and winced.

"Find something else," she hissed.

I tossed the stapler onto my nightstand and nodded.

"Yeah okay."

Digging out the staple with my nails, I returned to my office to scrounge some more. While not as painful as being stabbed, being stapled wasn't exactly great either. I wiped the small droplets of blood and forced the uncomfortable pain away. I'd live, but if I didn't figure out how to close Evie up soon, she might not.

I dumped drawers and threw things off shelves, looking for something, anything, when my phone started to ring. Pausing, I pulled it out and saw it was Bryce. Answering quickly, I started speaking before he could.

"Hey, where are you, I need help."

"Oh, I'm out of town. I was just calling to ask about—"

"I need to close a stab wound." I cut him off. Bryce went quiet.

"At home?" he asked. The tone of his voice and the background noise suggested he was with company that shouldn't be hearing this conversation. "Hold on."

"Yes, I don't have needle and thread, or glue. Staples are not an option." I looked down at my arm and paced, tugging my hair.

"Staples? Jesus, Seb, you're gonna make it worse. What about string and a paperclip?"

"What?"

"It ain't gonna be pretty, but if you heat it up some with a lighter to clean the metal it could work. I've had to do some quick clean ups a time or two."

I racked my brain, trying to think. Did I have either of those things?

Yes!

I returned to my messy desk and shuffled the contents tossed on top around, finding a handful of paperclips that had been in a drawer. They were covered in dust.

"Sebastian, you there?"

"Yeah, I just gotta find string." I said, wiping the paperclips off with my hand.

"You got any fishing line?"

I blinked. Did I?

"Thanks. I gotta go." I hung up and ran downstairs out to my garage. Bryce and I had gone out on his boat a handful of times. Quickly, I found my tackle box and pulled out a spool of fishing line. Staring at the two objects, I knew this wasn't ideal, but I took it back up to Evie anyways and showed her the paperclip and thread. I dropped to my knees at her side.

"Okay, Final Girl, you really need to work with me. We need to seal this up here. If we take you to the hospital, they'll report it, and you were just filmed on television at the charity event. They'll start putting pieces together, and we can't have that. Can you sit still, *please*?" I pleaded with her, placing a kiss on her damp forehead. She closed her eyes and nodded.

Straightening the thin metal instrument, I pressed the thread against it and poked her skin, and it refused to go in. Frowning, I thought back and remembered what Bryce had said.

"What are you doing?" Evie asked as I leaned back and pulled out my cigarette case. "You really need a cigarette right now?"

I ignored her, opening it and removing the lighter. Flicking it on, I ran the paperclip over the flame.

"Relax, Final Girl."

"What are you doing?"

"Sanitizing before shoving it through your skin."

"Sanitizing?" She stretched her neck to see.

"Yeah, it's a fucking paperclip I found on my desk covered in dust. Do you really trust that it's clean?" I pointed out.

She scrunched up her nose and relaxed back, breathing slow and steady.

Unsure of when it would be hot enough, I decided to just estimate, waiting until the silver metal turned bright red. I then blew on it impatiently, counting to sixty before taking my other hand and pushing her skin around the wound together to shove the makeshift needle through.

Evie grunted loudly, as if I'd socked her in the belly, and she whimpered as I pulled the line through. Despite feeling the urgency, I knew I had to take this slow so as to not do more damage.

This was going to be a long process.

I kept going as methodically as I could, muttering low words of comfort to Evie as I worked. Sweat built on my brow, dropping onto the bed, until finally, I pulled the last of her wound closed. Using the lighter again, I separated the line from the spool and tied it as neatly as I could.

As I'd worked, Evie slowly had started to relax, but only once I stood and announced it was done did her body untense. A moment later, she started to sob. I helped her lie all the way down, and then I crawled into bed with her, clothes still on, and comforted her as best I could while paying attention to the wound. She fell asleep in my arms, and I fell asleep sitting up, guarding her.

She woke in the middle of the night, and I got her more water and pills, thankful we didn't have work today or tomorrow. Hopefully, she'd be walking by then.

By morning, she was resting peacefully.

I stayed by her side all day, getting her anything she needed when she was awake and doing what investigating I could while she was asleep. I knew it was Arthur Englund who'd stabbed her.

I just wasn't sure why he did it in such a public place and why he hadn't finished the job. Was he sending a message, or was he that bad at murder?

Evie sat up for the first time almost twenty-four hours after the attack. She was sore, her face puffy from crying, but she was alive.

"You're really fucking lucky." I chuckled, still in disbelief that I'd managed to seal a wound with a paperclip and fishing line.

"This isn't funny," she snarled.

I paused, surprised. "I didn't say it was. I just— It was scary for a minute. I wasn't sure you—"

"I what?" She stood, wobbling on her feet.

I jumped up to catch her, but she pushed me away. She limped to my closet, pulling a shirt off a hanger, along with a pair of basketball shorts, slid the clothes on. I stood to watch so I could catch her if she fell.

"Evie, you need to rest." I sighed. "We can't have a repeat of last night."

She winced as she dressed and sat down on a nearby chair, breathing heavily. What was she thinking? There was no way she should be up right now.

"The closer we get to finishing off the men on my list, the more dangerous it's going to get. I know that. You don't have to throw it in my face." She glared at me.

I sighed. "That's not what I was saying. Evie..." Inhaling deeply, I braced myself to bare my heart to her. "I thought I was going to watch you die, and the thought killed me. I don't want you to be in a position like that again."

She stared, her face softening for a moment before returning to a deadpan expression.

"Well, I lived," she muttered. "Please take me home."

"Home? Evie, you can't go home right now. You're—" My mouth fell open, and I laughed incredulously. "I'm not driving you anywhere. You need to lie back down."

She shook her head. "You want me to stop, but I can't. I won't.

You want me to be scared, but I'm just angrier. Arthur and Elliott are dead." She gritted her teeth. "If you won't drive me home, I'll call Skye or Bryce." She reached for her purse, pulling her phone out and quickly tapping on it.

She mumbled that Bryce was on his way and dropped back down into the chair, exhaling deeply.

"Evie—please," I begged. Cujo and Precious, hearing our voices grow louder, bounded up the stairs carrying their rope toys. They ran to her and set them on the ground for her to play with them, and I shooed them back to give her space.

Shakily, she stood, wincing as she did.

She shuffled out into the hall, and I followed behind, grabbing her arm to help stabilize her. Despite wanting to lift her up and toss her back in bed, I forced myself to assist her downstairs. I wasn't going to force Evie to stay if she didn't want to.

"I'm leaving. Don't follow me. Actually—I don't want your help at all anymore. I'm going solo for the rest of this. I'll kill Arthur and Elliott on my own."

"You literally can't," I snapped, putting my hand on the front door to hold it shut. "It was going to be nearly impossible *with* my assistance. They'll eat you alive if you try to do this alone."

"I'm not going to let them. I'm going to finish this, then sell my house and my fucking YouTube channel and fly to Mexico to live off the money. Let me go, Sebastian," she said through gritted teeth.

"Evie, come on," I pleaded. "Don't do this. I—" My face crumpled. "I was watching *The Exorcist*." My voice cracked as I said the magic words.

She stared, taking in my confession. The sound of blood pumping rushed in my ears as I waited for her to do or say anything. My chest rose and fell in quick bursts, pleading to not be let down.

Evie stared at me, her lips pursed and her eyes slowly turning down.

"You're my Final Girl."

The words slipped from my lips, a whisper of defeat.

A horn honked from outside, and we glanced through the window to see Bryce's truck. We turned our attention back to each other.

Evie shook her head. "I'm really not." She reached up, yanked the necklace I'd given her just the day before off her neck, breaking the clasp, and handed it to me. "I'm no one's Final Girl. I'm my mother's avenger. After I finish what I came here to do, I hope they kill me."

She opened the door and stumbled out, pressing her hand to her wound.

"That way, I won't have to think about what I've done. Goodbye, Sebastian. Don't call me."

CHAPTER 57
SEBASTIAN

The Rewrites

"Ha. Good fucking luck." I continued picking the food from my teeth as I leaned back in my chair, listening to Dante tell me he wanted to do one more bedroom shoot with me and Evie.

He slapped my boots down from the table in my trailer, causing me to fall forward and put my feet on the floor. I glared at him as he tossed me the rewrites.

"Yeah, the producers don't care about your little fight. They want a bunch of extra shit I hadn't planned for. I don't know where exactly it's coming from, but someone wants a fuck-ton more scenes. It's stupid because it'll all get cut anyway, but they're paying us, so go shower, get naked, and get to set."

"Did you tell Evie yet?" I scanned the new pages. There wasn't much to them, just setup for the sex. Pages and pages of various setups.

"Are we doing a montage?" I asked, seeing that we were filming in more than one location. We were moving from the bedroom set to Ronny's office, Riley's desk, the stockroom at the grocery store, a tree. There were almost a dozen places they wanted us to film. Why?

"Yep, and no, I haven't spoken to her. I'm going to tell her the same thing. Figure out your shit and get to set. I want to see you in an hour."

He left my trailer in a huff, and reluctantly I followed him out, heading to hair and makeup.

I made it to set right on time, where a scowling Dante greeted me.

"Smartass." He shook his head as he looked at his wristwatch. "It doesn't really matter if you're here. Evie's throwing a bigger fit than you for once."

I'd be lying if I said his words didn't hurt my ego. I looked up at the ceiling and squinted.

"Is she coming at all?" I asked, careful with my words. "I'm not going to sit here with my pants down waiting for her."

"She'll show."

Suddenly, Arthur Englund strode out from the shadows behind a set piece, hands in his suit pockets.

Dante groaned. You knew things were bad when the studio executives came out of their offices to hang around your set. Before more could be said, Evie strolled up, looking absolutely pissed.

"You're late," Arthur said. "Every minute costs us money."

"Sorry, the makeup artist was struggling with how to cover this up." Evie lifted her shirt, revealing the bright-red wound, still healing. It had barely been a week since Arthur had stabbed her at the charity event. The wound looked inflamed and painful.

Almost as if she'd been sewn together with a dull paperclip and fishing line.

"What the hell? How did that happen? Who stabbed you?" Dante leaped off his seat and hurried to examine the scar.

Evie's eyes went right to Arthur as she answered our director. "Some pussy too coked out to finish the job." She pushed her shirt back down and straightened. "So, apologies for my tardiness. We decided the gash was too fresh to put makeup on."

"Are you okay? Did you go to the hospital?" Dante fired question after question, but Evie ignored them.

Arthur interjected. "She seems perfectly fine. Let's get this shoot underway. Time is money." He waved as if swatting a fly out of his face.

"Right. Of course. Why don't you and I talk while everyone gets in place, Arthur?" Dante gave us a knowing look as he went to the executive, put his hand on his back, and urged him off set. "I still don't understand why we're doing all this new stuff."

Evie and I didn't speak as we prepared for the scene. She spoke only to the assistants and crew, taking direction from them, rather than discussing it with me. We hadn't talked since she'd dropped her necklace in my hand and walked out of my house. It was obvious to anyone with eyes that we weren't on good terms. I'd never felt so...embarrassed.

Dante returned looking haggard and called us together.

"Okay, today will be a lot of changing sets and costumes. Let's just leave our personal feelings here, get our work done, and go home. You are actors. This is what you're paid for—pretending you like each other. Got it?"

We both muttered various forms of agreement and walked to our places. The first set was Ronny's office. Evie hopped onto the desk, and I stepped between her legs. With the energy she was giving off, it felt like any other non-explicit scene. There was no passion like there'd been in past shoots. Dante called, "Action!" and we came to life, kissing, pulling clothes off. It was all mechanical, and when we weren't giving him the fire we'd had before, he called cut, lectured us, and when we started back up, he began to yell directions. He told us where to put our hands, move our heads, and what to do with our mouths. Finally, he got something that could work, and we moved to the next set.

It was a long morning of costume changes and dry, cold make-out sessions with Evie. We made it through three scenes and then cut for lunch. The moment the bell rang, Evie left set without a word, which was the last straw for me. I stormed back to my trailer to eat and shower. Despite wanting to strangle her, my dick was hard. It was nothing more than a biological reaction, I tried to tell myself, but I knew it wasn't true. Throwing my next costume change on, I stomped out of my trailer and over to hers. I pounded on her door and got nothing. Instead, her assistant walked by.

"She's already on set. I was told not to let you into her trailer." She shrank as she confessed her orders.

"Fuck this," I snarled and took a cart to set, gripping the wheel tight, growing more and more pissed the closer I got. She was angry because I wanted to keep her alive. How ridiculous. I parked, and when I saw her standing next to Dante, my lips curled upward.

Perfect.

They'd dressed her in a skirt.

I sauntered over, shoving my hands into my pockets like Arthur had done this morning.

"Sebastian, good, you're here. I was just running Evie through this scene. You're gonna bend her over a tree and whisper in her ear as you pretend to fuck her. I don't care what you're saying to her. Music will be put over the montage. This is going to be a longer scene, as this is when Riley sees you two and starts to plot Lucy's murder, but that'll be shot a different day. You ready?"

"Always," I said and offered Evie my hand, to which she promptly stuck up her nose and walked the other way.

Dante sighed, but I only laughed and followed behind her. We got into place. Action was called, and I wrapped my arms around her, whispering in her ear.

"You think you're doing something by ignoring me. It's not working. I'm not letting this go."

We had no actual dialogue in this scene, so anything I said wasn't being picked up with boom mics. She let out a fake moan and let her head fall back.

"You have to. I'm not giving you the choice anymore," she said.

"Speaking of not giving you a choice..." I pulled away and swiftly spun her around, bending her over the fake tree trunk that had been built to look like an L shape, the branch sticking out to fully bend her over and cover our middles. I kicked her feet out and stepped between them, glancing at the camera just feet away from our faces. I bent down, pushing her hair from her face.

I licked her ear and whispered, "This is number four, Final Girl."

"Belt!" Dante called.

I stood up straight and made a show of undoing my belt for the cameras. They circled around us as I pushed my pants down so they could get the shot of my bare ass. I lifted Evie's skirt like the script told me to and waited until they circled back to our front before I stepped back to speak to her again.

"Don't you dare," Evie growled.

I ignored her. Moving her panties to the side, I ran my fingers down her slit.

"We had a deal, Final Girl," I murmured, bending down to kiss her exposed shoulder. "I get five chances to use your body how I see fit. You don't get a say. Do you trust me?"

"What?" she said through her heavy breathing.

"Do you trust that I won't let them see you coming all over my hand?" I bit down on my lower lip as I spread her pussy and slid a finger inside her. She gasped, and I grinned wickedly as my gaze darted to the camera catching every moment of this.

"There we go. Finally!" Dante called out his approval.

Evie gripped the tree trunk and arched her back. I pressed my hard cock into her backside as I fucked her with my fingers. When I added a second digit, she let out a groan.

"I trust you," she panted as her finale began to build.

I ground myself against her, putting on the performance of a lifetime as she coated my fingers with her arousal.

"I know you're mad at me for trying to stop you from completing your mission. And I won't try to stop you anymore. But you need to let me help you."

"How?" she demanded. "You want to take things slow, and I—"

"Want to finish now?" I grinned at my double entendre.

"You're a bastard." She pushed her hips deeper into me.

"Yeah, but I'm your bastard. That's the thing, Evie." I shoved my fingers deep inside, curling them. She gasped. "There's no going back now. We're in too deep. I know too much. You know too much. At the end of the day, you'll always be my Final Girl, and I'll always be your Psycho—"

"Killer," she cried out as her body pulsed deliciously, gushing her release all over my hand.

"That's right." I continued to fuck her through her finish.

Dante yelled cut, and I pulled my hand away and pulled up my pants. "Don't fucking forget it."

Evie adjusted her clothes and turned to look at me, her face a beautiful post-orgasm flush.

"I— I won't. Ever." She sighed deeply and moved closer, pressing her body against mine. Reflexively, I leaned down to kiss her.

"We can take things slower," she relented. "But I want to be the one to deal the final blows."

"Deal." I kissed her again, and Dante called for us to reset the scene and do it all over again.

CHAPTER 58 EVIE

The Motivation

I shoved my clothes back into place and fixed my messed-up hair. I could feel the flush in my cheeks, and mild mortification flooded me, making it worse. They'd filmed Sebastian fingering me to completion, and there was a chance it would make it into the final cut.

"That was great, Evie! You were gorgeous! Take fifteen!" Dante called from his seat.

I ran off set toward a bathroom to splash water on my face and hide. Sebastian slipped into the small space a beat later, causing me to sigh deeply and turn.

"It's been a long day, Sebastian."

"I know. I just... I've missed you." He gave me a bashful smile.

Guilt made my belly tight. I'd been so angry with him trying to stop my mission that I'd stopped hanging out with him.

I'd missed him too.

"Want to have dinner at your place tonight?" I offered. "We could figure out the next part of our plan while we eat, and I cuddle with Cujo and Precious?"

I'd also missed his dogs.

Sebastian's gaze darkened, and he didn't speak for a moment. "How can you be okay with dying for this?"

I shrugged. "When you've lost everything, nothing really

matters anymore. I know the risks. I'm okay with them." I finished washing my hands and reached for the door handle.

"I love you."

I turned back to look at him, my mouth open. "What?" I'd heard him, but the words were foreign coming from him. There was no way.

"I said, I love you."

My brain refused to compute his words.

He'd dropped the code.

The last, and only time, he'd ever done that was...our first time together. Tears welled in my eyes as the memories of that special night, before it became awful, flooded my mind.

"Don't—don't say that." My chin trembled as the words spilled from my mouth. He couldn't love me. He shouldn't love someone with a death wish. I stepped back until I hit the wall, then I turned the door handle. "You're lying."

"What? Why would I—Evie, I'm not lying." Sebastian came closer and tried to touch my face, but I brushed him away.

I sniffled, wiping the tears from my eyes.

"Evie."

"No, Sebastian. I'm not doing this again. We... We had our moment, years ago. This was just...a mistake." I started to open the door, and Sebastian's hand shot out, holding it in place.

"A mistake? We could never be a mistake. Evie, please, don't do this again. Don't leave me. I can't take you breaking my heart again," he pleaded.

I let go of the door and turned, narrowing my eyes.

"Breaking *your* heart?" My chest seemed to tighten as I looked at him. "You were the one who broke my heart."

"What are you talking about?" He shook his head. "You left without a word and then refused my calls and texts. You dumped me."

I stepped out of his reach. "No, I didn't. Sebastian, you broke up with me."

"Bullshit," he snarled.

"Really? Because I still have the voicemail."

His brows furrowed in confusion, and my heart ached. He didn't remember.

There was a knock on the door, and we stepped back so an assistant could poke their head in.

"We need you two on set. Sorry." They cringed as they backed out.

"This isn't over." Sebastian pointed at me then left.

I followed him, and we finished the rest of our day tossing backhanded comments at each other while we pretended to be madly in love. When we were done, I tried to go to my trailer alone, but Sebastian insisted on following me inside and demanding I play him the voicemail.

"I think I'd remember breaking up with the only girl I've ever loved," he shot at me as I dug through my bag for my phone. I pulled it out and started going through my password-protected files. Finding the one I'd listened to so many times I could recite it word for word, I lifted the phone and pushed play.

A younger, sixteen-year-old Sebastian came through the speakers. "Evie. Evie Reyes." I looked up at him. Sebastian's green eyes grew wide, recognizing his own voice. "You dumb bitch."

Sebastian took the phone and sat down on my couch as the voicemail continued.

"I got your voicemail. I don't really know what to say. Do you really think I'd leave everything behind? I worked hard. My family has sacrificed everything for me. Heather—Heather has done so much for me. To ask me to just give it all up to go with you... wherever is fucking selfish, man. You're delusional. If you want to leave... you're on your own. There's too many people here that need me. The world is going to know my name someday, Evie Reyes, and you should feel like shit for even asking me to choose. You're just as spoiled and entitled as your mom was. Get fucked."

I mouthed each word. It was the first monologue I'd learned by heart. Sebastian watched me with careful eyes as he listened. When it was over, he played it again. When it was done, he set the phone down and shook his head.

"I— I don't remember that. This is weird. If you left me a voicemail, I didn't get it. I would..." He paused and ran a hand through his hair. He came to sit with me, taking my hands. When I tried to pull away, he held me firm. "Evie, you have to believe me. If you'd asked me to leave, I would have. That's not me in that message. It can't be. This message feels like something..." His eyes glossed over. "Something isn't adding up."

He stood, letting go of my hands. "Can you come over tonight? I have to do some digging, but I think I have proof that the voice on that message isn't me."

When I didn't agree right away, his expression turned soft, his eyes pleading. "Please, Evie, give me a chance to prove my innocence."

I stared at him for a long time. Could I believe that it was all a hoax? "Fine. But right now, I don't believe you. I spent the last five years listening to that message, thinking I was the worst human in the world for asking you to sacrifice your career to come stay in some small town in Michigan. I can't go through that again."

"If I'd gotten the message, I would have." His voice was firm. "You won't go through that ever again. Just come over. I think I know exactly what happened."

Later that night, I stood on his doorstep, hands in my hoodie, feeling awkward and ready to run back to my car. He answered, the dogs barking excitedly at his feet.

"Come in. I found it," he said, pushing the dogs back with his bare feet.

Even now, I wanted to hate him, but as I walked behind him, I found myself admiring his shirtless back and all the muscles and ink on it. The memory of what he'd done to me this afternoon on set while we filmed sent me blushing and my body pulsing.

I hated how I responded to him, each and every time.

Sebastian took me to his living room, where he had a movie paused on the TV. He reached for the remote. "Sit."

I did as requested, and my space was invaded by his loving

pets. I laughed through the pain radiating from my side as they licked my face and tried to climb onto my lap.

"Listen to this," Sebastian said, pushing play on the TV.

I pushed the dogs away and leaned forward. A younger Sebastian was on the screen, talking to an older man—a teacher, it looked like. They were discussing him falling asleep in class because he'd been running from Simon Says all night. He paused the scene and looked at me, eyebrows raised.

I shook my head. "What?"

"Listen again." He rewound and played it again. "That's not me. That's a voice double. His name is Wes. He came in and did voice stuff for me all the time when I had scheduling conflicts. That voicemail was from him."

"How do you know?" I shook my head in disbelief.

"Pull up the message," he requested, and I had to muscle through another listen. He paused it. "Right there. Listen when he says your name. I don't say your name like that. Never have. Heather must have paid him to record this."

We replayed that small part a few times, and my eyes widened as I heard it. Holy shit.

"What does this mean?" I gulped, pushing down all the emotions I was feeling at that moment. I wasn't even sure what I was feeling. Hope? Nervousness? Relief? All of that and more was washing over me in droves, overwhelming me.

Sebastian snickered. "It means we have a pit stop to make. You're going to get your revenge, and I'm going to get mine. Let's go."

CHAPTER 59 SEBASTIAN

The Casting Couch

Five Years Ago

I stared down at the blank screen on my phone. Nothing. It'd been six months of nothing. Evie left town five days after Lita died—five days after we'd given our virginities to each other—and I hadn't heard from her since.

I'd tried to get in touch with her. I called, text, emailed even. She'd blocked me from everything. Or alternatively, which made my heart feel worse, I wasn't blocked. She saw my name on her screen every day and simply ignored it. I'd almost rather be blocked.

Evie, what is going on?

"What are you doing?" Heather's shitty attitude was felt before seen. She stormed into the green room, where I was waiting for my cue to go on stage. I'd been invited on one of those late-night talk shows to discuss the dark fantasy movie, *Surrender to Forever*, I did last year. It was finally being released in theaters.

I shook my head and shoved my phone into my pocket. "Nothing. Just waiting."

Her gaze flicked to my pocket and rolled her eyes. "I don't know why you do this to yourself. She's made her choice clear, I think."

I sat up hurriedly. "What do you mean, choice? Have you heard from her? Anything?" I regularly searched her name on the internet, hoping something would pop up. It was borderline obsessive, but she'd just dropped off the face of the earth with no goodbye. After what we'd done, our history?

I thought she loved me.

"No, and I doubt we will. Seb, she wants to be left alone. Let her. Her mom killed herself, for Christ's sake."

My eye twitched, and I bit my tongue to stop from correcting her. There was no way in Clive Barker's hell that Lita Reyes committed suicide. We'd seen her body. We'd seen the blood. But I refrained from arguing with my agent. The last time I did, she slapped me so hard my head spun and I hit a wall. I didn't need my shit rocked right before I went on live TV.

"Right." I looked away. "It's force of habit. Sorry."

Heather, in her signature fuchsia pink, straightened her jacket and dragged the chair from the vanity table over to me. She plopped down in it once she was right in front of me, and she reached for my hand.

"You know what they say the best way to get over someone is?"

I forced myself not to pull away. Heather often pretended to have a motherly affection toward me, but her words, actions, and sometimes hands, told a different story. Heather wasn't a loving mother. She was more like a drunken, angry father.

"What's that?" I humored her.

She beamed, thin lips tightening as she grinned.

"You get under someone new. Sebastian, we need to get you a new girlfriend."

The very idea jolted me. I yanked my hand away and jumped up, moving away quickly.

"Heather, that's—" I bit down on my knuckle. I couldn't believe she'd even suggest that.

She stood and sighed, crossing her arms. "Seb, she's not

coming back. First loves are always the hardest. But I think it's time to try to move on. You're the hottest teenager in America. You can literally have any woman you want, your age or not." She raised her eyebrows pointedly.

I grimaced. What was she implying?

"Pick someone, or I can do it for you." She pulled her phone out and began tapping furiously. "What about your co-star from *Surrender to Forever*? A showmance always sells. She's very pretty."

I shook my head and ran my hand through my hair. "Heather, not right now. I— I'm going to check on my time." I left, and thankfully, an assistant caught me and let me know they were just about ready for me to go on. I waited and, when prompted, took a deep breath, put on a smile, and walked out on stage, waving to the audience.

An hour later, I walked offstage not remembering a single word I'd said. Heather's suggestion had rocked me so hard, I couldn't think about anything else.

A new girlfriend? Never.

Heather and I went home, but I didn't speak much. The next morning, however, she surprised me with an afternoon date.

"I've lined up a handful of girls for you to see if anyone interests you. It's time, Sebastian." She offered vague threats, but I was used to them and zoned her out. I didn't really have a choice. Heather was my legal guardian. What she said went. I went on the date, but only in body. I ate, I sulked, and I left, not even learning the girl's name.

Heather saw through my bullshit by the fourth date and became more insistent. She joined me, made me drink, and despite myself, the alcohol loosened me up.

And soon, I found myself relying on alcohol just to get through. If I had to do these stupid dates, I could at least enjoy myself.

The second girl I ever kissed was at a pizza place, in the bathroom. She'd followed me in and let me pee before barging into the stall and forcing her lips on mine, and then she dropped to her knees and her lips found my dick. I was far too drunk to understand exactly what was happening. My body was complicit, so desperate for touch. I closed my eyes and imagined it was Evie, not... whoever, and was able to lose myself for just a few moments.

And after that, it got easier. Much easier. Makeouts and blowjobs turned into hands, hips, and tongues colliding in ways I'd only ever done with Evie. But maybe Heather was right. Evie didn't want me, but these girls did. Why not get off and go home? I could cry about the girl who broke my heart afterward.

Sex, something I'd considered special and important, became nothing but a release. Evie and I had put it up on this pedestal, saving ourselves not only for each other, but for the right time. Now, it was just something to pass the time in between auditions, commercials, photoshoots, speaking engagements, etc. I lost track of the names and faces. As long as we had a condom, we were good to go.

It was three months after I started dating that I had my first kiss with a guy. We were both hammered, and our lips just suddenly found each other's. And it wasn't bad. The scratch of his five o'clock shadow, his large hands on my hips—I was just as hard for him as I was for the girls.

We'd found my bed, and just as my shirt was coming off, the door opened and Heather walked in.

"Oh!" she yelped, her eyes widening as she took in the scene.

I froze, prepared for her to yell at me, but she didn't. She was smiling. She stared and then slowly backed out, leaving us be.

I should have known then that she wasn't simply okay with me being into both guys and girls. No, it was the next morning that I understood what had her smiling.

"I've lined up an audition for you. It's a good one, and everyone is gunning for it. But you have an edge. We're going to use it."

I looked up from my breakfast shake. "What's that?"

"The director likes you." She was grinning like a shark, just having seen the sign for Amity Beach.

"So?" Lots of people liked me. I didn't get why that was meant to be exciting.

Heather came over to me, her eyes bright and shiny.

"Sebastian. If you want this job—and I promise you, you do—then you need to seduce this man. Or let him seduce you."

Seduce?

I furrowed my brow. "I don't understand."

She sighed deeply, and her shoulders fell. "Sebastian, flirt with him. If he wants more...do more."

My mouth dropped open as I finally got it. "What? No, that's—"

She reached for my shoulders, pulling me into her, gripping me hard.

"We need to do this. This is your chance to get out of the cheap horror movies. You'll get to show off your range. Don't you want to be up for an Oscar or an Emmy? Horror won't get you any of those. But this one can. This script has legs. It has money behind it. It just needs its main lead, and if you let him fuck you, we will make millions."

Let him fuck me?

My mind was reeling. I had to sit down. I fell into a chair, gazing off into the distance. Could I? It was unethical, cheating to get the job. Couldn't I get it based on my own abilities? I'd taken a million hours of acting classes. I knew what to do at auditions to get the job. Was that not enough anymore?

Heather crouched in front of me, forcing me to make eye contact with her. "Seb, I know this is different for you. But if you can turn off your feelings, just consider it part of the audition, you can take us far. You're finally ready."

I chewed on my lip and steadied my breath so I didn't get sick.

Could I do what she wanted?

Turn off my feelings.

Consider it part of the audition.

I studied her words. *Take us far.* This wasn't about just me. It was her career, as well as the others we employed. There was a lot of responsibility on my shoulders. If I couldn't pay them what they deserved, that felt...bad.

What did she mean—I was finally ready? Had this been why she'd wanted me to start dating in the first place? So I'd be comfortable sleeping with people to get work? So I could shut off and stop thinking so much about Evie to get my job done?

Well, it worked.

I was utterly broken. Fuck Evie Reyes and what she'd done to my heart. I didn't have one anymore. But I did have a pretty face and a cock that people wanted. Might as well use them. I braced myself, pressing my lips together, and nodded.

"Fine."

CHAPTER 60

EVIE

The Re-Creation

"I never thought I'd see the day when your name appeared on my screen again, Sebastian Shaw." Heather, a woman I hardly recognized now from all the work she'd had done, sat across from us at the restaurant. Sadness and a bit of pity flooded me as I stared at the botched work. I was never one to shame someone for trying to feel more comfortable in their own body, but whoever had done her lips and facelift had done a bad job. It all looked... painful.

"Yes, well." Sebastian cleared his throat and shifted his weight from side to side. "Me neither, but my girlfriend is in need of an agent."

"I see." Heather's eyes flicked to me with disinterest. "Who are you?"

Reluctantly, I put my hand out. She stared at it, and I slid it back under the table.

"This is Evie Reyes, Lita Reyes's daughter. You've met before." Sebastian's annoyance was clear in his tone, but he quickly reined it in.

Heather scrunched her nose and motioned for the waitress to return to the table. She ordered a martini and then turned back to us.

"Sorry, I don't remember you. You need an agent?" She sighed, clearly bored.

My stomach tightened with nerves, and I nodded. "Yes, ma'am. My previous agent passed away."

"Don't call me *ma'am,*" she snapped. "You look older than me."

My eyebrows shot up as I pressed my lips together. She couldn't be serious.

"Anyway," Sebastian interjected. "I thought we could have dinner and talk. Maybe work something out."

"Yes, well, you and I were always able to do that, weren't we?" She looked at me and winked, and my mood faltered. What was she winking for? Was she implying that she and Sebastian had been... lovers? No. I could believe a lot of things, but that was not one of them.

Sebastian ordered for us all, per Heather's request. She spent the evening flirting with him, blatantly ignoring me, and repeatedly asking if they should take another, more private meeting to discuss his career, not mine. If I didn't know his plans for her future, I'd be jealous as hell, which was new for me.

After our meal, Sebastian paid the bill and offered to escort Heather to her car.

"Actually, I took a ride here. Did you two take separate cars? Maybe I could get a ride from you, Sebastian," she purred, leaning on his shoulder. She'd had far more to drink than what was professional. I'd had one beer to her five martinis. She was sloppy drunk, which I thought served well for this moment.

"Sure. Let's get you in the car." Sebastian led her to his vehicle and helped her inside.

I took the back, albeit a bit begrudgingly.

"Oh, sweetie," she slurred as I crawled into the back seat. "It would never work out. You're not pretty enough to act. You need to lose all those tattoos, get bigger lips, a new nose, less of a tan." She snickered.

My eyes widened as I took in her disgusting comments.

Excuse me?

Less of a tan?

"I'm Mexican. This isn't a tan—it's my skin color," I snapped, unable to keep it to myself.

She hiccupped. "I've been in this industry a long time. I just speak the truth."

"Right. Well, let's talk about how true that is when you wake up." Sebastian plopped into the driver's seat and pulled out a syringe.

"Wha—"

He plunged it into her neck, injecting a tranquilizer into her blood. Heather went limp. He tossed the syringe into his glove compartment then started the car. "Groovy."

"Where did you get that?" I asked. He'd told me he was going to sedate her, but he hadn't said how.

"I was in a movie with horses and made friends with the wrangler. He was a drug dealer on the low and used to give us all ketamine as a 'sample.' I never sampled, so this has been in my cabinet for a while."

I stared out into the dark, surprised again by another secret in this dark town. "What now?" I asked as he pulled onto the highway.

"It's not a movie, but you've seen *Dexter*, right?"

Heather roused to life a few hours later, and I breathed a sigh of relief.

She flinched at the harsh light over her head.

"What the—" She tried to move and quickly realized that she'd been restrained with plastic wrap. "Sebastian?" she whimpered.

I stood in the corner as Sebastian stepped out of his, looking like the titular TV character.

My heart pumped wildly, admiring how good he looked in the tight olive thermal and cargo pants. He walked to her, plucking the apron off a hook and making sure she watched him put it on.

My stomach hitched with anticipation. While I had looked

away when he'd torn apart Glenn's body, I planned to watch this.

"What are you doing? Why am I here?" She fought the restraints, but it was useless. Sebastian and I had used a metric fuckton of the plastic. Even the Hulk couldn't get out of it.

"See those?" He pointed his black leather–gloved hands at the wall. She turned her head as much as she could and squinted, trying to see the images. He really was having his *Dexter* moment—and as much as it scared me, I wanted this for him. After what he'd told me on the way to the restaurant, he deserved it.

Heather was an asshole.

"Those are the people you pushed me to sleep with. Do you remember any of them?"

Heather's wide eyes turned to slits in an instant, and she stopped fidgeting. She narrowed her eyes, and her blown-out lips attempted to sneer.

"Pushed you?" She laughed. "Hardly. I seem to remember you being more than eager to get on your knees for a bigger role. I may have suggested it, but you didn't hesitate."

"What were my choices, Heather? If I didn't do what you sent me to do, not only did I not get the job, but I knew these men's secrets and could've been blacklisted. I had little choice."

"Did you get off?"

Silence filled the room. Sebastian's eyes flicked to me, and I pushed myself deeper into the corner. I'd told him over and over in the car that none of it mattered. Erections and orgasms were just biological responses. They were not an indicator of consent. Putting his hand in his back pocket, he pulled out one of my knives, revealing it to Heather.

She paled.

"You lied. Tonight, at dinner. I know you remember Evie. Tell the truth."

She scoffed. "Is that what all this is about? Because I was a bitch to your boring girlfriend over drinks?"

"You broke us up," he accused.

"What?" She squinted, as if trying to recall, and then her eyes widened again as her lips formed an *O*.

"Wes. You deleted the voice message Evie sent me and crafted a reply with someone else so that I'd never know."

Heather was silent, albeit squirmy. "So?"

My attention flicked to Sebastian. His eyes had gone wide, and his mouth had fallen open in shock at her aloofness.

"So? So?" Sebastian turned and kicked a wall. "So? That's all you have to say for yourself? You made me a whore."

"Oh, come off it, Sebastian!" she yelled back at him. She swung her head toward me, then back to him. "Is this all because of her? Are you ashamed suddenly? She's not fit for Hollywood if she can't handle the truth about how everyone wheels and deals."

"Fuck you," I blurted, stepping out from the edge of the room. "I don't care what he's done. I care that you hurt him."

"Honey, I didn't hurt him," she groaned, refusing to look at me. "He wanted every last bit of it. He hired me to make him famous. I did just that, and then he fired me. Sorry to break it to you, but your boyfriend isn't telling you the truth."

"No, you're the only one lying." I pulled out the other knife and grabbed her hand, pricking it. A small drop of blood dripped from her finger, and she yelped as if I'd full-on stabbed her.

"You're psycho. Both of you. Is this some sort of reality show? I've seen *Dexter*. I know what this is. I'm not signing a waiver for this to air."

"This isn't TV, Heather," Sebastian said, striding confidently to the photos. "This is reality. How often did you go through my phone?"

"Fuck this," she muttered.

I pricked her again, and she let out a scream for help.

"It's pointless. We're in your garage. No one's coming for you," Sebastian snorted.

"Like you could really kill someone." She snickered. "You're just a scared little boy playing pretend, Sebastian," she taunted him.

"I've killed five men now, actually. Starting with your buddy

Michael Thornton."

"Thornton?" she asked, her smile falling.

He ripped a photo from the wall and brought it to her face.

"Michael Thornton, producer? Remember him? I killed him, if you didn't know. He was going to force me to suck his old cock in exchange for green-lighting *Simon Says Six: Six Six*, and I was done. I killed him and didn't bat an eye. He was my first, and since then, we've been picking away at his friends. And now, you're going to be dead soon too. But before we do this, answer me. How often did you go through my cell phone?"

"Is this a threat?"

Sebastian lifted the knife and pushed the tip into her chest, right between her surgically altered mix-matched breasts.

"Yes, Heather, it is. Answer."

"All the time," she rushed. "It was my job to keep your career safe and growing. You'd be nothing without me."

A slow grin spread over her botched lips. "When you heard that voicemail, Evie, how long did you cry? I hope it was a long time. I gave Wes a great script."

"You bitch," I snapped, raising the knife. Rage flooded my veins. How could she say she cared for Sebastian and then admit to doing all these awful things? I understood now why Sebastian was helping me on my quest for revenge. In this moment, I needed him to have his.

"Evie!" Sebastian yelled, stopping me from finishing this.

I swung it down to my side and hung my head.

"See, I did the right thing." Heather smiled. "Even now, he's choosing me. Sorry, sweetie, but men like him will always choose money over sex. I was doing you both a favor. Without me, you'd be nothing, Sebastian. You shouldn't be trying to kill me. You should be thanking me."

"Thank you, Heather," Sebastian snarled and, without hesitation, lifted his arm and slammed the knife into her chest, missing the plastic wrap. She gasped as blood splattered the room. It hit my face, and I winced in surprise.

Heather's throat gurgled as blood flooded her mouth and poured from her puffy lips. Sebastian removed the knife, and blood flowed from the wound, covering her orange skin and the table underneath with deep red. The plastic wrap holding her down grew slack as her body went limp. I trailed my gaze down her body, noting the occasional muscle twitch, ending with her curled fingers. And then finally, as we watched Heather's soul leave her body, I watched the tension leave Sebastian's. It was as if he'd taken a large breath for the first time in years. He fell against the wall and sighed, and then a slow, dry laugh came from his chest.

"How do you feel?" I asked, twisting my hands.

"Fucking glorious."

I couldn't wait for that feeling.

"What next?" I asked.

He smirked and kicked off the wall, going to the other side of the room to pick up the chainsaw. "You said you watched the show. Stay back if you don't want to be sprayed."

CHAPTER 61

SEBASTIAN

The Wrap Out

"Want some?" I offered Evie a swig of the mouthwash I'd already used several times during the grueling process of taking care of Heather's body. On top of the blood, gore, bones, and brain matter, the floor was also littered with both Evie's and my vomit. We'd tried to dismember my former agent, but we were struggling. I'd quickly abandoned the chainsaw in favor of some larger butcher knives I'd found in Heather's kitchen. The job took longer, but it didn't spray blood like a chainsaw did.

I just had to make sure I didn't slip on any vomit.

"Yes, God yes," Evie groaned as together we slid down the wall and stared around the bloodied room. She accepted the bottle, took a large swig, and then spat it out on the other side of her. "Can we never do it this way again, please?"

"Yeah, lesson learned." I took my goggles off, wiped the sweat from my brow, and sighed. This was way worse than breaking Glenn's face with my fists. This was...disgusting. "Real life isn't like the movies. Who could have guessed cutting someone to pieces was this..."

"I'm gonna be sick again." She launched forward on all fours, and I patted her back as she threw up all over one of Heather's arms. "Oh my God, it twitched," she groaned. I wasn't sure if that was possible, but the very idea made me feel sick too.

"Let's grab the trash bags." I stood and went for the box, pulling out a bag. I began the process of stuffing my former agent's body parts into the bag for disposal. When Evie stopped gagging, she stood and did the same. We stuffed the bags into my car and, on the way back, grabbed the garden hose and a bucket. As Evie tore the plastic down from the walls, I washed all the blood down the drain at the center of the garage floor. I grabbed a broom and pushed all the pieces of gore toward the hole, stomping them down with my boot, hoping they didn't create a clog.

"Can you stop waffle-stomping her entrails, please?" Evie gagged again.

I looked down at my feet and realized I'd been going so hard that whatever piece of Heather I'd been stepping on was now the consistency of chunky, bloody oatmeal.

"My bad. We're almost done." I hosed down the bottom of my boots and then went to her, wrapping an arm around her. Kissing her head, I said, "Thank you for helping me do this."

"Of course. I want you to have the same peace I hope to have soon."

I wondered, as we finished cleaning up the garage and removing all evidence of our visit, would I have peace?

Yes.

"Are we really getting a boat, like *Dexter*?" she asked as I drove to the marina with the chopped-up body and a box of bricks in the back.

"Yeah, Bryce has one docked there. He's taken me out fishing a few times. I called him earlier. It's private and doesn't have cameras. He told me where the spare keys are."

"They choose to not have cameras?" she asked. "I guess that says something about their clientele."

That it did.

"Do you know how to drive a boat?" She raised an eyebrow at me.

"I do, actually. I worked on a movie where we had them, and I put in my contract that I got to drive any boats my character needed to, instead of a stuntman."

I turned up the radio. Whitesnake blasted through the speakers, and when I snuck a glance over at Evie, she was smiling softly.

I understood her questioning things. I was supposed to be the confident one in charge, and yet, there had been so much vomit from us both in the garage. So much so that it had covered up the smell of Heather's insides.

We parked and headed to Bryce's boat. I'd been on it more than once, so it was easy for me to identify the green and white pontoon boat. It was the dead of night, so no one was around to watch us load all the bags and bricks.

Soon, I was pulling away from the dock and breathing a sigh of relief. In an hour or two, this would be over, and—as Evie hoped—I'd have peace.

Evie came to sit with me in the passenger seat and silently reached for my hand. I drove one handed and relaxed, enjoying the cool breeze and water lightly spraying my face.

"What are you thinking about?" I asked after a while.

"I'm thinking that a boat ride is often considered a date. If we were two people in a different world, this would be our second date," she sighed dreamily.

"Why can't it be? A boat ride in the moonlight?" We got a decent distance from shore, and I cut the motor. Regretfully, I let go of her hand and went to the back of the boat, where I started to tie the bricks to the bags of Heather.

"Most dates have fewer chainsaws and less vomit." She laughed dryly.

"Less, but not none." I smirked and raised a bag over my shoulder. "You know, maybe I am a psycho," I mused, tossing it over the side of the boat. "I should feel guilt, or sadness, or disgust over what happened tonight. I don't."

Evie came and helped me unload a second bag.

"I wrestled with my feelings for a long time before I came back. Why didn't I feel bad? They were humans, with people who loved them. Some have kids. Pets too. I just...don't care." She watched me toss another bag over. "They didn't care about me. And I may not be the only one they've hurt like this. How many suicides were actually murders in Hollywood?"

She wasn't wrong.

Together, we finished disposing of Heather's body and then dropped to the floor of the boat. She cuddled against me, and I pulled her close, enjoying every second of intimacy she offered. I knew that in a moment, it could be ripped from me, never to be felt again, so I had to savor it.

"I'm sorry she did all that to you," Evie said. "She deserved to die."

"You think?"

"I do."

Evie was just as cold as I was, and I liked it.

"I've always felt conflicted about what she did to me. She didn't *force* me into being with those men and women—but she had me convinced that if I didn't sleep with them, then all the people who relied on my money would lose their jobs. That I'd never be rich and famous, and so many people were depending on me. It was so much guilt, and she made it seem like I was the bad guy."

"Well, you're not. At least not for that." Evie smirked. She stretched up and gave me a peck on the lips.

My chest tightened, and my belly warmed. That was the first kiss she'd offered me willingly, not out of lust or because we were working. What did this mean?

"Do you...like bad guys?" I wiggled my eyebrows suggestively.

She laughed and fell back against my chest.

"Anthony C. Hopkins, Sebastian."

I held her tighter and placed my chin on her head. If we only had tonight, I'd die a happy man.

"I've enjoyed a lot of people's bodies, but I've only enjoyed one person's soul. Evie, I know you're still hellbent on this suicide mission, but I just need you to know—I'm going to do everything in my power to not only keep you alive, but to get you to stay here with me when this is all over." The words started slow, then, as I kept talking, all at once.

"I see. And what if none of that happens?" she asked. "Even if I don't die, which is unlikely, what if I want to leave Hollywood? Heather said it herself, I'm not really the look this town wants."

"Fuck this town," I snarled. "You want to leave, give me a day to pack my bags. We'll take Precious and Cujo with us. We can get one of those motor homes and travel the country if you want. Or just live a quiet life in the woods, or on a beach, or in the fucking Arctic. I don't care, as long as it's with you. I mean it, Evie," I said when she started to snicker.

I straightened, causing her to sit up and look at me. "I'm sorry Heather tricked you with that voicemail. If I had received it, I would have left this town with no hesitation. This place chews you up and spits you out. If I have to choose between the world loving me for my face or you loving me for who I am underneath it, I'll choose you every time."

"You say that now..." Evie shook her head, a small smile curling up one side of her face. She rose to her feet and went to the side of the boat where we'd dropped Heather off. She gripped the edge and spit into the water.

"Wait until this is all over. You might decide I'm the psycho, not you."

I joined her, wrapping my arms around her from behind. I brushed her hair back and kissed her neck.

"I think that'd only make me want you more, Final Girl."

CHAPTER 62
SEBASTIAN

The New Deal

"Another rewrite?" I slapped the new script onto the table and leaped up. "This is bullshit. They are purposely prolonging this movie, and for what? There's no way the sixth movie in a franchise needs this."

I went to my mini fridge and grabbed a Red Bull. We'd been at this for weeks. Rewrite after rewrite. The studio executives kept adding more scenes. They had Skye and me do sex scenes, Evie and me do *more* sex scenes, and everyone had a million extra fight scenes. They filmed me dying, Evie dying, Bryce—the main character of the entire fucking franchise—meeting his final demise. It was becoming torture.

"I've never been on a film this long," I yelled at Anderson as he came to the set—after I'd told Dante to fuck off when I was sent another new script.

"I know. I agree with you, Sebastian. I'm not entirely sure what the studio is doing either. They seem to be throwing more money at this movie to keep the cameras rolling. I'm going to ask for a higher salary for you."

"You bet your ass you are," I snarled. "I need a fucking break."

"You want a break? I can do that. What do you want? Two weeks?"

"I want to be off this fucking set for good," I groaned.

My agent watched me have a meltdown in my trailer, then nodded. "Okay, let me see what I can do."

An hour later, I got a text that I had a meeting with a studio executive. Under normal circumstances, I'd be elated, but when I saw the name of who I'd be speaking to, my mood sank.

Arthur Englund.

The man who had stabbed Evie. The next man on her list.

I'd convinced her to take a break from her murder spree. I'd promised her that once the movie wrapped, I'd help kill them quickly, but the movie wouldn't fucking end.

Connor, my assistant, drove me to Arthur's office. I slammed my energy drink just as I walked through the door with his name on it. I tossed my can in the trash, wiped my mouth with the back of my hand, and plopped down in the chair in front of his desk, propping my boots on the edge.

"You called?"

Arthur looked a bit taken aback but quickly recovered. He cleared his throat and shifted papers on his desk.

"I heard you're unhappy with the film schedule."

"What schedule?" I laughed. "This is a joke. You've pushed back the wrap date every Friday for a month."

"Yes, well—"

"No 'well.' Stop pussyfooting around and just spit it out."

Arthur's bumbling demeanor shifted. His smile dropped, and his eyes narrowed. "Remember who you're talking to, Shaw." His voice was cold, and I raised an eyebrow.

"You want to be done with all of this?" he asked and looked down, pulling out a drawer in his desk. "I have good news. We want to be done too. All of this...nonsense. Let's finish it once and for all."

His tone didn't match his words.

"If I'm being candid, Sebastian, we've been filming more scenes because Evie has made it clear she will not be returning after this film. We want to get our money's worth for flashbacks and things like that. When you create a franchise as prolific as

Simon Says, you have to plan not just for the movie you're currently working on, but the next five or six." While he spoke, he continued looking in his desk, shuffling things in each drawer.

"Evie wasn't even scheduled this week." I crossed my arms. "I call bullshit."

"Yes, well, we are also planning for your possible exit."

The words hung heavy in the air. He wasn't talking about killing Ronny McCoy, the character I'd played since I was a kid. He was talking about me.

I slid my boots off his table, dropping them to the floor as I leaned forward. "What are you talking about? I'm not going anywhere."

He stopped and looked up, a smirk playing on his face. "I think we both know that might not be true."

"So, this is why you're holding us hostage and making us film more every day? Because you're preparing to kill us?"

He ignored my direct question, sidestepping it with ease. "Sebastian, I know what you've been doing. Rumor has it, your extracurriculars are going to be leaked soon, and you might not be Hollywood's golden boy anymore."

I froze but forced myself not to react violently. I regretted slamming the Red Bull as fast as I had. I was beginning to feel jittery.

"What extracurriculars are you referring to, Mr. Englund?"

It was a fair question. Even before this film started, I wasn't exactly Steve from *Blue's Clues*. It could be a plethora of things he was talking about.

Was it the sex or the murder?

He shook his head, his lips turning down into a sneer. "The deeds I am referring to are you deep throating this town's top producers and directors to get gigs. Apparently, there are photos and videos of you doing whatever it takes to land a job."

I laughed. He was mad about me being a slut for roles? No, this was just the excuse they'd be taking to the public. He knew. Otherwise, he wouldn't have stabbed Evie.

"What is this? Are you jealous you didn't get topped before I got taken? I'm sorry you were a little too late, but I can ask my agent about securing a deal with a dildo company. Maybe we can make some molds of my cock for the Hollywood elite."

"Enough!" he yelled over me.

I shut my mouth, satisfied I'd gotten a rise out of him.

He slammed his hands on his desk and stood. "There's a good chance you'll never work in this fucking town again once people know what you did to land those jobs. Now, if you want all this to end, I need you to do something for me."

"I told you I was taken, Arthur," I snipped.

"You're a goddamn child. Actually, fuck it. I'm done. We know you two have been killing everyone involved in Lita's death. People aren't fucking happy."

"People as in Elliott Bradley? You don't know shit, and neither do I. I'm sorry people have been killed, but I can't help you, Arthur." I stood, but he lifted his hand quickly.

"Wait!" His voice held a desperation that interested me.

I paused, giving him a careful look. Why had he changed his tune so quickly? Did Elliott Bradley have something to say about this meeting?

"I want to make a deal."

"A deal?" I cocked my head to the side.

"Please, sit back down. Let's work this out." His face flushed bright red.

Humoring him, I sat down and leaned back in the chair.

"We know it's her and that she's had help. Jason and Charles—those men were too large for a girl so small to take down on her own. If she's anything like her mother, she could convince anyone to do what she wants. We know it was you."

"Do you now? What proof do you have?" I asked.

Arthur glared at me but didn't answer. "I thought giving her a good poke would be enough to scare her, but it didn't do anything. If you agree to leave Elliott and me alone, I'll make sure all that unsavory audition footage gets squashed. And I'll give you a producer credit and a good-sized bonus." He pulled a paper from the stack on his desk and offered it to me.

I scanned the contract. The offer for a producer credit and bonus was a number I'd never seen offered to me in my life.

"What if I'm not the killer? What if you die anyway? Then you've just made this offer for nothing." I set the paper on his desk and reached for a pen.

He pointed to the bottom of the contract. "You'll see at the end, if Elliott Bradley or I die in the next ten years, regardless of cause of death, the deal is off. Any monies paid will be owed back to the studio, and the proof of your sordid affairs with everyone in town will be released."

I pulled away, pen still in hand, and shook my head. "No thanks. It's clear someone has an issue with you. It's not my fault if you get what's coming. Release whatever you want. I'll figure it out." I stood to go, and he stopped me again.

"New deal!"

I sighed.

"One more scene. I want you and Evie to film a stand-off." He shuffled papers and offered me a thin packet.

I took it and scanned the script.

"We don't have proof it's you helping her, but we know she's the mastermind. We need you to scare her."

I smirked. "Explain to me again why I would help you?"

"Because if *you* don't get her to stop, *we'll* have to do it. And it won't be a quick jab this time." His smile fell off, and he stared me down.

I shifted, and scanned the packet, suddenly a little interested. "And how am I going to do that?" I looked up from the script.

Arthur's thin lips spread into a slow grin as he slid his hand inside his suit, pulling out a small, gray bullet.

"You're going to stun her. Scare her a little, that's all." He offered it to me, and I took it, bringing it to eye level and turning it between my fingers. "You ever hear of an *Ich lüge* bullet?"

CHAPTER 63 EVIE

The First Screening

"He's left us no choice. Sebastian Shaw is a monster."

"A monster?" I stared blankly at the executive who'd pulled me into his office after working a twelve-hour shift.

I was exhausted and just wanted to leave the studio.

To go home.

To go to Sebastian's.

"Yes. He has killed four of my friends. I'm not sure why, but we think it has to do with trying to cover up his past indiscretions. We need to keep Hollywood safe, Evie. And we can't do it without you and this *Ich lüge* bullet."

I smiled at Arthur as he nodded enthusiastically. He was telling me all about his grand idea for the final scene they wanted to shoot. I prayed I hadn't accidentally agreed to something, because I wasn't listening. How could I, when my mind was full of the text Sebastian had sent me right before I walked into Arthur's office.

Psycho Killer

This isn't fucking *Heathers*.

At first, I didn't understand what he was trying to tell me, and then Arthur produced the bullet, and it clicked. Those were the same bullets Christian Slater's character JD used in *Heathers*. There was no such thing.

Ich lüge means "I'm lying."

Arthur's hands waving in front of me brought me back to his office.

"Picture it. You and Sebastian, clothes torn, covered in dirt and cuts. Epic fires behind you, sirens blaring in the distance, and then, it's just you two. You lift your gun, he follows, and then you say—"

"Simon says, motherfucker," I finished his sentence, having already scanned the script.

He laughed and clapped, like one of those toy monkeys with the little cymbals.

"Yes! And then you shoot him! He'll drop, you'll run to him, not realizing it was a real bullet. As with any shoot with a gun, there will be proper staff on set to take care of him. He'll be stunned, but nothing more. The *Ich lüge* bullet was made just for this."

"For movies?"

"No, to scare the piss out of people." Arthur sat back and sighed heavily. "I'm sorry you got wrapped up in this, Evie. I'm not entirely sure why he's doing all of this, but Sebastian needs to be stopped. You're our last hope."

"What if I miss? This seems dangerous."

"It won't matter. Even if it hits his heart, the bullet can't pierce his skin. You have to trust me. If we don't do this, you might be his next victim," he warned.

I parted my mouth to speak, but I had nothing to say. When I realized I wasn't reacting, I gasped loudly. "He wouldn't."

"Oh, he would, and he might." Arthur came around his desk and put his hand on my shoulder. I forced myself not to flinch away. This was the man who'd stabbed me. Memories of that night flashed through my mind as he continued speaking so close to me.

"Sebastian Shaw is a monster we've kept at bay for many, many years. It started with your mother, but we think your return to Hollywood must have triggered something in him. He's hellbent on killing all the people he thinks have wronged him, and you may be next if he suspects you're trying to sabotage the film that is going to turn him into a household name. I've heard whisperings that a certain superhero franchise has been watching him. He won't let you ruin that for him."

"Because I don't want to keep filming?" I asked. This entire meeting was set up because I'd complained about the number of rewrites. Now, they were scrambling for excuses to keep us here. Sebastian and I both knew they were only prolonging this so they could keep an eye on us. Arthur's reasons were flimsy at best. It felt like he'd come up with this story just a few moments before I walked in. None of it made sense, but I went along with it, hoping he'd hang himself.

"Exactly. But I've convinced him this is the last scene needed. He wanted to keep filming, but we knew you were getting exhausted, and the longer it goes on, eventually, he'll kill again. It's time to wrap. So, what do you say? Let's stop this beast."

I thought about the text again.

Even if I hadn't received it, I wouldn't have believed a word from this asshole's mouth. He really thought I'd believe Sebastian killed my mother? This dude stabbed me.

"What are your hesitations?" Arthur asked.

"It's hard to believe he had something to do with my mother's murder," I said honestly.

"Understandable. Unfortunately, I was the one who watched the security cams. It was without a doubt Sebastian Shaw who raped her, stabbed her, and later staged her murder to look like a suicide."

I stared deep into his eyes, studying him. How could he lie so easily? He continued his fabrication without batting an eye.

"The studio made the mistake of covering it up. Why ruin multiple lives? We thought we were doing the right thing—keeping a boy with a bright future free but on a short leash. His urges had gotten the best of him, we thought. We were sadly mistaken and now need to take him down."

"And a fake-out is going to do that?" I lifted the bullet, deciding to play his stupid fucking game. It didn't feel rubber, although I'd never felt a real bullet to compare it to.

"Yes. He'll see it as a warning."

"Is that why you stabbed me? A warning?"

He was silent for a long time, then nodded. "Yes. I thought you were Sebastian. I didn't look before I thrust the knife." He hung his head, seemingly in shame. He was a good actor. "I am deeply sorry, Evelyn. I never meant to hurt you. You were never supposed to return."

This man really thought he had me convinced. I gripped the arms of my seat. If I had a gun, I'd use the *Ich lüge* bullet right now and test it.

I seethed inwardly. I needed to get out of here. I couldn't fake this anymore. Arthur walked across the room to a mini fridge. He opened it and pulled out a blue Red Bull.

"Are you thirsty? The blueberry is my favorite."

I peered into the fridge and spotted a red can. "I'll take peach." He pulled it out and handed it to me, then offered a toast.

"What do you say? Are you in?"

I stared blankly at the wall behind him, then lifted my can. "We have such sights to show you."

"What's that?"

"Nothing." I smirked. "Of course I'll do it. It's for the greater good."

THAT NIGHT, I sat in my home theater, freshly showered, wearing one of my mother's flowing pink nightgowns, watching her first film, *Missing You, Missing Me.* The storyline was shit, but her performance was impeccable. She was around my age yet appeared so much older.

Not physically. She was stunning until the day she died. It was the way she carried herself, the confidence she always exuded. She walked into a room with the expectation that everyone was there just for her. She took no shit and yet was soft as a kitten. I glanced at the rest of my couch, a small twinge of loneliness pulling at my heartstrings. If this were Sebastian's house, I'd be surrounded by dogs. Sebastian would be wrapping a blanket around me and handing me a bowl of freshly popped popcorn with M&M's, and we'd be snuggling in for another night of movies. But it was mine, and I had no one to warm my feet or cuddle under my arms. There was no popcorn with M&M's, and there was no Sebastian.

I missed him.

I pulled a throw blanket up to my chin and continued my melancholy reflection of my mother's body of work. Tomorrow, I was expected to kill Sebastian. They really thought I was stupid. Did they forget the internet existed?

They literally fed me the plot from *Heathers*, for Christ's sake. *Ich lüge* bullets? Come on. I made a living watching and deep diving movies. Did they really think I wouldn't catch that reference?

I had a feeling everything would change tomorrow. Someone was going to die. Whether it was me, Sebastian, or someone else, I could feel it in my bones. There was going to be an incident.

After the movie finished, I left the home theater and drifted through the house, my feathery robe trailing behind me. My mom had been so much taller than me, I felt like a little girl playing dress up. I tightened the robe and went out the back door to stare at the moon.

Sebastian had asked me several times what I wanted after this was all over. I hated to admit, but I'd begun thinking about it. Up until now, I'd made a point not to think of life after my revenge because I was so sure if I made it through the whole list, the police would gun me down on the front lawn after my last kill. But what if they didn't? What if no one ever learned about what Sebastian, Bryce, Skye, and I did? What then?

I was starting to think it was time to sell this old place. I could get a pretty penny for the home of Lita Reyes—the *Simon*

Says Final Girl.

Even if she hadn't been a star, the house was impressive enough on its own.

But then what?

I sell this place and then...

"You want to leave, give me a day to pack my bags. We'll take Precious and Cujo with us. We can get one of those motor homes and travel the country if you want. Or just live a quiet life in the woods, or on a beach, or in the fucking Arctic. I don't care, as long as it's with you."

Sebastian's words from our unofficial second date—out on the boat, disposing of his ex-agent's body—filled my mind. I hated how quickly my heart betrayed my brain. It wanted all those things so strongly, it was willing to change course, abandon all plans of murder, revenge, and peace, in favor of...love.

Could I?

"Penny for your thoughts, Final Girl?"

Spinning around, I found Sebastian leaning against the doorframe of my house. His arms were crossed, and his playful smirk danced on his lips.

"What are you doing here?" I asked, rushing to him. I threw my arms around him and inhaled his scent deep into my lungs. Oh, how I needed him right now.

"I couldn't stay away," he admitted, embracing me tightly. "What happened at your meeting with Arthur?"

I pulled back and took his hand, leading him out into my backyard. I didn't come out here often, but as I gazed around, admiring the heart-shaped pool and all the pink furniture my mother had painstakingly picked out, the idea of selling this place hurt my heart. I took Sebastian to the edge of the pool, where we pulled our clothes up to our knees and put our feet in the water.

"He wants me to kill you."

"Oh my God," Sebastian gasped dramatically. "Same!"

We shared a look then burst into laughter. He gave me the rundown of his meeting, and then I told him about mine. We'd both caught the odd bullet name from *Heathers*. In the movie, Christian Slater told Wynona Ryder they were stun bullets. He assured her they were safe to shoot, and then when they shot at the school bullies, Kurt and Ram, she discovered that he'd been lying, and they were real ones. That was what Arthur and whoever had helped him plan this were doing. They'd told Sebastian and me two different stories but given us the same lie about the bullets.

I wasn't surprised by any of this, but I was a little bitter that I hadn't been offered a producer's credit.

"Even in the business of murder, women aren't paid the same as men." I reached for Sebastian's hand and laced my fingers through his.

"So, what do we do, then?" he asked.

Good question. I stared out into the water. A tiny little plastic swan filled with chemicals drifted by, and I focused on it.

"We perform like we never have before. We pretend like we're going to go through with things. And then...we don't."

"We could turn the guns on them," Sebastian suggested.

I nodded. "We could. Although if your goal is to keep me alive, that isn't the way to do it."

"True." He tightened his hold on my hand. "I do enjoy you being alive."

I leaned close, resting my head on his shoulder. "We'll figure it out. It's funny that they tried to pit us against each other, and they thought you were self-centered enough to take the bait, and I was too stupid to see through them."

"That's Hollywood, Final Girl." He turned and kissed my forehead.

We relaxed and spoke of other things for a bit, but we'd both had long days and would have another long one tomorrow, so we pulled our feet from the pool, and he took his leave.

I stood on the front steps, waving and watching him drive off. He would have stayed, but the dogs would miss him.

So would I.

A cold shiver ran through me, making me shudder. Going

back inside, I locked the door behind me.

Tomorrow, I decided, I would make decisions. Plan a future with Sebastian if things went well. Or maybe, if things ended badly, I'd hide inside a closet upstairs and insist they break through the door and shoot me down, like I'd always planned. What a way to go.

People would paint portraits of my end.

Or I could abandon it all—for happiness.

Why did both ideas make me uneasy?

I went to bed, shutting off lights and checking locks as I moved through the house. I drifted to my mother's old bedroom, my current room. I paused, staring at the spot where Glenn had thrown up and died.

What a shame. We could have saved him and my carpet if he hadn't been such a pig.

As I lay in bed, preparing to fall asleep, my phone chimed. I knew who it was before checking, but still, I reached over and read the message.

Psycho Killer

Whatever happens tomorrow, just know... I was watching *The Exorcist.*

I set my phone down, wishing I could respond. I closed my eyes. The reply I couldn't type danced on my lips in a heavenly sigh. One day, in person, I'd finish the quote and truly tell him how I felt.

Oh, Sebastian, it got me thinking of you.

EVIE

The Sequel

"Groovy."

I stood with Sebastian as we sipped Red Bulls and waited patiently to step onto the set. We'd just gotten the fire safety speech and were watching as the professionals went around, lighting various props on fire. We chatted and pretended as if it were just another day.

"Tropical?" Sebastian tilted his blue can my way, and I lifted my yellow one.

"They've grown on me."

"Yeah, I use it to manage my ADHD." He shrugged.

"You have ADHD?"

"Who doesn't?" He smirked. "I tried the meds when I was younger. Wasn't a fan. I found ingesting a fuck-ton of caffeine does the trick."

I wondered if that was why my brain felt so clear lately. My thoughts weren't as jumbled. I'd grown fond of the caffeinated drinks.

"By the way, I learned something interesting. Dexter didn't use a chainsaw. In the show, it was a reciprocating saw. No wonder there was so much..."

"Vomit?"

My stomach turned as the image of Sebastian waffle-stomping

intestines into the drain while splashing both of our bile with each lift of his boot flashed in my memory.

"I guess we know for next time." He cackled, and I looked up to see the edge of his lips twitching. He finished his drink and pushed off the wall, going over to Dante to chat. "I'll see you later, Final Girl."

I stared after him, my heart longing for words I couldn't say.

Two figures pushing through a door just out of the corner of my eye caught my attention, and I turned. Fear slid down my spine as my eyes settled on two men in suits striding through, laughing and chatting excitedly.

Arthur Englund and Elliott Bradley.

What were they doing here?

Arthur saw me and nudged his friend. They stopped abruptly and turned my way. I stiffened and shoved down the nerves in my stomach.

"Well, there's the Final Girl." Arthur beamed.

Don't call me that.

I fought back a snarl. "Hello," I said politely.

"You've met Elliott Bradley."

I shook my head and forced myself to take his hand when it was offered. "I've seen you around." I studied him, looking for features that matched mine. I did this for each of the men on my list, and I was still no closer to the truth. I was my mother's daughter through and through.

"Yes, same here. It's nice to finally meet Lita Reyes's most important legacy. I've heard only great things."

There was a beat of silence where both men stared at me, giant smiles on their faces. It gave uncanny valley vibes, as if he were trying to appear human but wasn't quite selling it. The idea made me uneasy.

"I should get back to it." I tried to brush past them, but Arthur put his hand on my shoulder, stopping me.

"Where did you get that?" Arthur asked, pointing to the can in my hand.

"Craft services. Are we done here?" I snapped.

"We just wanted to see how you were feeling about the plan I laid out yesterday. Is this still going to happen?"

"It does this whenever it's told," I said bitterly.

They exchanged confused glances.

"What?" Elliott asked.

"I don't think I have a choice, do I?"

Elliott shook his head grimly. "You don't. Just do the shoot, and we can all go home."

"Groovy." I looked at my shoes, and they left, satisfied in their silent threats.

Once they were far enough away, I looked up. Sebastian was coming my way. He'd seen me talking to them. He raised an eyebrow, but I shook my head. We couldn't talk about this now.

"Dante is calling for the gun safety meeting. Let's go over."

I followed him and listened to a speech that didn't really matter. My gun, maybe Sebastian's as well, were likely loaded with real bullets. We could kill each other today. Or, God willing, we'd both miss.

I couldn't focus with Arthur and Elliott standing off to the side, watching us carefully. They wanted to make sure the job got done.

After our talk with the professionals, we were allowed on set to work on blocking without props. Dante was not a fan of guns in his films or on set at all, so he wanted to get it in one shot.

Which, if we did as asked, was all it would take.

Arthur and Elliott made sure to stay in view of me at all times. No matter where I turned, I knew they were there. Sebastian and I shot the hand-to-hand combat scene and then broke for lunch, during which I was finally able to get away from their intense gazes. I grabbed my hoodie off my chair and ran to my trailer, and as soon as the door closed, I settled into a wonderful, much needed panic attack.

I couldn't do this. I couldn't even pretend. This was bad. My pulse was rushing in my ears. This was real fucking bad. If I didn't shoot Sebastian, there was a chance he'd shoot me. Intentionally or not. What if his finger slipped? I paced until I dropped to the floor and started tugging at the roots of my hair.

I couldn't do this. There had to be a better way.

There was a knock, and the door opened an inch.

"Cleaning!"

I wiped my face and stood, rubbing my head. "Right. Come in, Bambi." I fell onto the couch as the woman who cleaned my trailer came in with her caddy and broom.

"How are you today, Evie?" she asked kindly, setting her equipment down on the table. "Sorry I'm here during your lunch hour. I got a little behind today."

"You're fine. I'm just stressed. I am so glad we're wrapping today."

She nodded, replying on auto. "I bet. It's been a long shoot." She usually had her headphones on as she cleaned, not one for pleasantries.

I let her do her thing and tried to relax. I went to my mini fridge by the table and bent down, grabbing a Red Bull. I stood back up and paused as my eyes settled on Bambi's caddy.

"Hey, Bambi? I'm done in here," I said, grabbing a small bottle of tablets from her bin. Tossing my hoodie on and putting my yellow Red Bull back in the fridge, I left my trailer and returned to set, keeping the bottle in my hoodie pocket. I rolled my eyes as I went to craft services and was flagged down by Elliott Bradley.

"Evie!"

I ducked my head into the fridge, grabbed a blueberry Red Bull, and opened it. He was a distance away, but not far enough. I only had a moment. I popped the tab and pulled the bottle from my pocket. Hopefully, my plan worked.

"Evie, did you not hear me?" Elliott raised his voice.

I turned and shut the fridge, hiding the bottle in my sleeve. "Sorry, what?" I smiled tightly.

He glanced with disgust at the drink in my hand. "Those are going to kill you."

I took a deep breath and pretended to be calm while I cocked my head in confusion.

"The caffeine. Those are so bad for you." He stared me down and his expression softened, and suddenly he reached out his hand. He stroked my cheek with his knuckle. "You look so much like her."

I bit back a sharp word or two, but the look on my face must have broken his trance. He pulled back and cleared his throat. "Right. Sorry. I just wanted to thank you for helping with this unfortunate matter. It's so awkward having to drag more people in, but if we can get this stomped out..."

"Of course." I nodded. "We wouldn't want more *accidents*, would we?"

Just then, Dante caught sight of me. He'd been walking with Arthur, and they both turned our way. Dante rolled his eyes at the can in my hand.

"Let's go. Take off the hoodie and toss the drink."

"I just opened it!" I protested, excitement flooding my veins as everything was going as I'd hoped. I had to dial my emotions back. "I haven't even taken a sip."

"I don't think they care about you wasting it." Dante rolled his eyes.

I made a show of taking it to the garbage to toss, when Arthur came around from the other side.

"I'll take it. I like blueberry. I thought you liked the yellow ones?"

I handed it to him. "They're out," I lied. There was an entire row of them.

Elliott clicked his tongue at his friend. "Those are going to kill you."

I hurried off with Dante, tossing my hoodie onto my chair as I went, making sure the bottle I'd taken from Bambi's cleaning caddy remained tucked inside it. Back on set, I found Sebastian already in place. I was handed my gun. My chest tightened as I felt the weight of the deadly weapon. This was it. The prop master gave Sebastian his and then left the stage.

Dante yelled out, "Action!"

Sebastian and I locked gazes and slowly, in sync, raised our weapons.

"Is this how it ends, then?" he said his final line, and I smirked and shook my head for the camera.

"Simon says, motherfuck—"

I was cut off by a loud choking sound and screams from the crew. We dropped our stances and turned, watching as Arthur collapsed, the energy drink in his hand spilling across the floor. His face turned purple as he convulsed. I stared, a satisfied feeling seeping into my belly and soul as I watched the life leave his body—not one person jumped to help him.

Elliott was right.

Those energy drinks *would* kill him.

CHAPTER 65

SEBASTIAN

Damage Control

I'd never been harder than in that moment—watching Evie's eyes light up as Arthur's dulled.

She was a fucking psycho, and I wanted to take her behind a fake hill and bend her over.

Actually, fuck it.

I stormed across the sound stage and wrapped my hand around Evie's wrist. I squeezed, causing her to drop her gun. I tossed mine down beside hers.

"Come on," I growled, dragging her away.

"Where are we going?" She giggled, as if we hadn't just witnessed someone die. As if it hadn't been her who'd caused it. I'd watched her hand Arthur that fucking can. She'd put something in it.

"I need to fuck you," I told her the moment we were out of view from the cast and crew. I pulled her behind a tall wooden backdrop that was shrouded in shadows and pressed my body against hers, making sure she felt the strength of my desire. "Bend over and put your hands on the wall."

"This makes five." She giggled again.

I studied her face. Dilated pupils, flushed face, deep, shallow breathing... Apparently, she was just as hot about murdering as I was.

"Fully aware," I said, spinning her around to face the wall. I pushed on her back, bending her over. With my other hand, I undid my belt and pants and shoved them down just enough to free my cock. She threw her arms out, palms hitting the wood. I shoved her skirt up and her panties aside. A groan escaped my lips as I slid into her pussy with an ease I hadn't felt before.

"Fuck, Final Girl. You're soaked."

"What can I say?" she moaned. "Something about getting everything I wanted turns me on. I hope you never rest, Arty, you fucking clown."

"Focus on me, Final Girl," I snarled and pounded into her. "This is going to be fast."

She squealed and arched her back. "I'm already halfway there," she said.

Fuck, she was so tight, so wet, so fucking hot. I leaned down, reaching to play with her clit. I made slow circles, swirling her arousal around her small pleasure button. She panted and gasped and begged for me to go faster, harder, and deeper.

It does this whenever it's told.

I listened to her orders, performing as she needed, and just as her body seized and began to convulse, my balls tightened and I joined her over the edge, spilling myself inside her. Pulling out and righting our clothes, I took her hand and pulled her away from set.

"Let's get out of here," I growled. "I know we said five, but I think I could go again. What about you? Want to make it six?"

She stopped and turned back to the set, where everyone was fawning over the dead executive. She slid me a sly smile. "I'm not opposed."

My cock sprang back to life, and I gripped her arm, tugging her to me. "Let's motor."

She giggled and nodded to the set, where people were still circling Arthur. "Wait. Let me go get my hoodie."

I WOKE UP to fifty notifications of missed calls, texts, and alerts from the internet. A quick glance caused my eyes to roll to the ceiling. Today was going to be a very interesting day. And not in a good way. I sighed and decided to take my morning slow. I took the dogs out and walked around my backyard. I was supposed to host a wrap party tonight, but considering a death on set, plus today's headlines, I doubted it was safe to do so now. I paused, still in my boxers, standing at the edge of my pool. It was my favorite thing about this house—the pool. I wondered for a moment, if I sold this place and moved in with Evie, could we add a red liner to her heart-shaped pool?

That is, if she wanted me to.

We were still avoiding talking about anything beyond finishing her list, which was now officially just a single name.

Elliott Bradley.

The dogs came back inside, and begrudgingly, I followed them into the house. Only then did I pick my phone up and start the phone calls, clicking on Anderson's name first.

"Sebastian, holy fuck. Are you—have you—".

"Yes, I've seen the news. It's..."

"A big mess."

"I was going to say not untrue, but yeah, that too."

He swore. "We are getting PR in on this. I'm fucking pissed."

I wanted to be angry. Getting outed as a Hollywood whore wasn't ideal for getting new roles. But I was more annoyed than upset. I didn't really care all that much about my career anymore. The moment Evie came back into my life, everything changed. My priorities had shifted from making myself a billionaire and a household name to making Evie mine. I hadn't been lying to Evie that night on the boat. If she left Hollywood, then so would I.

"Get showered. I'm gathering a team to come over and fix this. We'll be there in an hour."

"What's there to fix?" I asked, but my agent had already hung up.

My next call was to Evie. She answered, and it was immediately clear that her only concern was my mental health. It soothed me like a hot shower after a brutal workday.

"Hey, you okay?" she asked.

"I'll be fine. This isn't how I ever planned on the world finding out I'm kind of a slut, but it is what it is. If I lose some fans, then they weren't really my fans, anyway."

"Do you want me to come over?"

"Because of this? No. But in general, yes. Always. Evie..." I bit back the urge to bring up what I'd been thinking about near the pool. We could tackle living situations once this was all over. Once Elliott Bradley was dead.

"I'll be over in a bit."

I got up, showered, and answered what texts I could with quick replies, assuring my friends who'd seen the news that I was fine. Evie showed up at the door, and as I was toasting her a bagel, Anderson and the movie's PR team came running in. The frantic expressions on their faces were confusing. I licked the cream cheese off the knife and shook my head.

"I topped some producers, not shot them. Calm down."

"Sebastian," Stacey, the leader of the PR team, sighed. "People think you're gay."

I did a double take. This was what she was focusing on? "Yeah. Bi is on the list. LGBTQ—B is smack dab in the middle. My sexuality is no secret."

She shook her head. "But you're supposed to be dating Evie."

"So? I can be with whoever I want."

"Not if you're also sleeping with all these *men*!" She slid into a seat. "I spent the last few months building this magical fake relationship to sell this movie, and now the world thinks you're fucking every male studio executive in Hollywood."

"So we just explain that I'm not anymore?" I looked around the kitchen at the concerned team. "I don't understand the issue.

I'll be honest with you, Stacey. This all reeks of homophobia. If you're really interested in the details, there are plenty of women on the list of people I've fucked for work. I'm not going to hear you out if this is the vibe."

She looked at Anderson, who stared at her, nodding. "Sebastian is right. Him sleeping with men isn't the issue. The issue is that—"

"You used sex to get jobs." Another team member shook his head.

"My previous agent encouraged me," I explained, hanging my head lower. My gaze slid over to Evie, who was watching intently. I cringed, heat flooding my face. "I'm not exactly proud of all this."

Stacey perked up. "Who was your agent? Can we find her? Maybe we can shift all of this to her instead."

"Good luck," I snickered.

Evie shot me a look, and I forced myself not to react. "I haven't spoken to Heather since I fired her."

The dogs began to bark from the entryway, and we all turned.

"Knock knock. Sorry to intrude. I heard everyone was here trying to put out a fire?" Elliott Bradley came in with a smile and wave. "I'm here to help."

Stacey and the rest of her team turned and visibly swooned. Their eyes went wide, and gasps and whispers rang out among them. "Hi, Mr. Bradley," Stacey said.

My jaw ticked at the sight of the bastard in my kitchen. "We don't need your help," I said through gritted teeth.

"What if we have Evie break up with you, and then you apologize in some big show and you reunite for the premieres?" Stacey suggested.

"Or I can just apologize for using sex to get work," I offered instead. When she didn't even look my way, I snapped, "I'm done with this."

"All right. I think I'll take it from here. You can go." Elliott waved the PR team out.

Stacey shot him a disgruntled look. "With all due respect, sir,

I was hired for moments like this. If we work together to strategize, we can—"

"I agree," I interjected, the attention snapping to me. "I trust that Elliott can help me. You guys go, and we'll update you on things."

Elliott nodded his approval and looked at Stacey. "I'll make sure my assistant brings a couple of signed merchandise baskets to your offices next week."

The team began to murmur among themselves excitedly, and Stacey gave in, shaking Elliott's hand and quickly taking her team and leaving.

"You can go too," I told Anderson.

My agent hesitated but took his exit too, leaving just the three of us.

Once we heard the front door shut, Elliott raised his hands and began a slow clap.

"Congratulations. You've made it to the top. Arthur is dead, which I'm sure you saw. They found bleach in his drink. You know, the stuff they put in toilets? You know anything about that, Evelyn?"

We turned to her.

She pursed her lips and shook her head. "Those energy drinks have all sorts of things in them. You said so yourself."

He scowled at Evie, then turned back to me. "Right. Well, I hope you're happy. Now everyone knows how bruised your knees are. You'll never get work again. No one's going to risk taking you on. Either of you."

"Is that why you came here? To brag and throw your weight around? Revenge porn feels a little lowbrow, even for you." I crossed my arms over my chest.

"I came here to warn you—back the fuck off. My friends were stupid and over-confident. If you want a fight, you're gonna get one. Don't fuck with me, Shaw."

"Or what?" I smirked. He didn't scare me. Nothing short of losing Evie scared me anymore.

He grinned and turned to leave before turning back and repeating the words he'd said to me that day on the studio lot.

"Or this will end in a bloodbath." He pointed his finger at me and then started toward the front door.

Evie, who'd been mostly quiet this whole time, suddenly bound from her seat. I chased after her and caught her around the middle as she screamed.

"It was you! You'll pay for murdering Antoinette!" She choked out a sob.

Elliott turned, a slow smirk spreading over his face as he stared at Evie. "I don't know what you're talking about." He clicked his tongue and shook his head. "And that is no way to speak to your father."

CHAPTER 66 SEBASTIAN

The Blind Spot

Elliott's cackle echoed long after he was gone.

Evie sat at the kitchen table, staring at the wall. I didn't try to talk, instead letting her soak in what she'd just been told. I'd had my suspicions, but it didn't feel like my place to say anything. Now, it was as good as fact. Elliott Bradley—the model turned actor turned superstar turned murderer, not necessarily in that order—was her biological father.

"I kind of figured," she said after a while, slumping in her seat. "I had a feeling it would come down to me against my father. And well, top of the food chain and all."

I sat across from her and took her hand. "It's not coming down to you against him because I'm going to protect you. I'm not leaving your side until he's dead."

"How? That's impossible."

"Move in with me," I blurted, instantly regretting the impulsive request.

She shook her head, almost as if she hadn't heard me correctly. "What?"

I braced myself, sat up straighter, and doubled down. "Move in with me. Or I could move in with you. I don't care. I just hate us living in two different houses. I want to see you every day. Whatever you want, I'll do. Just..."

"I can't make a decision like this now. Or ever. I don't know. I came here to show you support." She pushed her chair back and stood. "I need to go."

"Go where? I'll go with you." I followed her through the house.

The dogs found us and began circling, trying to get our attention with toys.

"Will you guys get down!" I hissed.

"I— I don't know. I need to process everything. Don't you have a party to get ready for?"

I stopped walking and threw my hands up, incredulous. "You really think a party is a good idea right now? A dude died on the last day of filming, and I've just been outed as the most desperate actor in Hollywood."

"What better time to surround yourself with friends? I'll be back later," she said, and left before I could protest.

I swore and kicked the air. She drove me nuts, and I hated how much I'd miss it if she were gone from my life.

I sulked for an hour out by the pool with my pets before deciding not to cancel the party. I started calling, getting food ordered, and ordering a keg. Skye had promised she'd help decorate, so I shot her a text. She was over an hour later, blowing up balloons.

"When does everyone arrive?" she asked as night began to fall.

It had been a long day. I was stressed to the max, having not heard from Evie for hours. I'd called and texted, but she'd left me on read. Skye was entirely too excited about decorating, and for a while, it helped distract me. There had to be a couple hundred balloons in my backyard, all blown up by her. My housekeeper was going to be pissed when he came to clean and had to look for a thousand pieces of popped latex.

When the sun went down, I turned on the music, and members of the cast and crew began to show. With each new car, my hope spiked and was then popped like one of Skye's balloons when I saw it wasn't Evie. I kept trying her phone, and after an hour, once most everyone had shown, I started to panic.

Finally, she called back. I was in the middle of a conversation with one of the tech guys when her name flashed on my screen. I showed him the name and excused myself.

"Evie, where the fuck are you?" I hissed.

"Sorry. I spent the day with my mom. I'm in your driveway right now."

I ran toward the house, shoving past people to go inside and get to her. I met her at the front door and lifted her up, spinning her in my arms.

"Anthony C. Hopkins! Sebastian, let me go!" she giggled.

"Are you okay?" I asked, setting her down. I took her hand and led her through the house to the party in the back.

"I'm fine. Great, actually. I sat at the cemetery and just had a long visit with her. I got a lot off my chest. I feel really good."

I paused at the glass doors that led to the outside. I wasn't ready to hit the loud party.

"Really? Like..."

"Like maybe I'm okay stopping."

Stopping? She wasn't going to kill Elliott?

"And this isn't just because he said he's your—"

"Hell no," she scoffed. "If anything, that made me want to kill him more. No, I just think my priorities have changed a bit. Do I really want to go out so soon?"

"I don't know. Do you?" A loud click came from behind us, and we turned. There, Elliott stood, holding a gun aimed right at her.

"What are you doing here?" I asked.

His hair was slightly disheveled and his suit wrinkled. The smell of alcohol wafted through the room.

"I'm here to watch you guys. I want to make sure you don't go killing the rest of my friends. We have more movies to make. More people to help make their dreams come true."

"Don't you mean lives to destroy?" Evie asked.

"Same thing," he snickered and tilted his head, nodding to the glass door behind us. "Let's go have a good time, shall we?" He stuffed the gun in his pants, under his jacket, and together, the three of us exited my house into the backyard.

What should have been a joyous night with my girlfriend turned into a tense, stressful one. I was on constant alert, watching Elliott like a hawk. He'd shown up drunk with a gun. If something were to set him off, this could turn deadly.

The party kept going until close to morning, and eventually people began to slowly take their leave. With each person who left, I grew more and more nervous. Elliott was still here. Everyone was starstruck and kept asking me how I'd convinced him to come. I wasn't sure what to say, so I avoided the topic. Instead, I stayed close to Evie, making us look like the most in love couple that had ever existed. Any paparazzi who'd snuck in to capture some scandal would have tons of photos of us kissing for next week's magazines.

A few people mentioned the sex scandal, but I just laughed it off. More than one of them told me they'd had similar experiences. That was the thing. Bodies being sold was nothing new in this industry. People just didn't like to face the truth. The truth about Hollywood was ugly. That's why we tried so hard to make it look pretty.

Their plan to destroy my career had gone nowhere. I was sure that some directors might refuse to see me, but from the email I'd gotten from Anderson earlier, I felt comfortable that I'd still be making good money for the foreseeable future.

Eventually, Elliott took his leave, but not without a cold warning and another flash of the gun in his pants.

"Another time, perhaps. We can talk all about your mother, Evie, and how you came to be. I'm sure there'll be some conflicting stories we should get cleared up. I think you'll find I'm not the villain in this story."

"And who is, then?" Evie asked boldly.

Elliott smirked. "You are."

He left, and when we looked around, I realized it was just Evie and me. We cuddled on a beach chair and watched the sun rise.

"I meant what I said earlier," I said. "I want to move in with you."

"I know. Can we talk about it when I've had some sleep?" She yawned.

"I'd love that."

I closed my eyes, prepared to sleep near the pool with her in my arms, when my phone rang. With a groan, I answered it.

"Yeah?"

"Sebastian? It's Bryce. I popped a tire about a mile from your place. Do you have a tire iron?"

I groaned and gently moved Evie off me. I rubbed my face and stood.

"Yeah, I'm on my way. Evie, you want to come?" I asked.

She stretched and looked around the yard. "I'm really tired. Would I be a bad person if I said no?"

A small smile spread over my lips as she crawled back onto the chair. I bent down and gave her a quick kiss. "Not at all, Final Girl. Rest, and I'll be back in an hour, tops."

"Perfect. See you soon, Psycho Killer," she said as she closed her eyes.

I pulled my keys from my pocket and left, going through the house. I got to Bryce in a flash, and we got his tire changed and his car back on the road. He thanked me, and as I got back in my car to drive back to Evie, I checked my phone and saw a notification from my door camera. Someone had come in shortly after I'd left.

I clicked on the app to pull up the camera and see what the hell was up, and my blood chilled. The bastard had waited for my car to leave before pulling right back into my drive and walking to the door.

Elliott Bradly had come back for her.

CHAPTER 67

EVIE

The Boss Fight

My phone rang from the beach chair I'd been yanked out of a moment ago. Both Elliott's gaze and mine shot to it. Elliott walked over, picked it up, and smirked.

"Psycho Killer is calling. Interesting. I thought I was right here." Without a second glance my way, he softball pitched it into the pool. It made a plopping sound as it hit the water, sinking like the rock in my stomach.

Taking a steady breath, I lifted my hands from where I lay on the concrete. "Elliott—"

"You can just call me Dad, Evie. Gives this little reunion a personal touch. Lita would have liked that."

I sneered. My mother hadn't wanted me to know my father. In fact, she'd told me many times that it was better to not know him. He may be my biological father, but he'd never be my dad. But he was the one with the gun.

"Okay... Dad." I nodded. The word was foreign and felt gross in my mouth. "Should we talk?"

"What's there to talk about? You killed all my friends. Why shouldn't I just kill you now?"

"You spent twenty-one years in hiding. Don't you want to know your daughter, *Dad*?" I spat the last word.

He laughed. "Oh, you don't believe me." He nodded. "I see it on your face. Sorry to tell you, but that slut begged me to get her pregnant. She wanted the most beautiful child to have ever existed and didn't think her boyfriend was up to the task."

The bravery left my body as a flash of a memory hit me.

"You're the most beautiful girl to have ever existed, Evelyn Reyes. I made sure of that."

She'd said those words to me time and time again throughout my childhood. Back then, I thought it was just her boosting my confidence, making me feel loved, but now...

Had she been saying those words to brag?

"There are cameras everywhere," I warned. "If you kill me, people will know."

"You think a recording has ever stopped a damn thing in my life?" He scoffed and lifted his jacket, pulling out the gun he'd flashed earlier in the evening. He cocked it and pointed it at me. "I prefer an audience."

Every muscle in my body was stiff and screaming. If I moved, there was a good chance he'd shoot. But I had to get out of here somehow.

"Aren't you afraid Sebastian will be back soon? Killing me will be pointless if he kills you too."

"I think we both know that none of this matters anymore. Come sit, Evie. Darling daughter of mine. Let's catch up before I do this. I'd like to have something to reflect on later." Using the gun, he pointed to a table, and slowly, keeping my hands up, I went over and sat. He joined me, setting the gun on the table, making sure to point it in my direction.

"Now, tell me about yourself. What is your favorite color? Favorite film? What do you like to eat? I hear you're a YouTube star. How well does that pay?" He leaned in, putting his chin in his hands and smiling at me.

I studied him, searching harder for a version of myself in his face. Elliott Bradley was a strikingly handsome Hispanic man. He'd been on the cover of dozens of magazines as the world's sexiest celebrity. It was understandable why, if my mother had *chosen* who would father her child, it had been him. It also helped hide the paternity. If I'd had a father with, say—green eyes, blond hair, or dark skin, my appearance may have reflected that. But with both my parents having brown eyes, black hair, and light-brown skin, he was able to hide in plain sight.

He stared at me, his dark eyes shining. This was just a game to him. I didn't care to play, but if I wanted to stay living a little longer, so be it.

"Red. *The Exorcist*, 1973. Cereal—specifically corn flakes from Dollar General. My job has a lot of passive income, so it pays enough for me to live comfortably. What about yourself?"

"Maroon. *The Fly*, 1958. Red wine and a good steak. My job has made me wealthier than any man should ever be."

His dark eyes reflected... excitement. He loved this back-and-forth. He was a cat, playing with the mouse before he ate it. The snake, encircling its owner, measuring it and getting ready to swallow.

"Why did you say yes to my mother? To...fathering me?" The very concept turned my stomach. Elliott was a bad man, and my mother should never have been subjugated to him.

Elliott grinned. "Ego. Lita knew how to play to a man's need to be wanted. She used it often, and I was just one of her many pawns. She was on a mission, and I can clearly say it was successful." He waved to me. "She's the only one, you know, to have carried my seed. To my knowledge, you are my only child."

Lucky me.

"Why are you killing us now?" he asked, leaning back in his seat and crossing his arms. "I find it fascinating after all this time."

"I was just a kid when you murdered her. I needed time to grow up and find out who you were."

"Yes, but the plan was messy. You'd think with so much time, the deaths would have been cleaner, and yet, you allowed everyone to find the bodies. Why?"

"Because I don't want to hide. I wanted you to know I was coming for you," I answered truthfully.

"Interesting. There's no self-preservation in you."

"There really isn't." The words only felt somewhat true. I'd said them in various ways a million times in the last few months, and every time, they'd been correct. But this time, Sebastian rang in a tiny recess of my mind.

I gulped as nerves began to slowly take over. How long would he be gone? Would Sebastian be too late? The idea of him returning home to find me dead on his lawn was enough for me to lunge forward and grab the gun off the table. I shoved the chair back, and it clamored to the concrete. I pointed it at him, and he raised his hands slowly and stood, keeping eye contact with me. As he slowly rose, a smile followed, making me uneasy. We circled each other, walking around the perimeter of the pool. I forced him backward, hoping he'd stumble.

He stopped and chuckled. "You really think I'd put a loaded gun on the table for you to grab? That gun is filled with rubber bullets. But this one isn't." He reached around and pulled another gun from the back of his pants. "You shoot me, and I'll shoot you."

I stared at my father. "Who did it? Who was the one to put the knife in her middle and then hang her up to be found like that?" Tears slid down my cheeks as the memory of that morning flashed through my mind. The gun in my hand shook as rage took over.

Elliott took in my question, then laughed. "Who do you think? The one who gave her that *Simon Says* job, or the one who helped set up the meeting? Or what about the lawyer who created her contract, or was it the ex-boyfriend?" Elliott laughed. "Or maybe it was the one she fucked purely to get his perfect genes."

"Who was it?" I shouted.

He rolled his eyes. "It was the one with the most to lose. Me."

I pulled the trigger. The kickback made me stumble into the grass—and then a second bang rang out. All the air left my body as pain burst from my left shoulder. I collapsed, forcing my head up to keep my eyes on Elliott. He'd lied. There was a bright-red hole in his abdomen. He'd banked on me being too scared to shoot.

Joke was on him. I wasn't truly scared of anything.

Except Sebastian finding me dead.

The thought rang out in my mind, and I knew then that I had to fight back. Truly fight back. I couldn't let Sebastian find me like that.

Elliott stared at the wound on his belly in shock. I looked at the one on my left shoulder, then scanned him from top to bottom. Struggling to breathe, I forced myself to my feet. Slapping my hand over the bullet wound, I stalked over to him. He was fighting to stay upright, one hand on his belly and the other waving wildly to maintain balance. Elliott's eyes lit up as he tried to reach for me, but instead of saving him, I reached forward and pushed on his chest, and he fell into the red pool.

My ears still rang from the gunshots, but his scream pierced through as he splashed and fought to stay afloat. I collapsed and watched him flounder. He looked like he was drowning in a sea of his own blood. The pain in my shoulder was blinding, and I knew I didn't have much time before I fell unconscious.

If I could just watch him die first, I could follow in peace.

No! my mind screamed.

I straightened myself and looked back at Elliott. He'd fallen into the deep end, but he'd found his footing and was trying to swim. I was too tired to survive a physical brawl. I needed to end this now. Getting back on my feet, I walked slowly to the opposite side of the pool. Elliott was moving slowly, but...

There was a small metal box I'd seen Sebastian use often. He was always afraid Cujo and Precious would get out when he wasn't around and jump into the water. I opened the box and scanned the buttons, grateful that they'd been labeled clearly.

CLOSE POOL.

I pressed it, and the machine whirred to life. Turning, I watched the black cover slide out and slowly make its way across the water. It was so close to the surface, there was no room for air.

Elliott heard the noise and spun around in the water. It took him a moment to see what was happening, but he wasn't fast enough. He was pulled under as the cover overtook him.

He pounded on the tarp, but it was useless. The cover finished its journey to the other side of the pool and locked into place. I watched as my biological father, one of the most famous men in the world, pushed against the seal for a moment, and then stopped.

Something in my soul knew when he was gone. I stared at the spot I'd last seen movement, and then my legs gave out, and I crashed to the ground. My eyes closed as I heard barking and then Sebastian's voice.

Good, I thought as the darkness overtook me. I'd made it at least until he got here.

He didn't find me dead.

Just...nearly dead.

CHAPTER 68

EVIE

The Closing Image

"That should do it."

Bryce's voice pulled me from the darkness. My eyelids were heavy, but I fluttered them open. I wasn't outside anymore. I was... Where was I?

"See, you're already waking up. How ya feel, Final Girl?"

"Don't call me that." The words came out soft and painful. I needed water.

Bryce chuckled and patted my thigh. "All right, Evie Reyes. Whatever you say."

I placed my hands at my sides and squeezed the softness of the bed underneath me. There was so much pain, but it was more of a deep soreness than a shooting pain like before. The longer my eyes stayed open, the more I gained comprehension of my surroundings. I'd been taken to Sebastian's bedroom. I was lying on his bed.

"What happened?" I asked, pulling myself into a sitting position.

Just then, two figures appeared in the doorway, and my heart breathed a sigh as Sebastian and Skye walked in. Skye was holding a cup, and I reached for it, my throat screaming to be quenched.

"You are a badass motherfucker, Evie Reyes." Bryce laughed. "You took on fucking Hollywood is what happened."

"Elliott Bradley?" I asked after draining the cup. "Where is he?"

"We left him in the pool while we got you cleaned up," Skye explained, sitting down by my feet. She squeezed one and smiled. "You took a gunshot and survived. That is so freaking badass."

"It hurts," I admitted.

"No shit, Final Girl," Sebastian said—and the world around us disappeared. The seriousness of the situation was gone for a moment as I looked up at him.

"Hey, Psycho Killer. About damn time you made it." I smirked.

He scowled and sat down beside Bryce at the foot of the bed. "I had to go through and delete all my camera footage from the last twenty-four hours."

Bryce continued. "Sebastian called me while on the road, and I followed him back. We got there right as you dropped. Thankfully, I know a thing or two about removing stray bullets, from growing up on the ranch." Bryce lifted his hand and flashed the bullet. "I was able to pull this baby right out."

My hand drifted to the wound. He'd sewn it up. It wasn't clean, but it didn't feel terrible.

"I'll put some wrapping on it here in a bit. Gotta go to the store," Bryce explained.

"What now, then?" I asked the room.

Everyone had ragged looks on their faces, and they still wore the clothes they'd been wearing at the party. Skye was wringing a towel between her hands, and Bryce's hair was more disheveled than I'd ever seen it. And Sebastian, he just looked sick. He was pale, sweating, and covered in blood. Guilt pooled in my belly as I took everyone in. They'd done so much for me, and at what price? My return to Hollywood had aged them.

They shared looks.

"Well, we have a dead body in my pool," Sebastian answered. "I'm going to wait until noon and open it like I normally do. That's when I'll find Elliott—drowned."

"He was shot," I told them.

They all shared the same puzzled look. Had they not looked at the body?

"I shot him, then he shot me. Then, I pushed him into the pool and closed the tarp. That's how he died. How are you covering up a bullet wound?" I asked.

There was a beat of silence, and Bryce opened his mouth, but Skye cut him off.

"I swear if you suggest another AI suicide letter—"

"I've got a plan." Sebastian stood and left the room. He was gone for a long time, and in that time, Skye and Bryce asked questions about Elliott Bradley's last moments.

"Elliott was my biological father," I confessed to them.

Their eyes widened.

"No shit," Bryce said.

I nodded.

"Did he want anything from you?" Skye asked.

"Just to kill me." I shrugged. What else could the man who had everything want from someone like me?

"Are you okay?" Skye reached for my hand, squeezing it softly.

What a loaded question. I thought about it for a long while. Was I? I sighed deeply, tears for my mother rising to the surface again. I brushed them back with my free hand and nodded to my friends.

"I am. I finally feel like my mother can rest in peace."

And so could I.

I'd reflected a lot on my grief journey yesterday while visiting her grave. Her headstone had been decorated with pink flowers and other trinkets from fans. I'd picked up each and every item, thinking about the people who'd gifted them. They loved her so much for the woman she was on screen, never knowing the woman she was off it.

My mother experienced more than I would likely ever know. Good and bad. And now that the men who hurt her for the final time were dead, I could move on.

Skye reached for something from the floor and stepped over to Sebastian's dresser. She'd found my knives. Lita Reyes's final gift to me were the tools I needed to claim my freedom from the pain of losing her. The words carved on those knives echoed in my brain.

Good For Her.

Good for me.

It wasn't until we heard sirens that Sebastian returned, drenched head to toe.

"I'm about to be interviewed on the news. Anyone want to join me?"

The group helped me put a clean shirt on and go downstairs. I took a couple of pain pills Skye had pulled from her purse. People flooded Sebastian's yard. He took my hand, leading me through the front door. We could hear screaming out by the road, and when I looked, I saw twenty people, at least, with cameras and boom mics, waving and yelling to get our attention. Together, the four of us went down to speak to them.

"Sebastian! What happened? How did Elliott Bradley end up dead in your pool?"

Anderson, Sebastian's agent, appeared out of nowhere, pushing his way through the crowd. He stood beside us as Sebastian gave his statement to the public.

"I have spoken to the police, but I will say it here as well. Yesterday, the news came out that in the past, I have had relations with many people—many of whom were closeted men—in this industry, and in exchange, I received roles or higher salaries. I told my agent that I was going to come clean today. Elliott came and threatened me not to. He had a gun. He shot once, and the backfire caused him to drop it. I picked it up, and when he came for me, I shot him in self-defense. He fell into my pool and drowned before I could save him."

"Why did he want you to keep quiet? Did you have sex with Elliott Bradley?"

I held my breath as Sebastian took the fall for my murder.

"No, I did not. But I have had sex with many of his colleagues. I won't be giving out names, but it happened. And to be honest, I really, *really* do not care." He paused, taking my hand and squeezing. He lifted it to his lips, kissing it gently. "Hollywood is a town full of secrets, and I and many others like me are a part of that. While I know it's not a good look, and I'm sure that many great, more deserving people lost out on roles to me simply because I had no shame, I can't take back what has happened. I'm sorry to anyone I hurt while trying to advance my career. I won't be partaking in that kind of audition process anymore." Sebastian squeezed my hand as he said his public statement.

We turned to leave, letting Anderson step in to answer questions.

We went inside and spent the rest of the day repeating our story to the police over and over again. They were trying to make one of us goof up, but all four of us were tight-lipped and told the same story. Eventually, everyone took their leave, and only Sebastian and I remained.

He helped me shower, and despite knowing I could finally sleep in peace, he insisted I stay the night with him.

"Neither of us is in good shape to drive," he said as he came into his room from his own shower. I'd been given one of his T-shirts and had already climbed into bed. He dried off, put on boxers, and joined me under the covers. I snuggled closer, and he took care not to touch my wounded shoulder.

"We did it," I said sleepily. "My mother is finally at peace."

"And you're gonna be soon, too," he said, and I gave him a look.

Realizing how ominous that sounded, he laughed and backtracked. "My bad. I meant because you're falling asleep. Don't worry. I'm not gonna murder you. I won't even touch you."

My belly fluttered, and I rolled to face him. I winced as I put weight on my left side.

"What if... I wanted you to." I placed my hand on his warm, bare chest. His muscles were always so...

I sighed and looked up into his beautiful emerald eyes. Even in the darkness, they shone. For a brief moment, I reflected on how we'd gotten here. This man had murdered for me and still looked so innocent, so happy, so perfect.

He furrowed his dark brows, and his lips formed a thin line as he shook his head. "You gave me five chances to convince you to stay. I used them all, and I'm no closer than the day we reunited. You're off the hook, Final Girl."

My mouth fell open as my heart sank. No, that couldn't be. Was he really saying no after all this time of begging me to say yes?

"I'm bad at counting," I said, rolling back onto the pillows. "Has it really been that many?"

"Unfortunately. Which was your favorite?" He grinned and bent down, placing a tender kiss on my lips.

I kissed him back, raising my hands to his cheeks to hold him there.

"The *Psycho* house is definitely a top contender, but I think..."

My mind went blank. All cleverness left my brain, and I stopped kissing him, pushing him back to look him in the eyes. Quick flashes of the moments we'd had together on this journey flooded my memories—so many hot moments—but there was more to our little affair than that.

Sure, the sex was fun, but what about the inside jokes, the dogs, movie nights, popcorn with M&M's, and working together? This had been more than just some cathartic journey of revenge for me. I hadn't just found peace. I'd found Skye, Bryce, Cujo, Precious, and...Sebastian.

"I want to stay."

"What?" He inhaled, sitting up slightly as his eyes widened.

I nodded. "I'm going to stay. I want you, and Cujo, and Precious, and your red pool, and I want to be your Final Girl and—"

"Groovy." He cut me off with a deep kiss that said more than any words ever could.

Careful not to touch my bullet wound, he rolled onto me,

pressing his cock against me, showing me the strength of his desire, his love. I shifted my hips to make us comfortable.

"So, this doesn't count as extra, right?" he asked, tugging his boxers down and assisting me out of my shirt.

"Beep beep, Ritchie," I teased.

He shut his mouth quickly, and as we made love, truly made love for the first time since that first time so long ago, I knew that this was it. I was in too deep, and he'd won. The Psycho Killer had made me his Final Girl, and I wouldn't change a single fucking thing about it. My heart, mind, and soul were finally at peace.

We came together, and afterward, we lay tangled in each other's arms. I didn't want to pull away. I could live like this forever, and with that thought, I shifted to face him. I licked my lips, suddenly scared in a whole new way. My heart was in my throat as I stared up at the man I hoped to never part from ever again. Then I spoke the words he'd been waiting for.

"I was watching *The Exorcist...*" I started, my gaze holding firm with his.

A slow grin spread over his face as he replied.

"It got me thinking of you."

THE END

EPILOGUE SEBASTIAN

The Bonus Content

One Year Later

"Evie! Body Count Bimbo! Over here!"

I fought an outward reaction as paparazzi called for Evie instead of me—on the red carpet. We'd been invited to an award ceremony for the film I'd been the star of for most of my life. I smiled and urged my Final Girl over to them, joining her a step behind.

Evie was stunning in a sparkly off-white gown. Her hair and makeup had been styled to resemble a starlet from the Golden Age of Hollywood, which felt fitting for a woman as amazing as she was. Her tattoos, piercings, and stretched ears were a stark contrast from her styled look, which made her a complete bombshell in my eyes.

"I don't really go by that name anymore," she told them. "I've since retired the channel and turned the brand into a makeup line."

They asked a few polite questions about the career shift, but they weren't all that interested. They never were about the things that mattered. They just wanted gossip.

"How excited are you about the nomination for Best Breakout

Actress for *Simon Says Six*?"

"*Six Six*!" she replied.

I bit my tongue to avoid joining her in the joke. This was her moment, and I wanted to make sure she shined. I was just her arm candy for tonight, nothing more.

"I love your necklace. Where did you get it?" a journalist asked.

Evie lifted the charm off her chest and glanced my way, causing me to flush.

"Sebastian gave it to me during the filming."

I leaned into her and gave her a quick, tender kiss. I then spoke to the reporter, giving her a good sound bite.

"She's my forever Final Girl."

The paparazzi went wild, and they started shouting questions at me as well.

"What about you? You are nominated for Best Actor. Do you think you'll win?"

We moved on down the carpet, and Evie beamed as they snapped photos of her. I was dragged in for a few, but we all knew who the real star was tonight. We were joined by Bryce and Skye and some others who worked on the movie and then were shown our places inside the venue.

We were seated in a relatively good spot. Horror wasn't a genre often honored or respected in Hollywood. However, she and I both had names that got us recognition. Bryce and Skye sat with us, and the ceremony started soon after. These things were pretty boring, in my opinion. I'd been to so many of them, it was just part of the job now. We all pretended to be excited about dressing up and having our photos taken, but most of Hollywood would gladly receive their awards from the comfort of their homes.

I'd take a movie night with the dogs and Evie over this any day.

That was the plan for after this. I kept that in mind as award after award was handed out, none of them really interesting. Oftentimes, it was obvious who would be winning what.

Finally, someone familiar walked onto the stage. It took me a moment to recall her name, but Evie leaned over to remind me.

"That's JoJo Perkins. She interviewed us for the movie ages ago."

Oh, right.

JoJo did her speech and then listed off the women nominated for Best Breakout Actress.

"And Evie Reyes, for her role as Lucy in *Simon Says Six*!"

"*Six Six*," the table muttered low so only we could hear. The cameras panned to us as we laughed. Evie waved, then watched as the woman who was nominated for a romantic comedy took the award.

I squeezed her hand under the table. We'd known she wasn't getting it. This woman had already taken four other awards before this one, but that didn't make it sting less.

A few more awards were handed out, and then finally, they got to my category. An actor I couldn't stand in real life came out to present. I gave my professional smile when he said my name and they flashed the cameras to us, and then I stared at the stage until he opened the envelope.

"Sebastian Shaw for his role in *Simon Says Six: Six Six!*"

I stood, honestly a bit surprised. Horror hardly ever won awards like these. Applause exploded as I hurried to the stage to receive my trophy. I grabbed it and went to the podium.

"Wow. I mean, I know I showed my ass a few times this year," I paused for awkward laughter. The scandal regarding me sleeping my way to the top hadn't gone unnoticed. I'd been dropped from a few projects, but people had started calling again, so the town was moving on. "But who knew one of those times would get me an award?"

I looked around the room and zeroed in on my table. "I just want to say thank you to my girlfriend, Evie, for staying with me through all of it, on screen and off. This would have been a lot worse if I'd gone through it all solo. Evie, can you come up here?"

The room began to whisper as the cameras went to her. She

looked confused and mildly embarrassed, but Skye and Bryce encouraged her to get up, pushing her toward the stage. Slowly, she joined me.

"What are you doing?" she hissed.

"I'm your number one fan." I slipped into our secret language, offering her an apology as I dug into my pocket and dropped to one knee, holding a black velvet box.

Her mouth fell open as I lifted the lid, revealing the most expensive ring I could afford.

"I came here to chew bubblegum and kick ass, and I'm all out of bubblegum. Evie Reyes, will you be my forever Final Girl?"

Tears slid down her cheeks as she stared at me, then at the ring, then back at me.

"Groovy."

"What?" I asked.

"Groovy! Yes! Yes, I will!" she cried out, her arms reaching for me, pulling me up to standing.

The room erupted in screams and applause as I slid the ring onto her finger and swung her around, dipping her into a kiss.

I knew Hollywood was going to hate me for stealing the attention, but I'd gladly pay whatever fee or punishment came my way. This wasn't one of the big shows anyway. Although it didn't matter if it was. I got my Final Girl.

There was movement out of the corner of my eye, and in a flash, Bryce and Skye had rushed the stage and were joining us to celebrate. Bryce took the microphone and yelled out to the crowd.

"*Simon Says Six: Six Six* was one helluva ride, and we didn't take home all the awards tonight, but it doesn't matter because my best friends are getting married and we're already getting ready for *Simon Says Seven!* Whoo!"

Evie and I shared a look, and the world around us fell away.

"What do you say? Want to do another movie?" I asked. "It'll be..."

She nodded. "Groovy."

ACKNOWLEDGEMENTS

I feel a little like Sebastian and Evie in the epilogue, up on stage, a statue in my hand, with lights on me to give a speech. Who do I thank for this? Lots of people, I suppose. I guess let's go in order of how *Good For Her* came to be.

Aiden Pierce, my near and dear and oldest friend in the dark romance circle of Romancelandia. Around January of 2025, I messaged you and pitched you *Good For Her* as a cowrite, and you said 'no, that concept is all you. You write it'. So, I then pitched it to my agent, Heather, at 1852 Literary. Thank you, Aiden, for seeing what this book was before it was even written, and knowing that I was the one meant to create it.

Heather Roberts, my agent! I'll never tire of bragging that I have an agent and an agency to help me navigate my career and work out deals. You picked me up when I wanted help with *Slash or Pass*, and you had faith in me and my work. I will never forget when Aiden passed on the cowrite and I then pitched it to you, and you said 'Yes. That's the one. That is the book that will get picked up' (more or less).

At the time, I was writing my Gatsby retelling, *Beautiful Little Freaks*. Heather was chomping at the bit for *GFH*, and so was I, but I had to finish my other book first.

And then I managed to get nine chapters to pitch, and we were off. And, much like Heather said would happen, it did not take long for people to be interested. That level of confidence during that time was just what I needed to give *GFH* my best shot, and would you look at that, the book got picked up.

I'd also like to thank Becky at 1852 for helping me better understand the industry and give me space to vent and ask questions when I needed it. Also that pizza place you took me to when we met in Ohio? Let's do that again, soon.

I'd also like to thank some of the friends I've collected and kept during what I like to call, 'After Slash or Pass'. These are friends who have never treated me as someone they could get something from, but someone they could commiserate with. These are the ones I speak to daily and distract me when I should be working. Aiden, Aurelia, Amy, Emma, Raissa, Claire, and Cori, my dark romance boos. Meika, Christina, Gwen, Alby, Stephanie, Erin, Katherine, Alyssa, and Liz—my SPANK boos. And last, but never least, Dakota, Krista, and Victoria, my special boos.

While I couldn't tell many (if any) of you guys details about things, you were so supportive, before and after the announcement and I thank you for being genuinely good people.

This list is just gonna keep going, but hey, this is my first traditionally published book, it's important!

At the heart of my romance books will always be horror. It is very important to me that people acknowledge me in horror spaces and note the difference between dark romance and horror romance. While many don't really care, there are some that do and saw me when others didn't. Never have I felt more seen in those moments, and for that—thank you. Thank you Cassandra Celia, Harry Carpenter, Dorian Sinnott, Teresa Beeding, Heather Roberts, and Page & Vine for seeing me when others didn't.

Speaking of Page & Vine, I want to say large, large thank you to everyone there. First and foremost, thank you so much for trusting me. I know this is your first dive into the darker areas of romance, and while I trust you to help me publish the best story we can, with marketing and opening doors that had remained locked for me, you trusted me to deliver. I told you I could do this, and you said okay—let's go.

It's been an incredible experience, switching from indie to trad, one that while is exciting, is also, exhausting. I'd like to start direct the thank yous with Jordyn, my editor. That final round of edits nearly sent me over the edge. The first round I almost cried, the second one wasn't terrible, but seeing the third one in my email a day or so later? My brain deflated like a balloon! But, you made the book better, truly you did. Not only that, when I had questions, you were so kind enough to sit with me for hours while we worked through things, so that I could better understand this new world (trad) and how we could make *Good For Her* successful.

A second thank you goes to Victoria. You have been great at communicating with me on things and while I had been extremely nervous to work with you the most, you have been so welcoming to my ideas it makes the transition in my career easier. Thank you for being so kind.

Next I'd like to say thank you to Amber, who I had the privilege of meeting in Boston this summer. You only hear about meeting your publishing house in movies! For me to get that chance to meet someone in real life was such a dream and thank you for letting me talk your ear off! It really made me feel important and heard and I look forward to catching up soon.

And lastly, (although I know I am missing people), I'd like to thank Meredith and everyone else at Page & Vine for taking a chance on me. You saw only a few chapters of this book and pounced. The book wasn't even done and you didn't care. The level of trust you put in me is something I will not forget, and I want to thank you, for giving me this opportunity to show you what I've got.

Thank you also to my readers, my Whorror Babies. You guys are amazing and I so, so love seeing you in the wild or on my socials. You guys make my days, and I wouldn't be here without your voices. I appreciate you being so understanding while I switch my career over, being patient with waiting. I promise you, it's worth it. Thank you, thank you thank you thank you.

And lastly, thank you to *Slash or Pass*. I will admit, it was extremely hard for me to acknowledge that my breakout book was not going to be my first traditionally published book. I cried. But, taking a step back, I thank that book and 2023 Ty for publishing it.

Slash or Pass walked, so *Good For Her* could run.
And run it did.

AUTHOR BIO

Tylor Paige (she/her) is an Amazon Top 3 bestselling author of what her readers have lovingly labeled, whorror.

Tylor is proof that horror doesn't have to be serious to be effective. It can be self-aware, playful, and at times romantic--while still telling a solid scary story. In blending her passions for both romance and horror she's not only creating something that's both risqué and bloody, she's bridging the gap between the hopelessly romantic and the hopelessly haunted.

At the time of this publication, Tylor has published sixteen full length novels and four novellas independently. *Good For Her* is her debut into the traditionally published world.

ALSO BY TYLOR PAIGE

Good For Her
Camera Stays On (Fall 2026)
Surrender to Forever- a Goblin King reimagining
Beautiful Little Freaks- A Gatsby retelling

Final Girl Series:
Slash or Pass
Slay Less
Knife Comment Share
Thots and Prayers (a Slash or Pass novella)
Final Ghouls Series:
Hips, Lips, Apocalypse

Final Girl Featurettes: (100 page novellas!)
Like Father Like Slaughter
Life Begins At Possession
All I want For Christmas Is Boo

Little Deaths: a Vampire Mafia series
Seven Little Deaths
Lay Your Body Down
Bury Me in Blood

STORIES WITH IMPACT

WWW.PAGEANDVINE.COM